Georges Montbard

The Land of the Sphinx

Georges Montbard

The Land of the Sphinx

ISBN/EAN: 9783337389475

Printed in Europe, USA, Canada, Australia, Japan

Cover: Foto ©Andreas Hilbeck / pixelio.de

More available books at **www.hansebooks.com**

THE LAND

OF

THE SPHINX

WITH ONE HUNDRED AND EIGHTY-SIX ILLUSTRATIONS
BY THE AUTHOR

NEW YORK

DODD, MEAD, & COMPANY

1894

PREFACE.

WHENEVER a biped's bile gets beyond control and his gall-pouch overflows, or his too-excited vital spirits fly tumultuously to his brain, banging against the walls of his cranium, riotously cavalcading amidst the winding coils of his encephalon, he feels the necessity of discharging this bile, forerunner of jaundice; of emptying the gall-pouch that is corroding his tissues and souring his temper; of opening a safety-valve for the vapour of his seething brain, and freeing it of all dross. The manifestation of this intellectual epuration is to be found in the tangible form of a book, an exudatory by means of which the patient displays, either diluted or condensed, in an indefinite number of pages, the morbid state of his brain, beset by the relentless irritation of acrid, pernicious, and abundant secretions. The invalid is saved, but the unfortunate public who receive the deleterious shower are attacked: they catch the disease; the bacilli develop a million-fold in the fungus of imagination, stubbornly pursuing their detestable work, and the epidemic rages everywhere. I have been bitten by the terrible animalcule, and in my turn I save myself by an emission of my bile!

When acting thus one is so thoroughly conscious of committing an aggressive action against society, of being a disturber of human stupidity, that one instinctively feels, unless one is absolutely perverted, the necessity of excusing one's self, of uttering one's *mea culpa* in the form of a very anodyne and extremely sweet preface, which the public, that old *blasé*, as artful as a Red Indian, never reads! I have too much respect for routine not to steal a march upon readers whilst performing my little act of sly contrition—and the public would not be the public if it departed from its laudable habit of skipping the hypocritical preface.

Well, I was at Marseilles, and already the symptoms of the malady, the paroxysm of which was to produce the lucubration occasioning this preface, were showing themselves with vigorous intensity: my gall was fermenting like a vat of new wine; the impetuous ebb and flow of rebellious bile and uncontrollable blood rose and fell at their own sweet will! My disease was at its height. One day I was sadly sauntering in the shade of the trees of the Cours Belzunce, digesting with difficulty an indefinable *bouillabaisse*. After a while I stopped to listen to a quack who was making a remarkable speech in the midst of the silence of a gaping crowd. Amongst other marvellous cures performed by this learned disciple of Æsculapius, and related by him, there was one which particularly struck me, owing to its prodigious originality. In narrating this incredible event I cannot do better than textually quote that portion of the eminent doctor's oration, of which I scrupulously noted the terms; so here it is :—

"In Africa, I was at Cairo, when they brought me a young girl who, fifteen years before, had fallen asleep on the banks of the Nile; a little crocodile had crawled into her mouth, then into her stomach, and finally into her intestines, where, ever since, it had been causing the most frightful agony. What did I do? Gentlemen, I had this young person laid on her back, I rubbed her well with my balm, and at that very instant the whole body opened to the extent of three feet, and those present beheld, with as much awe as admiration, a monstrous crocodile issue from the body of that unfortunate young person. Gentlemen, in assuring you that it was fifteen feet long, and as big as a yearling pig, I am guilty of no exaggeration."

This was a revelation. These words produced a deep and ineffaceable impression on me, and settled the choice of the locality where the phases of my malady should develop, the frame wherein I would present the fruit of my labours to the public. From that moment I was dying to see the country where the crocodiles, by an inevitable law of atavism, take board and lodging in the bodies of the inhabitants, and grow and fatten there as did formerly the gods in the bodies of the sacred animals, and then clear out with such amazing facility!

I started for Egypt.

Since then I have overrun the valley of the Nile; I here describe its strange and varied aspects, dwelling complaisantly upon the present, plunging occasionally into the sombre recesses of the past, in order to stir up its venerable cumulations and bring to the surface a few amusing bubbles, with the muffled echoes of vanished times!

Having travelled a great deal, and read numbers of historians, modern ones especially, I have acquired an incontestable skill in the art of relating fables, of distorting facts, and of arranging them to suit the exigencies of my mood or the requirements of the moment —the reader will easily perceive this.

I have added a few thousand years to the vertiginous number of centuries so generously accorded to Egypt, thereby following in the wake of her ancient and venerable priests, those circumspect gossips, as cunning as the cleverest of quacks, who told such yarns to the credulous Greeks who came to interview them.

I have admired the beauty and proportions of the lineaments of the Sphinx, that monster which possesses nothing remarkable but its size, less to render homage to truth than from deference to the strange enthusiasm of its irrepressible admirers. For the same reason I have enlarged upon the praise awarded to the temple of this same Sphinx, a sort of slightly rough-hewn cavern of troglodytes.

I have stood enraptured in the presence of the imposing masses of the Pyramids, Cheops especially, the cuneiform character of which makes it, by right, the grandest thing in Egypt—because one is expected to be suffocated with admiration before those " barbarisms in hewn stone."

I have described the elegant profile of the obelisks, those stupid big landmarks, those pales of Titans.

I have noted without a smile the " robust delicacy " of the temples of the valley of the Nile, the genius of their architects, the prodigious art which presided at their erection, while I felt convinced that this debauchery of limestone congestions and piling up, on a large scale, of heavy and unsightly edifices proved absolutely nothing in favour of the art or the genius of their pretentious architects. On the contrary !

The glaring ornamentation of the tombs of the Valley of Kings, a description of twopenny coloured pictures on stucco fixed to miles of walls, did not please me ; and the bats which swarm in those funereal tunnels annoyed me immensely. Nevertheless I did not fail to " tremble beneath the breath of memories of the past," with a few romantic Cookites who had poked themselves in there, and who, in spite of their respectable emotion, were extremely anxious to get out again.

I have not missed bestowing the epithet " sublime " upon those stiff and gigantic statues of gods, which are in magnitude what a

Chinese magot is in exignity. I have showered praise on the isle of Philæ, that pearl of Egypt, which, after all, excepting the hypæthral temple with its three meagre palm trees, is only a mass of rubbish scorched by the sun, of gutted temples and fallen columns. The cataract, that grandiose result of the freak of an angry god, recalled to my mind Shakespeare's play, *Much Ado about Nothing*!

The burlesques of the incoherent theogony of Egypt, its ridiculous menagerie, reminded me of the inmates of the Zoological Gardens and the masquerades of Mid-Lent, but in no wise predisposed me to believe, like a great Egyptologist, that "at the summit of the Egyptian Pantheon towers a unique, immortal, uncreate, and invisible god hidden in the inaccessible recesses of being"; for, if anything does tower there, it can only be the memory of the immense and cruel madness of those who conceived the laughable silhouettes of this fantastic Olympus, audaciously casting as food to the imbecile imagination of ignorant mankind those headless and tailless myths, which so long misled bewildered humanity in its search after truth.

I have generously alluded to the wisdom of the "most grateful of all men," but regretted that, instead of bequeathing us indirectly that famous wisdom from which we are now seeking to be freed, they did not preserve it for their own private use ; this would no doubt have suited them remarkably well, and us even better!

I have extolled the Nile, boasted of the "limpidity" of its muddy waters swarming with insects and fucus, and the "variety" which occurs in the dispiriting uniformity of its banks, where from time to time are washed up the swollen carcass of a Soudanese negro, an Arab, or a camel covered with bluish sores. Cook the Great, the Tourists' Cook, the Circular Cook, that enterprising manager of universal locomotion, King of Upper and Lower Egypt, Prince of the Nile River and its intelligent showman, would never have forgiven me for inconsiderately attacking its fluvial fame, and disturbing the flow of his Pactolus!

To bathe in its waters is, it appears, the most agreeable of pleasures. I speak from hearsay, never having done so myself, for fear that a facetious and greedy monster might have played me the same trick as the one which was so fatal to Osiris and made Isis for ever inconsolable.

I found Nile water a delicious beverage; and when one remembers that the Princesses of the blood of the Ptolemies, wedded to foreigners, had it sent them to far-off countries, I should be very much looked down upon were I to state here that the water is brackish, that it produces pimples on the skin, especially during the first days of flood, and that the ancient Egyptians never drank it unmixed.

The Nile without crocodiles would not be the Nile; so, to avoid being accused of having confused this divine river with some common stream, as a certain general did the Seine with the Marne, I have mentioned crocodiles. In fact, I saw—one! as big as a lizard, and hanging to a string held by an Arab, who wished to sell it to me for twenty piastres. I had the tact to refuse, not wishing to deprive the great river of the only crocodile it possessed from Cairo to the first cataract; and from a certain fear too lest, yielding to the temptation of leading it away with me by a string, Typhon, finding himself insufficiently housed in that narrow carapace, should seek to change his residence and take up his abode in my far more ample person; the gods are so capricious and so fond of comfort!

Dreading extremely to be despised by Orientalists orientalising, I stood enraptured in presence of the worm-eaten marvels of unstable equilibrium of Arabian art; at the pleasing imagination displayed in its geometrical interlacings, at the surprises of its arabesques, and at the grace of its ornamentation—not daring to own that these edifices resemble wedding-cakes, the interlacing pattern a tangled caligraphy, and the ornamentation is the gaudiest of daubs.

I have commended the picturesque appearance of an Arab's rags, swarming with vermin; the purity of the atmosphere of the bazaars, reeking with the smell of burnt incense, rose-water, and the dung of asses and dromedaries, combined with the unsavoury effluvia of all kinds of commodities piled up in stalls a few feet square, and with the penetrating goatish odour of the fellaheen.

I have pitied these last, because every one pities them, especially those amiable philanthropists who, in Egypt, diligently tickle their backs with the courbash.

I would not criticise the gait of the worthy asses of Cairo, those cabs of the East, but yet I cannot deny the fact that after half an hour's ride one's person feels extremely sore; and lucky is the rider who has not been thrown, once or several times, by a jerk of the back, as sudden as unexpected, which is quite peculiar to these steeds.

The camels, which we leave unnoticed at home, interest us enormously so soon as we set foot in the East; so I have paid the tribute of admiration due to the ship of the desert, with its double motion of pitching and rolling, which, when you are seated on its hump, gives you a similar feeling to that which you experience on the deck of the Dover and Calais steamer, when your stomach is not quite as it should be.

In order not to alarm the interesting idlers, the well-to-do people plunged in the delights of the Luxor Hotel, that Capua of Upper Egypt, I have exaggerated the salubrity of this land of—sun-stroke, dysentery, ophthalmia, intermittent fever, bubos, frightful hypertrophy, and tuberculous leprosy; this land infested with reptiles, scorpions, flies, and mosquitoes.

Fearing to turn away from the journey persons with delicate tympanums and civilised ears, I have been silent respecting the eternal and excruciating grinding sound of the *sakiehs*, the shrill complaints of the *rebecks*, the monotonous hum of the *daraboukas*, the piercing and snuffling voices of Arab *cirtuosi*, the prolonged and discordant bellowing of the trombones of their orchestras, the unbearable cacophony of the Khedive's band.

I would not deprive Gérôme of his illusions by declaring that the Almehs sheltered at Esneh are now frightful jades, old and ugly, wearing boots down at heel and a kind of flowered dressing-gown of glaring colour, who fuddle themselves with vermouth; or by telling him that the sword-dance and the dance of the wasp are now no more than a bad and very repugnant *cancan*, which takes place on the beaten earth floor of a noxious hovel, lighted by a candle stuck in the neck of an empty bottle placed on a rickety deal table. It is even much against my wish that I am obliged to state that no Arab with the least claim to respectability ever sets foot in these low filthy taverns, and that they are only frequented by a few soft-brained tourists taken there by smart dragomans, who are on the best of terms with the "friends of these ladies."

I must admit, alas! in spite of all my respect for our venerable ancestress, that the whole of the vaunted wisdom of Egypt is resumed at the present day in the immodest acrobatic performances of Karaguenz, her science in the juggleries of her Psylli, her religion in the epileptic convulsions of impure santons, the waltzing of a band of dancing dervishes and the hideous distortions of their howling companions. Her imposing ceremonies of by-gone times have given way to the feast of the Return of the Carpet, a pretext for a priest drunk with hasheesh to trample under his horse's hoofs the fanatic faithful; and to the bloody anniversary of the death of Hussein and Hassan, when another variety of bigots take delight in hacking themselves and transpiercing their cheeks, to the accompaniment of most horrible yells.

I have treated tourists in general, and English tourists in particular, rather badly, because it is understood that an English tourist, who, in reality, is very well-behaved and much less annoying than others, should be nevertheless described as a most disagreeable person. It is true that I quite lost my temper with a fellow-countryman who persistently bawled out at the top of his voice some music-hall choruses in the hypogeum of Thebes; and that I saw a German coolly break and carry off some bits of the Beni-Hassan mouldings as though they had merely been pieces of common work; and if some very curious specimens of painting on stucco, at the temple of Abydos, did not disappear into the secret receptacles of this same Teuton, it was owing to the energetic intervention of English tourists, indignant at an act of vandalism as barefaced as it was barbaric.

TO THE READER.

THE most salient feature of that which precedes, and of that which is about to follow, will be the evident discursiveness which prevails from one end to the other; it would be no mistake to behold in this the faithful likeness of the state of my mind, the immediate consequence of that of our crazy century, consumed by a colossal and incurable athumia. It will be observed that I have often wandered away from my subject; this has happened to me each time the subject annoyed me, and I returned to it so soon as the digressions, which had led me astray, themselves commenced to bother me, a practice due to the habit of playing truant acquired in my school-boy days!

An absurd and precocious liking for noise, changing in course of time to an intemperate taste for the big drum, whose mighty rolls procured me indescribable delight, has clung to me in my mature age and exercised regrettable influence on my literary style. Hence the sonorous rumbling of some of my periods, as empty as the insides of those worthy asses' skins, the delight of my childhood, the favourites of my youth!

I have indulged in many Latin quotations, not for the purpose of laying claim to an erudition I do not possess, but from a mere instinct of the barbarian fascinated by the unknown, and an irresistible attraction for the mysterious, an invincible propensity for uttering enigmatical words! I must have had some speakers of oracles or Pythonesses among my ancestors. I am obliged, however, to admit that I understand the meaning of some of my quotations, those which I learnt by heart at college, but I must own that they please me infinitely less than the others, the meaning of which escapes me; for me they have no longer the attraction of forbidden fruit; they are, as to Eve after the apple, without the relish of a taste of risk.

Every time that I could, I have disguised truth with a veil. It smacks too much of a fable, truth stark naked issuing from a well, of all places in the world. To begin with, it is indecent, and besides it gives one the shivers. The Athenians, those witty ways, the ingenious inventors of this piquant allegory, but rarely brought her out of her humid dwelling, preferring to let her cool her heels there, with quite Hellenic discourtesy and absolute want of gallantry. The Greeks were right, and it is not I who would give her a hand to help her to come up, as I consider it very ill-bred to let people know what you think of them, and extremely disagreeable to be told the truth about oneself.

I have quoted, according to circumstances, all the well-known yarns—those inoffensive old stereotypes which lulled us to sleep in our infancy with their stately and monotonous lullaby; and, out of love for the picturesque, I have respected the legend of Cleopatra stung by an asp, instead of displaying the bad taste of stating, on the authority of Baron Larrey, of the French Academy, that the seductive heroine put an end to her existence by means of a bushel of charcoal, just like a simple Parisian grisette.

Through an excess of modesty, which will be readily appreciated, I have rarely believed what I have written, considering it most reprehensible to have too much confidence in oneself. It would, indeed, be too great impertinence if, when passing our existence in conjuring up the wildest illusions, in revelling in the most deceptive chimeras, we carried our simplicity so far as to believe in those illusions, our ingenuousness to the point of giving a body to those chimeras, our stupidity to the extent of becoming ourselves dupes of the artifices of our undisciplined minds, and if, to cap all, we had the singularly overweening pretension of imposing our belief on others.

I have been rather lavish with cant, the spice of modern literature, more anxious in its Byzantine refinement suitably to chisel out phrases, tastefully to encrust carefully selected words upon them, and to listen rapturously to the music of an empty and discreetly sonorous prose, than to find lodging for an idea in this dazzling palace of verbiage.

Amongst other faults which I possess, and which I will not mention here, lulling myself with the sweet illusion that they will perhaps escape the perspicacity of the reader, is that of being extremely talkative. This is unfortunately a propensity of which I have never tried and never wished to free myself; and one which, by long dwelling with me, tolerated at first, indispensable afterwards, has ended by making itself quite at home with me for good, and by becoming altogether part of the household. I beg the reader to show for this untoward habit some of the indulgence I have displayed towards him, without, however, wishing that the ugly weed should acclimatise itself with him as it has done with me, where the soil was perhaps more suitable for its self-cultivation!

CONCERNING THE ILLUSTRATIONS.

When expressions have failed me for withdrawing becomingly from the inextricable tangle of my ideas, I have had recourse to drawing: hence the number of pictures which bedizen this book, and which are deserving of just the same amount of confidence as the text, the pencil having only accentuated and finished the fantastic vagaries of the pen.

A GREETING TO GOOD OLD EGYPT, THE GRANDMOTHER OF NATIONS.

O EGYPT, "Gift of the Nile!" Land of Osiris! Thou Land of Pharaohs and fellaheen, of the courbash and baksheesh, of the lotus and papyrus, of beetles and crocodiles, of the Book of the Dead and mausoleums, of ophthalmia and elephantiasis! Sacred charnel‑house! Holy valley of everlasting tears and regrets! Venerable Egypt, who restest slumbering in thy innumerable mummies, in the gigantic void of thy colossal and useless edifices, in the undecipherable secret of thy hieroglyphics,—I salute thee!

Glory to thee! mysterious Ancestress of the world; indefatigable Seeker after sublime nonsense; questioning death to understand life; elaborating, whilst meditating amidst thy deserts during thousands of centuries, the elements of the human idea; a laborious parturition which cost thee thy existence, and bestowed on us that superb civilisation of which we, thy sickly grand-nephews, are dying, incapable of bearing the strength of its powerful effluvia!

Glory to thee! mother of justice, laying down with Thoth, in the hermetic books, the bases of science, that vertiginous accumulation of hypotheses; the A B C of wisdom, that of law and conventional civility in nations; the principles of justice, "that sovereign extravagance, that generous imbecility."

Glory to thee! generative mother of the gods, insane with genius, whose phenomenal brain invented that mournful and picturesque fancy of the rite of the judgment of the dead; audacious mystical lore, establishing at the same time the profound principle of palingenesis and the unfathomable stupidity of the human race; giving birth to the dogma of metensomatosis, and to that monstrous and enormous pantheon, an insoluble enigma, so irritating to the anxious and unhealthy curiosity of our declining century, feverishly tracing all back to its origin, bent upon the impossible reconstruction of an uncertain past.

Glory to thee! who, for the greater jubilation of inept tourists, lost in amazement in the presence of thy stiff-limbed idols, didst carve the strange images of thy apocalyptic divinities in the granite and the limestone of thy mountains; bestrewing thy plains with the temples of Titans, chiselling on their massive sides thy interminable hieroglyphics; erecting with perfect art and prodigious science thy hermetic obelisks, thy fantastic pyramids, thy marvellous sphinx, thy labyrinth, that stupendous feat of thy architects; digging out of the Arabian and Libyan rocks those gloomy recesses, those funereal hypogeums with their walls illuminated like the leaves of an old missal of the middle ages; shedding with unheard-of profusion that infinite multitude of tiresome mastabas; executing with inconceivable sagacity and surprising skill more gigantic works than now, after five thousand years, we take in hand timidly and complete with effort!

Glory to thee, illustrious vanquished! For a Power that is

mightier has mastered thee, thee the dread subduer! It has destroyed thy celestial menagerie, strangled thy gods, dispersed their Therapentæ!

May they rest in peace in Amenti, to the Occident, beyond the lake of Osiris; thy sacred animals, those homes of the souls of thy divinities, those hairy, feathery, or scaly personifications of the attributes of the primordial might, of the sole uncreated god, begetting and bringing forth himself in infinite space!

Gloria victis! Glory to you! holy and revered beasts, habitations of the gods!

Enviable cow, who concealeth in thy broad flanks the soul of Isis-Athor, the gloomy Venus, with the pale golden skin, the pure oval face, the straight profile, the long velvety eyes; ardent and inconsolable spouse of Osiris; unknown and impenetrable, mother and substance of that which is, mysterious source of all things!

Goose of the Nile, within whom resides Seb, the layer of the egg of the world, the matter containing the germs of life; husband of Nout, father of Ra!

Scarabæus, ornament of the brow; lion with the luminous hide, who art the habitation of the cabiric Phtah, of the demiurge, the lord of wisdom, the light which accomplishes all things!

Black ibis of Ethiopia and cynocephalus with the azure rump, ye. the two habitations of Thoth Trismegistus, the hierogrammatist, the speaking column, the living verb, the guide of souls, showman of the shades, prince of undertakers!

Serpent coiled about thyself, who containest the "absolute," the divine breath, and Knouphis the androgynus, who himself fabricates the generative mother of the gods!

Jackal with the sharp muzzle, temporary lodging of Anubis, latrant, guardian of tombs, watcher of mummies!

Bennou, with the gold and crimson plumage, friend of Osiris, the god of Abydos, the lord of Amenti, the nocturnal sun, the good intent, for ever fructifying Isis!

Lumbering hippopotamus, habitation of Set, the spirit of evil, the enemy of Osiris!

Sacred hawk with the lightning wing, emblem of the solar gods, of the sun in his radiant course of Ra, erect amidst his crew of Akhimou-Ordou and Akhimou-Sekou, with a Hor at the helm and a Hor at the prow, in the sacred boat which roams, enveloped in the coils of the serpent Mehen, upon the celestial Oner-ness!

Great tawny vulture, symbol of maternity, dedicated to Mauth, the mother-goddess, in whose womb was self-conceived Ammon-Ra, the bull, the generating principle above all, to whom the ram and the cerastes are consecrated!

Cat and lioness of Sacht-the-Great, the cherished friend of Phtah, the creative and dissolving power, she who purifies and she who punishes!

Famous Apis of Memphis, born of a celestial ray! Muevis of Heliopolis, with the black and bristling hair! Onuphis of Hermonthis, the good genius! Peaceful and preposterous receptacles of divine incarnations!

Winged Uræus, with the venom-swollen throat, who circlest the heads of gods and kings, terrible symbol of their inexorable sovereignty!

And ye: lascivious goat of Mendès! Wolf of Syont! Ichneumon of Heracleopolis! Crocodile of the Arsinoït nome! Owl of Saïs! Falcon and shrew of Butos! Mouse and dove of Isis!

Ye, sacred fishes: seal, eel, carp, phallivorous oxyriux, honoured throughout Egypt!

Ye, garlic and onion, respectable vegetables, by whom the people swore!

Thou, palm tree almost human, all tremulous with love, who moanest at touch of the knife! Acacia, whose trunk secreted Osiris! Persæa of Isis, the guardian of hearts!

Your reign is for ever at an end, O fantastic medley of beasts, trees, plants, vegetables, incongruous types of a complicated theogony; disjoined links of the most admirable web of extravagant mystifications the human mind ever conceived!

Grave and solemn throng of priests, with shaven heads and eyebrows, with long garments made of flax, cease your hyssop-scented lustrations; your gods are dead! the boat of Isis has capsized!

Dreaded prophets, bespangled with collars of gold, laden with charms, you will never again consult the entrails of the victims, or study the course of the planets, to learn and predict the future!

Hierostolites, you will no longer deck the images of the gods!

Learned Arpedonaptes, pluck off the plumes which adorn your heads; the ink of your canon is dried up, your calamus is broken; you will no more carry your sacred tablets covered with hieroglyphics; you will no more indite your funereal rituals!

Horoscopists, cast away your hour-glasses and your palms; you will never again draw conclusions from the movements of the sacred beasts!

Hieropsaltes, no more will you chant the hymns of the gods and the rules of life for kings, taught of Hermes, while accompanying yourselves on golden *sistra*!

Sphragistes, you will no more place your seal on the victim destined to the sacrifice!

Pastophores, guardians of the temples, you will no more bear the *baris* of Isis, or the beds, or the utensils of assistance!

Melanephores, the black veil of Isis is rent; you will place it no more on your shoulders!

Comastes, you will no more preside at the banquets on *fête* days !

Neophores and Zacores, you will no more have to watch over the objects of worship—there is no more worship !

Undertakers, your ministry is useless !

Designator, thou wilt no longer mark on the left side of the dead the piece of flesh that must be removed !

Operator, thou wilt no longer use thy Ethiopian stone to make the incision indicated by thy colleague, and thou wilt no more have to fly amidst the curses of the crowd, pursued by the stones of the bystanders !

Embalmers, leave there the natron, the palm wine, the cedar gum, the myrrh, the cinnamon, and the perfumes of all sorts with which you anoint the dead, the bandages you wind round them, the brushes and colours that serve to adorn their coffins. Your part is played ; Anubis is no more. We no longer make mummies ; we render to the earth what belongs to the earth !

And you, inhabitants of both Egypts, you will eat no more honey or figs on the day of the feast of Thoth ; you will no longer celebrate, in the month of Pao-phi, the feasts of the pregnancy of Isis and of the stick of the sun ; in that of Athyr, that of the loss of Osiris ; at the solstice of winter, anniversary of the birth of Harpocrates, you will no more give the first-fruits of your gardens, and you will no more lead a cow seven times in succession round the temple, in honour of the search for Osiris ; in the month of Tybi, in memory of the return of Isis from Phenicia, you will no longer offer her cakes, bearing the figure of a hippopotamus in chains, symbol of Typhon vanquished by Isis and Horus ; no more will you celebrate, on the first day of Phamenoth, the entrance of Osiris into the moon ; and, at the Pamylies, you will no longer carry the representation of the triple phallus, in honour of the delivery of Isis ; in Pharmuti you will not weep over bundles of corn while invoking Isis ; in Payni you will not attend the sacrifices with cakes bearing the effigy of a bound ass, telling each other " not to give food to the ass," " not to wear golden rings "; on the 12th of the same month, the day of the feast of the inundation, you will no more offer the Nile his magnificently adorned bride ; the tear of Isis, the solitary drop of dew, which purifies and drives away all corruption, will not fall on that night, or ever again, for the eyes of Isis are closed for evermore ! No longer, on the 30th of Epiphi, will there be the feast of the eyes of Horus ; and no more, on the last day of the year, in Messori, will you present the first vegetables to Harpamtes !

The time for feasts is over ! The era of prolonged mourning commences.

And you, redoubtable and resplendent Pharaohs, with the pschent surmounted by the threatening Uræus, your protracted slumber has been disturbed; they have uncovered you, as quarrymen at times disclose by a blow of the pickaxe some belated toad, who has remained a prisoner for a couple of centuries in his cell of hard stone. They have violated the secret of your sepulchres !

Your mounds of blocks of stone, the mystery of your hypogeums, the silence of your hieroglyphs, have not defended your royal remains against the avidity of the conquerors of the Nile valley, the disrespectful and indiscreet curiosity of learned Europe. They have discovered the obstructed or walled-up entrances to your last dwelling-places, penetrated within your mortuary chambers, raised the heavy covers of your basalt or porphyry sarcophagi, burst open your cedar or sycamore coffins, four within one another, torn the masks from your mummies, plucked off their ornaments ; profane hands have untied the bandages which imprisoned your stiffened limbs !

The lynx eyes of Egyptologists have found the key to your mysterious hieroglyphs and translated the long rolls of prayers of your papyrus!

Grave men examine you with the magnifying glass, analyse parts of your sacred personalities; they measure your facial angle, the length of your nasal organ, the form of your skull; they discuss your authenticity between a pinch of snuff and a cigarette; they send your mummies about in a most irreverential way; the distrustful custom-house rummages in the cases containing them, as they pass, in fear lest the remains of Rameses or Sesostris, forwarded carriage paid, should serve as a pretext for smuggling in a quart of brandy or a box of regalias! Cook or Barnum exhibits you at reduced prices to the snobs of Great Britain, the idlers of Paris, the Yankees of the New World, the idiots of all countries! You are simply an object of curiosity and commerce; money is made by retailing you to tourists, colours by subjecting your swaddled-up limbs to chemical treatment. And the great tramplers of people under foot, they who occupied so much room in the world, now held within a modest little zinc tube, ticketed "Mummies' Blacks," have for sarcophagus the colour-box of a mocking canvas-dauber, and serve to sketch out some mad conceptions of the studio.

Your bodies exhibited in the glass cases of our museums serve to astonish nursemaids and Tommy Atkins; it is a thing, a curio, a souvenir of Egypt! People place one of your hands, a middle finger, or your great toe on a row of shelves between a Chinese magot and a Japanese vase!

You are old furniture, numbered, classed, very well catalogued, frightfully messed about by the descendants of those same Tamahon with white skins, blue eyes, our ancestors, represented six thousand years ago by your scribes on the walls of your palaces, with arms bound, heads laid beneath the heel of the Pharaohs, who were the great conculcators of nations. . . . *Sic transit gloria mundi!*

The fanatic Theophilus has cast down the tottering edifice of your worn-out Pantheon : the rotten statue, full of rats, of Serapis, the last incarnation of Osiris, outcome of the supreme convulsion of your agonising worship, has been broken by blows of the hatchet by a legionary of Theodosius ; its remains, set on fire, flamed amidst the hooting of the Nazarenes, and even, alas! amidst the bitter sarcasms of its worshippers, exasperated at the complete inability of their god to defend itself!

Thy gods are dead. *Dolorosa mater!* Poor Egypt! congealed in thy hieratic majesty : eagles mute on the shoulders of thy colossi, which are cracking ; vultures repose on the ruptured summits of thy monuments; the screech-owl lodges in the cornerless capitals of thy temples ; the jackal prowls by night among the shattered columns of thy hypostyle halls ; the hideous horned snake crawls beneath the ruins of thy fallen pylons ; the colossi of Memnon, son of the Aurora, no more address their hymns to the rising sun ; thy masterpieces are disappearing in crumbs in the pockets of tourists; thy uprooted obelisks are transplanted to all the capitals of the world. Thy grand monuments, which marked the stages of thy prodigious civilisation, disappear little by little, buried beneath the desert sand—a moving winding-sheet, which slowly spreads itself over thy past glories!

De profundis! Old Egypt has passed into the shadow of death.

CONTENTS.

CHAPTER I.

CONTENTS.

CHAPTER V.

CHAPTER VI.

CHAPTER VII.

CHAPTER VIII.

CHAPTER IX.

CHAPTER X.

CHAPTER XI.

CHAPTER XII.

CHAPTER XIII.

CHAPTER XIV.

The *Saïd* leaving Marseilles.

CHAPTER I.

En route.—Corsica.—Cook and Son's living parcels.—Those rogues of note-books.
—Secret warfare between the Cookites and the unlabelled.—The authentic
Baronet.—International confusion.—Where the reader makes the acquaint-
ance of Jacques and his friend Onésime Coquillard.—*A propos* of frontiers.—
The consequence of having studied geography in France.—Departure.—What
Jacques, followed by Onésime, wished to see in Egypt.—Onésime.—Gaiety in
the forecastle ; frightful dulness at the stern.

ON October 8th, in the year 188–, at six o'clock at night, at the
"green hour," all perfumed with alcohol, when, upon the
Cannebière, the Marseillais, intoxicated with his own tongue, tempers
his superb loquacity with an absinthe cut with a dash of anisette—
at that seductive hour the steamer of the Messageries, the *Saïd*,
put out from the port of the Joliette.

Leaving on the left the old port, the Pharos, the Catalans ; on
the right the islands of Ratoneau and Pomègue ; then, doubling the
Château d'If, she steamed close to the sharp rocks of Mairé Island,
and continued her course to the south-east, burying herself in the
twilight, where one caught a glimpse of half-lost capes, islands, and
promontories.

The dinner-bell summoned all the passengers. An hour afterwards
a few vague shadows wandered about the deck, where the bitter

1

emanations of tobacco mingled with the odours of the breeze. The red tips of the cigars piercing the shadow of night alone indicated the indistinct smokers. These lights went out one by one, little by little,

The deck of the *Saïd*.

and there was silence, disturbed only by the dull, jerky moaning of the machine and the shrill calls of the captain's whistle.

The next morning the passengers, with heavy eyelids and wrapped up in their rugs, were assembled at the stern, gaping, coughing, stretching themselves out in the sun; till, relaxing the torpid muscles, the contracted nerves, the warm effluvia appeased by degrees the suppressed irritability, the painful twitches of refractory rheumatism.

Through a slight vapour rising sluggishly, slow, transparent, and as if with regret, one perceived on the right an uncertain streak of grey. The breeze rose, drove away the lazy fog, and all at once, beneath a caress of the sun, Corsica, with its barren shores, appeared—rugged, vindictive, and proud.

"Corsica!" pronounced a telescope; and English, French, Americans, Russians, Germans, Italians, Spaniards, *rastaquouères* of all shades—all the various specimens of humanity grouped on the deck gazed ahead.

One heard a febrile rustling of pages: it was the living parcels forwarded by Cook and Son from various countries to Cairo, carriage paid and insured in case of accident, turning over the leaves of their guide-books in search of the descriptive note, which, slightly mutilated, and enlarged by their personal impressions, was inscribed, after due meditation, and with a thoughtful air, in their note-books.

The note-books! How many does one find, especially in the United Kingdom, of those famous note-books that have come back from Egypt, placed treacherously, with subtle art, with affected negligence, upon the most prominent piece of furniture, on the drawingroom table between Shakespeare and Longfellow! They are spread out provokingly, those impudent little rogues, under different headings : "Souvenirs of Egypt" ; "A Trip to Cairo"; "My Impressions."

Corsica.

"My Impressions" is the title generally selected by those who have this ambition developed.

Besides Cook and Son's bundles, unlabelled Englishmen sought insidiously to widen the distance between themselves and the former, while these, like consummate strategists, exerted themselves none the less insidiously to diminish it. The struggle was silent, stubborn, incessant. On both sides recourse was had to the cunning ruses of Red Indians ; on the one hand to come into contact, on the other to avoid doing so.

An authentic Baronet, who had broken out of bounds of Parliament, cold, correct, was the radiant star round which all these planets in aberration gravitated ; and his perfect indifference to both parties avenged the Cookites, somewhat, for the disdain of the adverse faction.

From time to time a complex glitter shone like a flash of lightning, followed by a metallic rattling of tubes roughly torn from their cases, and tall, bilious-looking Americans, handling lengthy telescopes with their long hands, pointed them at the land in view.

The unlabelled Englishman.

Dark, full-blooded Frenchmen, with sun-burnt skins and hair cut close to the skull, were chattering like magpies, stamping on the ground with a debauchery of gesture which exasperated the telescopers, deranging the stability of their instruments.

A German in "us," a Doctor Herr Reptilius—they are all doctors in Germany, and all end in "us"—consolidated on his bulbous, subproboscidate nose his gold-rimmed spectacles—they all wear spectacles in Germany—reflected profoundly, and extracted from his huge pocket an immense map, in which he buried himself, the studious portion of "the second-hand colossus!"

Olive-green Italians, with low foreheads and loud voices, expressed regret through their nasal organs that Corsica was French, Nice the principal town of a French department, and Savoy annexed.

A taciturn Spaniard, full of dignity, rolled a cigarette and digested his chocolate.

An exsanguinous Russian, returning

The Frenchman.

from Siberia, smiled languidly through the silky threads of his long fair beard.

Amidst all these appeared the delicate features of pretty young diaphanous Misses, with fine heads, all pink and white like Yorkshire hams, and vigorous appetites; they were chirping and uttering little cries like frightened larks, while elderly ladies, grave and ugly, full of concentrated respectability, blew their noses like sonorous trumpets beneath the brazen sky!

Merry Frenchwomen were conversing with each other gaily, talking very lightly of extremely serious matters, beside beautiful Italian women, with dull complexions and harsh profiles, who, enveloping themselves in the *morbidezza* that is essential to every Italian woman who respects herself, spoke in a most serious tone of matters that little deserved it. A group of sentimental German women, temptingly plump,

Doctor Reptilius.

with fair skins, limpid eyes the colour of *vergiss-mein-nicht*, in the aureola of their golden hair, were blushingly murmuring tenderly poetical nothings, and in such long words that when they reached the end they had forgotten the commencement, those exemplary spouses, those incomparable housewives, " without rivals for making jam and fabricating children."

The island showed itself in full, with its hard outlines slightly clouded by the last remnants of the fog ; the cliffs stood out clear, in dusty violet tones, in the rays of morning. A few fishermen's boats, with white sails, were resting at anchor, similar to enormous sea-mews dozing, fatigued, upon the blue water of the Mediterranean.

The Spaniard.

" I say," exclaimed a young man in French to his friend, " look at those sun-bathed shores, at that pretty bit of ground ! "

" Pooh ! Corsica, a miserable place," answered the other.

" A miserable place ? "

" Yes, a miserable place, where the people pass their existence in mutually suppressing each other, in popping one another off from behind hedges ; a pastime as amusing as it is dangerous, which they call the *vendetta*. They indulge in this attractive sport in the 'maquis' with which the country is covered—probably for that purpose. Bonaparte, who was born in this charming cut-throat isle, of which he is the glory, excelled at this amusing game. Europe learnt it from him at his expense ; it cost her twenty years' warfare and millions of men."

" And why ? To be on one side or the other of a river, of a mountain, or of a certain line of demarcation, of which the custom-house officers are the landmarks—for frontiers, in fact."

" Exactly ! "

" But are frontiers indispensable then ? "

" Probably, as they are maintained."

" But what is the use of them ? "

The Vendetta.

" What is the use of them ? Why, it is this noble, but dangerous wall of national life, that makes us French— and proud of being so ! Suppose, for a moment, that you were to suppress the Pyrenees —we would at once be scraping the guitar and dancing the fandango ; the Alps—we would be eating macaroni and speaking through the nose ; the Jura—we would be sounding the *ranz des vaches* through a bugle ; the Rhine—we would be stuffing ourselves with sauerkraut and sausages ; the Straits of Dover—we would be singing psalms and reading the Bible ; the

Belgian custom-house officers—then we would be speaking pigeon French and drinking 'faro'!

"But a biped who strums on a guitar and disports himself in a fandango; swallows yards of macaroni and speaks through the nose; bellows the *ranz des vaches*—and through a horn too; revels in sauerkraut and sausages; chants canticles and reads the Bible; speaks negro fashion and intoxicates himself with 'faro,' —you will agree with me, is not a Frenchman. He may be an Albino, a Caraïb, an anthropophagus—perhaps a rational animal— anything you like except a Frenchman. Therefore, the frontiers being our guarantee against the guitar and fandango, macaroni and nasal intonation, the *ranz des vaches* and the bugle through which it is sounded, sauerkraut and sausages, psalms and the Bible, the Flemish language and 'faro,' we are indebted to them for being uncontaminated, and remaining what we are—that is to say, free from all those exotic eccentricities, the absence of which is our most beautiful ornament and the most appreciable of our qualities. You see that one cannot do without frontiers if one has the least desire to belong to one's country: *Nemo potest exuere patriam.*"

"Yes; but apart from the glory of being French?"

"There remains the advantage of always having a quarrel on one's hands—in case of need. Quarrels are so useful—especially when you are in the wrong."

"There is no necessity to quarrel — when there is no cause. *Sublata causa, tollitur effectus!*"

"But the frontier itself is the cause—the permanent, inevitable, fatal cause! Did you ever hear of two landowners, separated from each other by an intermediate wall, keeping up a good understanding? — Never! They always end in going to law, and, if they are obstinate, in ruining themselves. Well, frontiers are the inter- mediate walls of nations; only the dispute is settled by cannon balls; but it terminates in the same way as the other: people become obstinate, and both sides are ruined, or nearly so."

"But could not these terrible frontiers be abolished? There would be no more fighting about them."

"Abolish them! Why you are suggesting the destruction of the entire human race, unhappy man! When we no longer fight, we shall cease killing each other, and humanity, in a body, will die of *ennui*."

"The nostalgia of the cannon, eh, madcap? It's of a driven-in paradox that you'll die!"

The French Frontier.

"And you too, for having listened to me."

Then the two friends walked away laughing, arm-in-arm.

Jacques, who had spoken the first, was a curious type. His name was Jacques—Jacques, nothing more. He had seen the light of day on the rich slopes of Burgundy, that pearl of France, that admirable cellar which excites the bitter envy of the grotesque tipplers beyond the Rhine—as if those divine vintages had been produced for their barbarian throats. He was an artist. One fine day, without any warning, he had closed his studio, placed the key under the door-mat, writing in chalk on the door, "On a visit to the sons of Osiris," and had taken a ticket for Cairo, just as if he had been going to Asnières or Meudon. For since we have had a colonial empire, or rather a colonial republic, in France, with a special Ministry and Minister, like the old neighbour on the other side of the Straits, we have become prodigiously daring in the way of travels.

The study of geography, which previously had been very much neglected, according to what some people say, has become quite fashionable since 1870. The Government, to credit these wicked tongues, animated by noble ardour, rivalling Cook, of tourist renown, largely contributed to develop this taste. They first of all organised, at the cost of the State, cellular voyages to New Caledonia, Noumméa, Pine-tree Island, and the neighbourhood. *Audaces fortuna juvat.* Emboldened by success, they rushed towards other shores ; they wanted to do something grand ! Glory trips were organised for Tunis, Madagascar, Tonkin. In this instance the voyage was not gratis ; the passengers, selected by chance, paid with their skins, and most of them left them there ! Those who returned brought back bundles of laurels—and fevers !

They sacrificed thousands of men and millions, said the pusillanimous and chicken-hearted souls. The last Chinese adventure was particularly expensive. While, at Tunis, the Bey could not blow his nose without permission of the Republic ; at Madagascar, France became the titulary dragoman of her Malagassi Majesty, who was governed by English Methodists ; there she abandoned her Sakalave allies to the Hovas ; China, after an honourable and costly exchange of hostilities, undertook to entrust to French engineers—*if it pleased her*—the task of laying down a problematical network of railroads ; in Tonkin outlets were to be opened to—foreign commerce !

There were colonies—but no colonists to place there, continued the luke-warm patriots, with severe irony. There was a gap. Nations that had colonists and to spare — and no colonies, filled it up.

France had again spent her blood and gold for others, and had unconsciously pulled the chestnuts out of the fire, being treated with egregious bad faith.

Fortunately, beside those timid characters, those people devoid of initiative, of narrow views, restrained to an unproductive policy, there are some wiser minds, of a wider breadth of view, imbued with a more enlightened idea of patriotism and a more correct notion

The study of geography.

of the mission of France. More profound and sagacious, farther seeing politicians, have perceived in this cleverly provoked thirst to expand the Republic a way to give new outlets to her commerce, and the extension of French ideas.

They thought that the French nation, that Gallic race which has been described as " so apt to conquer the world, but so powerless to keep it," at least knew after the conquest how to open her purse to assist in the prosperity of her colonies, instead of enriching herself

at their expense and mercilessly exhausting them, after the example
of other nations that are more—colonising.

Perhaps these over-daring partisans of a colonial policy are only,
after all, simple visionaries, dupes of exaggerated jingoism, magnifying beyond measure their belief in the destiny and importance of their
country ! Perhaps those adversaries whom they accuse of timidity
are merely prudent pilots, anxious lest the fortunes of France
should be wrecked in a policy of adventure.

Jacques and Onésime.

The future will show us
whether the daring or circumspect were right.

Jacques, however, had
dared ! On the way he had
met his friend Onésime Coquillard.

" Where are you going to ? "
inquired the latter.

" To Egypt."

" What for ? "

" To see."

" See what ?   See whom ? "

" The country—the sons of
Osiris."

" I'll go too ; you'll introduce
me ; we'll see together."

" Come on ! "

" Let us be off ! "

And they had boldly set out, so thoroughly had the love of travel,
which had seized hold on the Government, infiltrated itself, like
healthy inoculation fluid, among the masses, and driven them forth
to the four quarters of the globe.

A painter of merit, a draughtsman of talent, Jacques had wished
to see Egypt ; he wanted to bow to the grandmother of nations, to
interrogate the Sphinx, contemplate Bonaparte's forty centuries on
the summit of the pyramids ; see if the Orient was a myth invented

by a facetious Rapin and Orientalism a superfetation ; whether Gérôme's Almehs and Bashi-Bazouks existed elsewhere than on his canvases ; whether Regnault and Fromentin had shown greater imagination than they should have done ; whether the so much vaunted water of the Nile deserved its reputation ; whether the stick was made purposely for the backs of the fellaheen, as a great patriotic statesman had affirmed at the French Tribune. His dream was to bring a crocodile back with him, into his studio, a real one, and to return with a little sunshine at the end of his brushes.

Physically he was a tall, strong fellow, well built, supple, firmly set upon his muscular legs ; the sinews of a hunter ; light reddish hair ; clear, penetrating, grey eyes, with a bold, mocking look about them ; the nose was straight, firm, finely modelled ; the mouth well furnished, revealing an expression of banter beneath a fawn-coloured moustache. He had a good appetite and the stomach of an ostrich. In a word, he was well armed to engage in the battle of life—and win it. The man was original, his aspect sympathetic.

Morally speaking, a giddy head, a warm heart ; a clever brain, with a fair amount of wit and a good many ideas ; joking seriously, always astride on a paradox, with a horror of fools and fleeing from them as from the pest. An able linguist, he was gifted with a peculiar scent for discovering suspicious and fantastical etymologies.

Onésime Coquillard, from Paris, his friend, in accompanying him, had been actuated a little by the want of occupation, a great deal by a desire to be with him, in a measure also by curiosity, but not at all by an inclination for travelling.

Left an orphan at an early age, a comfortable little income— *aurea mediocritas*—permitted him to live without working—and he took advantage of his position! As lazy as a dormouse, he had buried himself in his cheese, like the rat in the fable, purring away with the beatitude of a Capucin the existence of a porter's cat. Dark, short, fat, dumpy, bearded, hairy, downy, low on the shanks, a good fellow, with a beaming countenance, happy, he rolled through life quite slowly, without jolting. He was very fond of Jacques, a friend from childhood, who returned his affection. He was content to see others work ; the task of looking on, the only one that was not antipathic to him, sufficed. "One cannot do everything at once," he often remarked to his active Pylades ; "you work, and I am resting for you." He was witty, at times, when his laziness gave him an opportunity. He handled irony rather skilfully, lost his self-possession rapidly—on the surface, and regained it with even greater rapidity. His sudden displays of temper, factitious rather than real, broke out suddenly about nothing, and ended in the same way. A spoilt child of nature, he just allowed himself to live quietly, making of wisdom a pleasure, not an honour; of his idleness a virtue, not a vice. He detested revolutions by nature, loved liberty by egotism, hated war by instinct, but fought bravely—out of self-respect, he said. He was rather indifferent about religion ; but, if brought to the subject, he thundered against all religions, and scoffed at their ministers.

Feeling convinced that all the great thoughts of man come from the stomach, "that sublime alembic," he had vowed consequently a profound, devoted, and scrupulously rational worship to that agreeable organ. Gifted with a delicate sense of smell, a subtle taste, a very respectable power of absorption and assimilation, he loved the table and behaved very well there, eating steadily, drinking neat, expanding his good humour around him. He was polite during the first course, gallant with the second, tender at dessert, enterprising at the champagne, daring afterwards ! The aspect of a bottle of Clos-Vougeot, of a famous year, of venerable age, affected him considerably. The arrival on the table of a truffled turkey at once paralysed his power of speech.

His slumbers were as tranquil as his conscience. He advanced indifferently towards the inevitable end, armed with his charming egotism, satisfied with himself, thoughtless about others, finding that everything was for the best, in the best of worlds possible. When Jacques laughingly called him a gasteropode, Onésime retaliated with cephalopode ; they were living and inseparable antitheses.

The two friends had installed themselves fore'ard, amidst a group of sailors, where Jacques must have been up to his games, judging by the noisy hilarity that reigned around him.

But astern a sinister *ennui* weighed on every one ; black, dull, somno-lent *ennui* ; an unhappy product of bad, over-satiated stomachs, sick livers, affected pancreas, overflowing bile, choked-up ganglions, empty brains.

The hoarse sighs of the machine, with its dull, regular, monotonous strokes, scanned with their merciless rhythm the grotesque snoring, the strange gasping, the doleful gaping of this mournful assembly of undertakers' men, with ossified, zygomatic muscles ; of these unhappy victims of spleen !

Reptilius on the deck.

CHAPTER II.

The silhouette of Reptilius.—Where it is seen that Jacques has a spite against the Germans and a grain of ill-temper against the Italians.—Outburst of ultra-patriotism on his part, complicated by excessive socialism.—Exhibition of principles.—Dismay of Onésime ; his horror of the cataclysm.

AT this moment Reptilius had just left his neighbours the Italians, with whom he had launched out at a gallop into a burning discussion, the subject of which rolled upon the road Italy ought to take in crossing the Alps and penetrating into France in concert with Germany, which would invade it by the east. He was advancing fore'ard, gravely promenading his odd silhouette of a bird of ill-omen ; a sardonic smile wrinkled his pallid face, while his eye ran over the map he held in his hand as he walked along. He passed near the group, absorbed in meditation, and on the overhanging margin of the unfolded map Jacques was able to read, "The eastern frontier of France, drawn up by Herr Berghaus and Karl Vogel."

"So they have the eye always fixed on our frontiers, from which a slice has already been removed. watching a weak point that will serve to open a new breach in them," said Jacques, in a hollow tone of voice, in which anger was blended with a sort of contemptuous irony ; and a flow of blood reddened his cheeks, while the bitter flood of souvenirs rose up and oppressed his throat.

16

" O blond and geographical Germans!" he exclaimed, in a stifled
and restrained voice; " men of strong breath, all perfumed with
healthy and homely smells of beer, tobacco, sauerkraut, and pork;
virtuous Saxons, whose oily pores exhale those penetrating effluvia
which envelop your heavy bodies, precede your presence, and announce
you from afar, fatal messengers to people with a delicate sense of
smell and debilitated stomach; picturesque myopes with unctuous
hair, who confound in one immense predilection science and beer,
philosophy and sausages; chaste
and pure Germans, with square
heads, rounded bellies, enormous
loins, large feet, and phenomenal
intestines, which you have twelve
feet longer than less privileged
mortals; automatons disciplined
with the stick; grotesque calli-
pyges of whom the sons of
Rabelais have rendered the name
of Prussian immortal by making
it synonymous with that part of
the body which begins immediately where the loins end;
kleptomaniacs of clocks; indiscreet spectacled serpents, who
have raised espionage to a virtue;
cumbersome race that has burst
spontaneously into life, whose

Cultivating espionage.

prolific wave threatens to cover the world and to destroy the superior
species that generate more discreetly; practical people who made
the war with France a matter of business, in the names of ' William,
Bismarck, Moltke, & Co.,' which brought you five milliards of francs
and two provinces,—take your rest, honest brokers, booted, spurred,
armed, helmeted, paid bailiff's men, sanguinary usurers of the battle-
field; rest in peace on your laurels and your milliards, rocked to
sleep by your heinous ' Te Deum,' and, satiated boas, digest in

tranquillity your conquests!   France is still healing her wounds,
and if your black eagles have for their motto the barbarous war-cry,
'Might before right!' our standards have, inscribed in their folds,
that immortal device of humanity, 'Liberty, Equality, Fraternity';
right in its turn will stand before might!

"And you, Italians, you the sister nation who implore a smile
from Bismarck, who looks upon you as a *quantité négligeable*; you who

"Rest in peace on your laurels."

abandon France, who made you free! you who, with a superb independence of heart, cannot forgive her good services; you who shout,
'Stop thief!' when she hands you a kingdom in exchange for a town
and a few mountains covered with a handful of sweeps; who grabbed
Rome from her and had an eye on Tunis when she was gasping
beneath the heel of Bismarck,—take care that the *gendarmes* do not
arrest you, O illustrious effete; you, who were Romans, and have
retained their formidable appetite, without having preserved their
power of digestion.

"Have you forgotten the record of your august ancestor, the wolf's suckling, whose ferocity he inherited? who, slaughtering his brother, robbing his neighbours, violating their wives, implanted himself, sinister bandit, in the Aventine with his gang of worthless followers?

"Ambitious victims of neurosis, do not stir up a past that would crush you; trouble not a present which disdains the prattle of a people in long clothes, and do not obstruct the future by those deleterious dreams of universal domination which pollute your sick brain and impede your growth! Impotent race, you have lost the

Italy imploring a smile from Bismarck.

strength, forgotten the language of the masters of the world, your ancestors; you cannot and do not know how to say, *Civis sum Romanus*; S.P.Q.R. no longer means for you *Senatus populusque Romanus*, for you they are now only four letters without meaning; *Urbs* is no longer on the seven hills; it is everywhere where civilisation engenders progress and bestows a freedom; one is no longer a Roman citizen, but a citizen of the world! Rome is dead—dead and buried like Marlborough. You will not resuscitate it! One does not rise from one's ashes; the last Phœnix has been killed! There are no more Romans; the species is for ever destroyed, and nature does not recommence species; there are only Italians, a rudiment of people, a nation in an embryo state, an old geographical expression that has been revived. Lucullus no longer dines with Lucullus, he eats *ravioli*; Tiberius smokes halfpenny cigars; Vesuvius smokes for tourists; your old crumbling monuments are falling to pieces; your old boot, transformed into a museum of antiquities, is worn out. You are an old new thing!"

And Jacques turned round to the group of French sailors, who, with the mobility peculiar to their nation, were delighted with this ludicrous outburst against Italy, when an instant previous their fists had been clenching at the thoughts he had evoked about their own invaded country.

"You are treating them nicely, those poor Italians; what have they done to you?" said Onésime, taking Jacques by the arm and walking along the deck with him.

"Nothing. Only I feel hurt at their ingratitude to us."

"Yes, but we have in a measure deserved it, owing to the inept policy of Napoleon III., who, to pay court to Pius IX., who was laughing at him, and to keep his title of eldest son of the Church, so long left Rome to the Pope, who hated us, instead of giving it to the Italians, who loved us; he, in the place of completing our work of independence and handing Italy her capital, which she so warmly desired, thus ensuring her friendship and gratitude for ever, made, on the contrary, the service rendered weigh heavily upon her, affecting even to ignore that Italy also had fought valiantly beside us for her independence; he wounded the dignity of the young nation in the person of her King, whom the men of the Tuileries treated as a prefect of the Empire."

"I don't say nay; but Italy should not have held France, who spilt her blood to set her free, responsible for the stupidities of an imbecile Cæsar. She might have maintained her ill-feeling for the Emperor, but should have preserved us her friendship — and I reproach the hare-brained creature with her silly pranks with Bismarck; but I am without anger, and cannot feel hatred for a nation of our own blood."

" *Qui bene amat, bene castigat* ; that is the secret of your bullying her so."

" In a measure——"

" A good deal."

" That's true. Now! the peoples of the earth are gathering together in view of a supreme struggle for life ; and soon, disgusted, thinking better of her ridiculous mania for the great colossus, who is making fun of her, faithful to the instincts of her race, guided by a more lofty ambition, the beautiful sweetheart of the arts will throw herself into the arms of her big sister, France, to form with Spain, that other proud and noble sister, the triple league of the Latin races which will break up German unity."

" I shall illuminate, that evening."

" And you will do well ! But for the day to come, *delenda est Germania !* "

" You hate them very intensely, then, these Germans ? "

" Yes, I hate them, these parvenus of victory ; but I shall never hate them so much as they execrate us. Their hatred has most vivaciously survived their victory.

" We are, at any rate, not capable of such dire animosity as they cherish since 1870 in the contemplation of their glory, crystallised in the continuous apotheosis of their triumph ; we are not persecuted, as they are, by the microbe of an intense rage, which has reached the acute stage, and which all the prophylactic of Pasteur could not cure ; and never could a Frenchwoman soil her heart and lips with that ferocious wish, expressed in 1870 by a woman—Germaine, Countess of Bismarck : ' to see all the Gauls burnt or shot, all, even the smallest children.'

" We cannot, as they can, slowly distil, drop by drop, for three-quarters of a century, the venom of an incurable hatred refractory even to satiety ; and if they were able to strike us down, it was thanks to that handful of Protestants whom the revocation of the Edict of Nantes drove out of France, and whose descendants now belong to the staff of those rapacious reiters who ' have robbed us of our way of fighting, as they have stolen our trade-marks ' ; military plagiarists inventing I know not what 'Furor Teutonicus' in opposition to our chevaleresque 'Furia Francese,' just as they set their sour little white wines of the Rhine against our admirable brands of Champagne. It is also due to the gallant souvenirs which the conquerors of Jena left amongst them during the passage of the great army, infusing into the veins of these cold-blooded animals a little fervent Gallic ardour.

"We know not how to hate in France ; we have never known how. We have had sublime outbursts of anger, which have produced terrible revolutions ; they bore in their fecund flanks Liberty, which freed the world, struggling desperately in the grasp of the priests during that atrocious nightmare of the middle ages.

"But each of those efforts exhausted us ; and when these Teutonic hordes, who had been making ready for half a century under the canes of their officers, swooped down upon France, like voracious vultures, eager for the spoil, they found her weakened by those repeated shocks and taken unawares. After a superhuman effort, in an unequal struggle, handed over at Sedan by a flabby Cæsar, betrayed at Metz by the infamous Bazaine, resisting Frederick Charles with her young recruits and the remnant of her armies, France saved her honour, in spite of her chiefs, in an heroic defence beneath the walls of Paris.

"At length, maimed in her four limbs by her revolutions, crushed by the enemy, losing blood at all her wounds, she succumbed a martyr to liberty, mutilated by her implacable conqueror, who amputated Alsace and Lorraine from her, emptied her pockets, teaching her hatred, of which she knew nothing, and paralysing her steady advance towards progress, by forcing her to enter in her turn on the path of revenge, which will end in a fatal duel, in which one of the two nations will perish !"

"Amen !" said Onésime. "I hope it will not be France."

"France will never succumb. The breath of liberty is in her, and liberty does not die ! France, republican and free, will kill monarchical and enslaved Germany, just as modern ideas and science have killed ancient superstition and ignorance. Then right will have conquered might ; reason, the priest ; liberty, kings. Then those immense armies, that unconscious and irresponsible scourge, which expands like

HEGEMONIE
ALLEMANDE
ITE
FRANKE

a gigantic cancer over the world and gnaws it to its very marrow, absorbing the purest part of its blood—living, dangerous parasite of the fruit of her colossal labour—will have disappeared for ever! Then humanity, delivered, will perhaps be able to lend her ear to the dull rustling stir of the lower social strata ; she will be able to attentively follow the slow movement, the profound, mysterious work of transformation which is taking place among those murmuring masses, bestirring themselves in the secular slough of eternal misery where the merciless forgetfulness of the rulers has left them. Already at intervals, which are shorter and more threatening each time, some have risen to the surface, wan forerunners of famished multitudes, provoked by an accumulation of terrible suffering, of despair without a name, struggling livid in those sinister depths, in that Gehenna, hungering for air, liberty, and enjoyment! And their appetites must be satisfied, their sorrows must be assuaged, their stigmas effaced, the sufferers consoled, and a place in the sunlight must be given to those despairing souls, if you do not wish to disappear in a universal panic, borne away by a frightful cataclysm caused by the explosion of the exasperated anger of the lower orders in revolt !

"Instead of stagnating in a secular routine, instead of fruitlessly discussing old texts of ambiguously worded laws, we must cast off this unhealthy torpor, march resolutely forward, burn the old barbarous codes, the old antiquated laws, take a new line, and, guided by eternal justice, seek out the evil, destroy it, and find the modern formula by which to the right to live will be added the right and possibility of enjoying life. We must rebalance this world, which has been thrown out of its equilibrium by an unequal distribution of enjoyment and misery ; where the unfortunate die of hunger in the face of bloated millionaires, who paper the walls of their smoking-rooms with banknotes ; where children, who have too rapidly become men, commit suicide ; where men, who relapse into childhood too soon, lose their brain power. We must put an end to this lugubrious mystification which has existed so long ! "

Onésime was blue ! an indigo blue ! He stood there gaping, nailed to the deck, with haggard eye, struck down by the idea of this colossal and approaching downfall which Jacques had just evoked. Onésime—the peaceful Onésime, honest Onésime, Onésime Coquillard of Paris, independent gentleman, bachelor, elector, taxpayer, a friend of order and the Government—felt a shudder of terror running between his epidermis and the fat coagulated in the flabby adipose membranes of his person. For a moment he felt as if suffocating—and not without cause !

He had performed the part of echo when Jacques had roared against the Germans, he was a " Jingo " ; he had echoed again when Jacques had given Italy a dressing, he was of a gay turn of mind ; he had continued to sound the echo when Jacques in a sentence had anathematised warfare, he hated it ; the social strata had left him indifferent, although a trifle suspicious ; the appetites—of others —to be satisfied, the stigmas to be effaced, the consolation to be supplied, the place in the sunlight to be given to the despairing, had alarmed him ; but what had routed him, brought him to the earth, crushed him, scattered him in pieces, was the last blow, that rude thrust at his repose, that death-stroke with which his income was threatened, that was the frightful thunder-clap of which he seemed to hear the distant rumbling, and which was to pulverise all ! All ! down to poor and inoffensive Onésime Coquillard of Paris inclusively ! That was the cataclysm at short date, that incommensurate calamity which had been suddenly thrust under his nose ; and he had quaked and trembled at the prospect ; in the agony of his despair he had wept over himself—internally, intonating in sobs the *de profundis* of his misery—always internally, for, with that exquisite and rare modesty which is the privilege of great souls, he concealed, true martyr that he was, his extreme suffering, just as the timid violet modestly hides her perfumed petals beneath the grass, and without faltering had drained the chalice to the dregs. Onésime was a man —a man !

He gradually recovered himself, for his strength of character was great, and while still overwhelmed with the anguish of his fright, he poked out his nose from his prostration and turned his eyes on Jacques. That look was a look of despair ; it was a mute, eloquent, profoundly sad appeal to the pity of him who, juggling with his tranquillity of mind, made his liver turn pale and his heart beat with his sinister predictions.

Jacques had a mad inclination to laugh at the sight of his scared appearance; he sought for a moment to restrain himself; but being unable to resist any longer, he roared out in the face of the stupefied Onésime.

"He's laughing"; and Onésime made a calm, grand, resigned gesture, expressive of the intensity of the bitterness that filled his mind.

"But just look at yourself," exclaimed Jacques; "you have got such an odd face, you look so peculiarly funny, that you would do the same if you could only see yourself."

"So—peculiarly—funny!" slowly punctuated Onésime, and he paused majestically. Then his long-suppressed indignation burst out full of noble wrath.

"But, son of a gun! what would you have me look like when you unexpectedly announce such topsy-turvydom, such a chaos of frightful things? Set fire to the Code! Trample on the law! Dismiss the gendarmes! Sweep away all the institutions! Break and rack everything! Sack! Pillage! Flay alive! Go on gaily! Act like madmen! And, when you are quite tired of the game, when nothing remains standing in this abomination of desolation, carefully rebalance this disequilibrated world! And then set the galley sailing on the ocean of ruins! That is your programme, Vandal!"

"Burgundian, if you please."

"Burgundian, if you wish, but you must surely have had Vandals among your ancestors; in fact they were in a way cousins to Burgundians—the Vandals! It's atavism that's playing you a trick; you are troubled with the monomania of revolution, the folly of destruction. Yes, your programme is a very nice one! With 'all to the sewer!' or something similar for motto and *nihil* for the password. And it is doubtless you, modern Columbus of this world, revised and corrected, who will hold the helm and steer the barque?"

"I will give you the office if you like."

" To me ! I embark in that galley ! Thanks ! I have not found, as you have, the formula of happiness and the way to make use of it, an easy prescription to follow in secret, and even when travelling—shake the bottle before using the contents—for you've bottled it, your social syrup, the universal panacea. They sell it at the chemists' shops, this marvellous elixir—great quack ! But it is you who are the lugubrious mystifier in all this, and you horrify me with your social strata, your famishing poor, your cataclysms, and the sequel of your future revolutions. Schopenhauer is mildly gay aside of you ! And you speak of this with a light heart, as of quite a natural thing that must happen—one can see that it will cost you nothing."

" And you ? "

" And my income—is that nothing ? It would be I then that would dance the carmagnole, engulfed in the furnace."

" Yes, that's true. Your income—I forgot that ! "

" It's easy enough for you to say so, you, who have your fortune at the tips of your fingers ; but how about me ? "

" You, my good Onésime ? Well ! you'd do as I do, work. That would be a change in your existence."

" Me, work ! But at what, saperlipopette ? At what ? I ask you, what am I good for ? I, who have never in my life made any use of my ten fingers ? Do what ? And, besides, I don't want to change my style of life ! The way I live pleases me—and very much too ! I have a weakness for it; I don't want to live in any other way. I have not got St. Vitus's dance. I am not like you, who have quicksilver in the veins ; who can't stay in the same place ; who come, go, think of nothing but changing your quarters; who are always on the move ; who hold forth in all seasons, at every opportunity, upon everything and against every one, against the Germans this way, against the Italians that way ; now you are against the whole world. Since you have found the bacillus of the social evil, your fixed idea, to cure this poor humanity that doesn't know what to try next, is to upset society head over heels ; you require your little smash-up that was wanting ; you must have your tempest, as in the ancient heroic poems, like Homer in the *Odyssey* and Virgil in the *Æneid*. But, ye Gods ! the wind does not blow with such force there as it does with you: they are contented with stirring up the waves on the surface ; you, you are going to shake them up from the lowest depths at the risk of bringing on a deluge."

" And then—what after ? "

" What after ? But I don't know how to swim ! Goodness gracious, what a hurricane ! It's enough to give you nausea ! It's no longer a tempest; it's a water-spout, a cyclone, a simoom, simply something terrible ! And then, above all, it's your cataclysm that upsets me ! That monster of a cataclysm gives me the shivers ; that frightful cataclysm weighs me down ; it's a veritable sword of Damocles, suspended above my repose ; and if the thread broke, good-night, my nice little income ; good-bye, my cosy, comfortable life, my dearly beloved idleness ! The mere thought of it makes my back feel cold. Look here ! if you have the least regard for my person, if you have the least bit of friendship for me, you will suppress the cataclysm ; you don't know how the mere idea of that sinister farce makes me nervous ; you can do without it, can't you? It is not indispensable to you? You only knew of it recently; you have not had time to get accustomed to it yet. Suppress it, I beg of you. Do that for me ! "

" All right ! I suppress the cataclysm—which is, moreover, very hypothetical—as it is so much in your way, and I will limit myself to my social strata," said Jacques laughing. " Are you satisfied ? "

" More than satisfied; you save my life; thanks ! I breathe again with a light heart. But you, wretched being, you must have swallowed a volcano to enter into spontaneous eruption like that ! You have stolen Vesuvius or Stromboli on the way, and have hidden it in your stomach ! You burst out like that, all at once, about nothing. One talks to you, and bang ! you suddenly begin to throw out lava immediately, without a sign of warning ! Vesuvius at least foreshadows his fits of anger by some preliminary indications ; one has time to get out of the way. But your crater is treacherous, the explosion sudden ; you burst out in a moment *ex abrupto*, without warning, like a volcano that has been badly brought up. It's wrong ! "

" Hold your tongue, or I'll introduce my cataclysm again."

"Oh, no! I beg of you, don't do that. Sheath your cataclysm; I'll hold my tongue."

"And, before accusing me of having stolen volcanoes on the way, wait until we have first of all met with them. Can the mere prospect of my cataclysm have already upset your brain?"

"Alas! the word alone drives me crazy!"

Vesuvius.

CHAPTER III.

"THE island of Elba in sight," exclaimed a sailor. "The island
of Elba," repeated a mocking voice : "an island where
generals of Corsican origin who make themselves emperors are deposited on a model farm. They pass their leisure in teaching such
of their soldiers as show an aptitude for country life farming—
escape is easy."

Passing by Monte Cristo, Jacques, who was still a prey to his
geographical attack, insinuated that it had been discovered by
Alexander Dumas, who had found in a cavern there the material
for a great romance, which was as interesting as the island itself
is the reverse.

They had reached the straits of Bonifacio. A little beyond
the promontory of the Bear they perceived a white house, half-way
up the heights on the island of Caprera, the house of the hero of

31

Italian independence, a rock upon which, according to Jacques, Garibaldi had chosen to end his legend.

He had conquered the hearts of the sailors, had Jacques, as had also the good Onésime. If the baronet was the star of the poop, Jacques was the sun of the forecastle, and Onésime was its moon. The frank and communicative gaiety of the two friends made them very popular with the sailors, whom they were always putting in a good humour.

On the first day Onésime, under the

"It's the men's plank."

influence of a maritime emotion, as involuntary as it was painful to his heart, had had the weakness in a more than usually violent attack to sigh after "the cow's plank." Here, "It's the men's plank!" a sailor who happened to be passing that way coarsely blurted out in his face.

Jacques' stomach was above every species of emotion of that sort, a quality that was far from injuring him in the estimation of his rough audience.

The Gulf of Naples.

The next day they awoke in view of the Roman country: a naked, desolate coast, here and there ruined towers, rare miserable villages; facing the mouth of the Tiber and the little port of Finmicino, a luminous white spot, the cupola of St. Peter of Rome, shines far out in the country. The coast continues low and sad, broken from time to time by the Albano and Velletri mountains, which dominate Mount Calvi. They pass Porto d'Anzio, Nettuno, the Pontine Marshes, the abrupt promontory of Mount Circello — and, suddenly, there is a complete change. It is nothing but charming, coquettish, wooded hills, gently sloping towards the sea : this is the beautiful Neapolitan shore unrolling, before the enchanted eyes of the travellers, the treasures of its rich and splendid

Cook and Son's parcels.

nature. They skirt the gulfs Terracina and Gaeta, the miniature archipelago of Palmarola, Ponza, and Vandolena, the island of Procida, Cape Miseno, and, amidst a glorious sun, the vessel makes her entry into the Gulf of Naples. Leaving Pozzuoli, the Castle of Baïa, the island of Nisida on the right, she coasts by Posilippo, and Naples appears—radiant !

Capri ! Ischia ! Adorable guardians of an admirable bay, at the head of which, sparkling with light, sprinkled with touches of pink, blue, yellow, green, drowned in an immense warm tone of melted silver, a white city rises up in tiers, casting its clear, luminous reflection in the azure of the bay!

Indifferent to the dull growling of Vesuvius, whose sombre silhouette, crowned with its smoking plume, shows its profile, a terrible menace, beneath a leaden sky, Naples reposes unconcerned at the feet of her colossal neighbour, a rough companion who, one of these days, will dash her to pieces as he did Herculaneum and Pompeii!

What a lot of *personal, intimate* emotions were extracted from the guide-books, and were transferred compendiously to the note-books, on that memorable day, when the *Saïd* having triumphantly doubled the last promontory, this vision, sublime in its pro-digious grandeur, in its exquisite grace, marvellous in beauty and charm, appeared before the dull passengers, incapable of transmitting to the brain, mercilessly closed to a perception of the beau-tiful, sensations that they could not feel!

Reading his impressions.

They wrote in an unsteady hand, the better to convey the full strength of the emotion experienced. A series of dots indicated it incommensurably; notes of exclamation accentuated it, and commas gave it a colouring. And when, later on, they read it for the hundredth time to friends who were fortunate enough to enjoy the ineffable happiness, they introduced into their diction the shaky aspect of the up-strokes, the vigorous intonations of the notes of exclamation, the shaded har-monies of commas indicated in the text: in the sonority of the consonants, in the vigour of the syllables, thundered the anger of the volcano; in the softness of the vowels one caught sight of the pleasant Neapolitan horizons ; in the countenance and expression of the orator one imagined violent, but restrained, vibrations. And when his voice slowly died away in a final earnest accent, it was very rare not to perceive a few politely flattering tears form pearls on the eye-lashes of the audience, none the less in earnest, a satisfaction expected and deserved by the author, who, very much affected, wiped his fore-head that was bathed in perspiration.

At two o'clock the *Saïd* stopped almost alongside the quay. The vessel had hardly been secured in her berth, when a host of petty dealers invaded the deck, while a flotilla of boats, painted all sorts of colours and of strange forms, swarmed along the huge sides of the steamer. From these craft adults with bronzed bodies, clothed with a simple medal

Indigenous music.

suspended round their necks, elegant in form, with supple muscles and boldly outlined heads, rose erect, beautiful as antique statues, of which they unconsciously assumed the attitudes. They dived, being the most expert and indefatigable swimmers, after small pieces of money, which the passengers on deck threw for them into the sea. Disappearing in the blue waters beneath the vessel's keel, they reappeared on the other side, smiling and showing teeth of pearly whiteness, like famished young wolves, exhibiting in one hand the coin they had found and begging again with the other.

"Lovely models," said Jacques ; "a harmony of muscles on which they have forgotten to place an encephalon."

"Well-shaped idiots," corroborated Onésime.

From other boats arose sharp, nasal sounds, singing with accompaniment of cracked guitars and screeching violins. The passengers were literally enveloped in harmony ; it entered by the nose, eyes, ears, mouth—everywhere !

Unfortunately the town sewers were perceptible ; and to the suffering of the acoustic nerve, frightfully knocked about by the native cacophony, was joined the painful sense of the grievously affected olfactory apparatus.

In the meanwhile the chattering hawkers had displayed their curiosities from Pompeii and Herculaneum : pieces of mosaic and a lamp from the abode of the Vestal Virgins ; the marble umbilicus from a statue of Vitellius ; the skin

The odours of Naples.

of Cleopatra's asp ; a piece of the woodwork of the seat on which Heliogabalus received the fatal blow ; a photograph of Nero ; one of Caligula's horse-shoes ; Cicero's wart. You could see a lock of Cæsar's hair there, the toothpick of Lucullus : the latch-key of Messalina, which enabled her to escape at night-time from the Imperial Palace and visit the slums of Rome, from which she returned—

"*Jam lassata viris, sed non satiata !*"

The razor with which Cato, the Stoic, opened his veins, was also offered for sale.

All these were guaranteed authentic ; one could even order an antiquity to measure at choice—and still authentic ! Italy was emptying her drawers of family souvenirs ; she was trying to realise a few little things to pay for a monster cannon that was being manufactured. She wanted to make a stir in the world. Children are so noisy !

In the way of modern articles Vesuvius and the sea supplied them all, and the inhabitants of Torre del Greco brought their curiously worked pieces of lava and their deftly carved coral. Chaplets made

Torre del Greco.

of myrtle, olive, and box-wood, with enormous beads, attracted the attention of the pious. Beside these, grotesque coloured prints had the pretension of representing the venerable features of the successor of the Apostles.

Reptilius purchased Messalina's latch-key ; the young ladies rifled the vendors of necklaces ; the " parcels " crammed their portmanteaux with Vesuvian souvenirs ; the horse-shoe became the property of a superstitious Englishman ; the Italians abstained—and with reason.

A shrill whistle conveyed the order to clear the deck, and the noisy crowd rapidly made off, relieved of a good part of their second-hand pacotilla ; the concert-boats widened the circle, carrying along with them their noisy harmony, while the *Saïd*, slowly turning round, set her bow towards Sorrento.

They had at last got rid of the stenches of Naples, of its lazzaroni, of its false antiquities, of the nasal accentuations of that tongue, so sonorous because it is so empty.

Passing between the promontory of Campanella and the island of Capri, the vessel stood out to sea, leaving smoking Vesuvius behind her, and on her left the deep gulfs of Salerno and Amalfi.

The shades of night were falling when the *Saïd* entered that admirable Tyrrhene Sea, dear to Homer and Virgil. Continuing her

Vesuvius.

nocturnal course, she doubled Cape Spartivento, crossed the Policastro Gulf, and passed by the Calabrian Mountains, and farther on Stromboli, that old accomplice of Vesuvius, which on dark nights lights up the Lipari Islands with its sinister glare.

Once within the Gulf of Gioja, they passed Cape Faro, leaving on either side the famous and inoffensive rocks of Charybdis and Scylla. At noon they passed through the Straits of Messina, at the moment of the second breakfast, and through the open port-holes they distinctly perceived the wild, denuded, and sunny coast of Calabria, where the train from Reggio follows the coast-line, and the shore of luxuriant Sicily, extending on the right, with its rich vegetation, its picturesque mountains, dominated by colossal Etna, with its snowy peaks, its sides striped by its streams of black and red lava, descending as far as the vineyards which cover its base to the sea, where slender Maltese speronari, with only one mast, glide by on the surface of the water.

When Cape Spartivento was rounded, they passed into the Ionian Sea, and this time the steamer's head was set direct for Alexandria.

Onésime has the spleen.

The sea was hopelessly beautiful, the sky hopelessly lovely; hours succeeded hours. The passengers, momentarily galvanised by the meal-bell, returned immediately afterwards to their torpor of lizards, their immobility of fossils petrified in thick layers of boredom.

Jacques thought the sea very beautiful, but also very blue. Onésime had been sulking in a corner since they had lost sight of land; he felt something like a commencement of nostalgia, he regretted his cheese! He was wondering how much longer they were going to navigate that basin of blue water, beneath that blue sky and invariably lovely sun, in the company of that band of coagulated dozers on deck. His round, hirsute little person was bristling all over; he was quietly changing into a porcupine.

A few gusts of mad notes, a few measures of a quadrille they were playing in the saloon, snatched him from his melancholy thoughts and his corner; he directed his steps towards the performer, a Frenchman, who was endeavouring to stir the venerable chords of the vessel's Pleyel, which by a miracle was in good condition.

This unusual sound acted as an antidote to the general discomfort. A slight rustle of gowns indicated that the feminine element was showing signs of life; a few inquisitive heads appeared at the open windows; some daring ones had the audacity to enter.

Reptilius had been one of the first to dash in there. He had walked, or rather fallen, into the saloon like a bomb. As soon as the music-stool was free, he bounded on to it and screwed himself down there, fatiguing the instrument beneath a febrile, rapid, masterly touch.

Seen from behind, he resembled a gigantic coleopteron: his enormous round back was shining in shades of black, glossy, worn at the shoulders, of his garment; the long skirts of his frock-coat, his pockets swelled with books and rolls of papers, beat a wild saraband on his immense feet, which crushed the trembling pedals. At times his head all at once disappeared between his two shoulders, and the nose, coming to the assistance of the busy fingers, struck a difficult note. The rapidity of his movements seemed to multiply his arms, giving them the appearance of monstrous moving antennæ; one would have said it was an enormous cockchafer, affected with melomania, improvising.

" Us " was a capital virtuoso; the effect was unexpected, the

" Us " at the piano.

success prodigious, mingled with a little anxiety on the part of the young misses, rather frightened at first at the strange contortions of this musical beetle, and on the male side by a little stifled laughter excited by the performer's peculiar movements. He met, nevertheless, with complete success. "Us" could legitimately enjoy his triumph. His pale lips, with white commissures, trembled in his wrinkled face; his eyes sparkled behind the blue glasses of his gold-rimmed spectacles; his rare grey locks at the nape of the neck fluttered; his scarlet nasal bulb, bruised by contact with the keys of the piano, seemed to emit sheaves of sparks; while a warm vapour of perspiration, produced by this gymnastic exercise of the muscles, this violent excitement of the nerves, escaped from his whole person, enveloping him in a cloud which hid him from the profane.

All of a sudden, during a waltz briskly engaged in by the Doctor, Onésime, who for some time previous, with sparkling eyes, beating time with his head and imitating the barytone in a low voice, had felt a terrible itching in his legs, seized upon an old spinster—who, while offering some outward show of resistance, at the same time clung to him with all her might—and impetuously dashed off with her.

Onésime and Miss Priscilla.

Then it was as if a discharge of electricity had communicated its shock to all the company. Couples were formed; started, they spun round and round, engulfed in this maelstrom of human waves, the whirling evolutions of which were scanned by the bewildered "Us" with a frenzy that increased as he proceeded. *Vires acquirit eundo!*

Little by little this moving chain stopped, as its detached links sank panting on the divans. Then there was a noise like a hasty flapping of wings, produced by nervously handled fans; one heard the hoarse sound of breathless respiration ; multi-coloured handkerchiefs wiped foreheads bathed in perspiration ; a muggish human smell, mingled with the odour of more subtle perfumes, escaped by the open portholes, while the terrible Doctor continued, continued playing still !

This musical tide, which had borne along in its furious course all these different elements, all these antagonistic molecules, had left them, on retiring, strangely grouped.

Onésime, while mopping himself at one of the ports, had commenced an idyl with his dancer, Miss Priscilla, who gave herself precious airs, contented that the brick-coloured red tint which the excitement of dancing had brought to the slightly tanned leather of her cheeks should be mistaken for respectable modesty on the alert.

Cook and Son's parcels were mixed up with the unlabelled English people without the latter making any effort to get away ; they even exchanged smiles, and more than that, they conversed affably together.

The baronet, who had left his cloud in the cloak-room, was talking to Jacques, who had just conducted Miss Madge, his daughter, to her seat.

Italians and Frenchmen offered each other cigars and took refreshments at the same bar.

The Spaniard chuckled inwardly and went in search of his guitar.

Jonathan. in his delight and in his mania for whittling wood, had ended by cutting away the legs of his chair—which was breaking beneath him.

The Russian shook off his last icicles.

The ice was broken everywhere ; all the rancour, all the antipathies, melted in this salubrious thaw.

In the evening they dined with peculiar gaiety and glee. The shock had mingled all these heterogeneous genera together to form one unique species, well determined not to lose an opportunity for amusement ; a little music, a small hop, had performed this miracle, by rounding off the angles.

The days following comprised an uninterrupted series of pleasant moments. Onésime forgot his cheese, Jacques showed a tendency to draw near to Sir Hugh Templeton, the baronet, especially when Miss Madge was beside him ; concessions on all sides rained as thick as hailstones ; the "unlabelled" diffused tepid confidences into the bosoms of the Cookites, half confessing that an excess of vanity had largely contributed towards making them turn aside from the seductive advantages offered by Cook and Son ; and the Cookites, gently flattered by this confession, regretted that their purses had not been equal to their desire, so as to enable them to travel in as noble and independent a way as the others. The baronet behaved as a simple mortal with Jacques, who, in Miss Madge's company, learned to correct his imperfect English pronunciation. The Spaniard, who had ended by finding his guitar, put all his gaiety into music. Jonathan, in quest of a new chair to annihilate, extended his limbs in a silent laugh. Italy smiled at France, and the latter, while pouting at Germany, behaved fairly decently towards her sole representative on board.

The *Saïd* had left Candia far on the left ; another day and they would be in sight of Alexandria.

One felt the East in the splendid warm tones of the sunsets, where the purple clouds, striated with gold, waved to and fro, marvellous in colour, beneath the immense canopy of heaven, the green of which merged at the zenith into infinite dark blue.

Jacques stood for hours leaning on his elbows, silent, in profound enjoyment of these grand views ; and when the enormous blood-like disc, descending slowly to the horizon, at last sank with a final beam in the mighty amplitude of its glory, he still remained there watching the shades of night advance from afar, lost in his rambling thoughts.

Onésime was astonished at this profound, mute, contemplative, almost painful admiration, he who expressed it loquaciously, diffusely, epidermidally.

On October 10th, at noon, they sighted land. The commotion was general. Attention was eagerly concentrated on the coast in view, which at every instant became more distinct.

A long, low, grey line of alluvial earth just emerges out of the sea : in the centre is the twinkling glass dome of the Viceroy's palace ;

farther on Pompey's Pillar shoots up isolated, high, dark, dominating a few slender minarets that rise above pink, white, dusty-looking houses ; a few scanty palm trees, numerous windmills ; to the east Ramleh, lost in a few tufts of green ; and in the background, to the west, a great even white line—the Libyan desert. It is Alexandria, it is the decayed city of the Ptolemies.

A boat comes alongside, a pilot climbs on board. A few more turns of the screw, and the *Saïd*, passing through the difficult channels at the entrance to the port, casts her anchor in the midst of a swarm of boats that immediately surround her, and whose strange crews, prattling and noisy, swarm over the deck like a cloud of locusts.

The port of Alexandria.

CHAPTER IV.

General hustle.—They land.—Onésime, a Count in spite of himself, and Jacques,
very much puzzled, are conducted to the hotel. — Double explanation. —
Jacques is convinced of the excellent quality of Nile water.—They make
the acquaintance of Doctor Alan Kéradec.—Satisfaction, disappointment,
and anger of Reptilius. — Rough sketch of history. — Jacques makes an
error in a page and "Us" in a volume.—Two erudites fall out.—Onésime
is devoured by mosquitoes.

AMIDST a most frightful uproar the motley crowd invade the
deck. As nimble as monkeys, they appear on all sides,
penetrate by the portholes, disappear down the hatchways, ascend the
rigging, climbing over one another, crushing the passengers, laughing,
yelling, vociferating, gesticulating, catching hold of everything that
comes within their reach. It is a general hustle!

The deck is in frightful confusion; the noise, the agitation, the
guttural cries, the variety of strange costumes, of crude colours,
the infinite diversity of types, quite dazzle the astounded travellers.

Jacques, seated on his luggage, stoutly defends it against the
attack of a great devil of a negro who insists on removing it. As
an artist he admires the energetic and bestial head, with dull ebony
shades, beneath a red cap with a blue tuft; the form of an athlete,
with muscles jutting out from beneath the white gandourah that

covers them ; but as a prudent traveller he fears that the safety of his trunks would be very much compromised in such hands.

At this moment Onésime, who had disappeared, returns, flanked by a magnificent blue Kawas, the scimitar at his side, who bows to Jacques and has the luggage removed, himself carrying the portmanteaux. He shows the greatest respect to Onésime, whom he calls Monsieur le Comte ; and he installs the two friends on crimson velvet seats, in the stern of a superb galley carrying the French flag, covered with a red and white awning, and which, vigorously propelled by six oars, proceeds rapidly towards the custom-house.

On the way they cross a correct-looking craft flying the British flag, and recognise Sir Hugh and Miss Madge, with whom they exchange bows. The boat comes alongside the quay ; two sturdy fellows in yellow gowns remove the luggage, while the blue Kawas caresses with his courbash the backs of some rather too inquisitive urchins, bawling themselves hoarse with repeated demands for baksheesh. At a word which he utters as he passes by the custom-house, officers raise the hand to the tarboush, and, without examining the trunks, hasten to open the gates.

Onésime, sedate and sardonic, Jacques, very much perplexed, pass through the stirring crowd of clerks, porters, beggars, in the midst of trunks caved-in, turned topsy-turvy, by the ruthless hands of the custom-house officers, and depart under the eyes of such of their unfortunate fellow-passengers of the *Saïd* as had preceded them. At the gate their amiable guide calls a private carriage that is waiting, and they seat themselves in it amidst deafening cries, in which the word " baksheesh," yelled by sonorous voices, predominates.

The man with the scimitar, erect at the door, inquires if Monsieur le Comte still intends putting up at the Hôtel d'Europe, and, on an affirmative sign from Onésime, installs himself beside the coachman ; the lash curls round the horses, two superb thoroughbreds, which start off at a smart trot, and the two friends, embedded in the soft cushions, make their entry into the city.

During their rapid drive they barely have time to cast a glance at the narrow streets through |which they pass, and which are en-cumbered by an active population of diverse races in bright costumes that shine in the sun. Onésime does not breathe a word, but smiles from time to time in his thick black beard in answer to Jacques' mute interrogations and bewildered air.

A moment later they passed before the Mosque of Sheïkh Ibrahim, and, turning to the left in Anastasy Street, came out on the Place des Consuls, where the coachman put them down at the Hôtel d'Europe.

The serviceable Kawas rushed to the door, which he opened, and, preceding the travellers, led them into the vast hall of the hotel; then he approached Onésime smiling, and placed his hand on a level with his tarboush, a quite discreet way of saying baksheesh without opening the mouth. Onésime understood, and the worthy personage withdrew satisfied.

The two friends chose their apartments, and then went down to the drawing-room, where Onésime burst into a wild roar of laughter in Jacques' face, who, finally joining in this contagious hilarity, also burst out laughing.

"Look here, Monsieur le Comte," Jacques began, "would you kindly explain to me the mystery of——"

"Of all this, eh?" interrupted Onésime.

"Yes; for I understand absolutely nothing."

"Neither do I; and the more I seek to fathom it, the less I understand."

"Explain yourself."

"I will endeavour to do so. You remember that I left you for an instant on deck, during the confusion on our arrival, to fetch my bag downstairs?"

"Yes. And then?"

"Well, while returning, I knock up against our blue bird of a Kawas, who bows to me very low, and whose bow I return, but a little less lowly, however. 'Monsieur le Comte,' he says to me, in that frightful jargon which is termed *lingua franca*, and the vocabulary of which has been borrowed, in a measure, from all known languages, dead and living, 'I was seeking for your Lordship.' I look at him angrily, thinking that he is making fun of me. Not in the least ! And he adds very seriously : 'Your boat is waiting for you, Monsieur le Comte ; if your Grace will show me where your luggage is, I will have it landed '; and he seeks to relieve me of my bag, with which I

Onésime and the Kawas.

refuse to part. I reply to him that I am neither Count nor Lordship, nor anything approaching it ; that I am simply Onésime Coquillard, of Paris, independent gentleman and a bachelor : that no boat is waiting for me ; that I am even looking out for one at that moment : and, I add, endeavouring to get away, that he must certainly be in error. 'I see that your Highness wishes to remain incognito,' he says with a sly smile, 'but I have my orders.' And he insists more than ever ; I do not laugh, and insist on my side ; we both insist ; his obstinacy has the best of it ; he is determined I shall be Monsieur le Comte. Count who? Count of what? I will try to find out. Tired of the discussion, I let him do as he likes. I allow myself to be bombarded Highness ; he seizes my bag, I join you on deck, and find you struggling with your black man ; you follow quite bewildered, we jump into the boat, the French flag at the stern ; our guide makes the custom-house officers, who should have searched us, bow to us, seats us in a carriage, brings us here, and disappears ! Now you know as much as I do."

"It's a regular tale of the 'Arabian Nights.'"

"With this difference, that it's absolutely true, and that here we are saved from the claws of the custom-house, in which our unfortunate companions are probably still struggling."

Onésime had hardly concluded his story, which he had related without stopping, and in a loud voice, when an elderly gentleman, of eccentric appearance, who had been listening to him with a smile, approached politely.

"You will pardon me, gentlemen, the display of curiosity that made me stay and listen to the account of your adventure ; my excuse will be that I was indirectly mixed up in it myself. If you will allow me, I will clear up the mystery in a few words."

Jacques and Onésime bowed. The elderly gentleman continued :—

"My friend, Count de M——, attached to the French Consulate, was expected to-day by the *Saïd*; the janissary on duty, whom you mistook for a Kawas, had been sent to meet him ; the Count had remained in his cabin to avoid the crowd on deck ; the description of my friend tallies sufficiently with yours, sir" (and he looked at Onésime), "for the janissary, the blue bird, as you have very wittily termed him, to have mistaken you for him ; he did not understand a single word of what you said to him, and acted up to the letter of his instructions. You were allowed to pass without having your luggage examined, thanks to the immunity enjoyed in such matters by members of the Consulate body. And that, gentlemen, is the very simple explanation of an abduction which I see has not been attended by any very disagreeable consequences."

"On the contrary," said Onésime.

"I am all the more pleased as you were thus spared the delay and annoyance that have been the lot of your less fortunate companions."

"I regret it profoundly," answered Jacques, "and I beg you to excuse us, for this foolish prank of schoolboys out for a holiday must have left your friend in a sad predicament."

"Not in the least, gentlemen. First of all, you gave way to force, which frees you from all responsibility; I will now add, to set your consciences quite at ease, that the Captain of the *Saïd* at once placed a boat at the service of Count de M—— ; I was awaiting him at the custom-house, which you had no doubt left just before I arrived —behind time, in accordance with my praiseworthy habit—and we have been here some minutes. You have therefore nothing to reproach yourselves with, beyond a slight delay caused to Count de M——, which enabled me to be exact at a rendezvous for once in my life, for which I feel very grateful. I am happy that this *quid pro quo*, which has been of some service to you, without having caused my friend any serious inconvenience, has procured me the pleasure of making your acquaintance"; and handing his card to the young men, he took theirs, and they cordially shook hands.

Then proceeding all three to the dining-room, they found Count de M——, to whom the old gentleman introduced his new acquaintances. They all laughed a great deal at the janissary's mistake ; and after dinner, at which Jacques had the proof that Nile water was an excellent beverage, and fresh dates a feast worthy of the gods, they met again in the smoking-room, where a little later on Doctor Reptilius and a few other passengers of the *Saïd*, who had also put up at the Hôtel d'Europe, joined them.

Some installed themselves on the large divans, others placed their chairs on the balcony ; and amidst the smoke of pipes, cigars, and cigarettes conversation soon became general.

The old gentleman whom chance had thrown in the path of the two friends was Doctor Alan Kéradec, a good doctor, an Egyptologist of distinction. He had come straight from Syria, after having made fruitful researches in the field of science, attracted by the renown of the discovery that Maspéro had just made at Deïr-el-Bahari in the plain of Thebes, where he had found intact the sarcophagi of several Pharaohs, that of the great Sesostris among others.

He intended setting out again shortly to visit Upper Egypt, where he hoped to unearth something, if it were only the error of a fellow-labourer.

He was a native of Brittany, a "Breton bretonnant"; medium in height, broad-shouldered; the head was roughly accentuated—voluminous at the top, thin at the bottom; the forehead was vast, prominent; green eyes with dilated pupils sprinkled with gold spangles, large, luminous, of a profound softness, gleamed in the hollow of their dark sockets, surmounted by thick powerful eyebrows. The visage of a tamed anchorite, which extreme pallor had made livid, sometimes coloured with a passing hectic flush, with an expressive physiognomy furrowed by numerous deep wrinkles, where a network of bluish veins showed up in relief near the temples, was overhung with a big, unkempt, thick, black, grey-besprinkled maze of hair and beard. White, sharp, regular teeth shone in this forest of hair. The arms were too long for the body; the chest bulged very much forward, the back was flat; the legs were slender; life had taken up its abode in the upper regions.

Doctor Alan Kéradec.

A tall silk hat of a mature age, and of reddish-brown tint, covered his enormous head. Whether he was searching the plains of Syria, crossing the deserts of Arabia, or penetrating among the sepulchres of the Valley of Kings, that hat never left him, immutable on his bushy skull like the pschent on the heads of the Pharaohs, engraven on the pylons of Karnac. The correlative part of his attire fostered, perhaps, the beneficent warmth which, fertilising his brain, incubated the embryonic egg of his thought, and gave birth to his ideas. He might forget his friends,

he never forgot his hat!   The latter might leave him, he never left it!
A creased frock-coat, always hermetically closed, enveloped his angular
body and fell in pleats on his heron-like legs.   The care that he gave
to study prevented him from devoting sufficient to his person, which,
in the result, was considerably neglected.

His erudition was great : he was an excellent dictionary badly bound,
somewhat diffuse, which one might consult
at any moment.   A very good fellow at
heart, who would step aside
rather than crush a worm.

Jacques, who had mono-
polised him, was already turning over the pages.   Answers
followed questions, rapid,
exact, with a neatness of
elocution, a happiness of
expression, a liveliness of
description, that were astonishing.   The former did
not cease making inquiries,
the latter giving information,
to the great satisfaction of
both parties.

Reptilius, sniffing a redoubtable
rival in this encyclopædia on two legs, had glided
surreptitiously into the discussion, opposing ob-
jections to the risky hypotheses, the contestable
affirmations, the historical facts, more correct in

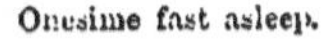

Onesime fast asleep.

appearance than in reality, of the terrible Armorican, who refuted
him with charming freedom.

" Us," wishing to crush his adversary, dashed into a cumbrous and
heavy compilation of facts, dates, anecdotes, with the pretension to
sum up the history of the greatness and fall of the ancient capital
of Egypt.   It was like a paving-stone launched amidst the audience.
When he had come to an end, Onésime was fast asleep, insensible to

the repeated bites that a mosquito was impudently treating himself to on his nose ; the other persons who had been amused at the slight skirmishes between Jacques and the old Breton had prudently fled before this charge of heavy German cavalry, which had crushed poor old Coquillard.

Alan Kéradec and his young friend applauded at the end of the tiresome dissertation. Surprised by the unforeseen attack, they had had to have recourse to all their patience to listen to the end, to all their politeness to suppress the yawning that overpowered them.

" Us," mistaking the fatigue caused by his indigestible dose for the discouragement of defeat, dissembled his immoderate vanity beneath feigned moderation ; he wiped the glasses of his spectacles, giving himself the airs of an old coquette, cackling quietly with satisfaction, assuming the aspect of a turkey strutting about with his tail spread out. At length, intoxicated by what he believed to be his success, encouraged by the silence of his audience, his conceit overflowed ; he sought to force out the compliments that did not come fast enough to please him.

" I tink, sentlemen," said he, with his head high, the nose forward, the nostrils dilated, the lip disdainful, his arms crossed behind his back, propped up on his skinny legs, with an air that bordered on impertinence, " I tink, sentlemen, it vood have been tifficult to have said as much in feuver vords ? "

" Or in more barbarous language," thought Jacques, *in petto*, horrified at Reptilius's frightful Teutonic accent.

" You forget, with laudable modesty, to add, ' and so well,' " punctuated Kéradec. " I repair that omission."

" I so much tislike speaking of myself," said Reptilius, fluttering beneath the compliment, " dat I ofden forget to to myself chustice. This ridigulous modesty vill pee my ruin. Yes, my tear tocdor, you have said zo, and I repead it, aldough plushing : ' as much in feuver vords and zo vell ! ' As you insist."

" Ah ! " observed Jacques.

" Is not dat your opinion ? " replied " Us," alarmed at this dubitative exclamation of the enemy, whom he had thought vanquished by his brilliant charge.

"What you have just set forth is no doubt very good," answered Jacques drily, provoked by the hypocritical ingenuousness and the extreme sufficiency of the Tenton, "but also very long; I think it might have been said more concisely."

"And one might even," let fly Kéradec, coming to his support, "have said much more in fewer words."

"And much petter, eh, Tocdeur Gueratec?" hissed Reptilius between his closed teeth, making a bitter allusion to the "so well" with which the Doctor had so pleasantly caressed his epidermis a minute before.

"Oh, I don't say that."

"You limit yourself to tinking it; I am opliged to you for stopping tere."

"There is no need to be."

"But, yes, tere is—stopping on such a peautiful road!"

"I have always known when to stop in time, Mr. Reptilius."

"Us" bit his lips. The shaft had gone home; he was struck with consternation, plucked of all his illusions; his adversaries, far from having been brought to earth, were making fun of him to his

Reptilius biting his lips.

face. He had made a mere vain attempt. These barbarous Gauls had not been able to appreciate his learned prose from the opposite side of the Rhine. *Margarita ante porcos*, he thought, to console himself; he must begin again! He dissembled his resentment and profound disappointment, and with constrained composure continued in a honeylike tone,—

"Vitch of fou, sentlemen, vill give me tee subreme satisfaction of proving vot fou have just advanced—dat fou could to petter and more priefly?"

"Really," said Jacques, "I think one could say in a page what it has taken you a volume to relate ; I will not go so far as to affirm that it will be better, but it will certainly not be worse."

"Speak, sir ; I vill have dat page engraved in letters of cold, and I vill present it to tee Berlin Museum, vere it vill remain as a motel of style and concision for tee great edification of chenerations to come."

"As you please, Mr. Reptilius ; write, it will not be long ; for if

Alexander and Dinocrates.

I unclothe your historical effusion and strip it stark naked, there will remain simply this, which I shall condense into a few lines :—

" 'Alexander, that soldier of genius with the vice of an arrant drunkard, the libidinous produce of an enterprising serpent and the bacchante Myrtalia, while on a visit to the Pharaohs, was one day promenading his own irascible majesty along the seashore, thinking of Hephæstion and dreaming of Bagoas, while working off the wine of the previous evening ; he halts before the little town of Rhakôtis ; the site pleases him : and, in accordance with the plans of his architect, Dinocrates, he has a city built there, which he baptises with his own name—vanity of a lucky warrior, who wanted to set up a monument of his reputation.

"'Like all cities, when once founded, it rises, grows, expands, and, after various adventures, topples over and falls, engulfed in a terrible catastrophe from which it has never recovered.

"'Artistic, learned, commercial, under the Ptolemies, it produces masterpieces, becomes the brain of Europe, and lives like a millionaire. Vicious with Cleopatra, it gets sick of the beautiful, leads the life of a punchinello, squanders its revenue, and from a mistress becomes a servant.

"'Beaten and plundered by the Romans, whom it feeds, it plunges into Christianity, loses the small amount of brains that it still possessed, and issues from the adventure stupid, a bigot, crippled with heresy. Its character is embittered ; it becomes pedantic, lunatic, ill-tempered, and wrangles indefinitely about trifles. It recovers for a moment a bit of strength, tussles with Amrou, who gives it a sound thrashing. After the victory he does not act too brutally towards it ; he quietly makes it Mussulman, reads it the Koran to divert it, teaches it to kill time by making pretty little mosques, ornamented with arabesques and dainty minarets as light as lace, with the pillars of its temples ; he heats his baths with the old worm-eaten volumes of its library, which had escaped the destructive zeal of the Christians, under Theodosius ; flirts with it, shows it the fidelity of a poodle-dog, and then suddenly leaves it to its own devices, to go and trace out the plan of Cairo, and make of Fostat what Alexander had made of Rhakòtis.

"'After that come the Turks, ill-bred fellows, who handle it roughly ; the Mamelukes, who behave like regular Pandours ; Bonaparte, who does not even look at it.

"'Finally, Mahomet Ali became infatuated with this corruption on the decline, and both he and his successors sought to renew its virginity ; but no, it was at an end ! The palmy days of Cleopatra's time are far away ; the people have been burning the candle at both ends ; and, with age, parturition has come to a standstill, striking with sterility the old but still bewitching coquette, who is now spending her last pence with a few shady bankers and unscrupulous shopkeepers who shamelessly live upon her.'"

"Us," in proportion as Jacques proceeded, had shown unmistakable signs of general uneasiness. When the latter had concluded this picturesque effusion, Reptilius made a prodigious leap in the air, like a carp, coming down on the feet of Onésime, who awoke with a start, and shouted out with pain, thinking he had fallen a prey to his bugbear—the cataclysm! Then, standing in front of the young man, "Us" examined him through his spectacles with mute, prolonged, cautious attention, as if he found himself in the presence of a dangerous and inexplicable phenomenon.

Onésime enjoyed this profound Teutonic stupefaction. "That rascal Jacques has been up to his games while I was asleep," he thought. And he looked merry, his ears wide open, while avoiding the attacks of the mosquitoes, attracted by flesh freshly arrived from Europe, and scratching his sore nose.

"Us" at length recovered speech ; he burst out,—

"But dis is an outrage upon science, an assassination of style ; it is hisdorical high dreason dat you have just gommitted ; this vandastical, I might almost say prutal and unseemly, inderbredation—— "

"You may dare," interrupted Jacques, laughing ; "do not stand upon ceremony."

"Of hisdory," continued Reptilius, "tisdurbs all recognised notions of tee metod of dreating tis nople pranch of human knowledge. It is bure fancy."

"Like his geography, in fact," thought Onésime.

"You have dold a story and not related hisdory ; and you vill not be surbrised if in my turn I find dat it is imbossible do say vorse in fewer vords."

"But, Mr. Reptilius," joined in Alan Kéradec, "what Mr. Jacques has just said is perfect in its way ; he relates history according to his temperament, you in accordance with yours ; to your interminable affectation he opposes his intended brutality ; his incisive ingenuousness astounds your inert crudition ; where you use the affirmative and cutting form, he juggles with words and plays with style ; you are long, he is brief, that is all the difference.   History is a mixture in unequal proportions of truth and falsity, in which falsity predominates ; now, you are prolix and Mr. Jacques is concise ; where you are in error in a volume, he only makes a mistake in a page ; all the chances, therefore, that he will commit fewer mistakes than you are on his side."

Reptilius smiled coldly behind his blue glasses.

"And you, Mr. Gueratec, in what way do you make mistakes ? "

Kéradec and Reptilius flinging arguments at each other's heads.

"In a vast number of ways."

" I vas aple to judge of dat a moment ago."

" And I trust I shall give you many other opportunities of doing so, Mr. Reptilius."

" To-night ? "

" I much regret, but I fear not ; I prefer remaining under the charm of your copious and learned dissertation, and of the original sketch of your adversary. However——"

Then he turned towards Jacques, and placed himself at his disposal, to accompany him the next day, and act as cicerone to him in Alexandria. "We will compose history on the spot," he added.

The evening was prolonged until the two doctors, after having tried each other for some time, ended by grappling together in earnest; and when the two friends, on taking leave, withdrew to their respective rooms, the savants, intoxicated by the science which rose to their brains, were well engaged, flinging arguments at each other's heads, bristling like fighting cocks, forgetting everything, forgetting themselves sometimes, in the heat of the struggle.

Jacques glided beneath his mosquito net, after having previously assured himself of the enemy's absence, and slept soundly, dreaming of the Ptolemies, of Antony and Cleopatra.

Onésime, the imprudent Onésime, who had not taken the wise precaution of making even a superficial inspection of the premises, and had left his mosquito net partly open, had a bad night, engaging by the light of his candle in a series of terrible battles with the mosquitoes that were thirsting for his blood, exasperated against his person.

View of Alexandria.

CHAPTER V.

Onésime's despair.—A turn in the city.—The Consuls' Square.—Jacques is dazzled ; Onésime is surprised at it.—Through the Arab town.—The island of Pharos and its old lighthouse.—Onésime's distress.—He has had enough of this steeplechase.—Alexandrian society.—Characters in the streets.—A few words about ancient Alexandria.—The Faubourg of Karmous.—Picturesque misery.—Pompey's Pillar.—Alan Kéradec and Jacques find Onésime at the Café Rossini.

THE next morning Onésime was not to be recognised. Exhausted, broken down by insomnia, a prey to smarting irritation caused by the bites of those abominable insects ; the visage puffed out, the nose tumefied and the colour of carmine ; an eye half hidden. beneath the red, swollen lid ; it seemed as if phlegmatic crysipelas had broken out all over his face.

When Jacques, after a capital night, went to wake him, and handed him, at his request, a mirror, Onésime almost fainted. In doubt as to his own identity, he wanted to think for a moment that it was his neighbour, not himself, who had just been awakened by mistake. When he was convinced that it was not an illusion, that it was himself whom he saw—himself, Onésime Coquillard—he sank moaning on his bed.

Jacques left him piteously facing his mirror, and went in search of a doctor. Coming across Dr. Kéradec in the corridor, who was then leaving his room, he gave him an account of the state of his poor companion. The doctor promptly accompanied him to Onésime. A friction with ammonia, followed by a comforting bath, made the latter himself again : and an hour afterwards, though still preserving honourable and painful traces of his nocturnal battle, he joined his friend and his deliverer, and sat down to the knife and fork breakfast with an appetite sharpened by the struggle.

Jacques was anxious to go through the city. The meal was briskly finished, and all three walked out on the Consuls' Square, the Mahomet Ali Square, where stands the bronze statue of the latter in the act of commanding.

Jacques was quite dazzled on entering this furnace, brought up to a white heat by the rays of the intense sun, where, in a strange confusion of shadows, of colours, of types, the hybrid population, hailing from all parts of the world, swarmed with a prolonged hum. This unexpected and faithful foretaste of the East very much impressed him.

While advancing, in the shade of the acacias of the square, towards the Tossizza Palace, he

Poor Onésime !

fully indulged his ocular enthusiasm, halting at every step to admire.

Here, a gigantic negro of the Soudan was shivering in his triple burnous in this temperature of 86° Fahr. ; there, a group of bronzed Bedouins, with small, white, even-set teeth, presenting a ferocious air beneath their kouffiehs of yellow silk, bound round the head by thick cords, enveloped in their loose brown gowns striped with white, in coarse material woven out of camels' hair.

Farther on fellaheen women, supporting great amphoræ with the

Baker at Karmous.

hand on their left shoulder, passed along with proud gait, the head
erect, covered with the yabrah, the corners of which touched their
heels, full of elegance in their ample dark-blue garments falling in
subtle folds. A black veil, fastened at their tattooed foreheads by the
bright bourou, hid the lower part of the face, showing only sparkling
eyes, half veiled by their long black lashes. With the other arm,
adorned with massive copper bracelets, made in heavy coils and
antique form, they gracefully gathered up the flowing folds of their
long gowns.

Then there were robust fellaheen, slender, muscular, the colour of
baked brick, with gentle physiognomies beneath their white takiehs ;
Arnauts, in petticoats, but each carrying a whole armoury of weapons ;
Montenegrins, with hard features, their belts bristling with knives and
pistols ; olive-coloured Jews, with hooked noses, restless eyes, black
turbans.

The Doctor smiled, slackening the pace, stopping with Jacques, not
wishing to disturb this first impression of a strange world.

Onésime, in the protecting shade of an immense white parasol,
lined with green silk inside, his eyes guarded by a tortoise-shell
binocle with smoked glasses, sought an explanation of the singular
enjoyment experienced by Jacques.

" What on earth," he murmured, " can he find beautiful in those
horrible negro faces, those ugly Bedouins, those water-carriers dressed
up in that ridiculous manner, those dirty fellaheen, those theatrical-
looking Palikari, those pasteboard Montenegrins, those filthy Jews ?
I admit that the sight is curious, even interesting ; but between that
and being lost in such ecstatic contemplation there is a long way ! "
And as Jacques had gone out without a parasol, he concluded that a
commencement of sun-fever was acting upon his brain and slightly
interfering with his intellect.

They walked round the square, deaf to the noisy solicitations of a
turbulent group of donkey-drivers, anxious to vaunt the qualities of
their respective animals. They passed indifferent in front of a stand
of hired carriages, in very good order, harnessed to small, sinewy,
frisky horses, with the elegant Arab coachmen in long white-and-blue

gandourahs and scarlet tarboushes on their heads, their enticing speech forming a striking contrast to the coarseness of their rude European brethren.

They halted for a moment at the angle of the square and the Rue Mahomet Tewfik, before the improvised shop of a money-changer, where a Bedouin was concluding a commercial transaction. Leaning with one hand on a rickety table, surmounted by a desk with the Sarraf's glass-case, seated on a staved-in and broken-legged straw-bottomed chair, he exchanged some small money for a paper which he placed in one of the numerous folds of his girdle. They approached and received a handful of piastres in return for a coin that they handed this open-air banker. Then, turning their backs to the Tossizza Palace, they entered the Rue Franque. Passing rapidly before the numerous covered stalls of clock-makers and jewellers, for the most part Italians, they noticed the red burnouses embroidered with gold, the light ornaments in gold and silver filigree work, damascened daggers, amber necklaces, long tchibouks with red clay bowls, and silk kouffiehs, displayed in a few rare shops where native produce was sold.

A money-changer.

They were very soon in the middle of the Arab town, which is built on the isthmus connecting the island of Pharos with the continent, on the same spot as the Heptastadia used to be. Lost in a maze of narrow streets, of winding lanes, stumbling into holes, floundering in sewers, they ventured into the long, low, and dark passage which forms the bazaar of wearing material, where silent Arab merchants, squatting down on their heels, between their narghilehs stuffed full of tombeki and their babonches, indulged in the sweetness of *kief*, or were selling European goods worked up in the country.

Frightful-looking old Jewesses, with impure gestures, gazed at them eagerly, quietly setting ajar the doors, so as to show pretty heads of young girls in the background.

Onésime, losing his equilibrium at every step, stormed, horribly disgusted with this, to his mind, senseless excursion, in these inextricable streets, amidst these miserable hovels.

They soon emerged from the labyrinth into the light ; crossing drowsy-looking streets, they perceived a few Arab houses, caught sight of some curious groups on the thresholds of the doors, of a few moucharabiehs at the windows ; and, after having followed an interminable length of white wall bordering the Grand Port, they came out at the eastern point of the island of Pharos, where the Fort Kaït-Bey rises on the site of the ancient lighthouse of the Cnidian.

Street in the Arab quarter.

An accumulation of rocks and hewn stone, which can still be distinguished beneath the water when the sea is calm, at the eastern point of the island, is all that remains of that splendid white marble tower, four hundred feet high, built in stories superposed one on the other, which was a marvel of the world.

"The Arab town, which we have just crossed," explained the Doctor, "covers the spot, considerably enlarged by land encroachments on the sea, where the Heptastadia, that gigantic hewn-stone dyke, seven stadia long, united the island of Pharos, where we stand, to the continent. It terminated with the lighthouse, which, according to some, exceeded in height the pyramid of Cheops, and, according to others, was only equal to that of the tower of Cordouan.

"This monumental jetty, intersected by a double line of communication, divided the port into two basins, which still exist: the Grand Port and the Port of Ennostos. The Grand Port, the New Port, now out of use, along which we have just passed, ended on the east by that narrow strip of land of the Pharillon which you see before you at the extremity of the gulf, the .Acro-Lochias of those days: at its base, facing the Palace of the Ptolemies, the Lochias, they had dug out a basin, the Port of the Kings, where the royal galleys remained at anchor. The other basin, that on the west, the Port of Ennostos which extends behind us, the Old Port at present, considerably enlarged by the Khedive, also had its private basin, the Kibotos, into which ran a navigable canal."

The Breton ended by recalling the trick, which was quite justifiable for the matter of that, of the architect of Cnidos engraving his name

on the stone, followed by an inscription, and covering the whole with
stucco, on which was displayed, in letters of gold, the name of the
supposed architect, Ptolemy Philadelphus, in the hope that the slow
action of centuries would one day remove this slender coating, and
proclaim his name to the admiration of future generations.   The
prevision of Sostratos was surpassed ; his fame outlived his work,
but the monument disappeared, carried away in the lapse of
centuries.

Continuing along the shore, leaving Fort Ada on the right, they
followed the axis of the ancient
island of Pharos, through the
burning solitude of a deserted
neighbourhood, and attained the
opposite peninsula, where they
visited the Palace of Ras-el-Tin, the
summer residence of the Khedive.
They ascended the superb Carrara
marble staircase, admired the grand
circular audience chamber, the
luxurious decoration of the ceilings,
the richness of the parquet flooring,
Then crossing the shady esplanade
which separates the palace from
the harem, they rested under the
trees near the fountain, contemplating with pity, at the western

The lighthouse of Alexandria.

extremity of the peninsula, the ungraceful silhouette of the modern
lighthouse, crushed by the souvenir of that of the times of the
Ptolemies.

Jacques filled a pipe, while Onésime, bathed in perspiration,
dabbed himself, furiously scratching his epidermis covered with red
papillæ, produced by the stings of those ferocious and obstinate
dipterons, and the old Breton, as dry as parchment, rolled a cigarette.

After this short halt, they passed before the arsenal, crossed the
magnificent floating dock, and, following the curb of the Old Port to

the custom-house, returned, this time on foot, by the same streets they had traversed the previous day in the comfortable carriage of Count de M——.

It was with considerable satisfaction that, fatigued and hungry, they returned to their hotel.

Such obstinacy, to tire oneself out, under the influence of an admiring sight mania, in the pursuit of insupportable ruins, of tumble-down bazaars, taking lessons of history in the open air, stupefied Onésime. This steeplechase was completely in disaccord with his indolent and barrack-like habits. Consequently, when the Doctor and Jacques, after the meal, rose to continue their excursion, he formally declined to follow them. He gave them an appointment, for six o'clock, at the Café Rossini ; and, going up to his room, threw himself on his bed, where, during a part of the afternoon, he regained in healthy slumber the strength exhausted by his fatigue of the morning and by the struggle of the night.

Jacques felt enjoyment in all the fibres of his being. His unrestrained emotion in the early part of the day was little by little brought under control, and, by reflex action, transformed into a sensation more calm, into a more just perception of things, which entered slowly, profoundly, into his brain, penetrating it and leaving an ineffaceable impression there.

After having cast a glance at the Mosque of Sheïkh Ibrahim, close to the hotel, a massive rectangular building, the base of which, at one of the sides, was entirely covered by a cluster of Lilipntian shops, guaranteed against the sun by miserable mats fixed to poles, they took the Rue Attarine.

The Doctor gave Jacques information as they walked along ; but the latter's mind was less attracted by these modern streets of the new quarter, ugly and pretentious, borrowing from Europe its fatiguing monotony, from native architecture its want of solidness, without the comfort of the former, without the elegance and graceful caprices of the latter.

"If Alexandria," said the Doctor, " is not the official capital, it is certainly the effective one, at least of the European colony, which by slow and continuous infiltration achieves the conquest of Egypt, a country which is for ever being conquered and for ever absorbing its conquerors! It is the centre of the operations of great banks, of wealthy commercial houses; also, alas! of impudent rascals, whose execrable reputation is the one thing that they have not stolen; who live here, thanks to the jealous and pernicious protection of their respective consulates, by extorted indemnities, by substantial compensations for imaginary injuries. It is here that daring adventurers, with easy morals, with elastic consciences, practise robbery and black-mailing on a large scale, following unavowed callings and engaging in wholesale smuggling with impunity.

"Despite the shameless speculation of these worshippers of Mammon, of these unscrupulous jobbers whom you loathe, the easy, charming life, the entirely Parisian flow of spirits, the absolute Oriental freedom of this Frankish city, attract you; the affable manner, the good humour, the attenuated atticism, but full of amenity and indulgence, of its inhabitants, on whom the souvenir of Cleopatra seems to have cast a last and pale reflection, enchant you; and its bewitching women, its passion for dancing, its love of music, its social gatherings, its balls, its garden parties, charm and detain you."

They stopped before the Greek Church of the Annunciation, a heavy monument with a bare exterior, of a Byzantine style, surrounded by gardens.

" You must see the return from Mass," the Doctor said to him, " if you wish to have a view of a long march past of superb creatures, modelled after the antique fashion, with adorable profiles, perfect purity of lines, with great, limpid, incomparable eyes, splendid dull complexions, slender limbs, grand, noble gait. Such must have been the lovely Alexandrian women in the days of the Ptolemies, when they hurried along, in search of pleasure and noise, in the streets of Bruchion, during the feast of Adonis, or during the Dionysia, those gigantic saturnalia, a single day of which cost millions to the Lagides."

At every cross-road ambulant tradesmen, Greeks from Candia for the most part, in long, untidy coats, a scarf twisted round the neck, a fez placed negligently over their long black hair, exposed for sale on a tray, placed on a frail folding support, their scanty edibles—red and white nongat, kolounia, dates, preserves.

Water-sellers made their copper goblets ring.

Arabs reposed indolently on the footpaths, grilled by the sun, troubled in their idleness, cursing these grand thoroughfares paved with long slabs, regretting the narrow streets of former days, where, sheltered from the sun, guaranteed against the heat, they could sleep at ease, and rest their fatigued limbs.

Barbers shaved their customers in the open air.

Porters, with canes in their hands, dozed on their kafas, made of the ribs of palm leaves, which were placed beside the open double doors, in the spacious vestibules of houses of white marble or hewn stone. Others conversed languidly between a couple of puffs from a tchibouk, which they passed from one to the other.

Berber women were returning from market with baskets full of vegetables, preceded by matrons beaming with pride; others, playing the part of nursemaids, a parcel of books in the hand, a little mantle on the arm, walked gravely behind babies and little girls returning from school, who prematurely spoil, by a commencement of arrogance, the lively charm of their pretty faces.

Then they passed a fat, proud Turk, crushing beneath his weight a little grey donkey, trotting along with small strides, followed by a diminutive donkey-boy, exciting the poor, tired-out beast with his plaintive "Ah!" and the point of his stick.

They passed stout, homely women, waddling along like fat geese, puffing and blowing beneath their white veils, putting aside with each hand the yards of black silk with which they were enveloped, resembling enormous leather bottles rolling along the ground when the wind, bursting in, inflated their robes.

Levantine women carelessly promenaded their indiscreet obesity, leaning on the arms of dried-up Levantine men, with cunning eyes.

Negroes, under the arches, were pounding coffee with heavy iron pestles.

At the Boulevard Ismaïl the Doctor stopped Jacques, and, pointing out to him some fragments of exposed columns, remarked : "Here we are in the midst of Bruchion, in the ancient Canopic way. Thanks to recent excavations, they have been able to find the foundations of the old walls and of the pavement of the streets of bygone days, which the progressive rising of the soil had covered with a thick layer of refuse, nearly seven feet deep, and to re-establish the plan of the city of the past.

"Beside Rhakôtis, extending along the banks of the Eunostos, rose Bruchion, skirting the Grand Port, separated by an enceinte from the remainder of the town, with its numerous monuments, its necropolis on the west its Jewish quarter on the east of the city. It was Ptolemy Soter, the successor of Alexander, the founder of the house of Lagides, who commenced its superb buildings.

"This neighbourhood was covered by a network of spacious thoroughfares, abutting on two great arteries which crossed each other. The largest of them, extending from the south-west to the north-east, connected the necropolis with the Jewish quarter, and ended on the west near the Canopus gate, the Rosetta gate of our own

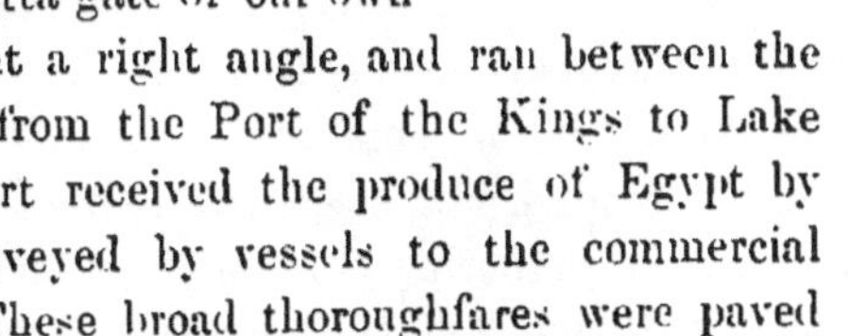

Pounding coffee.

days. The other traversed it at a right angle, and ran between the gates of the Sun and Moon, from the Port of the Kings to Lake Mareotis : there an interior port received the produce of Egypt by the canals, whence it was conveyed by vessels to the commercial ports of the Mediterranean. These broad thoroughfares were paved with enormous blocks of polished granite, resting on a thick bed of masonry, and bordered by palaces, colonnades, and spacious pavements sheltered by arcades.

"Apart from the water of the canal, which sprang from the Canopic branch ending at Kibotos, a number of cisterns gave Alexandria a supply of water in profusion, and the orientation of its streets gave its inhabitants the enjoyment, says Strabo, of a delicious season, thanks to the Etesian winds which blew from the north, and, after crossing a broad expanse of sea, brought pleasant freshness to the atmosphere during the heat of summer.

"At Bruchion, covered with royal palaces and public gardens, were the Museum and its library, where a multitude of philosophers and men of learning, screened from the material cares of life, laboured in calmness and meditation, in studying and in teaching science; the Greek temples; the Soma, where reposed the body of Alexander the Great; the circus and theatre, the gymnasium, the Stadia, the Poseidion, the Emporion, the Apostasis and other beautiful monuments, where a turbulent crowd bent on pleasure and a population of scholars, artists, and thinkers flocked together.

"In the Egyptian quarter of Rhakôtis, where we shall soon arrive, the Temple of the Serapeum, with its library recalling that of the Museum, towered up from the summit of its hundred steps.

"The Macedonian had taken a wide glance round, when, by a flash of genius, struck with the excellence of this admirable position, which permitted of communication with Egypt by Lake Mareotis, and, by a well-sheltered port, with the Mediterranean shores, he selected this site whereon to found his city.

"A vigorous current of emigration immediately flowed from all parts of Greece to this new emporium; adventurous fugitives from Syria came here, mingling with the cunning sons of Judea: workmen and merchants from the Delta awoke from their torpidity and reached the rising city in numbers. Under the successors of Soter, Philadelphus and Euergetes, Alexandria, rich and prosperous, was the commercial gathering place of the nations, while its letters, its savants and artists, made it the intellectual centre of the world. Euclid the mathematician, Demetrius of Phaleros, who commenced at the Museum the collection of books which was destined to become the finest in the universe, the painter Apelles, the sculptor Antiphilos, and many others gave matchless renown and lustre to its schools ; the Bible was translated into Greek, under the designation of Version of the Seventy : and later on, under Cleopatra, Dioscorides composed his works here ; the astronomer Sosigenes assisted Cæsar in introducing the Julian, or rather the Egyptian year. And now let us go and see Rhakôtis."

And the Doctor, taking Jacques' arm, turned to the right, following streets bordered by luxuriant gardens, exhaling delicious perfumes, and so quitted the city by the gate of the Nile, and followed the dusty road leading to Karmous.

The market, or rather fair, is held, on appointed days, on the large, dusty, arid expanse of ground adjoining the faubourg, and there flock Arabs, fellaheen farmers, with well-filled money-bags, their camels, their cattle ; there water-carriers and vendors of all sorts of beverages move to and fro. It is there that the Karagueuz goes through his lewd acrobatic performances, and where serpent-charmers renew the juggling tricks of Pharaoh's magicians.

Having crossed this Sahara on a small scale, they reach Karmous, the site of ancient Rhakôtis ; and through the openings in the double avenue of sycamores lining the road, they perceive in the distance Pompey's Pillar.

Here and there appear small dingy cafés with their few customers. Dislocated trellis work, half-covered with torn matting, shreds of old cloth rotting on sticks fixed into the masonry, hanging on cords stretching from the wall to the sycamores, cast a little shade on the rickety tables, broken-legged chairs, worm-eaten benches. Fowls peck about, pigeons swoop down, reddish goats with white spots, flat snouts, long, flexible ears, frail limbs, inflated bellies, come here for shelter.

Hosts of half-naked urchins, deliciously picturesque in their rudimentary rags, bound out of dilapidated houses. They raise clouds of dust in the wildness of their gambols, wallowing amid deafening cries in the ruts of the road, rolling pell-mell in the holes where voracious swine rummage with their black snouts in the stench of impurities and detritus of all kinds, and issue from them frightfully contaminated.

Farther on clusters of boys and girls, barely covered with a cotton chemisette sprinkled with red and yellow flowers, their eyes devoured by flies, are balancing themselves on rustic swings hooked on to the branches of the sycamores.

A goat.

Camels with undulating necks gaze vaguely about them with their great sad eyes, walking silently with their heaving motion, urged on by the voice and gestures of sombre Bedouins perched up on their summits.

Women with ravaged features, with sordid garments, pass by with babies seated astride on their shoulders. Little girls clutching their gowns with the hand, a leather amulet round the neck or suspended between the two eyes, in flowing chemises of a crude colour, the head

Café in Karmous.

bound in a fichu of torn spotted muslin, trot along beside them, supple as young snakes, shaking in the wind their fine plentiful black tresses. Their little arms are encircled with bracelets ; a smile plays on their sweet brown faces, casting a gleam into their dark eyes ; their pearly teeth shine white, moist, between their red lips, resembling drops of dew fallen on gaping pomegranates.

You pass by a butcher's stall in the open air, composed of a few planks surmounted by a weather board protecting a vacillating counter where a few pieces of blackish meat are drying, while a child armed with a palm leaf defends them against an onslaught of flies.

Women of Karnious.

Woman selling oranges.

Close at hand a poor Arab is striving to drive away those aggressive insects, which are besieging a quantity of reddish stuff placed on a tray on the ground— sticky goods called date bread, composed of that fruit kneaded into a glutinous block.

Near him, in a liliputian shop, a woman is selling oranges, squatting down in the midst of her fruit, which casts a brown-gold reflection on her face.

In the courtyard of a house a psylle—a snake-charmer—is

installed, making his hideous pupils go through their work: removing the cover of a basket filled with woollen rags, he plunges in his arm and draws forth a handful of reptiles, who hiss and twist about—grey snakes, vipers with brilliant horns, eryxis, scytalis. He first of

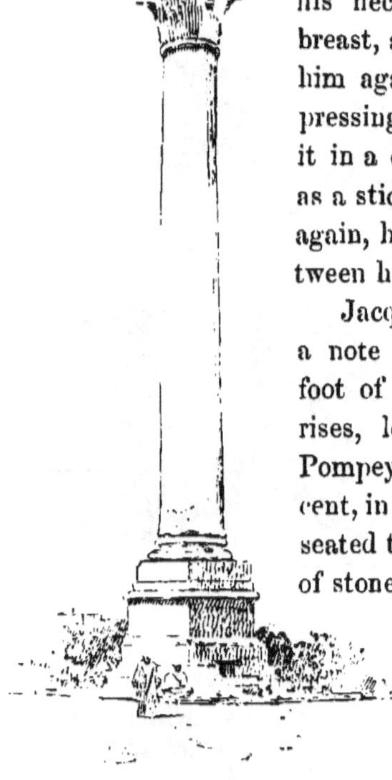

Pompey's Pillar.

all teases them with a stick, rolls them round his neck, his wrists, slips them into his breast, and makes the repulsive creatures bite him again and again. He ends, by slightly pressing the head of one of them, placing it in a cataleptic state and making it as stiff as a stick. To give it elasticity and movement again, he gently rubs the end of the tail between his two hands.

Jacques stopped from time to time making a note or a sketch. They soon reached the foot of the mound, on the summit of which rises, lofty and white, the column called Pompey's Pillar. They climbed the steep ascent, in a few seconds reached the upland, and seated themselves on the last remaining layer of stones of this remnant of the Serapeum.

It was close to here that Kleber was wounded while leading an assault; and it was at the foot of the column that the French soldiers who met their death in scaling the ramparts were buried.

This colossal monolith, measuring twenty-three feet in circumference by ninety-six feet high, was erected by a Roman prefect, one Pompey, in honour of Diocletian. The column, in polished red syenite, with its quadrangular socle and crowned by its dilapidated capital, on the top of which was perhaps a statue, is a masterpiece of proportion. According to an Arab legend it moves, bending in the morning towards the east to hail the rising sun, and in the evening, at sunset, to watch the sun speed away in the western horizon.

A Snake Charmer.

Disappeared! the portico surrounded by its four hundred columns, where tradition places the Serapeum Library. Disappeared! the giant staircase with a hundred marble steps leading up to it. The column alone remains of all those glories, a solitary and grandiose witness, testifying to the splendour of the edifice annihilated by men's anger, recalling in the decay of the present time the marvels of the past.

Tourists have inscribed their names on the pedestal, soiling with their vain egotism this imposing page of history.

From the high ground the eye sadly contemplates the Arab cemetery, which extends in an arid waste at the foot of the mound, with its innumerable sepulchres made of sunburnt bricks or pisé, and its accumulation of flat stones, sheltering swarms of scorpions, from beneath which a horned viper from time to time thrusts out its hideous head.

The two friends came down again, followed by a dozen boys and beggars, who kept at a respectful distance and strained their lungs by cries of " Baksheesh ! "

They soon re-entered the city by the Mahmoudieh Gate, following the Rue Ibrahim Pasha, at the rapid trot of their muscular little steeds, and at six o'clock reached the Café Rossini, where Onésime, who had rested, faithful to the appointment, had been waiting for them for half an hour.

The country of the Delta.

CHAPTER VI.

The Grand Port.—Alan Kéradec invokes the past.—Onésime's virtuous indignation.
—What he thinks of Cleopatra and her Needles.—Nocturnal run through
Alexandria.—A trip to Ramleh.—Onésime and his donkey.—Across the
fields.—The Mahmoudieh Canal promenade.—Its gardens.—The canal
banks.—Kéradec, Jacques, and Onésime take tickets for Cairo.

THERE was a splendid view from the front of the café, which
was built on piles, almost in the centre of the curve of the
New Port. The north wind brought some freshness, and the sun,
which was disappearing behind the Arab town, cast its dying
lustre on the opposite shore.

Onésime was not very sensitive to these effects of nature, to this
child's play of the sun, making, he said, such a fuss before going
to bed ; he sipped the contents of his glass, rolled cigarettes, enjoyed
his *far niente* like a man accustomed to it and who knew how to
appreciate it properly : thrown back in his chair, he inhaled the
breeze deliciously, listlessly lent his ear to the puffs of harmony
which escaped from the open windows of the café, and left the
two friends to their mania for admiring, and to their historical
reminiscences.

The rays of the setting sun, in a final glow, cast a purple glaze
on the gold and amber tones of this bay, full of graceful curves

and almost imperceptible sinuosities. In the distance Cleopatra's Needle stood out against the warm background of the sky, slender and rose-coloured in its elegant splendour. The Pharillon, with its forts on a level with the ground, gave a few brilliant touches of reddish white which were reflected harshly in the luminous calm of the gulf, where the pale whiteness of the tapering crescent of the moon was already delineated in an imperceptible quiver.

Fishermen were hurriedly drawing in their nets; in the water up to the waist, they formed a chain extending from the shore to a boat anchored a few feet from land. The little skiff, kept motionless by an old Arab with naked feet, white beard, and green turban, standing erect in the fore part, provided with a long boat-hook which he thrust into the sand, hardly swayed to and fro in the undulation of the waves which came to die on the fine sand, breaking in a thin silvery line. The men, with features tanned by the sea, bronzed by the sun, silently passed an interminable net from hand to hand. The last of them, on shore, withdrew the fish caught in the meshes, keeping the largest and casting the small fry aside.

Poor, half-naked children, showing their lean backbones, picked up the latter from the sand and placed it in baskets woven out of palm leaves.

Arabs, sitting down, wrapped in their burnouses, looked on, mechanically turning the box-wood beads of their chaplets in their hands.

Yellow, thin, famished dogs, with pointed muzzles, prowled restlessly about, with tail low, ears erect, fangs sharp, the nose to the wind anxiously scenting traces of carcasses to devour in the effluvia of the air.

Then all these, men and things, dissolved insensibly in a uniform tint of a bluish transparency, which the twilight slowly extended over this great tranquillity, and the cold shadows of night fell with their damp veil over the scene.

"How beautiful!" escaped from Jacques, turning towards the Doctor, who was also looking, with his elbows on the balustrade, but looking as one lost.

"Here we are," said Onésime to himself internally; "the fit has seized them. Admiration is about to be given uninterrupted sway. They have pulled the cord; look out for the shower-bath!" And he let out a puff of smoke, with a loud sound from his lips and a very contemptuous shrug of the shoulders.

"Yes, it's very beautiful," answered the Doctor, "beautiful in the beauty of the present and in the souvenirs of the past. Look!

"Poor, half-naked children."

we can reconstruct it in the mind's eye, this grand past, which weighs upon this fallen city; the scenery is still here."

"Ah! Here's the first act commencing; attention! The curtain has risen," murmured Onésime pleasantly; "let's listen to it!"

"Quite in the background, over there—that point of Pharillon which is facing us, with its two forts, the Mencharieh and the Jews—was the promontory of Acro-Lochias with the spur of its breakwater. At the base of this promontory probably rose the Palace of Lochias, at the foot of which, enclosed between its two dykes, was the private port reserved for the galleys of the Ptolemies. Follow the curve approaching our shore ; there were the arsenals, the Apostasia or royal storehouses, and facing them, the island of Antirhodes, with its little private port and palace. Those rocks, the tops of which you see peeping out in the form of a horse-shoe, indicate the site. A little below, and more to the east, upon another islet which no longer exists, rose the Timonium of Antony, connected with the land by a causeway leading to the steps of the Temple of Neptune, the Poseidion ; Cleopatra's Needles, removed from one of the pylones of the Temple of Heliopolis,—one erect, which we see, the other overthrown, half buried in the sand. Then, still nearer to us, the Cæsareum or Sebasteum, completed under Tiberius, where seamen came before sailing to implore the gods to be propitious to them, or to thank them for a happy return. Between the coast and the existing gardens of Antoniades was the Exchange, the Emporium, the centre of the commercial transactions of the three continents.

" Now if you could sound the depth of the gulf (the Great Gulf), you would find beneath the water, at a fathom or two from the surface, from Cape Lochias to Cleopatra's Needles, the traces of the quays that preceded these splendid buildings. There vessels of all countries came to discharge their goods and carry away the produce of Egypt : ships from Tyre, built with the pines of Sanis, with masts of cedar hewn down on Mount Lebanon, with oars fashioned from the oaks of Basan, seats of Cyprus box-wood, ornamented with ivory, sails made of Egyptian flax, dyed with the purple of the Hellespont, with their oarsmen from Sidon, their mariners from Djehal. Their spacious hulls contained purple, lapis, coral, and the jasper of the Armenians, wine from Kelboun, and dazzling fleece from Damascus ; polished iron, cinnamon, the aromatic reed from Javan, Dan, and Menzal ; rich carpets from Dedan ; slaves and brazen vases from Tubal and Mosoch ; ivory from distant islands.

" Boats from the Red Sea brought kids and lambs from the desert ; aromatic plants, precious stones, and gold from Yemen.

" Equi from Gades, their prows ornamented with horses' heads, discharged their heavy cargoes of iron, tin, and lead from the Orcades.

" The oneraria of all forms, loaded with furs and slaves from the North, Italian wines, thronged along the quays, beside light liburnes with two rows of oars ; other powerful liburnes, with their undershot wheels, set in motion by bullocks or athletic slaves ; galleys, from the simple unireme with one bench of oarsmen, to the colossal vessel of Philopator with forty, measuring 420 feet in length by 57 feet broad, and numbering 4,000 rowers, the thalamites at the prow, the zygites in the centre, the thranites, with long oars, at the poop, ending on either side with double blades. Amidst these splendid ships, poor looking lembès, frail epholsces coasting in the Mediterranean, mingled with covered thalamegia of the Nile, and with the leather boats, lined with wicker-work, of some adventurous red Gauls."

" That sounds very well," thought Onésime maliciously, " all that little classical nonsense ; one scents the university a mile off ; it has a savour of the library, a perfume of erudition which is quite troubling for rather rudimentary brains. And to hear them one would really think that it has happened—that they have seen those equi, oneraria, liburnes, lembès, epholsces, thalamegia. One would really imagine they had navigated on board those playthings all their lives with their thalamites, zygites, thranites. That is what they term re-establishing the past ! A fine past, indeed ! " And shrugging his shoulders, he hummed in thought, accompanying the last measures of the orchestra, which was concluding a melody of Beethoven.

" And now nothing ! " said Jacques—" nothing but this isolated monolith on the ruins of Bruchion, like Pompey's Pillar on those of Rhakôtis ! Two granite ancestors, humiliating for the weakness of their degenerate descendants ! "

" Who do not even understand the words graven on their face," concluded Kéradec.

" There ! That's it, bring out the big words," scolded Onésime, whose face was becoming overcast. " Mock the living ! Incense the dead ! Pronounce the panegyric of all these antediluvian antiquities ! It is impossible ! They must have made a mistake in the century of their birth. They must have missed their entrance at the period of the Ptolemies, these praters of ' dead languages ' let loose in the midst of the nineteenth century! Don't they cling on to the past?" And Onésime, whose face all at once became stern, felt the thorns of irritation which began to prick his muscles ; he felt the needles, the uneasiness in the legs, that with him was the certain premonitory sign of a storm which was brewing in the innumerable cells of the tissues of his person, and which disturbed their system.

"Ah !" continued the Doctor, "in this down-fallen Alexandria, given over to complete intellectual and moral disorder, under the successors of Euergetes, fallen under Roman tutelage, there must still have been vivid bursts of light when Antony, subjugated by the adorable beauty and marvellous mind of Cleopatra, followed her to Egypt ; when the amorous couple, magnificent in their furious love, ever in quest of a fresh pleasure, of a new sort of voluptuousness, untiring in their enjoyment, insatiable in the immensity of their desire, drawing from inexhaustible treasures, promenaded in the four quarters of the city the conflagration of their immense debauchery, of their unheard-of luxury : colossal orgies in which the fortunes of Antony were to founder, in which both were to meet death, he falling on his sword, Cleopatra by allowing an asp to bite her in the breast ! "

This was too much! The measure was full. They exalted Cleopatra, that old coquette of Egypt; they glorified vice ! Onésime's patience was exhausted. The storm burst, and the dark cloud, swollen with his accumulated exasperation, burst beneath the vigorous effort of virtuous indignation—and Onésime's indignation was no small matter. He made a superb movement, his movement on great occasions, that incomparable and inimitable start, that astonishing start, that sudden, bold, dominating action, full of design, which so furiously shook the heavy layers of his hirsute rotundity. Sometimes to this typical gesture, which was almost legendary, he added his *pollice verso*—another oratorical movement which also belonged to him, was absolutely his, but which he only made use of under very solemn circumstances, when he sapped the foundations of religion and spoke of placing Ministers of Religious Affairs in the presence of their Creator. On these occasions he was irresistible; everything gave way before him: he catapulted! This time he left his *pollice verso* in its sheath. His voice vibrated in a tremolo full of threats ; he used his

irony, his cold, bitter, sarcastic, corrosive irony. It burnt. It became impregnated with gall, bile, curare, and a lot of other things that were stirring within him. It bit, lacerated, smashed—for, when he broke out, he was terrible, Onésime, terrible! *Terribilis visu!* And he broke out, Onésime Coquillard, of Paris.

"What owls you make yourselves!" he exclaimed in his sudden explosion. "Always upheaving ruins, rummaging in demolitions, rebuilding in imagination a lot of old structures which have seen their day, kneeling before old ashlars like the negroes of the Congo before their fetishes ; the shadow of the past haunts your cracked brains and deranges them, my good

"Always rummaging in demolitions."

friends ; you are hallucinated with History ! "

"What ! " said Jacques, stupefied at this sudden outburst, which was quite unexpected, " hallucinated ! "

" Yes. hallucinated ; and hallucinated moreover in the worst way ! " And the peaceful pate of the excited Onésime bristled up. "Maniacs, if you prefer it ; pettifogging patchers-up of anecdotes, polishers of history, who have not even the tact to choose, but rush with the nose pointing right on to the ulcers of the disease, and laboriously describe its loathsome phases ; when you walk in such paths you should look where you place your feet. What a lot of fuss for a miserable block of stone and a slut who went on a revel with a soldier ! But leave alone that poor, ridiculous landmark which has been forgotten by the destroyers, as well as that

" Yes, hallucinated."

fallen creature Cleopatra, the Egyptian Messalina, who, like her imitator later on at Rome, was never satisfied, not even fatigued, the hussy!"

"But, Monsieur Coquillard," Kéradec ventured to observe, "this Cleopatra whom you are treating so cruelly, did she not, faithful to the instincts of her race, protect the Arts, restore the library of the Museum, which was burned during the siege that Cæsar conducted at Bruchion against the Alexandrians, and enrich it with two hundred thousand volumes? And that obelisk, that landmark, as you term it, why, it is a page of history."

Useless trouble! Onésime was not to be stopped like that; he would not come to terms when the revolt of his good sense was in action. They had roused his anger, they must bear it: they had imprudently thrown a lucifer upon his inflammable matter, and he had burst out in flames! They had blown oxygen on the latent fire of his drowsy indignation, poked up the live embers that were smouldering beneath the ashes of his longanimity, and the conflagration was raging! Onésime was in full combustion—*Ardet Ucalegon!* And in the frightful rumbling of his phrases, in the incessant crackling of his words, he roared out burning invectives which vigorously shook his robust framework as they issued forth.

"They were beautiful!" he exclaimed, in reply to Kéradec's imprudent interruption, "the instincts of your protectress of the Arts who prigged from the city of Pergamus the treasures of its library to make a present of them to Alexandria, and stock its Museum with them. The hussy! What would you say of a person who robbed you of a sovereign to present it to his friend? That he was an impudent thief. She was nothing else. As to your page of history, if all the old books of your Serapeum or your Museum had similar ones, the volumes

"The hussy!"

must have been of prodigious size and have occupied an enormous space! I pity those who turned over the leaves. Don't bother me with your genteel, beautiful, noble Cleopatra ! that insolent female who, instead of threading pearls, like a well-brought-up young lady, as she should have been, amused herself by swallowing them ! That wicked queen, who treated herself to perfumes the price of a single one of which would have swallowed up a quarter share in the business of a stockbroker of our times, and inundated herself with them ; who sat down to table smothered in a heap of roses before phenomenal dishes, and who could not go a step without a band of musicians at her heels ! That same Cleopatra, whose rabid restlessness never allowed her to pause ; that dissolute creature who disguised herself at night-time to frequent places of ill-repute with her Antony, after having married her young rascal of a brother at fifteen, and thrown herself into Cæsar's arms a year later ! And her husband, in the meanwhile, her poor brother and spouse, the luckless Ptolemy XIII. (bad number !), disappeared like a nutmeg, juggled away by his tender sister and wife, and despatched *ad patres* to sleep with his ancestors ! And the little boy Cæsarion, the fruit of her Cæsarian love, was left by his dear mamma in the kitchen with the servant-maids ! And it is that atrociously bad woman, combining so agreeably robbery and adultery, prostitution and murder, ending by suicide, whom you have chosen for a heroine ! You have been fortunate. Listen, shall I tell you ? Well ! Your historical figure is merely an hysteric figure ! Your page of history is unclean, and if it is necessary that it should be written somewhere, there are special gazettes for that—in England !"

In caudâ venenum ! It was the tail-end of the storm exhausting its anger in this last clap of thunder, which was to strike " *perfidious Albion* " beyond the seas.

Jacques and the Doctor laughed heartily at the virtuous indignation of their friend, whose chaste bourgeois instincts had been unexpectedly ruffled by this, according to him, immoral exaltation of one of the most marvellous women of antiquity.

" Laugh as much as you like," said Onésime, whose indignation, drowned in the tide of his own words, had given place to his customary sly good humour ; " I'll laugh also, to keep you company, and because

Street in the Arab quarter of Alexandria.

' laughter is the characteristic of man '; but all the same, it annoys me to think that there are many good, courageous, pretty, amiable, devoted little women, admirably staid and sedate, who present their husbands with beautiful brats, pass their lives in bringing up the latter and in coddling the former, performing prodigies of economy to make both ends meet, and who are never spoken of, whereas people do nothing but sing the praises of those ancient and modern wantons. Well! yes, there, I protest against this pernicious praise; it irritates me, it enervates me, it makes me jump ! "

" Jump ! my friend," said Jacques ; " you have rested enough this afternoon. But let us leave Cleopatra and her Needle and return to the hotel ; your *quo usque* has made me feel quite empty, and must have roused your own appetite."

" Yes, tolerably ; but as for Cleopatra, that shame of the Levant, that strutting historical slut——"

" That's understood ; we will send her to join the cataclysm ! There, are you satisfied ? "

" Yes."

" Well ! let's be off."

And the trio set out for the hotel standing at a few yards from the café.

At the corner of the Mahomet Ali Square they fell in with a crowd of Arabs advancing towards the Rue Franque amidst the noise of daraboukas, flutes, Indian bells, dominated by the resounding blasts of trombones, which overpowered with their metallic notes the human voices that were intoning a discordant melopœia. The men carried enormous paper lanterns. The procession was preceded by acrobats, and followed by a swarm of urchins with lighted *machallas*, which shed clusters of sparks accompanied by thick black smoke.

The Doctor explained to Jacques that this was a bridegroom being escorted to his bride.

After dinner Jacques and the Doctor, who were indefatigable, went out, leaving Onésime, who had sunk down on one of the divans of the smoking-room, behind them.

Night had thrown its sombre tint over the brilliant show of

costumes so dazzling during the day : the doors closed, the crowd became less compact : the sounds were muffled; the city was slowly falling off to sleep in the cool repose of the night, which at each moment became more obscure. The darkness of the streets, vaguely lit up by rare gas-burners, was broken here and there by streams of light from the European cafés ; they were plotting there the scandal of the morrow, or concocting between two drinks the business of the week; a few readers were looking through the European papers.

Vacillating lanterns were suspended at the framework of the worm-eaten doorways of Arab cafés, lit up inside by miserable lamps giving doubtful light. Morose old Turks were smoking their narghilehs beside natives, picturesquely squatting down in company with Levantines in coats. All were listening with rapture to the humdrum voices of the singers and story-tellers, mingled with the harsh grating of the rebecks. From time to time a prolonged "Ah !" plaintively modulated, was uttered in applause of the song or story of these troubadours of the East.

In the eccentric quarters they passed rapidly before gambling hells, where the dregs of the population were losing, amidst blasphemies, what they had earned or stolen during the day ; where the losers, knife in hand, mad with rage, were quarrelling with the winners for the money that chance had bestowed on the latter.

They walked by other suspicious-looking establishments, where a disgraceful human merchandise could be perceived through the half-open doors as a bait for belated passers-by, for desires that were not very refined. Furtive shadows entered, others came out. Sometimes the prolonged, heart-rending cry of a woman escaped from one of these dens. followed by a series of imprecations of a brutal, discontented male ; and hideous silence once more reigned around.

The two friends hurried on their way, and returned to the central thoroughfare.

Along the walls, against the closed shop-fronts, the night watchmen, wrapped in miserable-looking rugs, reclined on their

Arab café.

long palm-fibre cages, or, squatting down in packing-cases, yelled
their watch-cry in the silence of the night; this cry flew from mouth
to mouth, repeated by each of them, running along the street,
reverberating in the whole neighbourhood, lulling the ·slumbering
city with its humdrum monotony, disturbed
sometimes by the moans of a watchman whom
the courbash of the Sheïkh, the appointed
chief of the corporation, was punishing for
falling asleep.

They got home rather late, and found
Onésime and Reptilius claiming, each for
his own country, the glory of having
had Charlemagne for Emperor. As the
argument was approaching bitterness and
threatened to become still more en-
venomed, Doctor Kéradec made them
of one mind by delivering a judgment
worthy of Solomon.

" Cut in two this German, crossed
with a Latin," he said, "and let each
take his share ; he is a Teuton by
his name Karl, and French by his
qualities which obtained for him the
surname of Magnus : Karl is your
property, Monsieur Reptilius; Magnus
belongs to you, Monsieur Onésime."

This put an end to the discussion, and each of them retired to
his room.

Night watchmen.

The next morning, at eight o'clock, Kéradec, Onésime, and Jacques
were at the Ramleh railway station. An Arab boy, in a white
gown, with a wide-awake air about him, perforated their tickets ;
they were able to examine at their ease the rather stout station-
master in a stambouline and tarboush, and jumped into the carriage.

On leaving the station a few shafts of broken columns, brought to light in making the earthworks of the railway, made them think of Bruchion again ; they passed a small, almost dried-up watercourse over a little bridge, the only one on the line ; caught sight of fellaheen villages through the reeds ; and, a few minutes afterwards, crossed the " French lines," gigantic entrenchments thrown up by Bonaparte's soldiers in 1799, to protect the town on this side against the English.

Station-master.

On coming out on the plain the view was splendid ; it took in an immense horizon : on the left the intensely blue sea, with its cliffs in tones of burnt ochre ; opposite, the Mustapha Palace ; on the right innumerable fig trees, the Mahmoudieh Canal with its tufts of green and multitude of boats, the masts and sails of which seemed to rise from the earth ; and, right in the background, Ramleh with its white, pink, and blue houses coquettishly scattered amidst its gardens and palm trees. Then, close at hand, between the line and the sea, the solitary ruins of the old necropolis of the Jewish quarter and of the Eleusis faubourg of Alexandria, regular quarries of work, riddled with hypogea constantly turned topsy-turvy by the greedy hands of dealers in curiosities, while those hewn in the sides of the cliff are lost beneath the sea-waves, destroyed by the everlasting action of a violent maritime current from west to east.

After a short stoppage at Mustapha, the train went on again, passing the traces of the Oppidum, the grand ruins of which, still intact in 1871, served to build this little upstart Ramleh, which stands on the site of Nicopolis.

The three travellers got out at the next station, and made the three donkey boys whose animals they hired happy, while they disappointed the five others who were not chosen. They got astride their smart asses, and trotted through this agglomeration of villas of all colours, placed irregularly and built lightly on a foundation of sand. The guardianship of these country houses of the wealthy citizens of Alexandria, inhabited during the winter, is entrusted to the honesty of the Arabs, under the responsibility of their Sheïkh.

Onésime made prodigious efforts to maintain a most unstable equilibrium, first losing one stirrup, then the other, clutching the reins with one unsteady hand, while with its companion he feverishly grasped the handle of his parasol, which acted as a balancing-pole, describing fantastical curves in space ; he resembled thus a fat, drunken Silenus brandishing his thyrsus. All at once a plaintive " Ah ! " uttered in a hollow tone of voice and followed by the vigorous stroke of a switch, applied to the loins of the ass by the young fellah in a blue gown, white turban, and yellow babouches, who was running behind the uncomfortably seated rider, produced a sudden and unexpected effect, which was disastrous for Onésime's stability, already so much in danger. Surprised at this doleful exclamation, he turned his head to ascertain the cause ; at the same moment the animal set off at a full gallop, and the unfortunate rider, losing both stirrups together, letting go his parasol, with his spectacles disarranged, his hat blown off, his hair wafted by the wind, had only just time to seize the large red pommel of the saddle with both hands and to clutch it firmly. Frightfully shaken on the back of the quadruped, whose gallop was accelerated by the stirrups beating his flanks, he had quite the appearance of a badly fastened bale of goods. After a final and fruitless struggle to preserve this problematical stability, he at last lost his balance, emptied the saddle, and spread himself out in full on the sand, while the disburdened animal continued his course faster than ever, followed by his owner, who ended by catching him.

Onésime rose free from all harm, rather confused at his fall, but nevertheless laughing at the mishap, while he picked up his helmet, spectacles, and parasol, which lay strewn on the scene of his discomfiture.

The Doctor and Jacques had at once turned bridle, anxious as to the result of the accident ; but the appearance of Onésime, who was on his legs in the twinkling of an eye, completely set them at ease ; and, enlivened by this incident, at which the victim was the first to laugh, they gave him a little good advice, urged him not to use his stirrups and to follow as much as possible the same road as his animal, and then set off again at a slow trot.

"Animal!" grumbled Onésime, looking askew at his donkey boy, " let me catch you warbling your idiotic 'Ah!' again, and I'll warm your shoulders for you!"

Farther on, a few phlegmatic Englishmen watched them pass. They reached Bulkeley, where the battle of Nicopolis was fought in 1801, between the English under Abercromby and the French wretchedly commanded by Menou; stopped for a minute at Bakos, the commercial centre of Ramleh, where Onésime got over his shock by drinking a large glass of raki and water at the Hôtel Pericorne; then, passing along the side of the Mosque and the shops with broad cloth awnings in the bazaar of the Arab village, they continued through the fields and charming gardens of Seffer, prettily situated at the foot of a rather elevated mound, and reached Schutz Junction.

Giving their asses a little breathing time, they alighted, and proceeded towards the sea, where are still to be found, half buried in sand, Roman baths hollowed out in the rock of the cliff, and into which water only penetrates by a narrow opening. Onésime would have willingly bathed there if the salutary fear of being devoured by a shark had not prevented him. Far away, on a rather elevated point of earth, the blue mass formed by the abandoned Zizinia Palace stood out against the curtain of palm trees on the Siouf oasis. They soon rejoined their steeds, and, cutting across the fields, proceeded on their way back.

Lean bullocks, with hanging fetlocks, conducted by little fellaheen, were manœuvring *sakiehs*, which gave a sharp, hollow, grinding sound as their horizontal brake-wheels were made to revolve. These set in motion a series of other brake-wheels, which, in their turn, drove round perpendicular ones, provided at the extremity of their spokes, on the outer circle, with jars of baked clay, fastened with cords made of palm fibre. The latter, in their constant rotation, scooped up water from the wells by means of their jars, and poured it into basins, from which it ran along narrow gutters, dug at right angles in the earth, and spread out like the silvery meshes of an immense net covering the entire plain.

Fellaheen, barely clothed in a pair of cotton drawers, their head covered with a hemispheric skull-cap in thick white or maroon felt, alternately filled and emptied the leathern pails of their *shadoufs* with their copper-coloured arms. The slender cross-beams of these primitive machines, weighted with a rough counterbalance of loamy

A sakieh.

earth kneaded into a ball, and see-sawing upon pieces of wall built of dry clay, rose and fell without intermission, drawing from innumerable arteries that beneficent water of the Nile, the foster-father of Egypt, to distribute it afterwards on the hard ground.

Dusky girls, with long slender hands, tapering fingers, the nails reddened with henna, a corner of their garment between their teeth to hide their faces, pushed flocks of turkeys before them along the borders of the fields. They walked slowly, the head raised, the gaze frank, and copper bangles clanked gently on their delicately moulded ankles.

Fellaheen stopped at their work, leaning on their hoes, smiling with an eternally peaceful smile, and gazing with their great soft eyes. Beside them enormous sheep, dragging, like cannon-balls, the weight of their tails, deformed by a strange growth, raised their sad heads and then turned back again to browse.

A shadouf.

Labourers, with their gowns caught up to their thighs and fastened to the waist by knotted belts, made out of bunches of thin, unplaited strips of leather, guided their wooden ploughs, to which oxen with small horns and tawny coats were yoked. Blue herons,

Ploughing in the Delta.

white ibises, hopped behind, and flights of pigeons swooped down around them.

Larks, lost in the sky, threw forth their light trills ; white-throats were warbling in the grey-green foliaged tamarinds ; pink - coloured flamingoes with curved beaks were stalking tranquilly ; while storks wandered among the rushes ; sedate cormorants, with their eyelids half closed, lost in thought, were resting upright on one leg amidst the reeds; turtle-doves flew from palm tree to palm tree ; and high above, in the azure immensity, great fawn - coloured vultures described concentric circles.

They proceeded at a walking pace along the canals, amidst the magnificent vegetation, growing thick and fast beneath this burning sun, in this warm atmosphere, where swarms of flies, clouds of mosquitoes, butterflies of all colours, whirled about in the air, mingling their confused buzzing noise with the thousand dull sounds of radiant nature at work.

Labourer.

They soon found themselves at Bakos again. There they followed the line, trotting along the narrow margin of the embankment, at the risk of being crushed by a train perceived too late, or of tumbling down the steep declivity to the entanglement of branches, wire netting, rushes, and brushwood covering the swamps slumbering below. Then reaching the beautiful macadamised road, with fountains at every hundred paces, they followed it at a gallop, beneath the shade of its double row of sycamores, passing between plantations of fig trees. Next they went through the village of Kadra, where the ancient Eleusis stood, and re-entered the city by the Rosetta Gate.

All three were delighted with their little country excursion. Onésime, who had not met with a second spill, considered himself an accomplished horseman, "a real Numidian," he said; he even spoke at the café, after having vigorously handled his fork, of enlisting in the hussars on his return to France. Jacques complimented him on this masculine determination; but Alan, who was more prudent, advised him, before coming to

Rosetta Gate.

a decision, to wait until he had had experience of a horse, and, above all, of a dromedary, after which he would only be embarrassed as to the choice of the animal that pleased him best.

At about three o'clock the monotonous calls of the muezzins, launched from the height of the minarets, tore them from their delicious siesta, reminding them that they had much still to see; and, like new Wandering Jews, they went out and recommenced rambling about the streets.

The Doctor first of all conducted them near the Mosque of Sheïkh Ibrahim, in a dark narrow street, where industrious Arabs, provided simply with a pair of shears, a knife, and a marline-spike, displayed matchless dexterity in weaving mats, cords, halters, and nets to hang

A muezzin.

at the sides of camels, out of the bog-rush and the

cortical fibres of the palm. The spike-stalk of the leaf was used to make brooms, cages, stools, and also the kafa, that sort of long cage which, covered with a light mattress, serves Egyptians as a bed. Then they hailed a cab and were driven to the Mahmoudieh Canal, the favourite promenade of the Alexandrians.

Fridays and Sundays are the days on which the elegant Christian, Jewish, and Mussulman society of the city assemble there in their costly and handsome carriages purchased at Vienna or Milan; and in which charming women, in bewitching toilettes, forwarded direct by the best Parisian dressmakers, recline supinely on the cushions, saluted by fashionable horsemen trotting amidst the vehicles. Nimble sayces, with naked feet, the *chirwal* falling to the knees, sleeves of floating white muslin, crimson or sky-blue velvet waistcoats, covered with thick gold embroidery, a red cap on the head with a long blue silk tassel striking their shoulders, and a stick in the right hand, precede the equipages, and overtake, indefatigable runners that they are, the most high-mettled steeds. Great negroes, with cheeks slashed with bluish scars, are watering the road; and the footpaths are encumbered with pedestrians of all races and all shades. Everywhere the tarboush in the way of masculine headgear predominates.

A sayce.

This promenade, with the long avenue of acacias and sycamores forming for some distance a thick arch which is a guarantee against the sun, is delicious; and while the Mahmoudieh Canal, which borders it on the one side, affords a pleasant freshness, the masses of foliage about the sumptuous villas which bound it on the other give repose to the fatigued eye, from the dusty whiteness of the city.

In this line of gardens, that of Moharem-Bey, amongst others, which belongs to Nubar Pacha, the Garden Pastré, that of Antoniades, are really admirable. There grow in full vigour the cactus, aloes, daturas, mimosas with yellow flowers, red euphorbia, acacias, of rapid and sometimes gigantic development ; olive trees, bananas full of vitality ; here and there large scarlet leaves stand out like great drops of blood in the dark groups of verdure. These barely permit one to catch a glimpse, through a few rare openings that perforate the thick shrubbery, of the barred windows, the high walls of houses mostly inhabited, and behind which imagination assists one vaguely to discern bewitching odalisques and sombre tragic incidents of the harem ; there, also, are banian trees, a single one of which contains generations of forests, and the secondary stems of which, starting from the trunk and branches, grow downward to the earth, which they penetrate, forming new trees which spread indefinitely.

In the spring the orange and lemon trees shed around their exciting perfumes ; the rose bushes disappear beneath their bloom ; the male palms, trembling in the caresses of the sweet breezes, incline their rounded plumes, shaking in the air the white dust from their fibres, the pollen, which, borne away by the warm breath, goes to fecundate the female palms with the quivering stems. The oleanders, the bougainvilleas with broad trails of rose, the multicoloured pinks, the chrysanthemums, violets, zinnias, periwinkles, snapdragons, mignonnette, pansies, petunias, narcissus, jonquils burst out into tints that are exquisite in their delicacy and variety.

The transition is sudden when one passes on the other side of the canal. There Egypt commences, the real Egypt, with its poor villages built of clay, cooked and recooked by a burning sun ; with its huts of earth covered with dry sorghum leaves, scattered irregularly here and there ; its cafés built of loam and straw and rickety planks, where exhausted beggars sleep in sordid rags, where poor peasants devour a donra cake and drink a cup of coffee.

Women, in long blue gowns, fetch water in their heavy clay pitchers.

A ferry-boat goes across. Men returning from work, women with bundles of clothing, camels loaded with sugar-cane, asses bending beneath bulky bags of rice, encumber the deck. The ferryman, an old, muscular Arab, presses in his arm-pit the well-used end, made shiny by usage, of a long pole, the hook of which is buried in the

Incident in the Harem.

mud, and, holding it with his two sinewy hands, pushes as he walks along the flat edge of the ferry-boat, which glides slowly towards the other bank.

Naked children, with their head shaved with the exception of a little tufted lock on the summit of the skull, begrimed with mud or grey with dust, dabble on the shore or roll on the bank ; emaciated, surly dogs rummage in the ground, or bark in a lugubrious way ; large boats, loaded with corn, carrying a whole family sheltered

The Mahmoudieh Canal.

beneath an old piece of cloth stretched out tight, meet beautiful, well-appointed yachts ; old dahabichs, with their cabins and sterns immoderately elevated, their massive rudders, their long lateen-yards and triangular sails, resembling sick old sea-mews, slowly pass ; weighty barges follow the banks, towed along by camels, or by the bargemen chanting in a nasal tone a monotonous complaint.

Large grey buffaloes, with horns curling backward, little hair, wrinkled skins, thrust their shining snouts out of the water : from time to time a grey heron, which has been disturbed, escapes from the reeds ; a plover flies off with a quick jerk of the wing ; while voracious white Pharaoh's chickens hover overhead, watching with their piercing eyes a prey on which to fall ; taciturn pelicans perched on one leg, keeping their beaks warm beneath the down of their wings, are reposing amongst the papyrus near a blue lotus, the plant dear to the Pharaohs, which one finds engraved everywhere on the walls of their temples. This plant, male and female, whose calyx is the maternal breast of the august Rhea, which sees the mystery of the union of Osiris and Isis accomplished in that of stamen and pistil, that symbol of immortality, of the earth again watered by the Nile, of the creation of the universe by the waters, the emblem of Phallus and Myllus united one to the other, is similar to the Joni-lingam of the Hindoos !

And far away extends the luminous country of Egypt, losing itself in the admirable transparency of bluish distance.

In the evening they were almost alone at the hotel, with a few unknown new-comers : the Cook and Son packages had been despatched the previous evening for Cairo ; Sir Hugh and Miss Madge had left the day of their arrival, as well as the Americans, and were installed at Shepheard's Hotel ; " Us " had disappeared in the morning, proceeding to Tantah ; some of the other passengers of the *Saïd* were distributed in the different hotels of the city—at the Hôtel Abbat, the Messageries, and others ; the remainder, composed of persons employed at Alexandria coming back from their holidays, or of merchants, had returned, the former to their desks, the latter to their business.

Jacques and Onésime had seen nearly all that was interesting in Alexandria, thanks to Alan Kéradec. Jacques, whose appetite was sharpened by this first glance at the East, aspired to penetrate it further ; Onésime agreed to everything ; the Doctor had delayed his departure for Upper Egypt to be with the two friends a few days. Briefly, they decided by common accord that they would leave without delay for Cairo ; they talked a little, smoked a few pipes, puffed some cigarettes, and separated early to fasten up their portmanteaux.

The next morning, at 9.30, they were at the Cairo railway station, where the Doctor, at Jacques' earnest request, took three third-class tickets. He wished to see the fellaheen at close quarters. Onésime

Women fetching water.

pouted a bit on seating himself on the hard seats of the carriage, where a central alley allowed of passengers walking up and down, and placed himself as far away as possible from a group of Arabs who were engaged, on their own persons, in a hunt that was as determined as it was fruitful.

The whistle of the locomotive blew ; the train was set in motion. They would soon see the pyramids.

View of Cairo.

CHAPTER VII.

Desert sand in the carriage.—Lake Marcotis.—The Delta country.—Kafr-Dawr.
—Bakshcesh.—Damanhour. — Tel-el-Barout. — Kafr-el-Zaïat.—Tantah.—The
carriage is invaded.—Onésime's suffering and regret.—Benha-'l-Assal.—The
travellers breathe a little.—Touck.—The pyramids!—The Mokattam.—
Khalioub.—Cairo.—The arrival.—A turn in the Esbekieh.—Onésime imagines
himself in Paris.—The crocodile quarter.—By the light of the moon.—Onésime
sulks with Osiris.—His tenderness for Isis.

THE houses and villas disappear, and fine, impalpable sand penetrates through all the openings of the carriage, which is devoid of glass. It falls on everything : the travellers swallow it; breathe it ; get it into the eyes, the ears ; one's clothes are covered with it. You shake yourself, dust yourself, wipe yourself. Labour lost ! It is necessary to begin again five minutes afterwards. The Arabs wrap themselves in their rugs ; the Doctor lets himself be sanded like the Sphinx, without a frown ; Onésime grumbles, sports his spectacles, and covers his head with his handkerchief ; Jacques stands the avalanche without a murmur.

On the left, turning the back to Alexandria, the Mahmoudich Canal, dotted with boats, runs parallel to the line, with the Aboukir Lake in the distance.

On the right, the sun glitters on Lake Marcotis, now an immense expanse of lagunes, formerly a wide basin dug out into large ports, containing innumerable fleets and bordered by fine country houses, by superb vineyards, yielding a delicious wine, that was highly appreciated in ancient times.

For a moment the line, like a regular jetty, advances into the middle of the lake ; the water splashes against the embankment on either side ; then the Mareotis disappears, and the luxuriant country spreads out on either side.

The corn is waving as far as the eye can see, with squares of lucern standing out in raw green on its blond ground ; fields of linseed, indigo, sugar-cane, alternate with patches of motley-coloured poppies ; vigorous vines, with powerful shoots, creep over long arbours made of reeds, and cotton plants display their white fleece on the frail entanglement of their withered-looking branches ; innumerable canals, glittering like silver, run through all this fertility.

The wheels of the *sakiehs* turn without intermission ; the beams of the *shadoufs* rise and fall incessantly ; and the patient fellaheen, bent over the ground, work—for the Khedive, to whom the greater part of these lands of the Delta belongs.

Buffaloes, buried in the water up to the breast, take long drinks, then remain motionless, the neck extended, the head stretched forward, bathing their big forms in this attitude ; others, guarded by a mere child, browse in a field or meadow, in company with herons, bullock-keepers, some of whom have the impudence to perch on their backs. Here and there is a picketed cow or a lean goat, and swarms of pigeons everywhere.

The train follows, without deviation, the bank of a canal which runs beside the high road ; there is a continuous passing of men, women, animals : an Arab galloping on his horse ; a group of fellaheen in good humour returning from a village ; a woman loaded with a heavy bundle toiling painfully along, a child astride on the shoulder, others clinging to her skirt ; stout peasants in easy circumstances trotting on little asses, which they strike with one end of a sugar-cane, while they gnaw the other. Files of camels pass by, each of them with his head attached to the tail of the one preceding him ;

others walk along at a swinging pace, balancing their bales of cotton, their bundles of sugar-cane; a few, kneeling at the side of the road,

On the route.

groan deeply while their masters load them, and others that are quite young gambol at their side.

Villages follow villages, always the same : the hovels of poor
fellaheen, of Nile mud kneaded into a cubic form, with branches and
palm leaves for roofs ; houses of well-to-do peasants, in brick made of
broken straw and clay mixed together and baked in the sun, placed
against high towers which are gigantic pigeon-houses.

Goats sleep before the doors ; dogs rummage among the heaps
of refuse that are rotting in the middle
of the road, or contend with vultures
for a carcass abandoned in the vicinity.
Enormous tamarinds shelter with their
shade these humble refuges grouped
beneath their giant branches. Date trees
tower up among lebakhs of India
and caronb trees, and acacias
covered with long bunches of
flower perfume the neighbourhood.

The train stops at Kafr-
Dawr ; the dust diminishes, one
sees better. Women with baskets
of oranges on their heads approach the carriage ; young girls offer
pitchers of cool water ; blind men,
leaning on long sticks, implore the
pity of travellers ; and an army of
beggars and urchins jump on to the
steps of the carriages, hang on to
the doors, and deafen one with their
demands for gratuities. " Baksheesh !" mutter the bass voices of

Arab village.

the old people. " Baksheesh !" harshly resound those of adults.
" Baksees !" squall out younger throats. " Bassis !" lisp the infantine
tongues of urchins. " Sis !" prattle brats hardly weaned.

This demand for a present or a gratuity, of baksheesh in fact,
is the rallying cry of Egypt against the foreigner ; henceforth it

will resound in his ears from the Mediterranean to the confines of Nubia.

Second stoppage at Damanhour, the old city of Horus, the little Apollinopolis of the Greeks, where Bonaparte, who preceded the army with a weak escort, narrowly escaped being carried off by a party of Mamelukes.

A branch-line on the left goes to Dessouk, where rose, farther towards the west, the ancient Naukratis, which, previous to the founding of Alexandria, was the only city in Egypt open to the Greeks for residence and trade.

After a short stay at Tel-el-Barout, the junction of the railways of Upper Egypt, the train starts again. It crosses, with a rumbling sound like thunder, the iron bridge thrown over the Rosetta branch of the Nile, near the village of Daharieh, and stops at Kafr-el-Zaïat, where, taking advantage of a break in the journey of twenty minutes, the three friends take a snack at the buffet, regretting that they cannot visit the ruins of Saïs, situated a quarter of an hour distant.

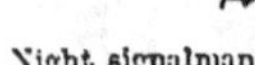

Night signalman.

They are soon at Tantah, where the fairs, particularly that in honour of Seyed-Ahmed-el-Bedaoui, recall in a coarser way the scandalous saturnalias of antiquity. A multitude of fellaheen, of women, of Bedouins, await the train; they precipitate themselves upon the carriages, which they literally take by assault, even before the train has stopped; bursting in all together by the doors, which open

Young Bedouin girl selling water.

at either end of the one compartment, thus preventing those who have
reached their destination leaving, they pile themselves on one another, pushing, swearing, fighting,
amidst bags, bundles of all sorts, cages full of
fowls, young turkeys fastened by the feet—
all these heaped up, pell-mell, in one human
avalanche : it is a regular Noah's Ark !   A few
who have not found room in the inside
climb on to the roofs of the carriages,
and, notwithstanding the stones which
the employés throw at them to make
them come down, spread themselves out
flat on their bellies and obstinately refuse
to move.

The three friends defend
themselves as best they can
against this invasion, bringing with it rank smells of
sweating flesh, of the

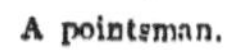

A pointsman.

droppings of buffaloes, of sick poultry.   Half suffocated, they succeed with great trouble in keeping a
part of their places.

Onésime, crushed against the woodwork on one
side, is flanked on the other by a stout Armenian
schoolmaster with bleary eyes ; a Bedouin woman,
whose smile, stereotyped on her face, very much
irritates him, is squatting at his feet.   She holds in
her arms a dirty little black pig, which grunts con-
tinually, and on her knees an enormous bundle.   At
every moment Onésime sees the horrible little animal
rub its wet snout against him ; sometimes even, to
his extreme terror, he fancies he feels its teeth in
search of his calves.   The Doctor is no better off.
There is no possibility of moving ; they are
immured, packed up like herrings !   Onésime is

A signalman.

furious; at a look of reproach that he casts on Jacques—as badly treated as himself—the latter answers him by that remark of Guatimozin on his gridiron : "And me, am I on a bed of roses ?"

At Birket-es-Sab half of the fellaheen get out, which is a relief; the carriage, none the less, remains completely full. They cross the Damietta branch of the river, and at Benha-'l-Assal—where, a little to the north-east, are the ruins of Athribis—a second lot decamp;

Village in the Delta.

the three friends breathe, and Onésime, at length freed from the Armenian, from the Bedouin, from her pig and her bundle, stretches himself with a sigh of satisfaction.

"Ye gods ! If you ever catch me again taking 'thirds'—in Egypt—I'll be roasted," he exclaims, grumbling ; then he breathes hard, and mops his forehead.

"Like you are now," answers Jacques, laughing at Onésime trickling with perspiration, which by a thousand streams has found a way through the sand which the wind had deposited on his face. "You look like a monument disappearing under the sand, or being submerged in an inundation."

"It's very funny, is it not? And you think it's amusing to travel like this, covered with sand, suffocated, crushed!"

"But you have seen the fellaheen at close quarters."

"Alas!"

"And have been able to study them at your ease."

"Yes, at my ease! Between a fat, stinking, bleary-eyed fellow, who flattened me against the side of the carriage, and that creature tattooed blue, with hands green with muck, the owner of that horror of a little aggressive negro pig, her suckling; that's what you call ease! And all that to make nice, pretty, intimate little studies of life. Well, my dear fellow, in future you can make them all alone, your studies of life—at least, of that kind; I have had enough of them!"

"Have patience!" says Jacques; "in an hour we shall be at Cairo."

"Fortunately!"

Little by little the plain becomes less green, the valley is contracted. At Touck the pyramids, roseate beneath the sun, appear on the right, through the palm trees, against the yellow tones of the Libyan desert; to the left, on the arid groundwork of the Arabian desert, are the heights of Mokattam, with the Citadel and the Mosque of Mahomet Ali, the dome of which shines brilliantly between its two tapering minarets.

At Khalioub one perceives to the west the great brick towers of the Barrage of the Nile; to the south a forest of minarets, of cupolas, of white walls; the train enters the suburbs of Cairo; villages appear, and villas. We have arrived!

Amidst deafening cries and furious pushing, the three friends possess themselves of a cab, which takes them to the Hôtel d'Alexandrie in the Esbekieh quarter, where the landlord, a friend of Kéradec, a charming man, formerly holding a post in the Suez Canal Company, installs them in clean and spacious rooms; and he finds Jacques, besides, a large apartment facing north for a studio.

After vigorous and repeated ablutions, the travellers, free from sand and refreshed, go, guided by Kéradec, for a turn in the Esbekich Garden—formerly a lake, surrounded by trees and habitations ; at present, after successive metamorphoses, a landscape garden of a rectangular form, with the corners cut off, surrounded by iron railings and tastefully laid out. A basin, with swans and ducks, has succeeded the lake where the old sycamores reflected their thick foliage, and European hotels have taken the place of the picturesque houses lost in shady lanes. A restaurant *à la carte* stands on the spot where slowly turned a sakieh manœuvred by buffaloes ; Europeans walk along carefully · sanded paths, where Arabs of the desert, perched on their camels, passed in the dust of the roadway.

An infantry soldier.

This oasis is none the less a very delightful cool nook, with its strange trees brought from the interior of Africa by Doctor Schweinfurth, its blocks of foliage and green lawns, beneath the limpid blue Egyptian sky, the magnificent Eastern sun, which bathes all its green freshness in the pure transparency of its radiant light.

What affects the eyes disagreeably, and contributes to take away what still remains of the Oriental in this half-Haussmannised quarter, are the modern establishments installed in the garden : cafés, beershops, restaurants, photographic pavilions, etc. ; the gardeners with their long pipes on wheels recall to you the watering men in the streets of Paris ; the river emptying itself into the lake, its waterfall and the artificial grotto surmounted by its belvedere, make you think of the Bois de Boulogne ; and when from four to nine o'clock at night a military band performs its European repertory, you could easily believe you were in the Tuileries gardens.

Jacques noticed with regret this clumsy imitation of the manners, this commonplace adaptation of the industry of pale Europe in the former capital of the Arab civilisation, now accepting with passion the vices of the West, but refractory to assimilate its virtues. Onésime chattered like a magpie, happy to find in the land of the Pharaohs something to remind him of his dear Paris. The restaurant, especially, attracted him in an irresistible way ; the three friends took their meal there, and this finished putting him in a good humour ; when they sauntered along the walks, after coffee, with cigars only removed to let out lively words and laughter between the lips, he was beaming with joy.

Stealthy shadows passed by—veiled women, whom Onésime eyed with most impertinent conceit ; men in silk gowns of various colours, government clerks in tarboush and stambouline, soldiers dressed in white. The Venetian lanterns and the lamps hooked to the awnings of the Arab cafés mingled their dull red gleams with the brilliant light of numerous gas - burners. Beneath these tents, sheltering Arab orchestras, daraboukas were droning, rebecks grating, guitars squeaking, blended with the harsh, piercing voices of the singers, applauded by the prolonged "Ah !" of their enthusiastic admirers.

A street in Cairo.

From there Kéradec took them to the centre of the Arab town ; they were lost in streets, where they could hardly walk two abreast ; in broader ones, where heavily loaded camels flattened them against the walls, where donkeys crushed their feet ; they stumbled over formless heaps of rags, which were the bodies of wretched creatures sleeping in the darkest corners ; then they all at once emerged into streets teeming with people.

Lanterns of all forms and sizes, hooked on to the fronts of rudimentary shops, brightly lit up the goods set out there with their streams of vacillating light. Here a fruiterer was seated in the midst of the vegetables, water-melons, melongenas, oranges, lemons, encumbering his stall, four feet in breadth ; there a saddler was actively engaged in finishing a magnificent sky-blue velvet saddle enriched with gold ; farther on a tobacconist was enjoying his narghileh, and speaking ill of his neighbour to a few customers with long tongues ; a woman was crushing corn between two mill-stones, while her husband idly smoked his tchibouk.

They turned the corner of a street, and suddenly passed into the deep obscurity of the narrow alleys, bordered by lofty houses, where the succession of corbels, of balconies, of moncharabiehs rose up in flights along the walls, hardly leaving space right at the top for one to perceive a square of the heavens sprinkled with stars. A few rare lamps lit up, with their dying and indistinct light, the capricious arabesques, delicately picked out, that adorned the wooden casing of monumental doors. before which swung stuffed crocodiles and hippopotami.

A woman crushing corn.

Strange shadows glided silently by ; great thin cats brushed against their legs or slid along the walls ; vague forms disappeared in gaping apertures ; their footsteps, muffled by a thick coating of dust, made no sound ; they barely heard, like an indistinct murmur, the hum of the stirring street they had quitted, which a vaporous glimmer of light indicated in the distance.

They were stranded in blind alleys, frightful passages without egress, amid houses that had tumbled in, where the quivering beams, suspended in space, threatened at each instant to fall down on their heads. They groped about on the rubbish, stumbled among the ruins, climbed over heaps of stones, avoided the sinister openings of caved-in cellars.

Other narrow streets in the Crocodile quarter had an appearance as accentuated, but of quite another aspect : there, high carved doors were half open ; on the thresholds, women belonging to all races, simply attired in a *kamis* of a raw colour, red, olive, or lemon-yellow, very low at the neck, smoked cigarettes.

Little negresses from Kordofan, supple, shiny, with flexible loins, hard, pear-shaped breasts, firm stomachs, monkeys' hands, naked delicate feet, ornamented with massive silver rings, soon blended with the shades of night ; the whiteness of their teeth, when they laughed, made a bright flash indicating the place of their heads.

Fellaheen women, of a caressing nature, with a smile of resignation, tall, light, slender, tattooed with blue on the forehead and chin, leaning their backs against the wall, were chatting with obese Turkish women with thick eyelids, eyes enlarged by antimony, fat fingers covered with rings, massive legs, heavy feet

Fellaheen women.

encased in white stockings and cramped in Parisian boots with high, worn-down heels.

Thin Jewesses, with olive complexions, aquiline noses, blood-red lips, brilliant eyes beneath hollow arched brows, of a gloomy countenance, troubled the passer-by with the intensity of their burning look.

Young Nubians modulated a plaintive song in a strange rhythm, gazing with their great wild eyes, of a golden brown, wide open, and showed in their whole manner something of the frightened air of the gazelle of their deserts.

Through the gaping doorway one perceived other women inside stretched out on mats. Near a chiselled bronze brasero old matrons, squatting down, in black gowns, the collar being embroidered with silver, the head covered by a veil, approached their fleshless hands

Old matrons.

to the fire, seeking a little warmth for their old blood grown cold. Motionless in a corner a sickly fellah, the shame-faced servant, gazed without seeing with his sparkless eyes !

They increased their pace. The cafés succeeded each other in the street, badly lighted, swarming with Arabs close together on dislocated forms ; performers on rebecks deliciously tickled the ears

Arab musicians.

of their audience, alternatively with young ulemas of the Mosque of El Azhar, who attempted to recite delightful stories of their own composition before a good-natured public, who received them with flattering applause. Tea, perfumed with a piece of amber fixed at the bottom of the cup, and coffee, were passed round amidst the smoke of tchibouks, cigarettes, and narghilehs.

In the streets, at every hundred paces, soldiers in iron-grey cloaks, with a tarboush on the head, the rifle slung across the shoulder, were smoking cigarettes and watching over public order.

Kéradec soon brought his friends into the Rue du Mouski, and from there to the Esbekieh.

It was a splendid night; the stars shone in the heavens with soft lustre, imperceptibly veiled by a slight transparent vapour, hardly disturbing the admirable purity of the atmosphere ; it enveloped the trees, the houses, the distances, with its diffuse light, accentuating the masses, softening the outlines, casting everywhere a sort of bluish, velvety glaze, exquisitely limpid and of extraordinary softness to the eye.

Decidedly the blinding ferocity of the tone of the brilliant Osiris, God of the Sun, was not equal to the downy touches and serene amplitude of his adorable companion, the gentle Isis, Queen of Night. Such, at least, was the opinion of Onésime : he considered that His Majesty the Sun became embarrassing, and did a little too much as he liked with poor mortality, whom he pitilessly roasted. Like a gallant Parisian, all his sympathy was given to good Isis, the Lady of cool evenings, the dispenser of healthy repose.

They strolled round the square, passed, at the angle of the Boulak Avenue, before the house where Bonaparte, during the Egyptian campaign, had established his headquarters, and, a little higher up, before the palace of the Defterdar-Bey, opposite to which Kleber fell under the dagger of a fanatic.

Five minutes later they were back at the hotel. Kéradec, whose slumbers were disturbed by visions of the laurels secured by Maspéro, had only a short time to remain at Cairo and devote to his young friends ; he traced out their itinerary for the following days. On the morrow they would visit Heliopolis, returning by way of the petrified forest ; then would come the turn of Memphis and the Pyramids ; on the fourth day he had to take the train to Assiout, and from there, by the postal boat, reach Luxor, where he was to be joined later on by Jacques and Onésime.

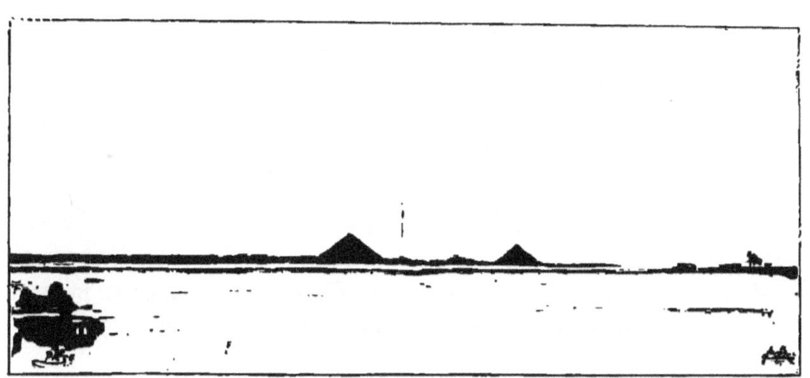

The Pyramids as seen from the Nile.

CHAPTER VIII.

Monsieur de Lesseps. — Telegraph and Gambetta. — Bismarck is beaten by
Monsieur de Lesseps.—In the garden of Matarieh.—A picnic.—The obelisk of
Usertesen I. and the Virgin's Tree.—The battle of Heliopolis.—Retrospective
glance at Heliopolis.—Onésime considers that the ancient Egyptians were
madmen and the Greeks cracked with genius.—He will not admit that Greek
civilisation was the offspring of that of the Egyptians.—He reproaches the
learned with having at times too much science.—The Egyptians invented
powder.—Causes of the greatness and decline of the Egyptians.—The petrified
forest.—What Onésime thinks of hypotheses.—Jacques a deicide.—Kéradec
pretends that if God hides his abode it is because he desires to preserve his
incognito, and that it would be wrong to seek to disturb him.—Different
hypotheses upon the petrified forest: that of Onésime.—A dash into the
desert.—Return to Cairo.

THE next morning they had hardly reached the threshold of the
hotel, when they were surrounded by a regular army of donkey
boys in light-coloured turbans, red skull caps, blue or white gowns,
showing glimpses of silk waistcoats with coloured stripes. They
pushed each other as hard as they could, and, by counter-shock,
involuntarily knocked up against their future customers. There were
shouts of laughter, exclamations, a flood of prodigious words ; they
quarrelled among themselves for the three friends, pulling them by
their garments, seating them almost by force on their animals.

"Good donkey, sir," said one of them to Jacques, whom he

endeavoured to appropriate to himself. "Fine ass! Good moke! Goes like lightning; Empress's donkey! 'Gambetta' goes like steam. Take my ass, Monsieur le Comte! Take Ahmed—good donkey boy, Ahmed!"

Jacques allowed them to do as they pleased, laughing. He was amused at the sight of this animated pantomime, of this exuberance of gesture and cries. The expressive features, the intelligent physiognomies, the innate elegance of these young fellaheen, their noisy

Donkey boys of Cairo.

gaiety, their constant good humour, all this "dash" of good spirits, interested him. He gave his preference to "Gambetta," a handsome black donkey, clean, shining, with a fine head, a flexible neck, and seated himself in the high saddle made of red leather, sewn with yellow silk; Ahmed took possession of his album, water-colour box, camp-stool, and, sure of his conquest, threw upon his comrades a superb look of satisfaction.

Kéradec had taken, not without difficulty on the part of the turbulent band, the ass of a poor little Arab, who, after having contended despairingly with his big companions to approach the travellers, had ended by abandoning a useless struggle, and, standing apart, a butt to the jeers of his turbulent associates, was shedding warm tears, while cuddling the head of his poor donkey. The animal seemed to join in his grief, and softly wiped away, with his tongue, the shower of tears that trickled down the cheeks of the unhappy little Abdallah. When the last-named saw Kéradec approach and jump on "Telegraph," his tears dried up in the twinkling of an eye. He gave a leap; "Telegraph," out of fellow-feeling, did the same, and the Doctor was almost unseated!

Onésime was the envied prey of two donkey boys, each of whom pulled him his own way, and would not let him go. One of them, Hassan, placed the reins in his hand, and endeavoured to hoist him into the saddle of " Monsieur de Lesseps." His companion, Ali, on the other hand, did his utmost to put one of his feet into " Bismarck's " stirrup, and seized him by the arm to tear him from his rival. Victory remained with Hassan and " Monsieur de Lesseps," a beautiful grey ass, on whom the clipper's scissors, no doubt in honour of the great name he bore, had cut out capricious arabesques, coquettishly displayed on the shoulders, and on the thighs and legs. " Monsieur de Lesseps " was really very bewitching, with his open woven stockings and embroidered mittens ; a sort of little rebellious tuft waved proudly on the top of his head, and small tassels of the same quivered at the extremity of his ears.

Onésime, worthy and imposing, fixed in his saddle, was proud of his mount, and the latter, without doubt, was proud of the noble appearance of his rider.

Hassan, like a thrifty fellah, had removed his babouches and held them in his hand ; Onésime formally recommended him to put away his plaintive " Ah! " along with his babouches, under the penalty of not receiving baksheesh if he disobeyed, and, for greater security, mindful of his misadventure at Ramleh, he borrowed his stick.

" Bismarck," beaten, returned with drooping ears, with Ali, among the group of rejected donkey boys. Onésime had begun the revenge under happy auspices : "Monsieur de Lesseps" had beaten Bismarck ; France had won the first heat !

The scuffle was at an end. Once the riders in their saddles, the squadron swayed, then started off at a gallop, raising a cloud of dust, in the direction of Heliopolis, amidst the sonorous shouts of "Guarda ! yaminee ! choumalee !" of the donkey boys running behind the animals ; the passers-by made way in the road, leaving the place free to the spirited cavalcade launched at full speed.

They were soon on the road to Abassieh. Turning to the left, they crossed the Khalig ; arrived in front of the former Mosque of Gäma-el-Dhaber, transformed into a guard-house ; then fell into the old road to Abassieh, bordered by acacias, which passed in front of the massive Palace of the same name, comprising the Polytechnic School, the Military School, the Observatory, and close to which was the old racecourse.

After a brief halt the party, slackening speed, follows the edge of the desert ; the road is dry, dusty, the air hot, the sun strikes fiercely. Onésime, forming the rearguard, cooks gently in his juice, notwithstanding his parasol ; Jacques' back is roasted ; Kéradec is at the head, with the happy Abdallah skipping, chattering, beside him, dividing his careful attentions between the Doctor and "Telegraph," who behaves very worthily, like an ass that feels that he has a man of learning on his back. They breathe a little when, leaving the border of the desert, they come into the lane, bordered by a hedge of lemon trees, which leads to the Viceroy's Palace. From that point the road crosses the fertile and well-cultivated plain of Matarieh, all covered with magnificent gardens, and at last they stop at that of the Virgin's Tree. This, with the fields surrounding it, is watered by a sakieh which draws up the element from the bottom of a well ; they put foot to ground close to the palings that surround Mary's sycamore.

After having rested here for a moment in the shade of the old tree, with its mutilated trunk, which is covered with all sorts of inscriptions, Kéradec and Jacques went for a stroll in the environs. Onésime made Hassan bring him a jug of fresh cool water, took

Street in Cairo.

some long draughts from it, then stretched himself out comfortably on the grass in the shade of the acacias, and, his head covered with his pocket-handkerchief, as a protection against mosquitoes, awaited the return of his two friends. Ahmed and Abdallah, installed some distance off, took a few bits of bread from their pockets, and began munching it beside their unbridled animals.

The Virgin's Tree.

When Alan and Jacques returned, after having had a look at the obelisk, recognised a few vestiges of inferior temples, and met with some remains of sphinxes, they found Onésime sleeping like one of the blessed, and Abdallah was doing the same between the legs of "Telegraph"; Hassan, after having wiped "Monsieur de Lesseps" and watered him, was giving him some crusts of bread while fondling his good old head; Ahmed had removed the saddle from "Gambetta" and was rolling on the ground with him, a game that seemed to please both of them a great deal.

The provisions were placed on a nice white table-cloth, spread in the shade of a grove of lemon and orange trees, on the ground, by Hassan, who had appointed himself butler to the expedition, while Ahmed brought a pitcher full of limpid water, drawn at the well of the neighbouring *sakieh*. They awoke Onésime, and a smile overspread his jovial face at the tempting sight of the table set out and of his two friends only waiting for him to commence the feast.

In this shady corner, cool, perfumed, they made a repast of sybarites. The excellent coffee that the ingenious Hassan had prepared was served by him and received with enthusiasm; then, with the cheerful calm and benevolent serenity of persons who have a clear conscience, a full stomach, robust health, and an inexhaustible fund of good humour, the three Gauls began to talk nonsense in the most amiable and witty manner imaginable. Alan rolled cigarettes and risked the most daring hypotheses; Jacques, between a couple of puffs of his pipe, rivalled him in ardour, piling paradoxes on paradoxes; Onésime blissfully followed with the eye the bluish spiral smoke of his cigar, an occupation that seemed to interest him infinitely more than the fantastic speculations of his two neighbours.

They at last tore themselves away, with regret, from this sweet retreat. The trio lazily made their way, across some insignificant ruins, towards the unique monument of Usertesen.

"But, Doctor, you have brought us into a regular wasps' nest," said Onésime, pointing to the monolith, covered with the nests of the mason-wasp.

"This wasps' nest, Monsieur Onésime, is the most ancient obelisk known in Egypt; and here we are on the spot where formerly stood, in all its splendour, the most ancient city in the world."

"And of this old and superb city," inquired Jacques, "there remains nothing, nothing but this obelisk and these few ruins?"

"Nothing but this *menhir*, of a geometric form, with architectural pretensions?" continued Onésime.

" Nothing ! The wish of Amenemhat I., the founder of the Temple of the Sun, who exclaimed, on laying the foundation stone : ' Let it not be destroyed in any space of time ! Once completed let it last !' was not realised ; and the heinous prediction of Jeremiah, the prophet of the Jews, 'those vile Asiatics, those accursed, those leprous, those pestiferous creatures,' as the Egyptians reviled them, was unfortunately accomplished !

" Chap. xliii., ver. 13 : ' He will also break the statues of the house of the Sun, which is in the land of Egypt, and he will burn with fire the houses of the gods of Egypt.'

" Only the obelisk of Usertesen I., escaped from the anger of the God of the Jews, put into effect by the vandalism of the Arabs, has remained to indicate the site of the venerable city, near that sycamore, in the shade of which, according to the legend, the Virgin and the infant Christ rested during the flight to Egypt, and in the hollow trunk of which they hid themselves to avoid those sent in pursuit of them ; a spider, that had spun its web at the opening, shielded them from the sight of their persecutors. As to the small spring that runs at the bottom of the well that you see there, tradition has it that the Virgin there washed the swaddling clothes of the Saviour ; it is added that everywhere where a drop of water fell from the linen a balsam tree grew."

Obelisk of Usertesen.

" That's an origin for the balsam tree that sounds somewhat like a fable, Monsieur Kéradec."

" If the legend does not please you, you can take history, which teaches you that Cleopatra brought the balsam tree from Judea."

"Where she, no doubt, went to play some of her pranks," interrupted Onésime.

"Something of the kind," replied Alan, laughing ; " she had gone to try the power of her charms on Herod."

" The provoking strumpet ! "

" I see she pleases you no more than this obelisk, this *menhir* of a geometric form, as you term it."

" I much prefer the latter; it at least keeps itself straight, although it doesn't say much."

" If the obelisk of Usertesen could speak, Monsieur Coquillard, it would say that they are, by the legend of the Virgin Mary, superseding Osiris, who, at first, hid in the trunk of a tree, and that the element that watered the ground beside it had made balsam trees grow thousands of years before Christ ; that, long before, Osiris had sent his son Horus on earth to save mankind by spilling his blood, as Jesus had redeemed the world on the cross ; that people took communion from him, that divine Lord, before taking communion from the Son of God. It would relate also the sanguinary battle fought on the plain of Heliopolis, when on March 19th, 1800, in an heroic struggle, 8,000 Frenchmen, commanded by Kleber, dispersed 80,000 Turks urged on against us by England, after the Convention of El Arish, and it would express astonishment that the souvenir of this glorious passage of arms had not effaced, even to the last vestiges, the pale Christian legend that has taken shelter in the shade of the old tree, wasted and worn out with age."

" And it would not be wrong," said Jacques ; " legends are the splutterings of humanity in the cradle, and history is the manly language of adult nations : to return to legends is to fall back into infancy, and the world is not old enough yet for that ! "

" So," said Kéradec, " let us leave this legend, more or less apocryphal, in its swaddling clothes, and talk a little about Heliopolis, or *AN*, as the Egyptians called it, the *ON* of the Hebrews, the city consecrated to Toum-Harmakhis (the rising sun, the setting sun), the City of the Sun, with its grand temples approached by interminable avenues of sphinxes, with innumerable obelisks before them.

" It was here that the bennou, the phœnix with the gold and crimson plumage, unique and without a mate, came from Arabia every five hundred years to expire and be re-born of its own ashes on the altar of the Sun; here that the lion with the luminous coat, with the golden claws, wearing round his neck triple collars of precious stones, in his ears pendants of gold enriched with emeralds from Ethiopia, and the ox Mnévis, with the black and bristling hair, whose horns were gilded and the points ornamented with turquoises from Sinai, his body partly covered with plates of delicately chiselled gold sewn with chalcedony from Thebes, delivered their oracles,—revered animals that were fed by special officers of an elevated rank, whose post was hereditary, honoured and envied; having their bathers, perfumers, hairdressers, valets, to attend to their toilet, to satisfy the caprices of their coquetry; their painters to reproduce their pictures; their sculptors to chisel their sacred features; their scribes to relate their deeds and gestures; their harems and their eunuchs entrusted with the duty of providing for their august amours; their singers, their musicians, to charm their leisure; their thurifers to burn incense around them, their priests to sing hymns in their honour; and a whole people to kneel down before them and spread out carpets on their way, respecting them to such a point that, in times of famine, men ate each other rather than touch the food of their adored animals, who wanted for nothing; that their death was a signal for public mourning; that, in equality with the Kings, they were embalmed with prodigious luxury and placed in splendid sepulchres; and that, like the gods, they shared divine honours."

" Good gracious! but those people were mad," said Onésime, " mad as hatters! Egypt was the Bedlam of Africa; its inhabitants had all a tile loose. The monsters! Eat each other in the presence of an enormous beefsteak on hoofs, of indecent corpulency! But it was pyramidal! It was pure anthropophagy, without attenuating circumstances too! The wretches had lost their brains."

" Not at all, my dear Monsieur Onésime; the Egyptians only lost their brains after their death, when the embalmers, with an oblique iron, drew them out of their nostrils."

" It must have been a regular sinecure then, and their oblique iron must often have searched in emptiness."

" The Greeks thought quite differently of the Egyptians, Monsieur Coquillard; Eudoxus and Plato came to study astronomy at this very place, at Heliopolis."

" Another nation of cracked people, your Greeks ! "

" The Greeks ! " exclaimed Jacques; "they are the heroic, intelligent, artistic, learned nation *par excellence* ! "

" Speak in the past tense, if you please."

" That nation was—— "

" Yes, was—*fuit*—— "

" The Prometheus of humanity."

" Its weakness is now the object of the pity of Europe."

" After having been by its genius the cause of its greatness. Respect must be shown for such ancients, and not pity ; the ungrateful sons of the Germans, the Dacians, Britons, Sarmatians, and Latins, forgetful of the services rendered in antiquity, must not come and bite the breast of the sublime wet-nurse, where their ancestors sucked the sacred milk which, from barbarians that they were, made them men ; all must, like the grateful children of the Gauls, pay their debt to old Hellas by guiding the tottering steps of her descendants; their weakness must be protected, and not threatened."

" To enlighten the groping efforts of Greece, clearing her road in the present, guiding her aspirations towards the future," said Kéradec, " is to bring another element to the great work of civilisation, and one of the most fruitful ! Greece, as well gifted now as formerly, brave, learned, philosophic, artistic, awakening from her long slumber, seeks to join the past to the present and to continue the glorious tradition of times that have disappeared."

" It is only Hercules who could have brought this work to a good end, and he will not spring up again from his ashes, like the bennou," said Onésime.

" That's true ; but he has left descendants who—— "

" Delight idlers at the fairs ; an agglomeration of muscles that has extinguished the brain," interrupted Onésime.

" Who desire nothing better than to follow in his footsteps," continued the Doctor ; " and it is here, among these madmen, as you call them, that the philosophers of Greece, then in full bloom, came to ask the priests of Egypt on the decline for the elements of that wisdom which had been bequeathed to them by the servants of Horus."

" Or rather to ascertain the degree of folly they had reached."

" Perhaps ! Nevertheless they adapted those principles to their versatile genius ; their brilliant imagination transformed them ; their light-hearted scepticism stripped them of the mystic formulas that enveloped them ; their common sense, so precise, threw light on the obscurities, lopped off the excrescences ; their fascinating elegance, their harmonious language, propagated ideas, casting to the four corners of the globe that triple germ of human thought, science, and art, the development of which was to give expression to our modern civilisation."

" I consider it very amusing all the same on the part of that good old Attica, coming to ask Egypt how to behave decently in life. Ogres conducting a philosophy class ! Mummy-manufacturers, who put the bodies of their relatives ' up the spout,' undertakers teaching the science of life ! Imbecile scribes, forerunners of Aristophanes ! Interminable litanies of an idiotic ritual, preparing the work of Æschylus ! Egyptian fables, inspiring Homer ! Hierogrammatists with their hieroglyphics, dry daubers of profiles, stiff stone-scrapers, clumsy sculptors of baboons on a large scale, constructors of chambers in the pyramids, forerunners of an Apelles, of a Phidias, of the sublime architect of the Parthenon ! These surveyors of nomes assisting Diophantes to work out his theorems, giving lessons to Euclid ! These ungainly adorers of animals teaching æsthetics to that noble, beautiful, elegant race, which had the sentiment of art innate in its mind, or in the blood, whose brain produced the myth of Prometheus, casting immortal masterpieces about in profusion ! You might as well say at once that this obelisk is the primal type of the Pallas Athene of Phidias, or the Faun of Praxiteles."

" Yes, indeed, Monsieur Coquillard."

" You decidedly know too much, you gentlemen of learning; you are able, like the Almighty, to make something out of nothing ; more powerful than Moses, who by the blow of a stick caused water to spurt from a rock, you make wisdom flow from folly. Continue, my dear scholar; explain us all these mysteries, divulge to us all the secrets that the monuments of your old friend Ægyptos have murmured in your ear ; tell us what the Colossi of Memnon related to you at sunrise, what the granite Sphinxes of Karnac confided to you ! Translate to us the most intimate confessions of this solitary obelisk and of this old sycamore, relics of a religion that has disappeared and of another that is agonising ; and if there remains somewhere, in some naos buried beneath the sand, at the bottom of the serdab of some mastaba forgotten by Mariette, in the entrails of some pyramid neglected by Maspéro, in the labyrinth of some speos lost in the Arabian mountain, a bit of this famous wisdom of Egypt, well ! ask this solitary mile-stone, this wasps' nest, to show you the way and to find you the place where this gem rests, this *rara avis*, and make a present of it to the fellaheen of to-day, who have great need of it ! "

" They are not the only ones," retaliated Jacques.

" You want your share ? "

" Yes ; to divide it with you."

" But if I told you, Monsieur Coquillard, that at the period when our ancestors, in mere barbarism, lived in caverns, struggling with arms of flint against bears and wild bulls, the Egyptians had their astrologers, their mathematicians, their architects ; that they practised all the arts, exercised almost all the trades known in our own times ; and that Egypt had already arrived at a high degree of civilisation before Babylon and Nineveh were founded ? "

" I would believe you, because you would affirm it to be true."

" And if I added that it was an Egyptian who invented gun-powder ? "

" An Egyptian ! "

" Yes, an Egyptian, born here, at Heliopolis ! "

" Then I would ask whether you were speaking seriously."

" And I would reply that I am speaking very seriously ; that this

Egyptian, crossed with a Greek, was called Callinices, that he lived in the seventh century of our era, that he discovered the composition of Greek fire, which is little different from gunpowder, the use of which was even known to the Egyptian priests."

"And the celebrated German monk? And Roger Bacon?"

"They would have invented nothing at all."

"But the Chinese, did not they have something to do with the invention of powder as well?"

"It was known to them from time immemorial, and as commercial intercourse existed between the east and west of Asia, perhaps their secret was transmitted to Africa and thence to Europe by Callinices, who took advantage of this discovery; but these are quite gratuitous suppositions. What is beyond doubt is that the Egyptian priests made use of powder, or of something similar, in the performance of their mysteries, or in their initiations, to impose on the people and frighten the neophytes; that Callinices found Greek fire, or gunpowder, and took his discovery to Constantinople."

"Well, I should never have thought them capable of such a thing."

"But," broke in Jacques, "how do you explain, Monsieur Alan, such an absolute breakdown of this people so profoundly original, so singularly tenacious, so attached to their old customs, to their institutions, to their Pharaohs, so opposed to all importation from the outside? How has such a complete metamorphosis been performed, which transformed the hardy soldiers of Thotmes into the timid fellaheen of the present day?"

"By that fatal law of nature which provides that all here below are born, multiply, and die."

"And begin again," remarked Onésime, "as the Greeks are budding again; at least, so you affirm."

"And begin again," acquiesced Kéradec; "that happens sometimes."

"With patronage; your spoilt child has doubtless attained a dispensation. I see arrangements can be made with science as with the Church: I was not aware that the noble daughter of Mnemosyne and Jupiter, the impartial Clio, sometimes lost herself in the undulating paths of the sweet disciples of Loyola."

"But you see exceptions at every instant, in everything!"

"To confirm the rule, is it not so?   And Greece is one."

"Yes, like all beings who, before dying out, left the germs of a new life."

"Ah! Doctor, give me, I beg of you, the secret of procuring a new life."

"Marry and have children," answered Alan, laughing.

Onésime made a grimace.

"Thank you, Doctor; I do not feel myself sufficiently near my end to wish to continue.   I'll wait."

"To revert to your question, Monsieur Jacques, travel back to the period when the Macedonian founded Alexandria, grafting a vivacious shoot on to the old stalk of Egypt slumbering over its mummies, exhausted by successive invasions.   Under the powerful impulsion of Lagos, the Greek city became the centre of intelligence, science, and art at the same time as the commercial rendezvous of the world.   The Ptolemies sought in vain to blend, in a fusion contrary to the traditional genius of Egypt, the sombre and angry character of the Egyptian with the gay and mocking nature of the Greek, and to implant in the decayed civilisation of the Pharaohs that younger and more pleasant civilisation of Greece; it merely grazed the surface of the old national mind, and, powerless to penetrate beyond, only weakened the ancient doctrines, which were altered and partly lost, as well as the sacred language of hieroglyphics, which disappeared for ever, some centuries later, stifled by Christianity.

"And when Amrou, at the head of a Mussulman army, invaded the valley of the Nile, Egypt was nothing but a corpse, which neither the genius of Lagides nor the astounding vitality of the Greek people —light of heart, turbulent, thoughtful, learned, artistic, of untiring ndustrial ability, of unrivalled commercial activity—had been able to galvanise; and while Egypt, inert, submitted almost unconsciously to the Arab invasion, accepting mechanically their customs with their religion, the Greeks, after a long and heroic effort, the last spasm of their dying energy, abandoned by the orthodox Byzantium, succumbed, exhausted and glorious.

"They bequeathed to their conquerors the brilliant remnants of the Hellenic civilisation from which is born that of the West.

"The Arabs, adapting to their genius, so original in its graceful fancy, this pure sentiment of the beautiful, this profound science of the Greeks, in their turn, guided by the victorious Crescent, carried the civilisation of the conquered as far as Spain. But the fatal principle of Islamism, which prevented them accepting it in its entirety, contained the germ of death, which would, in the end, stay the powerful flow of this astounding culture, and annihilate the Colossus which Europe is even now dividing in his lifetime.

"At the present day Islamism is breaking up; the mosques are crumbling to ruins before the eyes of the indifferent Arabs, who possess neither the courage nor the necessary science to repair them or to build new ones ; the Crescent, like the Cross, like the key of the life of Osiris, is on its way to join, amidst indifference and oblivion, all the worn-out rattles of our fathers, all those old accessories of annihilated religions.

"The fellah alone is left in the midst of his tombs, of his temples, of his mummies, unchangeable like the Nile, slowly absorbing his conquerors, consoling himself in his ardent affection for his beloved river, the Osiris of his ancestors, patiently waiting, bent over the dark soil, for the soul of Egypt, gone to the unknown regions of Amenti, to return and animate afresh its poor body."

"But where are the ruins of this city of Heliopolis? It is not possible to conjure away the remains of such a town like a nutmeg."

"One must seek for them at Cairo, in the foundations of the houses, of the mosques, of the ramparts. The Arabs built the new Egyptian capital with the ruins of Heliopolis and Memphis, reduced, alas ! to the state of quarries in full activity. *Væ victis !* The quotation is applicable to stones as well as nations."

While chatting thus together, the Doctor, Jacques, and Onésime had wandered about a good deal, and seen almost everything. Jacques had made a few sketches, Kéradec had deciphered a few hieroglyphics, and Onésime had conscientiously got over his digestion. They returned to the camp, jumped on their asses, and set out in the direction of the petrified forest.

In a short time they reached some sandy ground between Gebel-el-Ahmar and Gebel-Mokattam, in a desolate, arid spot. The donkeys advanced at a walk, the horsemen did not breathe a word ; the donkey boys also followed in silence, wiping away, from time to time, a few drops of perspiration with the back of their hands. An oppressive heat weighed on the little caravan. It laboriously ascended the slope of Gebel-el-Ahmar, and at last came to an expanse of table-land, covered with the remains of trunks of trees, some of a remarkable size, which were petrified, or rather transformed into a siliceous substance.

"These petrifications," said Kéradec, "which are also found at Gebel-Silsileh, in the great Libyan desert, in the Bayouda desert, in Abyssinia, and at Kilima N'jaro, seem to form part of an immense siliceous system, covering all Eastern Africa and disappearing under the sand, some parts only emerging, in places, on the surface of the soil. Different hypotheses have been advanced as to their origin."

"Ah ! the hypotheses," said Onésime ; " there they are coming to the rescue, those good-natured hypotheses, those perfidious charmers, those docile children of your restless imaginations, those vaporous forerunners of the realisation of your wishes, timid enlighteners of science, slight scaffoldings with which you prop up the extravagant speculations of your minds, so ardently captivated by truth, whose gigantic leap towards the unknown only equals the vertiginous depth of the fall, light bubbles escaped from the meanders of your seething brains, bursting, poor fools ! in the stern contact with cold reality."

" Certainly, Monsieur Onésime, for it is in the crucible of a severe analysis that our reasoning is refined ; logic is the touch-stone of our speculations, and we do not permit ourselves to be deceived by the delirium of our imprudent imagination."

" Your imagination ! It surpasses even your knowledge, gentlemen of science ; you jump on to the hypothesis as lightly as a poet leaps on Pegasus, and when, by chance, brutal truth seizes your

The Mokattam.

complaisant mount by the bridle and flings him down, it is almost with painful regret for an illusion that is lost, that, letting go the saddle, you quit your broken-down screw, to enter on the bitter and luminous path of reality."

" But, Monsieur Coquillard, it is by hypotheses that we arrive at truth."

" You might almost say at once that by lying we get to say what is true."

" The hypothesis, my dear Onésime," said Jacques—" pardon me, Doctor, the audacity of my hypothesis—is the dung on which grows the venerable mushroom of science."

" Good and evil, then," interrupted Onésime ; " for beside the wholesome mushroom often grows the venomous fungus ; and these two brotherly enemies are so much alike, that one must have a very sure eye to distinguish one from the other, and with these gentlemen, pioneers of science—your fellow-brethren, Monsieur Kéradec—if the mind is always powerful, the sight is sometimes weak, and the possibility exists that, through the glasses of their spectacles, they might mistake the two, and be guilty of errors, very excusable, no doubt, but much to be regretted."

" Don't worry yourself," said Jacques, " Monsieur Kéradec knows his business; you may have confidence in his long and learned experience."

" I have always appreciated to the full extent the great learning and clever good sense of M. Alan," answered Onésime, who turned smiling towards the Doctor ; " he has my entire confidence."

" Thanks for your good opinion of me, my dear Monsieur Onésime ; I will endeavour to preserve it by not making too frequent use of hypotheses, and you will do me a service by refuting them as I establish them ; they will thus be so many false scents exposed, and it will be so much to the credit of truth."

" Do not rely on me for that ; I am too much of a conservator to wish to bring accepted theories to destruction, however hypothetical they may be."

" And then," said Jacques, " there are some that have existed so long wrapped up in such universal veneration that you would fear to do the least thing to them. Attempt, for example, to touch that respectable hypothesis of the existence of God ; try to tear away that cloak of Nessus which man has taken and placed on his shoulders, and which he can't get rid of ; it is the oldest and most tenacious ; its age is the age of humanity ; it was born with the first man and will die with the last. It is true that some strong minds consider this hypothesis both useless and dangerous, like an insolvable equation which, during centuries, has tormented humanity, stupidly bent upon discerning the unknowable ; but the masses cling to it as to the last straw."

" Deicide ! You only required that," interrupted Onésime.

" Let us leave these fools, maybe these wise men, their antiquated hobby ! The modern idea is to dissect the earth, as formerly they scrutinised the sky. Tired of seeking God everywhere and finding him nowhere, of obstinately endeavouring to clasp what is not to be caught ; worn out, they respect a mystery they were unable to penetrate ; some through want of power or fatigue, others out of politeness or fear, have ceased to worry with their indiscreet curiosity the supreme manager, the great potentate of space, obstinately preserving his incognito and hiding his secret and his abode.

" In the face of this formidable unknown mystery, for ever escaping from the anxious investigation of thousands of human beings, since thousands of centuries, man, having no more strength, discouraged, has sunk down exhausted, bruised all over.

" At the present day he has recourse to heroic measures to cure himself ; pitilessly rejecting all vague aspirations towards imaginary worlds, better and eternal, he casts his eyes on that in which he was born, his real dwelling, his home, endeavouring by his ingenuity, his labour, and his wisdom to make the house pleasant and life agreeable, or, at least, possible, by doing his maximum in a minimum lapse of time. Instead of consulting the future, people study the present ; the alchemist has made way for the chemist ; the secrets of nature are wrested from her ; it is easier, and there is less probability of working in the dark. And I will now simply lay before you the hypotheses that have been presented on this corpse of a forest.

The tombs of the Mamelukes.

"Some admit the silicification on this spot of a pre-existing forest, produced by the eruption of thermo-siliceous springs, analogons to the geysers of Iceland. Another hypothesis, rejecting the idea of a pre-existing forest on the Mokattam, supposes that these blocks, already silicified, starting from Nubia, were brought down by the Nile, or by powerful marine currents, or again (following the theory of the erratic blocks of Switzerland), by the influence of great glaciers, and were quietly stranded on the heights of the Mokattam.

The desert.

"The first hypothesis seems the most rational, the second encountering almost insurmountable difficulties. What do you think, Monsieur Coquillard ? "

" I think, as we're playing truants in the fields of hypothesis, that we might just as likely suppose, simply, that this dead forest was mummified by some Pharaoh or other, who was a great admirer of trees ; in a country where people mummified everything—gazelles, ibis, hams, wigs—it is not illogical to suppose that they mummified a few trunks of trees."

" Your hypothesis is not wanting in originality, Monsieur Onésime, or in logic, particularly. You have the stuff of a learned man in you."

" Hypothetical," remarked Jacques.

" You're jealous," answered Onésime.

From the spot where they were, the view extended far beyond the motionless waves of the desert sand, undulating at the east and losing themselves in the distant violet of the twilight ; a few white bones here and there broke up the yellowish monotony of that silent immensity, calcinated by the sun for many centuries.

The three friends tore themselves away from the contemplation of this scene of desolation. Night was approaching ; it was time to leave. They turned along the road to Cairo ; they were soon at the bottom of the Mokattam, passed between the tombs of the Mamelukes Kaït-Bey and El Gowry, and as night closed in reached the gate of Bab-el-Nasr ; it was quite dark when they quitted their steeds at the door of their hotel.

The Pyramids.

CHAPTER IX.

On the road to Ghizeh.—The Pyramids in the distance.—Escorted by the Arabs.—
At the foot of the Pyramids.—Carried off by the Bedouins.—Jacques and
Onésime ascend Khout-the-Brilliant.—On the top of the Pyramid.—The
descent.—Onésime's annoyances.—He meets old acquaintances of the *Saïd*.—
Intra muros.—Kéradec's opinion of the monuments of the Pharaohs.—
Onésime's horror of the latter.—Hypotheses as to the use and object of the
Pyramids.—What history and legend say of them.—Onésime's theories of these
regular stone-faced tumuli and their authors.—History of Youssouf's hand.—
Digression on the descendants of the Crusaders.—Her-the-Superior.—Cook
and Son's packages.—Ur't-the-Great.—The watchman of the desert.—In the
shadow of the Sphinx.—Truffles and Clos-Vougeot.—To the health of Osiris !
—The Temple of the Sphinx.—Through the Mastabas.—At the hotel.

IT is seven o'clock ; a fine morning, sharp air ; the Doctor rolls a
cigarette, Jacques lights his first pipe ; Onésime, still half asleep,
pulls out a cigar, and settles himself down on the cushions of the
carriage that they have engaged in the Esbekieh. The coachman
takes them along at a pretty smart pace : they pass beside the
Kasr-el-Nil barracks, across the bridge of the same name, and, leaving
the Palace of Ghezireh on the right, drive through a tumble-down
village ; then the road becomes open and takes a straight line to the
Pyramids.

The highway, shaded on either side by a double row of limes, is
dreadfully direct; the atmosphere admirably pure and exquisitely

fresh and perfumed ; slight vapours glide over the damp ground, rise, mount, disperse, and disappear in white flakes in the dull blue of the sky.   In the distance, the Pyramids appear aerial, transparent, bathed in a silvery mist ; little by little they are freed of these last veils, the gauze is torn away, and, suddenly, quite naked, superb, inundated with light, they burst out radiant with their hues of reddish gold, their gigantic profiles standing out boldly against the sky.

The bridge of Kasr-el-Nil.

On both sides of the road the country undulates resplendent : the black earth of Egypt palpitates under the fiery kiss of Horus ; it awakes and smilingly presents its wide flanks to the robust fellaheen, its children, black as itself.   Naked to the waist, they indolently lean with their hands on the arms of primitive ploughs, which barely skim the surface of a marvellously fertile soil ; they are drawn by small, lean bullocks with short necks. Buffaloes graze ; fishermen laboriously drag long nets in the canal which borders the road ; flights of herons make away ; pelicans shake their feathers, erect on their long stilts. Villages appear like nests amidst the verdure.

The Pyramids grow big ; the eye can hardly distinguish the mutilations they have suffered in the course of centuries. The blue of the sky becomes more intense, the light more brilliant, the sun hotter. The road rises little by little ; the horses have slackened their pace. A swarm of Arabs, of Bedouins in black and white burnouses, appear on all sides, surround the carriage, follow it running : leaning one hand on the edge of the door or the hood, they, with the other, draw

Labourer of the Delta.

from the folds of their burnouses old coins, cats and figures of Osiris in bronze, stone beetles, earthenware chaplets, remains of mummies, shreds of papyrus, and the song of baksheesh commences, monotonous, irritating, imperious ; the voices are harsh, guttural ; the faces hard. the limbs muscular. The wild children of the desert have become simple ciceroni ; very talkative and disagreeable beggars ; but not in the least dangerous, notwithstanding their terrible air and bass voices.

All at once, at a turn in the road at a right angle, the driver wakes up his horses, ascends a steep incline at a gallop, reaches the high ground, and suddenly the mass of *audacia saxa* rises before the stupefied travellers ! The sensation produced by the sudden sight of this mastodon of architecture barring the horizon, invading the sky, covering space, cannot be defined. The idea that this colossus, of which "the indestructible mass has fatigued time," is a work imagined by the brain, executed by the hand of man, astonishes the understanding and disconcerts the imagination.

Jacques experienced a sort of giddiness ; he felt as if attracted by an abyss. Onésime gazed with a contemptuous pout ; this gigantic effort of man left him quite calm. The Doctor, to whom the Pyramids were old acquaintances, was bargaining for a black granite beetle, engraved with the cartouch of Thotmes III., with a Bedouin, who was asking him an extravagant price for it.

On their arrival another swarm of Bedouins, joining those who had escorted them, had surrounded them and almost dragged them from the carriage. These Bedouins, ciceroni in burnouses, under the orders of a Sheïkh, form part of a tribe of prey who, from father to son, possess the monopoly of showing foreigners over the Pyramids, a privilege which they strangely abuse ! These demons pester them with tedious perseverance ; the one who has a discussion with Kéradec insists on selling him his beetle, and disputes possession of him, *unguibus et rostro*, with his fellows. Jacques and Onésime are less fortunate ; deafened by the cries, blinded by the gesticulations, pulled about by the long hands of the rapacious band, they submit to being led off without resistance beneath a shower of demands for baksheesh set forth imperatively.

"Hold your tongues, brigands," shouted Onésime ; " you will awaken Bonaparte's forty centuries that slumber there, aloft ! "

On the way they meet other Europeans, like them prisoners of these barbarians, and enduring the same constraint ; this sight consoles them. Orange-sellers follow behind, and, passing their skinny arms over the heads of the jailers, offer their commodities in a shrill voice; a troop of donkey boys, resting in the midst of their animals in the large triangle of shade thrown by the north side of the pyramid, watch them pass by and laugh.

At the foot of the monument two of the Arabs leap upon the first step; each of them takes one of Onésime's arms and pulls him upward, while a third pushes him up from behind, and the comic but laborious ascent commences.

Jacques, at the sight of the fate that awaits him, escapes from his guardians, springs on the blocks, and, thanks to his strength and the flexibility of his muscles, climbs them tolerably briskly. The men with the black burnouses pursue and capture him. He endeavours to make them understand that he can and will go up alone. All in vain! The three guides surround him, gesticulate and halloa like maniacs. "Baksheesh! baksheesh! ketir!" is the only answer to his protestations; the discussion threatens to be everlasting, reasoning is useless; it is repugnant to him to use force, he has recourse to artifice; taking a handful of piastres, he throws them to the foot of the steps: in the twinkling of an eye he is clear of his persecutors, who dash off with emulation in search of the small money, pushing and swearing at each other, while he continues to climb by the strength of his limbs.

Ascent of the pyramid.

Half-way up he finds Onésime, out of breath, bruised, furious, his knees scraped, staring piteously at a large rent in his trousers, while cracking sounds of evil omen, which accompany each of his movements, announce other serious damages. He absolutely refuses to continue. Jacques comforts him as well as he is able; he at length becomes calm, and with returning breath recovers courage; he completes the ascent without any further accident, and after some trouble reaches the platform.

The sight is grand in the extreme; but, suffocated by the heat, dazzled by the sun, Onésime immediately beats a retreat, leaving Jacques to admire it at his ease. Assisted by his Bedouins, he descends a few steps on the north side of the pyramid, and there, in a retreat formed by a stone torn from its socket, in the shade, seated on the burnous folded in four of one of his guides, fanned by the two others, he rests from his fatigue, indolently allowing his roving gaze to fall on the landscape that expands below him. From time to time, the remembrance of his eventful ascent mixes a little bitterness with this drowsy quietude, and he is seized with a nervous trembling at the thought of the approaching descent. Apart from these slight vexations of an imagination too readily impressed, he feels as well as can be.

The eye hovers over an immense surface : to the east glitters the Nile, winding through a vast breadth of verdure, resembling a monstrous reptile asleep in the sun ; sheets of water shine like mirrors ; a few villages break up the dark green of the plain with touches of grey. Beyond, in a sparkling agglomeration, shine the domes of the mosques, the summits of the minarets, commanded by the citadel and the two slender needles of the Mosque of Mahomet Ali, standing out clearly against the reddish mass of Mokattam. To the south points up the Pyramid of Chephren, Ur't-the-Great, still covered at the upper part with its facing of granite, round which eagles are whirling; that of Mycerinus, Her-the-Superior ; then quite a long chain of other pyramids, of embryos of pyramids, of mastabas echeloned as far as the eye can see on the border of the desert. To the north, cultivated fields alternate indefinitely with strips of sand in the plain of the Delta. To the west, the desert : a gloomy succession of red hillocks, of desolate ravines, studded here and there with the violet heads of rugged rocks of indeterminable forms.

Sometimes, in the grey, dull shade that weighs on this redoubtable

expanse, strange glimmers, powerful effects of light, wild and unexpected, galvanise this spectral aridity for an instant by a sudden
and terrible flash of life. One feels oppressed by a sentiment of
inexpressible sadness in face of this accursed land, of this furnace
where blows a wind of death!

Jacques was all at once drawn from his contemplation by the
bantering voice of Onésime, who had just appeared on the platform,
his helmet on his head and his parasol in his hand.

"Pardon me disturbing you in your delicious *tête-à-tête* with Khout-
the-Brilliant, my dear friend, but we have now been roasting for a
good half-hour on the summit of this ridiculous tumulus with uniform
faces; suppose we were to think of descending?"

"Whenever you like."

"Very well, then, let us be off," sighed Onésime, whose jovial
face became all at once overcast.

"Is it regret at leaving that makes you sigh?"

"Almost, when I think of the ground I still have to get over."

"Such a picturesque road, so easy! where you descend all the
time, without the least hill to climb."

"Only your ribs to break, hey! You consider that picturesque,
do you?"

"Ah! You see, in clumsy hands," Jacques observed gravely, "you
run the risk of starting from here wholesale, and of being retailed
at the bottom. That has happened, and——"

"Will you hold your tongue, tormentor?" exclaimed Onésime,
half laughing, half trembling. "You make my skin creep with your
stories, and to do so you choose the very moment when I am clinging
to my courage with both hands to undertake this abominable descent.
Ah, traitor!" And Onésime, with ill-restrained emotion, places
himself once again in the hands of his Arabs.

Upheld, withheld, tossed about by them, he descends, or rather
allows himself to descend; but not without lively apprehensions for
the security of his person, and as to the resisting strength of the
seams of his clothing. Jacques, freed from his acolytes, bounds
lightly from step to step.

Half-way down they cross some tourists anxious to go and engrave their names at the summit of the monument of Cheops, and thus prove the truth of the proverb, *Nomina stultorum semper parietibus insunt*—idiots spending hours sinking the proofs of their stupidity into the stone. They exchange a greeting as they pass.

A prudish old English woman, rather roughly handled by her gingerbread-coloured lifters, gives utterance to the suppressed, sharp clucking of a hen, and exhibits, by reason of her efforts to try and hide them, deplorable defects in the contour which nature usually provides for mankind of the female sex. Onésime fancies he recognises one of his old acquaintance of the *Saïd*. A little lower down a precipitated halt attracts his attention : there is no longer room for doubt this time ; it is the six packages of Cook and Son, guide-books in the hands, note-books in the pockets, leather bag for souvenirs slung across the shoulders, who are being hoisted up. "A pleasant journey!" shouts Onésime. "Thank you; the same to you!" roar the six throats at the same time ; and the sextuple ascension continues.

Other parties follow. Then it is Jonathan, always phlegmatic, accompanied by his telescope, which one of the Arabs carries ; as he passes he presses the hand of Onésime as if he wanted to pulverise the fingers and disarticulate the shoulder. "Brute! lout!" thinks the latter, while delineating a doleful smile in answer to this Yankee politeness, and he withdraws his aching hand from the vice with a stifled moan, bows, and descends. "It's abominable to cripple people like that under pretence of greeting them!" he growls between his teeth, while separating his fingers, condensed under the high pressure of American handshaking, and, avoiding any new recognition, he allows himself to be manipulated by his bearers, who finally deposit him at the foot of Khout-the-Brilliant, where Jacques, who has arrived a few minutes before, is awaiting him with Kéradec, who has ended by purchasing the Thotmes beetle.

"Well, Monsieur Coquillard, here you are back again sound and well from your adventurous expedition!" said the Doctor gaily.

"Almost, Monsieur Kéradec, with the exception of a great scratch on the knee, a hand dislocated by an Iroquois calling himself civilised, bruised all over, my trousers with as many holes in them as in a strainer, my coat gone in all the seams, my hat all dented in, one of the glasses of my spectacles lost, two of the ribs of my parasol broken, the tattered appearance of a plasterer on the spree, and the positive symptoms of extreme soreness all over my body. With the exception of that," answered Onésime with bitterness, "I am not very much deteriorated."

At the foot of Khout-the-Brilliant.

"There are no roses without thorns, Monsieur Coquillard ; you know the proverb."

"I have felt the thorns, but as to the roses, I am still in search of them."

"You will probably find them inside the pyramid we are about to visit, for you will accompany us there."

"Faith ! While I am here I'll not stop on such a good road ; so much the worse if I leave the remains of my trousers there ! "

" What !   Onésime, you, a conservative by principle and hygiene, is it with perfect equanimity of mind that you contemplate the eventuality of returning from the interior of Khout *sans culotte !* "

" Alas, my friend, I shall not be in the least surprised if this internal visit is accompanied by some affliction of that sort after what the external experiment procured for me; but I will enter at any cost."

" If your corporation permits of it, though ; the passage is so narrow."

" My corporation !   Look at that lean man who wants to make me pass for a Silenus, because nature, in a moment of generosity, has bestowed on my person a comely plumpness, symbol of a charming character, and has graced me with this stomach so pleasingly round in form, with such pure lines, discreetly comprised within sober limits ! whereas she has shown herself a parsimonious mother in regard to him, forgetting to put a little of this coquettish fat on that angular individual with sharp edges, that composition of muscles, nerves, and sinews !   Confess that my well-bred obesity, so full of distinction, so imposing, shames your proletarian scragginess, and that the serpent of envy is gnawing your liver ! that you are jealous of my stomach ! "

" No, my friend; I only admire it, and I do not envy it you.   It would be too heavy to carry ! "

" Lazy fellow ! "   And Onésime catching hold of Jacques' arm, they both accompanied the Doctor, who conducted them to the northern side of the pyramid, where the entrance is, about five-and-twenty yards from the lowest layer of stones.

Preceded by an Arab carrying a candle, followed by two or three others, also provided with lights, they penetrate, bending down, into the square gallery descending in a gentle incline.   In proportion as they go lower the air becomes heavier, its closeness affects them in the throat ; numbers of bats fly round about in fright, graze their faces, occasionally extinguishing their candles with a blow of their wings. At the end of the gallery they turn round a block of granite which bars the way, and remount by a low corridor ending at a horizontal passage, where there is a bifurcation ; they follow the horizontal corridor, which leads them into the chamber called " The Queen's," situated in the great vertical axis of the pyramid ; the ceiling is composed of flags of stone most daringly fixed here.

Retracing their steps to the point of intersection of the two passages, they enter the grand gallery, more lofty, but not so large as the others, which ascends on an incline towards the centre of the pyramid. The pink granite sides are more than twenty-seven feet high ; one breathes more freely. The walls are smooth; a bench runs all along them ; some niches are hollowed out in the stone. The adhesion of the blocks is so perfect that one hardly perceives the joints. At one hundred and sixty feet from there, they arrive at a sort of vestibule, tolerably large, where vertical grooves have been made in the walls. Four slabs of granite formerly slid into

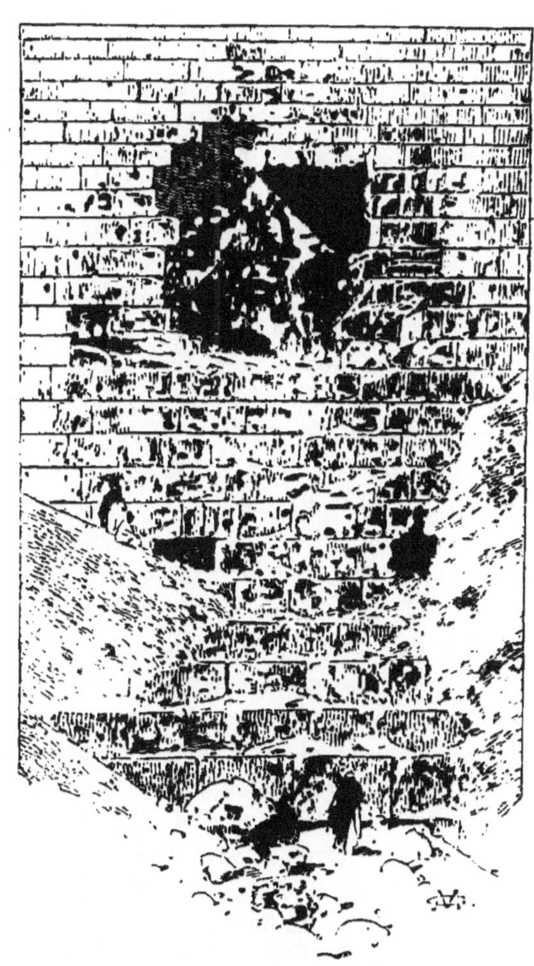

Entrance of the Great Pyramid.

them, and this quadruple door closed the entrance to the sepulchral chamber, which they now reach. The entrance is low, they have to bend down to pass, and they find themselves face to face with the sarcophagus of red granite, polished, without ornaments or hieroglyphics, which contained the Royal Mummy. The ceiling is flat. Above, five low chambers, husbanded by the architect, rise in stages at brief intervals, the last holding the two blocks which form the ceiling, leaning by their base on the mass of masonry, and joining together at the top, where they form a rather wide angle, thus diverting from the vault all the upper weight of the monument.

"And is that all?" asked Onésime; "and millions of men have been employed piling up those blocks, and in making the road which rendered it possible to bring them along solely to place a tomb there!"

"Solely for that, Monsieur Coquillard."

"And you don't call that madness, furious, criminal, accursed madness, on the part of this rascal of a Pharaoh?"

"What can you expect, Monsieur Coquillard—*alia tempora, alii mores!* We have the cemetery of Père Lachaise, the Egyptians have the necropolis of Ghizeh."

"The Egyptians did grand things, we do small ones," said Jacques; "that is the only difference."

"It was not during the Second Empire that things were done in a small way! Son of a gun, what a mania they had for working on a large scale at the Tuileries!"

"The only great thing of that unlucky period," said Jacques, "was the bill to pay—a heavy bill of blood and gold that the Emperor left to be settled by France, after having cowardly handed her over at Sedan and thrown all the gates wide open to invasion, while he went and hid his shame in England."

"You are treating him nicely!"

"Not worse than you treat Cheops."

"Oh! As for that matter I have no mercy for him; his folly of greatness outstrips all limits. Look here, Monsieur Kéradec, I ask you what is the result of this total of incredible efforts, if not to end in gigantic puerility? For what good? Why? What is the utility of it?"

"What is the utility of the Venus of Milo?"

"I can't say there is much, but it is beautiful."

" Well ! Monsieur Coquillard, the pyramid of Cheops is quite as useless as the Venus of Milo, but it is sublime ! "

" Sublime ? "

" Yes, Onésime," added Jacques, " almost as much so as your astonishment."

" What ! *Tu quoque !* Decidedly Pharaoh has bewitched you ; you are hypnotised ; you are under the influence of a mental suggestion, a physical illusion, which his shade, or rather his double, who wanders around us, has imposed on you. Brrr ! Let us get out of this mummy's hole quickly ; I am afraid of contagion."

" Be at ease, Monsieur Coquillard; this kind of disease only attacks certain kinds of brains."

" That is quite possible, but let us leave here, all the same. My brain only needs to be one of those ! "

" Fear nothing, Onésime ; there are privileged natures like yours that are sheltered from everything, even poverty, you happy mortal ! "

" Unfortunately not for long, if your cataclysm succeeds."

" But I suppressed it to oblige you."

" Excuse me, I forgot ! "

And following the guides, who had now gone out, they retraced their steps, and soon found themselves at the entrance, and then at the bottom, of the pyramid. A generous baksheesh delivered them from their conductors, and they went and seated themselves on a stray block in the shade of Khout-the-Brilliant.

" Ouf ! " sighed Onésime, sinking down on the stone. " Anyhow, one can breathe here "; and, addressing himself to the Doctor, who was rolling one of his eternal cigarettes,—

" Look here, Monsieur Kéradec, now that we are alone in the open air, beyond that unhealthy tunnel, and the pernicious influence of that rascal Cheops, and no longer fear his evil eye, now, seriously, do you consider that beautiful ? " And he extended his hand towards the pyramid.

" That, Monsieur Coquillard, that calcareous mountain ? "

" *Instar montium eductæ*," interrupted Onésime, with disguised gravity.

"*Portentosæ moles*," continued the Doctor, smiling. "This formulated immensity, hiding beneath a studied simplicity of lines prodigies in dynamics and statics, unheard-of perfection of detail, the beauty of a magnificent execution, is an indestructible witness of the implacable pride of the Pharaohs and of the grandiose audacity of the genius of their architect. He has marked his sublime work, of absolute sincerity, with the seal of eternity, of which it is the symbol ; he has created the most vast and durable product of art."

"Do you hear ? " said Onésime to Jacques, with an air of profound conviction. "Who would ever have imagined that there were so many things hidden beneath it ? "

"Certainly not you ! "

"Oh ! you, you would draw emptiness from life, as a companion picture to the famous 'Passage of the Red Sea by the Hebrews.' "

"Why not ? They photograph the invisible."

"The invisible ? "

"The invisible ; they photographed Mont Blanc during the night."

"Without candles ? "

"Without candles. But ask Monsieur Kéradec."

"Certainly, in 1883, at the commencement of September, M. Singer photographed Mont Blanc in the middle of the night."

"And he succeeded ? "

"Perfectly."

"So much so," added Jacques very seriously, "that Mont Blanc recognised itself at once."

"And no doubt immediately ordered a dozen album photos ? "

"I did not ask him that. And the pyramids served, Doctor—— "

"Simply as sepulchres. They were tombs hermetically closed, the colossal stone envelope of a mummy ; they were covered with a smooth casing like a cuirass, formed of brilliant and variously coloured stones, probably alternating in horizontal bands, red, black, pink, green ; a terminating stone crowned this gigantic mosaic, which, beneath the reverberation of the powerful rays of the sun, must have been brightly resplendent and have thoroughly deserved its name of Khont-the-Brilliant."

" It must have produced the effect of an enormous mirror for larks, and have horribly fatigued the sight," concluded Onésime. " It is not surprising that there were so many blind people at the period."

" And now ? " answered Jacques.

" Oh ! now they are only one-eyed, and that is by atavism."

" Near the eastern side," continued Kéradec, " was a mortuary chapel, where the scribes attached to the monument received the offerings and performed the prescribed rites.

"One of the three pyramids that you have noticed at a short distance from the eastern side is the tomb of the daughter of Cheops ; around it you see a series of long lines of mastabas ; those are the sepulchres of grand dignitaries of the Court in the vicinity of the tomb of their Pharaoh, who covers them with his great shadow."

" And, no doubt, Monsieur Kéradec," inquired Onésime, " you have quite an assortment of little hypotheses to explain the object or the use of the pyramids ? "

" Oh ! they are not wanting ; I will quote you a few ; but remember that they are only hypotheses, and that I am not the father of them. According to Pliny, the motive of the Pharaohs in building the pyramids was either not to leave their treasures to successors or rivals who might wish to supplant them, or to prevent the people from being idle."

" Generous souls ! Excellent Pharaohs ! Pushing their solicitude so far as to provide amusements for their subjects. Hearts of gold ! " murmured Onésime.

" Some believe that the perfect orientation of the pyramid shows its astronomical destination ; it served for scientific purposes ; it was a sort of indestructible metrical standard ; the construction and arrangement remained a rigorous demonstration of the quadrature of the circle."

" Demonstration of an absurdity ! Why not suppose at once that they served for a geometrical diagram in the open air ? "

" One has seen gnomons that measured the length of the days by the shadows they threw."

"That's it! A sort of belfry of Egypt. That idea must have issued from the brain of a clockmaker or a German doctor."

"Lighthouses guiding the traveller in the desert."

"Funny lighthouses! They don't say whether they had fixed or intermittent lights. That omission is unpardonable!"

"The Arabs of other days believed they had been erected in prevision of a deluge, to deposit there the treasury of human knowledge condemned to disappear."

"The loss would not have been great at the time."

"In the middle ages they looked upon them as granaries built by Joseph, or his tomb."

"They were capable of anything in the middle ages."

"Some persons have seen in them a strange prank of nature, like the Giants' Causeway in Ireland."

"It would be well if it were so, for the memory of the Pharaohs."

"The Copts believed, Monsieur Coquillard, that it was from the summit of the pyramid that Pharaoh reviewed his troops."

"That's an idea! They don't know if he had a lift to raise him up there?"

"They also attached symbolical ideas to them, established on the most ingenious speculation."

"No doubt in the style of those you mentioned just now, Monsieur Kéradec?"

"Yes, about the same. The Arabs call them El-Heramat, the old fairies, and believe that they were created by God long before man."

"He had a lot of time to waste then!"

"Time is God's, Monsieur Coquillard, and he can use it as he pleases."

"And waste it, if one admits that he is the author of this deformity in hewn stone, which would not be complimentary to his good taste."

"According to the Druses, the pyramids are the places where God keeps the register of the acts of all creatures, to consult it at the day of judgment."

" Do you hear that, Jacques? The chronicle of your misdeeds is there. Look out on the day of the Grand Assizes when they try without appeal ! "

" And you ! For yours is in the same pigeon-hole, and your irreverent observation in regard to the work of Jehovah, whom you reproach with his want of taste, will be entered there."

" Finally, M. de Persigny considered them a barrier opposed to the sand of the Libyan desert, the whirlwinds of which they broke up, thus protecting the cities erected between the Nile and the desert."

" M. de Persigny was very clever, in science as well as politics."

" The Arabs relate that, in the pyramid of Mycerinus, which is the most dreaded, there dwells a beautiful woman, who comes out at night-time and drives mad the traveller who allows himself to be ensnared by her charms. They add that genii, sometimes in the form of a child, sometimes in that of an old man who burns incense, walk round the monument. But," concluded Kéradec, " we are leaving hypotheses for the field of legend."

" The pyramids, then, have also their legends, Monsieur Kéradec ? " asked Jacques.

" Certainly ! Like all the monuments that have any respect for themselves, commencing with that of Cheops. If we are to place any faith in what the Egyptian priests related to Herodotus, whose credulity equalled his good faith, this is about what the father of history tells us :—

" ' After having extracted the blocks from the quarries at Toura in the Arabian chain, and dragged them to the bank of the Nile and from there carried them on to the other side, it required ten years to make the road by which they were conveyed from the Nile to the Libyan highland and to excavate the subterranean chambers on which the monument was erected. The pyramid itself took twenty years to build, and cost six hundred talents. One hundred thousand men were employed on the works, and were changed every three months.' "

" But that is not a legend."

" Wait a bit ! Tradition adds that ' Cheops, exhausted by the expense, reached such a point of infamy as to prostitute his daughter to get money, and that not only did she perform her father's will, but that, wishing also to have her own mausoleum, she requested each of her lovers to give her a stone to build her pyramid, which is between the two facing her father's.' "

" When I told you your Pharaoh was a worthless fellow," Onésime hastened to remark, " facts show me to be right."

" Only tradition, Monsieur Coquillard."

" Tradition is sufficient for me when it accords with common sense."

" Or rather with your wishes, Onésime."

" It's all one."

" Chephren, Monsieur Coquillard, also obliged the Egyptians to build him a pyramid, Ur't-the-Great."

" A good dog hunts by hereditary instinct."

" ' The Egyptians '—it's Herodotus who is speaking—' have such an aversion for the memory of those two kings, whose odious reputation of tyranny outlived their death for centuries, that they will not even name them ; they call these monuments, for this reason, by the name of a shepherd, Philitis, who in those days took his flocks to feed in that neighbourhood.' "

" You see," interrupted Onésime, beaming, " that I am not the only one who has them in horror, these monsters of Pharaohs ; already, in their own time, the people could not bear them."

" Always according to tradition, Monsieur Coquillard ; Diodorus goes even so far as to say that neither Cheops nor Chephren enjoyed their tombs, the people in fury having risen and torn their bodies from the sarcophagi."

" They were not hated without deserving it, those tomb-builders, if the thing be true."

" The successor of Chephren, Mycerinus, even-tempered and beloved of his subjects though he was, nevertheless had his pyramid built."

" I no longer follow you, Monsieur Kéradec. Why did the Egyptians show so much indulgence for this Mycerinus, who played them the same trick with his pyramid as Cheops and Chephren ?

I understand their hatred for these two latter, but I cannot comprehend their love for the third."

"That would seem to prove, Monsieur Coquillard, that either Herodotus has made a mistake or has been deceived, and that the Egyptians, after all, were not very discontented with their kings. It is also said of Mycerinus that, having fallen in love with his own daughter, he took her by violence; that this young princess having strangled herself through despair, her father had her body placed in a wooden heifer which he had had gilded, and that she received divine honours. It is added that her mother had the hands of her daughter's attendants cut off for having delivered her to Mycerinus."

"A model father. What else?"

"A short time after the loss of his only daughter he knew by an oracle that he had only six years to live, and that he would die in the seventh. The oracle, consulted again, having confirmed the prophecy, Mycerinus had recourse to stratagem. He had a great number of lamps made. When the night came he had them lighted, and passed his time drinking and enjoying himself without interruption either day or night. He intended, by converting days into nights, to double the number of years—of six to make twelve—and to show the oracle had lied."

"A nice family! One prostitutes, the other ravishes, his own daughter, and is then drunk day and night for six consecutive years; and that's the famous legendary wisdom of Egypt which was inherited by the Greeks. I wouldn't have accepted the legacy until I had seen an inventory of it!"

"Diodorus of Sicily attributes this pyramid to Inarus. Others pretend that it is the tomb of the courtesan Rhodopis, 'with rosy cheeks.'

"Strabo relates, in reference to this, the following charming legend: One day, while bathing, an eagle carried off one of her shoes, which was being held by her attendant, and took it to Memphis. The king was then meting out justice. The eagle, hovering above his head, let the slipper fall in his lap. The sovereign, surprised at this singular event and at the smallness of the shoe, had the woman to

whom it belonged sought for throughout the land. She was found at
Naucratis ; they presented her to the king, and he made her his wife.
When she died they gave her this pyramid for a sepulchre."

"That was very nice, anyhow," admitted Onésime.

"Herodotus, alas ! destroys this pretty Cinderella story in a few
lines. Rhodopis, whom Sappho calls Doricha, he says, was born in
Thrace. She was a slave of Iadmon, a man of Hephæstopolis, in the
island of Samos, a companion in slavery of Æsop the fabulist. She
was brought to Egypt by Xanthus, of Samos, to exercise the calling
of courtesan. Charaxus, of Mitylene, son of Scamandronyme and
brother of Sappho, gave a considerable sum for her ransom. Having
thus recovered her liberty, she remained in Egypt, where her beauty
procured her great wealth for a woman of her class, but much inferior
to what was necessary to build such a pyramid. Besides, the amount
of her fortune is known, a tenth part having been laid out by her in
purchasing iron spits to roast bullocks for the Temple of Delphi, so as
to transmit her name to posterity. Moreover, Rhodopis did not live
under Mycerinus, but under Amasis ; that is to say, many years after
the death of the kings who built the pyramids."

"So much the worse," said Jacques. "I liked the legend better."

"The truth is very ugly, then, for you to prefer the fable,"
remarked Onésime, jeeringly. "Fortunately, you are not an historian,
or you would relate fine things, with your fancy for the marvellous."

"You," responded Jacques, "if you were an historian, you would
hold a class on morality, or on the history of the *pot-au-feu*, from the
commencement of the world to our own times."

"Do not despise the *pot-au-feu* too much ! A Minister fell in
France because he did not appreciate it as he should have done in
politics."

"But what could have been, in your opinion, Monsieur Coquillard,
the aim of the authors of the pyramids ? I am curious to learn your
views."

"The aim, Monsieur Kéradec ? Has a madman any aim ? Does
one discuss the acts of a person deprived of the power of discerning ?
For this pretentious dolmen, as well as all its megalithic congeners,

is the work of a cruel fool served by a gang of imbecile slaves, under
the direction of an architect who is all the more blamable for lending
himself to this monstrous farce, as he possessed greater talent. One
should not squander one's genius on tomfoolery, even though it
assume colossal proportions. That is what I think of this calcareous
fetish, of this stupid and murderous idol ; this Egyptian Melkarth,
that, raised amidst the maledictions of an atrociously oppressed people,
absorbed for thirty years, without truce or mercy, the work and often
the lives of thousands of poor creatures, to satisfy the ghastly whim
of a vain Pharaoh, passing his life in preparing a first-class funeral
for himself.

"As to those symbols of eternity, those epithets of sublime and
other idle terms, *ejusdem farinæ*, with which you gratuitously muffle
up this massive extinguisher, which has so easily set your imagination in activity, expressions that would really make any one think
that an infinity of elevated and superhuman ideas had presided at
its erection—well, profound men that you are, grave Egyptologists,
they must be utilised elsewhere ; the skin does not fit the animal !
You have once more allowed your imagination to carry you away for
nothing. In face of the requirements of your too narrow logic and the
astounding abstractions of your thought, which will not admit the
uselessness, as absolute as evident, of such a work, you are in vain
puzzling yourselves to find a pretext, if not a reason, for its existence ;
you cannot or you will not get into your heads that this hybrid
mountain was built without rhyme or reason, and you are racking your
brains to find out the why, in proportion to its size, of a thing which
never had any other reason for its existence than the mad fit of a
despot afflicted with the monomania of a tomb on a large scale, a
disease which he transmitted to his descendants. It is Pharaoh, that
great conculcator of the people, as he called himself, who would
enjoy a good laugh if he could hear you confabulating in this way on
his masonry, striving to explain this riddle which he has unconsciously left behind him, unless one supposes that he did so with the
malicious thought of tormenting the learned men who would follow,
or attributes to him the intention of providing an income for the tribe

of Arabs who show his tomb—his descendants, no doubt. If it be so, it is the action of a good father, and quite in accordance with the habits of the country, where they live by their ancestors, where the sons retail the mummies of their parents to foreigners. If you think I exaggerate, look !" And Onésime, drawing with precaution something black, surrounded by wraps, from his coat pocket, took it delicately between the thumb and forefinger, and satisfied the curiosity of his listeners.

"What on earth is that ?" asked Jacques.

"That," said Onésime triumphantly, "that is the hand of Ouserkeres, in Egyptian Ousourkaf, first king of the old Memphite dynasty, Ancient Empire, first period ! That is what it is. At least that is what one of those Bedouins who hoisted me to the top of Cheops told me, when he sold it me in spite of myself, and who seemed as if he would leave me on the way if I didn't buy it ! I feel convinced that it's the hand of his grandfather, perhaps of his father."

"Or his own," said Kéradec, who had just attentively examined the pretended hand of Ouserkeres.

"Or his own ?" exclaimed the stupefied Jacques and Onésime in one breath.

"Yes, his own ! That surprises you ?"

"More than you imagine."

"You see that great fellow stretched out on the ground there, warming himself in the sand like a lizard ?"

"But that's the man who sold it me."

"I thought so. Well ! I know him, Monsieur Coquillard ; it's Youssouf."

"I believe you, but that doesn't explain to me how this hand——"

"Is his. Patience ! You have, or perhaps you have not, noticed that he has lost the hand of his left arm ?"

"Exactly, I remember it now."

"And your hand of Ouserkeres is a left hand ?"

"Yes, but still that would not prove——"

"No ! But it is of public notoriety that Youssouf, four years ago, mutilated himself in order not to serve as a soldier, that to make up for the loss of his hand he mummified it, and since then he has been endeavouring to get rid of it for a monetary consideration. He has ended by palming the unsaleable article off on you. Last year it was the hand of Amenhotep, after having been successively that of Sesostris, Rameses, and others."

" But how did this become known ? "

" Everything is known here, the Arabs are so talkative ! Moreover it was easy to guess: Youssouf had had his middle finger maimed, of course, previous to the amputation ; the small phalanx of it was wanting, and if you observe the hand that is in yours, you will notice that that anatomical part is absent. Besides, the rascal a long time ago acknowledged the deceit, not being able to hide it any longer."

" Well ! that's a crusher," said Onésime, throwing Youssouf's hand far away from him.

" Isn't it ? "

" Dissect and retail oneself ! "

" But, my dear Onésime, they do the same at home, less the mummifying, to avoid the conscription ; it's likely enough, even, that the Egyptians borrowed this habit from us, along with that of drawing lots."

" Anyhow, you will not tell me that we sell our grandfathers and live on their corpses ? "

" Faith ! almost : doesn't a nobleman live on his ancestors ? Is it not true that the consideration that attaches to an illustrious descendant of a still more illustrious family permits of his picking up a fat wedding dowry among the silly bourgeoisie, finding a little goose sufficiently vain and dazzled by heraldry to ' manure his lands,' according to the impertinent expression of these agreeable noblemen ? Free, it is true, once the marriage consummated and the wedding portion secured, not to receive the bride's parents, of whom he is ashamed, and to relegate to the loft, after her demise, the portrait of the intruder, tolerated rather than accepted by this society, which she entered with a golden key and left by the door of oblivion, unworthy to figure in the gallery of portraits of the family, who were already offended at seeing her there in her lifetime."

" And, nevertheless," added Kéradec, "the unfortunate woman had done more than darn the noble rag, and regild the faded coat-of-arms. She had put into the veins of the successors that her robust fecundity gave to her languid aristocratic husband a little of the vigour that labour deposits in the red blood of the plebeian class from which she came, enriching the blue blood pervaded by the scrum of those idle and morbid races, the bastard produce of the descendants of the Crusaders."

" Shall we be off ? " inquired Jacques, leaving his seat with the Doctor, and all three advanced towards the haunted pyramid of Mycerinus.

" I say, I hope we have finished with peregrinations and ascensions *intra, extra,* and, above all, *supra muros,*" sighed Onésime.

" Make your mind easy. We have time for a pipe and to take a stroll through a few mastabas to give us an appetite, and we will go and recruit our strength in the shade of the Sphinx."

" Recruit our strength ? "

" Yes. A surprise I have in store for you."

" By Jove ! what a splendid idea you have had, Jacques ! And is the feed to be a serious one ? "

" Serious as your appetite ; I joke with you, but never with your stomach: it is too captious in that respect. And," consulting his watch, "it is eleven o'clock," he continued ; " our automedon must be preparing the provisions. Our landlord, who is our amphitryon, has acted handsomely ; there are, among other choice things, truffles and a flask of Clos-Vougeot of a fair year—a feast for a king ! He knows your tastes, shares them, and it gives him pleasure to satisfy them, so far as he is able."

" Truffles ! Clos-Vougeot ! " repeated Onésime, whose face was all at once beaming. " Are you sure there are truffles ? "

" I affirm it ! "

" And Clos-Vougeot ! of an—age ? "

" Respectable."

" Oh ! what a good, what an excellent man this landlord is ! How can I express to him my gratitude ? Jacques ! you'll do his portrait ?

Truffles ! Clos-Vougeot ! and of a fair year, ye gods !　It's well worth
a portrait, isn't it ?　It shall not be said that I have been ungrateful
to so amiable a man."

"You mean that it is I who shall not have been ungrateful, because
I shall have done the portrait."

"Yes, but it is I who will present it, my friend."

"Oh !　Then it's different !"

"Reflect—you cannot do everything !"

"That's true."

And Jacques, although accustomed to his friend's ways, could not
keep himself from laughing heartily at the singular manner, so naïvely
suggested to him by his egotism, of paying the debts of his stomach
with the work of others.　Kéradec had the greatest difficulty in
keeping serious.

"Truffles," murmured Onésime.　"Would they be from Périgord ?"
and his eye inquired of Jacques.

"Ah ! as to that I am ignorant."

"And the year of the bottle ?"

"Equally so."

"Never mind.　It does not matter much, we shall see ;　I say,
J acques, are you sure your watch is right ?"

"Perfectly sure.　Why ?"

"It seemed to me it was later than you said."

"Gourmand !　It's your appetite that's in advance !"

"Perhaps !　After all, the alluring perspective, of which you have
just given me an idea, in the near future, has quite comforted me" ;
and as a proof Onésime danced about gaily, and, seizing Jacques' arm,
started off at a smart pace, humming a popular air.

"Not so quick," said Jacques ;　"reserve your strength, if only to
do honour to the lunch."

"Me !　I'd go to the end of the world now."

"It would not be difficult, Monsieur Coquillard : you can go there
without moving from where you are."

"How is that ?"

"The earth being spherical, the end of the world is everywhere."

" Oh, science, science ! "

As they talked, they reached the foot of the pyramid of Mycerinus, Her-the-Superior.

" It is much smaller than its two neighbours," remarked Jacques.

" Yes," replied Kéradec ; " but the interior chamber is more beautiful than that of the two others ; it is entirely built of granite, and the ceiling, hewn in the form of a vault, recalls the English Gothic arch; moreover, while in the axis of the pyramid, it has the peculiarity of being hollowed out in the rock, and below the base of the monument, which covers rather than contains it.

" It was formerly opened and closed again by the Khaliphs of Egypt. Since then it was explored, in 1837, by Colonel Wyse, who penetrated into the sepulchral chamber and found the sarcophagus, of brown basalt striated with blue streaks, which had contained the mummy of Mycerinus. He collected a part of the remains of the wooden coffin, and some bones and bands of the Pharaoh, which he sent to London to the British Museum. The sarcophagus, which was also sent to England, went to the bottom in sight of the Spanish coast with the vessel that was transporting it.

" The opening of other chambers and the existence of numerous passages obstructed by rubbish conveyed the idea that Her-the-Superior might contain, or have contained, another tomb—— "

" That, perhaps, of your friend Doricha with the rosy cheeks ? Supposing you were to make sure by visiting the inside."

" I should be afraid," answered Jacques, "of profaning the chamber where she reposes by my presence."

" And if she were not reposing there ? "

" Then to lose my illusions as to the reality of the existence of the charming Cinderella."

" And no later than yesterday you stood upon high terms to tell us in a peremptory tone that ' legends were the splutterings of humanity in the cradle,' and this and that, but now you grasp the first legend that comes like a drowning man who seizes the pole that is extended to him, and you cling on there. Ah ! you weathercock ! "

" I merely refer to the legend you fling in my face, out of pure

gallantry to a woman who desired that her name should be transmitted to posterity."

"At the point of a spit for roasting bullocks!"

"That is quite as good, in the interest of humanity, as going there
at the point of the sword."

"Hold your tongue, will you! Look here, you flirt with history
as you coquetted on board the *Saïd* with geography. In your hands
Nero would become a model of all the virtues, Lucullus would have the
sobriety of the camel, Messalina would be crowned a *rosière*, and so on
the others! And you would merely be imitating the bold innovators.
Thus, they quite recently made us a Bonaparte of a new model—
wonderful! Nothing of the old one, for example: oh, nothing! He
is perfectly new, this Bonaparte; a real treat for amateurs. 'Cast
in a rare mould, composed of different metal from his fellow-citizens
and contemporaries, a condottiere of mediæval history re-born; one
out of the ordinary, beyond comparison with Frenchmen born in the
eighteenth century; belonging to another race, to another age, in
whom one perceives the foreigner at the first glance, the Italian and
something else besides, with no similitude or analogy '—an impossible
being, in a word an algebraic formula; nothing is wanting, a unique
mould, special qualities of an exotic race and of pre-historic times, a
miracle of the *genus homo*, and yet a foreigner and an Italian, something strange, allegorical, which at the same time does and does not
resemble another thing that does not exist.

"This portrait of Bonaparte in a new manner is a masterpiece. It
has none of the features of the 'Scamp of St. Helena,' by another
fanciful writer, and which proves much in favour of the vivacious
imagination of its author, of his picturesque ingenuity, and of his
repugnance to keep in beaten tracks. He is the worthy emulator
of a certain mayor, profoundly learned, who, in a book entitled
' Literary and Historical Rectifications,' undertakes to convince us,
with a grand reinforcement of proofs and 'authentic' documents,
that Joan of Arc was never burned at Rouen, that she was saved
by devoted friends and married to a Lorraine nobleman. Well, my
dear Jacques, you handle facts in the same way: you take a tale here,

a piece of gossip there, a little anecdote somewhere else, an extract from secret memoirs; you look out some strange words, glaring, violent; you slip a little wit into all this, even a good deal, set it in a pictorial frame, improved by a well-turned style, with a phrase sometimes sufficiently incomprehensible for the reader to be obliged to admire, in confidence, a depth that escapes him, and you fly your little historical *canard* very prettily. It's a new system imitated from Alcibiades of twisting the tail of one's dog, and cutting the ground from under the feet of the learned, those impassioned erudites of science, those galley-slaves of study, bending over big folios, eager in the pursuit of truth; poor creatures, ignorant of life, passing their own lives in reading and re-modelling those of the generations that have preceded them."

"It's more honest than giving them sops, as some do, covering their inexactitude of facts by their daring assertions."

"You practise insinuation while others make use of intimidation, but you all arrive at the same result."

"That of?"

"That of misrepresentation!"

"My system, however, is more polite."

"But more dangerous ; your weakness for fable and your facility in accepting it can only be compared to your indifference for truth and your carelessness in ascertaining facts ; you consider the opportunity rather than the reality ; your history is a pretentious legend, witty or sentimental, attired in the garments of the historical; a bare-faced servant, who impertinently adorns herself in the gown of her mistress."

Jacques bowed, smiling.

The three friends, as they were talking, had almost got round the pyramid ; as they turned the angle on the northern side they fell into the midst of Cook and Son's packages.

"Hullo!" cried in a single moment the six voices of those tourists, with a familiarity that was rather disagreeable. "Where are you going, old boys?"

"Where you have probably come from," Jacques answered in English ; "we are going to have a look at Chephren's monument."

"Oh, Chephren!" exclaimed the educated one of the party in broken French; "very pretty. We've all got a little bit of the pyramids of Chephren and Cheops in our bags. Have you a small piece of the stone, Mounsieu Coqnwillarde?"

"Neither large nor small. I don't understand carrying off the pyramids of others, like that, in my pockets: I prefer taking away with me the esteem of the people I visit, rather than their monuments." "It's cool of those persons," he growled between his teeth, "to boast of such a thing. It was quite bad enough to murder my name, without going and stupidly tearing the epidermis away from these poor pyramids."

"And you, Mister Jack, have you secured some pieces of the old witches?"

"Not even the smallest. I consider that Time, the terrible destroyer, has no need of assistance, certainly not of such a zealous nature, in his ugly work. You ought, while you're about it, to put a little sunshine in your pockets; it would be welcome in London!"

"Very good joke indeed!" exclaimed the spokesman tourist; "it ought to be sent to *Punch*." And the sentence ran from month to mouth until it reached the sixth, while a phenomenal smile passed through the circle of inane and vulgar faces exhibited by these cockneys, who had been packed up in London, and here let loose by Cook and Son in the land of the Pharaohs. A shudder of disgust overran the usual serenity of one of the Parisians, and he instinctively recoiled before the tone which their conversation had taken.

"A very good joke indeed, Mister Jack!" This was the last echo of the mirth which, passing from one to the other, came and died on the lips of the sixth Cook's Tourist.

"A good joke it may be, but assuredly less offensive and more straightforward than the act of vandalism you have just accomplished. When people receive you in their homes and show you their knick-knacks, it is worse than bad taste to break pieces off and carry them away as souvenirs. I cannot congratulate you, gentlemen, and I wish you good day." And Jacques, touching his hat, continued on his way, while the six tourists, escorted by their eighteen Arabs, sprang forward to the assault of Mycerinus.

"Put that in your bags with your little pieces of stone," said Onésime, imitating the pronunciation of the Cookites. "How ugly they are, all the same! What bad samples of England!"

"If they were only ugly," replied Kéradec; "but they are also dangerous with that criminal mania which makes them attack everything and dilapidate right and left. If they are allowed to continue, in another century not a single monument will be intact; they will have done more damage in a few years than time in ages!"

"Chephren's pyramid, Ur't-the-Great, has at least had the wit to keep on a part of his outer clothing of granite, which protects him against the destructive curiosity of these idiotic tourists."

"I would bet," added Onésime, "that Bonaparte's forty centuries that formerly lodged on Khont sought refuge there to escape from these stupid lithoclasts; and one must imagine that they have led a hard life these poor forty centuries, for they have become two thousand years older since Bonaparte quitted Egypt."

"That was perhaps out of regret at seeing him leave them!"

Kéradec called their attention to a few traces, visible in places, of the basement or stylobatum on which is built the pyramid of Chephren, less buried in rubbish than its neighbours; then, to Onésime's great delight, they advanced towards the Sphinx; they soon reached a spot from which it could be seen.

But there Onésime could perceive the final preparations for lunch; with moist lips, sparkling eyes, dilated nostrils, he seemed to sniff from afar, in the air, vague odours of truffles, and to imagine he inhaled the intoxicating bouquet of the divine bottle of Burgundy, and his stomach thrilled with the violence of his eager desire! He hastened his steps, accelerated at each second; then, all at once, unable to restrain himself any longer, giving way to the imperious entreaties of his appetite, dashed along at full speed towards the object so ardently pursued, while Jacques and the Doctor stopped to contemplate the Sphinx.

The monster, with a human head, the body of a lion, hewn in the rock itself, rests squatting in its calm and powerful attitude, buried to the shoulders in its shroud of sand; the head alone emerges,

Tho Sphinx.

bearing the imprint of that imposing serenity which one finds every-where on the visages of the gods in Egyptian statuary. Its placid face, to which the mutilated nose, a deep incision in the forehead, and the broad gashes furrowing its cheeks, give a redoubtable appearance, contemplates the Orient, searching the desert with its melancholy look; its thick-lipped mouth, slightly curled up at the corners, has the vague and long resigned smile of the fellaheen; its

Chephren's Pyramid.

large ear seems to listen to every murmur, and on its giant-like neck the royal bands that ornament its forehead fall in rigid plaits.

This strange figure, "the marvellous production of the gods," is frightful in its solemn immobility; one feels oneself shudder before this mute guardian of Cyclopean tombs, this advanced sentinel of Egypt, whose mysterious gaze eternally fathoms the depths of the desert, listening impassive to the distant hollow sound of advancing hosts coming upon the land of the Pharaohs, as it once listened to the lamentations and despairing maledictions of the labourers who built the pyramids.

The flux and reflux of invasions have beaten against its stone breast without shaking it ; time has forgotten it, and for more than six thousand years the sombre visage of the genius of Africa continues to gaze at the Orient and to receive the morning kiss of Horus.

It is the ancestor, disfigured by pigmies, of that mute race of Titans hewn summarily in the granite, with astonishing delicacy of chisel, observing the centuries pass by, stiffened in their rigid attitudes.

It is "the Father of the Terrible" of the Arabs, who fly from this enormous head which rises out of the earth.

Finally, it is the monstrous enigma of the history of Egypt which, in proportion as one seeks to penetrate the mystery, removes farther and farther away the landmarks of an historical past, which is lost still more profoundly in the night of ages.

"Was it not a symbol? Did it not personify Horus?" asked Jacques.

"Yes : for the Egyptians it was Hor-Em-Kou, Horus in the brilliant sun. The Greeks called it Harmachis, Horus on the horizon, and also Agathodemon ; it symbolised the victory of Horus over Typhon, of light over darkness ; and personified the idea, reduced to its most simple expression, but boldly set forth, of the resurrection. Formerly it was overlaid with a coating of red colour, of which some traces remain. At the period of Cheops it was restored, which gives it then a respectable age, but one does not yet know to whom to attribute the foundation. Will the excavations that are being made at this moment give the secret of the enigma? Is there any-thing else between the paws of the Sphinx than the altar, the little model shrine, and the lion discovered by Caviglia at the commence-ment of this century, or in the granite temple found by Mariette in the neighbourhood? The future will tell us."

"And what was that granite temple, Monsieur Kéradec ?"

"It was the Temple of the Sphinx, at least it is thought so, but I see your friend Monsieur Coquillard, who is signalling to us to come ;

it would be unkind to make his stomach wait too long, and we should do well to go and join him."

"At last!" exclaimed Onésime, seeing them approach; and when they were all seated on a soft Turkey carpet, around an immaculate white table-cloth, on which Mahmond, their Arab coach-man, had placed the victuals, he gave a final glance, and seeing everything arranged to his desire, he said in a grave tone, "Now, gentlemen, to table!" and seating himself with his legs crossed

The Temple of the Sphinx.

Arab fashion, he took possession of an appetising truffled fowl, which he began to cut in pieces with surprising dexterity. There soon remained nothing of the succulent poulard but—the souvenir. The other provisions disappeared with the same rapidity. At dessert, Onésime, with solemn deliberation, uncorked the venerable bottle of Clos-Vougeot—"Your countrywoman," said he to Jacques. He was quite charmed when the perfume of its bouquet reached him, and it was with a sort of tenderness that he filled the glasses; listening attentively to the harmonious tune of its gurgling, he praised as a connoisseur the rutilant onion-peel colour of the infatuating nectar. Then, raising his glass, smiling at the rosy liquor : "Gentlemen," he said, "honour to whom honour is due. I drink to Noah, who was the first to plant the vine !" And he absorbed at one draught the contents of the glass. "To the last drop, gentlemen," he added.

"Your toast is wrong, Monsieur Coquillard," said the Doctor, setting down his empty glass ; "we should drink to the glory of the divine Osiris."

"Never ! "

"To Osiris," continued Kéradec, "who, after having instructed man in agriculture——"

"I don't care a bit for that ! "

"He found the vine in the land of Nyse, discovered the secret of cultivating it, was the first to drink wine, and taught the Egyptians how to make it and preserve it."

"Ah ! By Jove ! If that be true it was a stroke of genius on his part."

"The Greeks called him Dionysus, from the name of his father Ion and that of the town of Nyse, where he had been brought up ; they also say that he was none other than Bacchus, and that he went over the rest of the universe teaching mankind to cultivate the earth and plant the vine, and to renounce at the same time their barbarous habit of eating each other."

"Another glory overboard ! After all, I do not much regret it ! He was a pitiful drinker, Father Noah, who did not know how to carry his wine decently."

"And," added Kéradec, "he had children who were very badly brought up."

"I withdraw my toast. To Osiris then ! " and Onésime, filling the glasses again, warmly toasted the benefactor of humanity.

Then Mahmoud handed them the coffee ; the Doctor rolled a cigarette, Jacques pulled out his pipe and Onésime a cigar ; and there, in the shade of the Sphinx, beneath the blue sky, on that golden sand, they indulged in an indolent, delicious, idle doze, yielding to the sweet oppression of a voluptuous digestion. They suffered themselves to be slowly penetrated by the enjoyment produced by that subtle glow which irradiates from the stomach, the mysterious laboratory where the synthesis of our aliments is solved ; and whence the blood, after being aërated by the lungs, becomes charged with vital force, the gift of the sun, which causes to circulate in all our being happiness, strength, life.

Onésime was the incarnate personification of absolute beatitude ; his back against a cushion of the carriage, which he had made Mahmoud place between him and the rock, with arms crossed, the mouth half open, the eyes moist, he was no longer conscious of anything, if not of the well-being in which he revelled.

"You don't happen to have a looking-glass ?" he inquired languidly of Jacques.

" A looking-glass ? No. What for ? "

" To gaze at myself and contemplate my happiness."

" Sybarite, who wishes to enjoy the very reflection of his happiness ! "

" It's so delightful to be happy," murmured Onésime, while his eyelids closed. " Honest Osiris ! And it is to thee, the father of wine, that I owe this supreme felicity, and those idiots of Arabs, those inept water-drinkers, have called thee the Father of the Terrible, the brutes ! All the same, Osiris did not know our Clos-Vougeot, poor man ! " And Onésime's voice, become more and more weak, died on his lips with that last word, while a faint smile, full of soft irony, fluttered over his half-opened mouth : his head fell gently on his shoulder, and he slumbered in his happiness.

"Thotmes IV.," said Keradec, " also fell asleep on his return from hunting, four and a half thousand years ago, at the feet of the watchman of the desert. He dreamt that Horus ordered him to remove the sand that covered his image; struck by the dream and considering that it was his duty to listen to the warning, he cleared the Sphinx, and had the event inscribed on a stela that still exists."

" Happy Onésime ! " said Jacques; " let us leave him to his dear sleep; we'll ask him when he awakes whether Osiris appeared to him in his slumbers."

"Let us go for a turn to the granite temple, Monsieur Jacques; it's a few steps away."

"Willingly." And after having confided Onésime to the care of Mahmoud, who, armed with a fly-flipper, protected the sleep of this innocent, they proceeded towards the ruined temple, situated about two hundred paces from the Sphinx.

From the foot, or rather from the uppermost border of the edifice, which, buried in the sand, has its top on a level with the ground, the eye may wander over the interior, through the large open spaces of the caved-in roof.

"Here," said Kéradec, "is what Strabo dares to call an edifice 'of barbarian style.' Of barbarian style! This structure, unique in its powerful and taciturn originality, its huge blocks of granite matched with such perfect art, the vast rectangular halls of which, with walls lined with alabaster, are paved with the same stone, and the ceilings supported by quadrangular pillars, enormous monoliths of pink granite, admirably polished, fifteen feet high by three and five feet broad, set up with the greatest care!

"You can see that the walls on the inside are absolutely bare; neither moulding, nor bas-reliefs, nor mural paintings, nor inscriptions—nothing to indicate its destination or the period of its construction, nothing but a perfectly smooth surface. Outside, the same rigid simplicity; blocks of calcareous stone with plain surfaces, ornamented with long vertical and horizontal grooves cleverly crossed; in a corner a small door.

"In a deep well containing water, situated in one of the halls and now filled in, Mariette found several mutilated statues, engraved with the name of Chephren, among which was one of diorite, almost intact, beautifully sculptured, which is now at the Boulak Museum.

"Under what circumstances they were thrown into this well nobody knows. Nor has it transpired whether the place is a temple or a tomb. Was it the mortuary chapel of Chephren? Was it the tomb of the king who had the Sphinx sculptured? Was it the Temple of the Sphinx itself? So many questions here remain unanswered in face of the rigorous silence of these stones. It keeps its secret like the Sphinx ; like it, widens the horizons of history to an incredible distance, and tickles the curiosity of science, putting the ingenious perspicacity of the learned at fault."

" We find among this people," said Jacques, " a sculptor capable of hewing in the massive rock a colossus with such beautiful proportions as the Sphinx, an architect able to arrange the plan of this building, and workmen who could move these enormous blocks, set them up so skilfully, match them with such consummate art. This people must, at the period when these two monuments were produced, have arrived at a high degree of civilisation, and it would have required thousands of centuries to prepare that condition."

While chatting they had reached the tombs of the First Empire, dating from the Fourth Dynasty, at the end of the Pharaonic period.

Statue of Chephren.

" We are among what they term mastabas, I think, Monsieur Kéradec ? "

" That is the name they give them. The mastaba, you see, is an ædiculum of a rectangular massive form, containing one or several chambers, arranged from north to south. A single door gave access to the interior, which received daylight by that opening only. The walls of this room, or those where the relatives of the departed came on certain anniversaries to accomplish funeral rites, were almost always decorated with bas-reliefs, representing scenes of every-day life. At the end, facing the east, was a stela bearing a prayer.

Below the stela was the table of offerings ; it was granite, alabaster, or calcareous stone ; sometimes a statue of the deceased was placed there.

" In the thickness of the masonry was a corridor lofty and narrow, the serdab, with completely naked walls, which was closed up ; it contained the statues of the dead.

" In the great axis of the edifice was sunk a square well, the orifice of which opened either in the room itself or on the summit of the mastaba. That well penetrated vertically in the rock to a depth varying between thirty-six and eighty feet, ending at a very low, horizontal passage, which led to a vault where the sarcophagus containing the mummy was placed. The walls of this vault were bare, like those of the serdab; nothing is found there but great red pointed vases, small alabaster calyx-shaped cups, bullocks' bones, and wooden or alabaster head-rests. When once the mummy was deposited and hermetically shut up in the sarcophagus, the passage was walled up and the well filled and closed for ever !

" We shall also meet with tombs hewn in the rock, underground ; there are several in the neighbourhood, opposite the second pyramid, as well as near that of Mycerinus."

They now found themselves in the midst of regular rows of mastabas of the Ancient Empire to the west of the pyramid of Cheops. They stopped an instant at the edge of the peculiar tomb of Campbell, a well, almost fifty feet deep, containing another sarcophagus in black basalt. Then they wandered somewhat at hazard through these multitudes of tombs, spread round about the pyramids.

Jacques examined the various subjects represented on the walls with curious attention : here, scenes of farming, of the pursuit of wild fowl, of breeding cattle, of navigation ; groups of musicians or dancers ; farther on were people leading animals, others picking fruit and making wine ; games on the water, athletes wrestling ; one of the most interesting represented an Egyptian bandaging a mummy, while another was painting the mask that was to cover the deceased's face. The strange contrast offered by this series of pictures of exuberant life, graven on the walls of these aisles of death, powerfully attracted Jacques' attention, and Kéradec gave him the best information in his power.

At length, tired of this funeral procession amidst the tombs of princes, princesses, and high personages, they rejoined Onésime, who, rested by his excellent nap, had relit a cigar, and was sipping a second cup of coffee which the attentive Mahmoud had brought him. The latter ran to put the horses to, and at the expiration of an hour he set the trio down at the door of their hotel.

View of the Citadel.

CHAPTER X.

Onésime thanks his landlord.—How the wise are asses and the asses wise.—The Mosque of Hassan.—Neglect of the Arabs.—The Mosque of Touloun.—The legend of its minaret.—Onésime admires the Sultans and their mosques as much as he abhors the Pharaohs and their monuments.—His horror of religions and their ministers.—Oratorical explosion.—Onésime's *pollice verso.*— There ! — Polyandry among the Arabs.— The Citadel.—Joseph's Well. — Onésime will not visit it.—The Mosque of Mahomet Ali.—Onésime sleeps there on his feet.—Sudden awakening.—How Jacques saved his life.— Sunset.

ONÉSIME, in the ardour of good digestion, hastened to go in search of his sympathetic landlord ; he thanked him profusely, and persuaded him with some difficulty to accept his portrait painted by Jacques, in remembrance of his amiable services to the party ; then he rejoined the Doctor and Jacques, who were awaiting him.

"Well !" he exclaimed, on making his appearance, " our dear amphitryon accepts."

" Accepts what ? " asked Jacques.

" His portrait, which you will paint for him, of course ! "

" That's very kind of him."

" I had some trouble in persuading him, and in overcoming his scruples, but at last I succeeded. The charming man, he does not know what it is to refuse anything ! "

"That's a pity," murmured Jacques.

"You know," continued Onésime, who had not heard the interruption, "you must do his hands in the portrait."

"They shall be done."

"You understand, it would be stingy to do the head only."

"Oh! Absolutely stingy."

"Would it not? Especially as he was not sparing. What truffles! What wine! Be liberal, my friend, liberal!"

"We'll be liberal; the hands shall be there, even the feet, if you wish it."

"I hardly dared suggest that."

"I admire your reserve."

"But as you desire it——"

"It would be wrong on my part to raise any objection," answered Jacques, laughing and concluding Onésime's phrase. "That is the reply you wanted to make."

"You guessed my thoughts."

"I know you so well."

"A portrait from head to foot! I hope it will not be said that I eke out my gratitude."

"Nor that it costs you dear!" observed Jacques.

"Ah! you see I am not a Crœsus. I am sometimes obliged to reckon."

"Not with me though!"

"I never reckon with my friends," remarked Onésime, with dignity.

"Such a sentiment does you honour."

"And I thank you for appreciating it as it deserves."

"You are coming with us? We are going to see the Citadel."

"Is the Citadel very far away?"

"Half an hour's trot, on a donkey, at the most."

"That's reasonable."

"Here is the very thing," added Kéradec, who had just leant out of the window. "Our recent acquaintances, Ahmed, Hassan, Abdallah, and their 'learned ones,' must have been on the look-out for our return, for I see they are before the door waiting for us to go out."

"Their ' learned ones ' ? " inquired Onésime.

"Their donkeys, if you prefer it; it was thus that Bonaparte's soldiers designated the prancing Cairo donkeys at the commencement of the Egyptian campaign. Later on, they rendered to Cæsar what belonged to Cæsar, and the parties took their respective names again."

"And what was the origin of this distinction accorded to Master Aliboron, or of this uncomplimentary denomination of your condisciples Monsieur Kéradec ? "

"As follows : when the French army marched on Cairo, after the capture of Alexandria, the soldiers suffered cruelly from hunger and thirst; on the way they found nothing but abandoned villages ; the wells had been filled up, and a most oppressive heat struck down the bravest. Discouragement was general. They regretted France, and cursed the presumed authors of that unfortunate expedition, who had sent them into this frightful country, where they could neither, they said, ' make their soup, nor get a drop of brandy.' Recriminations and invectives had full play. Since, as a matter of fact, gaiety and joking are the base of the French character, and never lose their rights even under the most critical circumstances, sallies and jests abounded. The Commander-in-Chief, according to them, was a good fellow; he had allowed the Directory, who had a spite against him, to make a fool of him by transporting him into this country, which was not fit for a dog. And as they halted everywhere, if any vestige of antiquity was to be found, to excavate and make researches, they saddled the Egyptian Commission with the original idea of the expedition, and avenged themselves by calling the savants who composed it 'asses,' and the asses 'savants.' They accused old General Caffarelli, a man as courageous as he was learned, of having cajoled Bonaparte, and of having brought him into this hornets' nest. 'He doesn't care a bit which way it goes,' they said. 'He has one foot in France'; alluding to the leg he lost on the Rhine."

They were at the door when the Doctor had concluded his explanation, and sprang on their animals.

"None of your ' Ahs ! ' rascal," said Onésime to his donkey boy. "'Monsieur de Lesseps' does not require that to go along straight,

A Fortune-teller.

and it worries me. That's true, it makes me nervous," he added, turning to Jacques and Kéradec, who were getting ready to start.

"And makes you lose the stirrups—and the rest!"

Hassan swore by the beard of the Prophet that he would not open his mouth, and would only use his switch.

"Your switch! Still less, you ugly brute; leave us alone, my ass and me. Limit yourself to following us, and do that, even, at a certain distance." Then, settling himself in his saddle, he seized the reins.

The cavalcade sets out. Passing along the Esbekieh at a gentle trot, they reach the Place Atal-el-Kadra, and take the Boulevard Mahomet Ali, which ends at the Place Sultan Hassan. There they alight and approach a group of idlers.

At the corner of a doorway squatted an old negro. On the ground were a leather bag, a scrawl, and a copper inkstand; he was a wizard. Upon the fine sand which he had taken from the bag and spread out before him, a peasant woman had placed her flat hand; she withdrew it; the soothsayer examined the imprint with apparent attention, and scribbled some letters in Arabic on a scrap of paper, which he presented to the woman. The latter gave him a piastre, took the square of paper, carefully secured it, and withdrew.

They lend a deaf ear to the solicitations of this black Cagliostro, and, proceeding towards the Mosque, ascend a staircase of a few steps, and pass beneath the gigantic, vaulted, ogival gateway with corbels and stalactites. It is surmounted by a frieze bearing an inscription in magnificent Cufic characters, and a powerful cornice dominates the whole. Then crossing a vestibule, and a dark corridor furnished with stone benches, they reach a long room, where the attendants provide them with straw sandals. When this is done they enter the courtyard, paved with marble of all sorts of colours, and open to the elements.

At the sides are four gigantic bays, following the bold curves of two enormous arches, which unite at an imposing height to support an embattled wall. The largest is the entrance to the sanctuary. At the end is the *mihrab* of different sorts of marble, ornamented with graceful columns; close at hand is the *mimbar*, and in the centre of

14

the hall the pulpit for the readers, the *mastaba*, of a rather elegant aspect with its columns and pilasters. From the ceiling hangs an admirably chiselled chandelier of bronze, as well as lamps and ostrich eggs ornamented with tufts of silk. Vases of coloured glass, each of which is secured by a light treble chain to a long iron bar reposing on iron brackets fixed in the masonry, form a double line parallel to the lateral walls, along the top of which runs a frieze, a perfect arabesque of lacework, where verses of the Koran are inscribed in Cufic letters.

You enter the room containing Hassan's tomb by a door on the right of the *mimbar*. It is a vast square apartment covered by an enormous cupola,

Entrance to the Mosque of Hassan.

joined on the inside to the angles of the walls supporting it by a corbel of stalactites ; sentences from the Koran are written on a frieze decorating the walls above the marble which covers the lower part.

The flags on which they walk are broken; the slabs of marble lining the sides are falling off; the mosaics are shifting from their setting; the worm-eaten stalactites escape one by one from their decayed sockets; bits of wood which accumulations of dust have long since covered with a uniform grey tint, effacing all trace of painting, tumble down from old age or hang threatening above the heads of the faithful; birds build their nests there; spiders spin their webs; bats lodge in the crevices; and streams of light, coming through the dilapidated dome, strike the wall with their bright rays, ruthlessly illuminating the shameful wreck.

The fountain for ablutions in the middle of the court is in the same dreadful state. Its vast blue sphere-shaped cupola, surmounted by a crescent, is cracked in places; one still perceives the traces of a large zone, formerly covered with Arabic writing in gold; it stands on an octagonal wall supported by slender columns at the angles. Arabs perform their ablutions here.

Fountain for ablutions.

" What an admirable monument, Monsieur Kéradec ! " said Jacques, as soon as they were outside, casting a last look of admiration on the tall and severe façade of the edifice ; " it is a perfect marvel of boldness and elegance."

" It dates from the fine Arab period."

" Is it not related that Sultan Hassan had the hands of his architect cut off, so as to prevent him erecting another monument of such beauty anywhere else ? "

" Yes, that and a great many other things ; but I am much afraid that you accuse this poor Sultan Hassan wrongfully, for that story about the architect is far from having been proved. What is blamable is the unpardonable neglect of the Arabs, who allow such works to fall to ruin."

"Is this neglect general, or is this merely a particular instance of it ? "

" A particular instance ! It is the same throughout Egypt : men and things, from the sea to the cataracts, from the Arabian to the Libyan desert, suffer from this culpable neglect, from this fatal want of

Mosque of Touloun.

consideration, which, with the vandalism of tourists and the cupidity of the inhabitants, ruins the country, and causes even the last vestiges of its past glory to be mutilated or to disappear. But before visiting the Citadel we shall have time to go as far as the Mosque of Touloun ; it is five minutes from here ; you will then see that I do not exaggerate the frightfully abandoned state in which these monuments are left."

Taking to their donkeys again, they set out for the Mosque standing between the canal and the Citadel.

They are hardly inside, when a swarm of half-naked poor and crippled people, to whom the sanctuary of the Mosque serves as a place of refuge, surround them and pester them with demands for baksheesh. They are horrible to look at, and are with difficulty got rid of.

In the middle of the courtyard rises the ablution fountain, with the dome tumbling to pieces. On three sides of the court the naves, with double rows of columns, surmounted with ogival arches, which have been filled in, serve as a dwelling-house. On the fourth side the porch numbers five rows of columns. This part of the edifice forms the sanctuary, or the mosque proper.

Of the four minarets that flanked the four angles one only is standing, and is much decayed. Square at the base, then cylindrical, and finally octagonal, it is compassed by an exterior staircase half in ruins, the upper part leading to the summit of the minaret being impracticable. The sanctuary only is in a fairly good state of repair, with its ogival arcades hollowed out between the arches ; but the stucco coating the bricks is crumbling away, the Cufic inscriptions on the friezes are falling in lumps ; the antique mosaics of the slender marble columns of the *mihrab* are wasting away; the incrustations in ivory of the old walnut *mimbar* are leaving the worm-eaten wood ; the ceilings, in carved palm wood, are cracking and rotting. There will soon remain nothing of the beautiful light ogees, of the original columns, of the elegant arabesques, and of the thousand delicate ornaments of this mosque, founded a century before Cairo—of the Gam'a of Ahmed Ibn El-Touloun, the chief of the Toulounides dynasty.

" You probably know the legend connected with the building of the only minaret of this mosque that remains standing ? " Kéradec asked Jacques.

" I don't know the first word of it."

" I will tell it you. Ahmed, who was of a serious disposition, was one day holding a council, surrounded by the grand personages of his Court and the leaders of his army. Seated at a table, he was playing thoughtlessly with a sheet of paper spread out before him. His fingers folded and refolded it with apparent yet unconscious attention, absorbed as he was in a fit of musing which, little by little, had seized on his whole being. When he recovered from it, and suddenly returned to reality, he noticed astonishment displayed on all faces, and could not help reddening at his passing distraction. As he was not wanting in presence of mind, he wished to efface the impression he had produced by transforming the childish act to which he had unconsciously given way into one of profound thought. He examined the paper once more, again modified the form he had accidentally given it, and sent for the architect. 'That,' he said, handing him the sheet of paper, ' is the form you will give to the minaret of my mosque.' "

" He was a man of resources, this Monsieur Ahmed," said Onésime.

" He had, moreover, astounding luck. Thus, historians of the day relate that the entire Koran was engraved on the friezes of sycamore wood which ornamented the sides of the mosque ; and it appears that this wood was none other than that which came from the planks of Noah's Ark, the remains of which Ahmed had found on Mount Ararat."

" Let the friezes look out, then ! If ever Cook and Son's six tourists hear of their Biblical origin, not one will escape them. Just fancy, a piece of Noah's Ark ! They will split them into pieces and fill their leather bags with them, at the risk of causing the remainder of the building to tumble down on their heads. But, between ourselves, it was a wretched find, and since the Deluge must have been pretty well worm-eaten ! "

" This was only a commencement, Monsieur Onésime. He found better than that. Thus, one day, when he was crossing the desert, the horse of a slave thrust its hoof into a hole which suddenly opened beneath its tread, stumbled and fell, while the rider was thrown out of his saddle. Ahmed alighted, examined the broken ground, and saw that the accident had been caused by the fortuitous falling in of the arched roof of a cellar. He had the rubbish cleared away, searched the interior, and found a treasure there of the estimated value of a million *dinars*."

" Which would represent at the present time—— ? "

" About a million and a half francs."

" By Jove ! You don't find that every day under a horse's hoof."

" It was very common with him, for he is credited with the discovery of several other large treasures ; and it is only due to him to say that he turned them to the best account, devoting them to build his mosque, which was completed in two years, improving the standard of the coinage, and assisting the poor. With this view he placed a pharmacy near his mosque, where, once a week, by his order and at his expense, medical men attended to the sick and assisted the indigent."

" Those Sultans were, anyhow, men of heart and good taste," said Onésime, " and that did no harm. They erected temples full of pretty columns, with beautiful little ogees delightfully executed ; set up nice minarets in daring positions, with ornamental balconies of open work, like Malines lace ; they hollowed out in the courts of their mosques coquettish springs, covered them with light domes and numbers of pretty tiny columns, without mentioning those lovely niches for prayers ; those adorable *mihrabs,* all in marble and alabaster ; those deliciously carved *mimbars,* with delicate incrustations of ivory ; those beautiful mastabas ; those marvellously chiselled lamps ; those ribbons of capricious arabesques tracing prayers on the walls. They had taste, and, moreover, exquisite taste! Charming and original fancy ! And then it was put together in two or three years without an effort. A few bricks, a little plaster, some beams, sundry columns rifled here and there from some old Greek church out of fashion, marble casing carried off from some ancient Egyptian temple, were the materials. Pleasant labour, just sufficient to give the workmen an appetite and extend their muscles—a species of hygienic gymnastics ; that was all the trouble. A delicious jewel of a building and a happy people, who come and pass the siesta there, thinking of Mahomet, with their noses turned towards the Orient—that is the result obtained ! And no expense, because the treasures they found amply covered the architect's account ; at.least, it was so in Ahmed's case. Add to this a gratuitous hospital for labourers in case of accidents, an office for relief, and a dispensary for the poor. But it was high philanthropy, pure ethics in action! These Sultans were simply precursors of Montyon ; whereas those grand conculcators, the Pharaohs, with their great stupid heaps of rubbish, their massive pyramids, their heavy tombs, and their placid disdain for the lives of others, their—— Son of a gun! My blood boils at the mere thought of those brutes and their boobies of subjects, whose clumsy productions absorb all your admiration."

"If you hurt my Pharaohs," exclaimed Jacques, "look out for your Sultans!"

"Rest assured, Monsieur Coquillard, that we admire the mosques as we admired the pyramids."

"You might just as well admire a powerful draught-horse, harnessed to an omnibus, as equal to a thoroughbred."

"Certainly, Monsieur Coquillard; one is worth the other on the same terms—they are two different kinds of beauty."

"Just," continued Jacques, "as a lovely brunette is equal to a pretty blonde, a glass of amber ale to one of XXX stout, and an intelligent French poodle to a good-natured Newfoundland. Only I prefer the blonde, I drink stout, am glad to fondle the head of old Gyp, my Newfoundland, and like the grand powerful manner of the Pharaohs better than the refined and charming fancy of the Sultans. I admire the robust work of the ancient Egyptians, grand, simple, imposing, engraved with the cartouch of Cheops, Rameses, Sesostris, or others; and whether this brilliant, elegant, and fragile effort of Arab art be signed Touloun, Hassan, or Khalaoun, I consider it merely pretty. The long ribbon of paintings taken from life, covering the walls of the tombs of the sons of Horus, setting forth so naïvely, so faithfully, their mode of life, pleases me more than the twisted, flowery, and fatiguing caligraphy of the letters of the Koran, scattered over the friezes of the mosques. In a word, I prefer Osiris to Mahomet; and if you cannot feel all that is admirable, sublime, grand in the colossal work of the Pharaohs, well! my dear friend, it is because you have not the sentiment of the beautiful, and there is an empty cavity in your brain."

"An empty cavity in my brain!" repeated Onésime, laying stress on each word; "that is too much!"

This was the last drop of water that made the cup run over

Onésime, the gentle Onésime, revolted against this persistent Pharaonic
infatuation, as he had revolted against the outrageous praises bestowed
on Cleopatra, as he had condemned the ridiculous eulogy addressed to
the pyramids. Onésime had, above all, a just mind, a straightforward
character, an honest heart; he did not dally with his conscience, and
they had braved that conscience to his nose and to his beard! He was
always impatient of ill-placed, unhealthy admiration of matters which
he termed, with superb and deserved contempt, picturesque fancies and
ridiculous crazes, unworthy, he added, of troubling for a single instant
the trim of well-balanced minds. And he was well-balanced, he was;
he did not vibrate in space like that hare-brained Burgundian and that
old Armorican Druid, not he, Onésime Coquillard, of Paris, unique and
without a consort, like the phœnix, almost, less the plumage and
immortality. He wished, he, the rational being, the practical man,
the convinced partisan of the *utile dulci*, to whip with the rod of
common sense, to scourge with the thongs of satire, those frightful
exaggerators, those admirers beyond reason; he would, he, Onésime
Coquillard, he would *castigare ridendo mores!*

Erect on his short, fat legs, he threw back his shoulders, also his
head; that was his famous posture, that memorable attitude of grand
occasions, characteristic and inexpressible, which was assumed at the
outburst of his improvisation. It was the preface to his anger! His
right hand, round and plump—the other was always in his trousers'
pocket when he was merely ironical—described a graceful, regular curve,
in no way abrupt, the arm was extended horizontally, the fingers were
stiff, the palm of the hand turned towards the heavens, the thumb
raised. The position of the thumb was of great importance in his
oratorical gestures; raised thus it expressed bitter irony! The thumb
down—but one must not anticipate. By a simple effort of his will,
the mocking mask of refined, sharp, biting irony all at once took the
place of the placid and good-natured aspect of his usual face; and his
thick-lipped mouth, of a sinuous and well-formed outline, sarcastically
opened amidst the black bristles of his beard.

"Look here!"—and his voice, sharp as a razor, betrayed by its
bitter, wild energy how vigorous were the bellows of his lungs—

"your Egyptians, those stone-hewers, were nothing more than living-dead people, lunatics who began to scrape the rock and dig their own graves when they had barely come into the world ; they were the Trappists of antiquity, dull sad fellows, passing their lives in worrying themselves to death ; hypnotised by the dread of being badly buried, regretting the nothingness from which they came, and hastening to return there——"

*   *   *   *   *   *

And he continued for a long time thus, always ironical. without fatigue, without anger, calm, severe ; then resumed,—

" They were a nation of moles ! "

" Worshippers of moles, Monsieur Coquillard," rectified Kéradec.

" That was worse still ! " answered Onésime, who was not to be easily unseated ; " in worshipping moles, they worshipped themselves, so strong was the love of the beast in them."

" They gave the mole divine honours," said Kéradec, " because, considering it blind, it personified, in their idea, darkness, which they thought older than light."

" They were more blind than it was, that nation of moles, who, for thousands of years, discovered no better way of passing their leisure than in riddling their calcareous mountains with hypogei and in making a lot of heaps with even sides, in the midst of their plains, with the rubbish——"

*   *   *   *   *   *

And he continued, led away by the vertiginous vortex of his superb cerebration, until at length, intoxicated by his eloquence, which got into his head like strong wine, maddened by the constant rattle of his own words, the tumultuous multitude of which whirled round in his ears in a formidable racket, stunned by the clatter of his phrases, at the moment when he was about to suddenly soar to an infinite height, he felt himself, all at once, bitten by the demon of anti-religious hatred.   He drew his left hand from his pocket with a jerk, rested it proudly on his hip, and turned his right hand over with the thumb down—*pollice verso !*   That terrible *pollice verso* indicated with him that bitter irony would give way to cutting, implacable satire, branding

like a red-hot iron ; he was transfigured ; his features were contracted,
his eyes flashed, and amidst the thunder of his phrases, the clang of
his words, the sonorous roll of his deafening
sentences, he fulminated an impetuous pero-
ration, terminating with this crushing apos-
trophe, in which he pulverised priests and
religions, which, with the cataclysm, were his
peculiar bugbears.

"And it is this old Egypt, living stupidly
with one foot in the tomb, stinking of death,
that in one of its granite coffins one day
whelped, in a superb litter, those radiant
virtues of humanity, wisdom, art, science?
Never. This African troglodyte, in her long
association with the sombre spirit of Death,
felt in the end a monstrous desire for the

Pollice verso.

hideous lover, and in the terror of darkness conceived, in a horrible
union, the Hierophant—a monster ! who killed her at his birth and
vomited on the world the bitterness of religions, those antagonistic
sisters devouring each other, whom like a second Typhon he had be-
gotten with Night, his mother ! "

And Onésime paused, inhaled a breath of air, and then, examining
from head to foot Jacques and Kéradec, who were looking at him with
a sort of indulgent commiseration, he concluded with these words,
uttered in a calm, brief, well-modulated voice,—

"I have said, gentlemen. There ! "

That "there " was pronounced in a clear, firm, imperious tone ; it
was superb, that "there"; it smelt of gunpowder, shone like steel,
rang like bronze ; it fell like a blow from a mace, bang ! with the
grave and prolonged sound of a gigantic gong. No other than
Onésime could have accentuated it with that decision, that air of
conviction, at once resolute and audacious, which made an impression
in spite of all ; he said so much in those five letters, that word of one
syllable ! It was one of those words that remain, one of those sparkling words that illuminate with their flashes of fire an epoch of history,

and mark it with an indelible stamp, like the *Mene*, *Tekel*, *Peres* of Belshazzar, the *Veni, vidi, vici* of Cæsar ; and many others —*verba non facta*. But his was more laconic ; it was not three words, it was not two, it was one word, a single one ! But such a word ! Short, thickset, sturdy and stubborn, black and hairy like himself, terrifying in its stupefying conciseness.

" There ! " And he had said it simply, without fuss, in an easy-going manner, as Louis XIV. must have said, " The State is me ! " As Napoleon III., between two cigarettes, had said, " The Empire is Peace ! " As Tartarin of Tarascon had said, " Sword thrusts, Gentlemen, sword thrusts, but no pin thrusts ! " It was one of those words kindred—but a better brought up relative—to that of Cambronne, who also, on a momentous occasion, thus in five letters summed up, in a manner at once brutal and sublime, the unbearable annoyance that gained possession of him in presence of the crushing calamity of Waterloo—that immense disaster in which the fortunes of Napoleon were wrecked !

Then Onésime, in a noble, serene, Olympian posture, in a posture cast in bronze, Jupiter and Napoleon mixed together, crossed his arms. With him—for with Onésime the slightest gesture signified something, as in the old aerial telegraph—with him the arms crossed were his anger sheathed, his justice reposing ; it was the apotheosis of his victory, as Kneph was the personification of the goodness of Phtah, Neith that of his wisdom. It was also his revenge for the cataclysm. One saw in him the pride of accomplished duty, of vengeance satisfied, and he enjoyed as a man that pleasure of the gods. While Kéradec smiled with wonder, mingled with a dash of irony, and Jacques contemplated him with cheerful calmness, he continued in a brisk and rather sharp tone, which showed a little spiteful malice, notwithstanding his compressed dignity,—

" Well ! And then ? Even if you do look at me like that with an air of pinch-him-without-laughing ! Well ! Yes, it was I, there ! It was I who said that. I, Onésime Coquillard, of Paris, 22, Rue du Faubourg Montmartre, on the entresol, the first door on the left at the end of the corridor. Are you satisfied ? "

"And you called me deicide!"

"Certainly, for you are so, in intention."

"It's an accusation of tendency that you are bringing against me there."

"If you like. You deny God, because of your incapacity to understand him; his existence inconveniences you; that *Deus ignotus* irritates you—you are vexed because he will not be interviewed by you."

"Not at all! But I do not care about making the acquaintance of persons against their will, especially of the unknown; we don't meet, that's all!"

"You would perhaps like him to make advances to you?"

"Politeness indicates that he should take the first step; his high position permits of his doing so, commands him to do it even."

"I see there is a coldness between you."

"But I say your intercourse with him does not seem to me to be so very cordial, and the position between you appears to me sufficiently strained, if I judge by the way in which you arraign his ministers."

"His ministers! Those hybrid creatures who disguise him with every device, who have the audacity to represent him in their image and to make a terrible and ridiculous idol of him, and, what is worse, a stupid and cruel divinity, amusing himself in tormenting and destroying his own creatures, imposing on them the obligation of conforming to the humiliating practice of a long tedious series of absurd rites to deserve his good graces!"

"All the gods they manufacture, my dear Onésime, are cut on the same stupid and bad pattern! Saturn also devoured his children."

"Saturn! But that Kronos, Saturn; he belongs to the Egyptian Pantheon, that ogre, that voracious god. I think he was one of the three husbands of the goddess Athor."

"Precisely! His two collaborators were Phtah and Thoth, of whom the Greeks have made Vulcan and Hermes," answered the Doctor.

"That's immoral enough."

"Everything is permitted to the gods."

"Yes, but three men for one woman is——"

"Polyandry, neither more nor less. Besides, it is a custom rather common among the Arabs," said Kéradec.

"One woman is generally sufficient for a man's happiness."

"Or his misfortune!"

"When one is clumsy."

"Well, gentlemen," interrupted Kéradec, "we will take a turn through the Citadel before dark, if you like; it is five o'clock; we have an hour before us, let us profit by it."

The entrance to the Citadel.

They left their donkeys and donkey boys on the Place Roumeilieh, which they soon reached, to enter the fortress.

"Here," said Kéradec, "is the Château of Youssouf Salah-Edden, the famous Saladin, built under the direction of Karagueuz, his first Minister."

"That Karagueuz was a sort of cracked person," advanced Onésime.

"That is what is said of the eunuch, although his acts do not quite respond to the reputation he enjoys."

They found themselves facing one of the entrances to the Citadel called Bab-el-Azab, or Gate of the Mamelukes.

The gate, in pure Saracen style, with elliptic ogee, opens between two massive towers, striped with broad horizontal bands alternately red and white. They enter, and follow the narrow crooked lane which leads to the upper part of the stronghold.

"It was in this small defile," explained the Doctor, "that was performed that terrible butchery of the Mamelukes, which at one stroke destroyed the power of the Beys, and established that of Mahomet Ali, who ordered the bloody drama."

"And not one of them escaped the massacre?" asked Jacques.

"Yes, one, Emin Bey, the Arabs relate; his horse flew with a prodigious bound over the parapet of the rampart. If Hassan, your donkey boy, were here, Monsieur Coquillard, he would show you, without hesitation, the spot where the frightful leap was accomplished."

"Emin Bey's horse must have had wonderful legs," summed up Onésime, measuring the height of the parapet with his eye. "And Hassan would have tremendous cheek if he dared to affirm the thing and show me the place where it occurred."

"But every one believes it here."

"So much the worse for every one."

They had reached the inner courtyard. After having stopped for an instant before the old mosque, in the Byzantine style, of Khalaoun, almost destroyed, and the cupola of which has fallen in, they go towards Joseph's Well, which is close by.

"Do they make the sinking of it so ancient as the chaste Joseph of the Bible?" inquired Onésime.

"The legend does, but history affirms that it was Youssouf, the Mameluke Joseph, who had this well sunk. Another version says that the latter merely had it cleared of the sand with which it was filled up, but is silent as to the name of the person who had it bored in the first instance; so you have the choice between the two Josephs, the servant of Potiphar and the Youssouf of Saladin."

"Only a Pharaoh would be capable of such a fancy; he must have bored this pit to put a tomb there; and the Arabs, like practical people, transformed the mummy hole into a well, after having cleared it of the sand."

"That is an hypothesis like another: let us go and verify it, and examine this celebrated well, which is assuredly very curious."

Onésime approached the orifice, but firmly refused to take the snail's path that leads to the bottom.

"I go down there!" he exclaimed; "and who will bring me up again? Not I, for sure!"

"Very well! you will remain there. It appears there is a good Arab fellow down below who sleeps there; he will keep you company, you who like the Arabs."

"Pardon! the Sultans only."

"The depth is barely two hundred feet, Monsieur Coquillard."

"That is two hundred too many; and besides, you see, I do not care about wandering like that at the bottom of wells—it's unhealthy, one catches colds there. Go on! Do not stand on ceremony; a pleasant journey! Amuse yourselves well; I will await you here, and light a cigar." He installs himself on a stone in the shade, while Jacques and Kéradec descend.

The spiral path on a gentle slope turns round the wall of the well, which is provided with semicircular openings; about half-way down a large landing, hollowed out of the massive rock, comprises a stable for the bullocks and their guardian, a forage loft, and a large reservoir. The well is covered over by a circular wooden trap on a level with the landing; a mechanism set in motion by oxen raises the water and empties it into the reservoir, while another *sakieh*, established at the top of the well, takes the water from this reservoir, raises it to the orifice, and throws it into a trough, whence it runs to the different quarters of the Citadel.

Kéradec and Jacques were not long in reappearing.

"Well!" inquired Onésime, "is it nice down there?"

"Rather cool," answered Kéradec; "but it's very interesting to see. Let us hurry off and warm ourselves in the sun, and pay a visit to the Mosque of Mahomet Ali, before the daylight quits us"; and they proceed there at a brisk pace.

They had hardly entered before Onésime was quite bewitched by the luxury of the interior of the edifice. The sun, at that moment streaming through its broad European windows, cast warm shadows on the walls, caught all the twistings and windings of its pillars, gleamed on the alabaster columns, and formed great squares on the ground, where the pattern of exquisite colours of the Smyrna carpets covering the floor shone out in admirable brightness. He was somewhat of the opinion of his two companions, who found the *mimbar* too profusely gilded, the form of the windows heavy, the chandelier suspended in the centre of the arch more pretentious than beautiful, the *mihrab* all in alabaster very ordinary; he thought, as they did, that while the architect was about it he might have made the columns entirely of alabaster, instead of making the base and lower part of it, and painting the upper part in imitation. However, he did not go to the length of regretting, with them, the destruction of Saladin's Palace, on the site of which the Mosque is built.

But, in spite of all, he found himself affected by this luxury of refined taste, by this relative modern comfort; he basked in the lukewarm atmosphere which enveloped him in a soft caress. His footsteps, deafened by the thickness of the carpets, did not make the least noise; he observed with good-natured pity the faithful, slowly inclining in the silent performance of their devotions; he followed their ceaseless genuflexions with a look of tenderness; he remembered, not without some emotion, with which was mingled a pinch of jealousy, the delicious promises to true believers in Mahomet's Paradise, and had vague thoughts of changing his helmet for a turban; he felt himself gently becoming a Mussulman. Little by little, lost in his dream, his eyelids became heavy, the eyes closed, first of all for long intervals, then completely. He advanced mechanically; the voices of Jacques and Kéradec, chatting beside him, now only reached his ears in a confused hum; his head slightly oscillated, and he was about to give way to the sweet and irresistible torpor which was gaining possession of him, when Jacques all at once seized him by the arm and abruptly pulled him, at the moment when he was on the point of stumbling and tumbling on the back of a Mussulman devotee, absorbed in prayer, with his face towards Mecca.

"Halt there! Help!" cried Onésime in a stentorian voice, with wild eyes, his hands extended forward; all at once dragged from his dream by this abrupt jerk, and still under -the influence of his hallucination, he thought himself suddenly attacked.

"Hold your tongue, you unlucky devil!" Jacques said to him in a subdued tone. "Are you mad?"

"Oh! It's you!" he answered, looking at him in astonishment.

"Yes, it's me, of course! Who on earth did you suppose it was? Are you ill? What has taken possession of you?"

"Why, you have," said Onésime, now well awake and recovering all his presence of mind; "you are still holding me!"—and he looked at Jacques, who had not yet let go of him, in a rather cunning way.

"You were asleep then on your feet?"

"I would not swear to the contrary! It is so nice here; and I think, God forgive me, that I dreamt I was a Pasha, or something similar."

"With how many tails?"

"They had not yet grown; you awoke me too soon, or rather just in time, for the Sultan had sent me the bow-string; I was condemned to strangle myself. You have saved my life. Thanks!"

"Don't mention it. What is positive is that you were about to crush this child of Mahomet, so busy in assuring his salvation. I stopped you in time."

"It's all the fault of religions!"

"Of religions?"

"Yes; if there were no religions there would not be places of worship; if there were no places of worship we should not be in this one; I should not have fallen asleep here, and you would not have had to wake me with a start to prevent me from crushing one of my fellow-beings; it's very simple, as you see."

"What I see is that we should do well to bolt; your unseemly outcry has troubled the piety of the faithful; they are looking at us angrily; let us get into the courtyard, and go and see that splendid sunset."

The Citadel.

" When I told you that all evil came from religions ! " murmured Onésime, as they went away.

" You see," said the Doctor to Jacques, when, on reaching the grand court surrounded by an alabaster colonnade, they could take in the whole building at a single glance, " there is nothing remarkable but the size, and the wealth of materials used in building it. With its Byzantine cupolas, its two slender minarets with pointed roofs, it is nothing but a rather successful imitation of the great mosques of Constantinople."

" Whether it be a copy or not, it pleases me, this mosque ; it is kept cleaner than the others," answered Onésime.

" And one can sleep upright in it," retorted Jacques.

" Where is the harm, after all ? "

" There is none when one has a friend at hand to prevent it."

" The discretion of the person who renders you a service doubles the value of that service," said Onésime, sententiously.

" And I am not discreet, because I am an honest man ; I do not wish to double the importance of the obligations people may be under to me by my discretion."

" Paradox on two legs without feathers, go on ! "

At that moment they were on the terrace : the view was unique, fairy-like, with the splendid sunset.

At their feet spread out the city, immense ; in the near foreground they distinctly perceived the mosque of Sultan Hassan ; that of Touloun, with its strange minaret ; farther on the barracks in the Square Karameidan ; then, in a dust of gold, in a luminous swarm, rose an infinite confused mass of terraces, domes, cupolas, minarets ; and, amidst all these, a few black lines indicating the network of streets. The Esbekieh Garden made a green spot on this blond, vaporous expanse, terminated by the bordering of European houses in the wealthy Ismaïlieh quarter, which spread as far as Boulak. The Nile shone like a silver blade in a green belt of trees ; and, in the extreme background, standing out in the bluish, misty ground of the desert, the great silhouettes, of a deeper blue, of the Pyramids.

The sun sank slowly to the horizon. At one moment, before disappearing, there was a sort of prodigious dazzle of brightness, a species of gigantic halo filling the sky, illuminating space ; and the city, all streaming in light, became resplendent with endless scintillation beneath this brilliant glowing avalanche of purple and gold. The Nile glittered ; the fields suddenly became a more intense green ; for an instant the minarets shone like needles of fire ; the cupolas sparkled, the domes beamed in a general conflagration. Then the orb of fire disappeared on the horizon, and instantly all was pale ; the sky turned green, the streams of light died out ; the strong colours abruptly became softer ; the gold and purple of a moment ago were transformed into orange, violet, and then into blue tones ; the air suddenly freshened, the shadows increased in intensity ; and soon, almost without transition, all was lost in a great sombre tint, and night came !

"Brrr!" said Onésime, shivering and putting on his overcoat ; "that is done rapidly here ; the sun's in a hurry, he does not care about eking the hours out with lanterns on the horizon, twilighting as he does at home. He does not mince matters ; as soon as he has done his work, ' Good-night, all ! ' " He bows to the ground and turns on his heels ; then, addressing Jacques : "There, you're pleased now. You've treated yourself to your sunset ! "

When they found their donkey boys again on the Place Roumeilieh night was complete.

The Step Pyramid.

CHAPTER XI.

Onésime's gallantry almost gets him into trouble ; Hassan saves his equilibrium.—
Among the palms of Bedrasheen. — Local silhouettes. — The Colossus of
Rameses II.—A chaos of ruins.—Onésime steals away.—Jacques and Kéradec
go forward. — Sakarah.—A negro dance. — Round the town.—Picturesque
scenes.—Dealers in antiquities.—Meeting a saint.—In the desert.—The Step
Pyramid. — Onésime calls it a mischievous gossip. — The Mastaba of El-
Pharaoun.—The tomb of Ti.—Where one sees that the fellah was made for the
stick, and *vice versâ.*—From the dweller in caves to him on the Boulevards.—
How we return to the age of polished stone.—Digressions on Egyptian art.—
Description of the bas-reliefs of the tomb of Ti, and what Onésime thinks of
them.—Mariette's house.

"GEE up, Jackass!" It is Onésime who treats "Monsieur de
Lesseps" with this excessive familiarity, and the ass,
notwithstanding his rider's weight, scampers away at full gallop along
the road leading to the railway station for Upper Egypt ; Hassan, as
gay as a lark, with his babouches in his hand, runs along behind
him ; Jacques and Kéradec follow at a short distance.

Onésime, fresh and nimble, radiant, in a good humour, smiles
complaisantly in the black thickness of his well-combed beard, shining,
perfumed, embalming the air with subtle odours. From the height of
his beautiful red leather saddle he gives himself a lordly bearing,
holding the reins high, joyfully drumming with his elbows, which rise

231

and fall on his sides with the regularity of a pendulum. He makes his switch double round the thighs of his donkey, who is quite astonished at a behaviour so inordinate, and so completely foreign to the usual habits of the person riding him.

Making a frightful abuse of the only three Arabic words that he knows, *chimalan* (to the left), *yaminan* (to the right), *dogri* (straight on), he vociferates them constantly and absolutely without purpose in a tremendously resonant voice, and disdainfully casts a proud glance on the passers-by. The latter stop and gaze with curious astonishment at this fat, chubby-cheeked individual, provided with a white helmet and blue spectacles, sheltered by a gigantic parasol, and whose jovial face forms a strange contrast to his conquering airs ; then they smile, follow him for a few moments with their eyes, and continue on their way. Urchins, less polite, mock him, and in spite of blows from Hassan's courbash address somewhat uncomely epithets to him.

Onésime's exaggerated confidence in the stability of his equilibrium, which is all the more compromised by the stiffness of his attitude, plays him a nasty trick : at the corner of a street, agreeably tickled in his self-esteem by the killing glance that a slightly buxom and decidedly Levantine housewife casts at him as she passes along, he wishes to engage in a contest of gallantry, and turning round back- wards he sends a fascinating kiss with a most graceful curve of the arm. But, alas ! forgetting to warn "Monsieur de Lesseps," who bravely continues his gallop, of his intention, he spins round in his saddle, loses his stirrups, and is about to make a plunge into the middle of the road, when Hassan, who was watching the game out of the corner of his eye, and had foreseen the conclusion, catches him in the middle of his parabola, supports him in his arms, and re- equilibriates him in the saddle, without either him or his animal stopping for a second.

Onésime perceives himself, in the twinkling of an eye, fall, rise again, gain the saddle, and continue his furious gallop. It is a regular juggler's play. He is bewildered, and at the bottom a little ashamed. Hassan rises in his esteem ; however, he does not cancel his pro- hibition in regard to the " Ah ! " and continues to retain the stick.

"By Jove! I escaped it beautifully, thanks to Hassan," he remarks to Jacques, who has rejoined him and gallops at his side. "I almost fell"; and he pronounces those words with comic despair, which shows that his vanity has been severely wounded by this slur on his recent equestrian pretensions.

"Bah! Louis XIV. was once almost obliged to wait," said Jacques to console him.

"Yes, but he did not run the risk of breaking his spine, whereas I ——"

"You—you are Onésime Coquillard, you are not Louis XIV."

"That's possible, but I care as much about my skin as he probably did about his, I suppose."

"He particularly! who had a double stomach."

"A double stomach!"

"That excites your envy? that double stomach of a crowned head?"

"I own that, in case of need, I would have used it as well as he did, and without the least trouble; a spare stomach is not to be disdained," he con- cluded, as the cavalcade burst into the railway station at full speed.

They jump into the train, the donkey boys install themselves in a cattle-truck with their animals, and twenty minutes afterwards they are at Bedrasheen, a large village, full of shade and freshness. between the Nile and a forest of palm trees.

They drag the don- keys out of the truck; the railway journey has made them lively. "De Lesseps" prances,

A grove of palm trees.

" Gambetta " is restive, " Telegraph " vigorously scrapes the ground ; Hassan, Ahmed, Abdallah hold their respective animals with difficulty, while their riders get astride of them.

Onésime settles himself to his best on the backbone of " De Lesseps," whose petulance makes him feel rather anxious ; Jacques rises in the saddle, and gently caresses " Gambetta " with his hand ; Kéradec takes the lead, seated on " Telegraph."

The caravan advances at a slow trot along the road leading through a superb grove of palm trees. They grow thick beneath this blue sky, burying their roots in a fertile silt, a thick sheet of earth extended over those numberless generations of men who for more than six thousand years lived in the city of Menes.

On their left the ground is strewn with bricks, broken remnants of pottery, pieces of statues ; bits of sculpture, stumps of columns lie here and there, with blocks of granite covered with half-effaced hieroglyphics. To the right palm trees extend as far as the eye can see, bending beneath the force of the wind.

A swarm of little black creatures, half-naked brats, with squeaky voices, as nimble as squirrels, follow them, laughing, chirping in a shrill treble, incessantly extending their little monkey paws, making their throats sore with their demands for " baksisse."

Arab beggars.

If the party stops for an instant before some interesting lump of cornice, or fragment of a stela, the frightened boys fly away, pushing each other about, and, when once at a distance, continue their impudent litany in a more piercing tone than ever. They are like a flight of sparrows sporting in the sun, cleaning themselves in the dust.

Under the trees the light plays with the shadows, and produces unexpected effects, sometimes that of a powerful enhanced coloration, rendered deeper still by the opposition of shades of vigorously determined violet-black; sometimes of a softness, a harmony, a charm that are exquisite.

At the top of a palm tree, a fellah, his feet resting against the trunk, secured round the loins by a strap that encircles the tree, gathers well-clothed branches of dates in a kouffa, while another, suspended in the same way, makes a female palm tree fruitful.

Beside the road, his feet buried in the dust, an old fellah clasps a distaff; his shadow in the strong light falls hard and crisp on the wall at his back; his naked skull shines in the sun like a mirror; his features are drawn; his skin,

Fellah gathering dates.

strewn with tufts of white hair, resembles an old parchment. It is stretched so tightly on his bones that, in places, it seems as if it would burst. He mumbles a few words in a hollow voice as he sees them pass, while his long, thin, knotty fingers turn the spindle with a febrile movement. His dull eye stares vaguely into space. Death must have forgotten him.

And here is a handsome dark girl, a young peasant woman, her arms encircled with copper bracelets, draped in her blue gown, with a *goulah* on the head. She veils a corner of her face, and as you pass you notice the flame of her eyes, the pearly whiteness of her teeth.

From time to time green fields and fellaheen at work appear through an opening. On all sides are pigeons in innumerable quantities.

The air is admirably pure; Onésime assumes a grave and majestic air on his donkey, with the negligence of a Pasha, hardly listening to Jacques and Kéradec, who talk without stopping. They proceed slowly, quite impregnated with this freshness of the landscape.

Arab woman returning from drawing water.

In a pit beside the road lies a heap, without form at first sight; they stop, descend to the bottom of the hole; it is the Colossus of Rameses II., resting with the face to the earth. At close quarters the features of the Pharaoh are distinguished with difficulty. Every year the Nile comes and kisses the face of the "beloved son of Ammon" with its fertilising wave. Each year he sinks deeper and deeper in the coating of silt deposited by the inundation, and before long, if England, to whom he belongs, does not have him removed, or at all events set upright, he will disappear as have disappeared all the monuments of Memphis.

A little farther on, in a square of ground surrounded by a fence, are a few remains discovered by Mariette, which are waiting to be conveyed to some museum.

From time to time a mass of bare granite protrudes through the earth, resembling the back of a pachydermis buried in the mud; it is the shoulder or head of a Colossus about to disappear.

To the left of the road it is always the same: ground turned topsy-turvy, gaping holes, heaps of rubbish, sprinkled with fragments of pottery, crushed bricks, broken shafts of columns, miserable remains of the splendid city.

Leaving the road they adventure across this chaos of complete demolition. The air is warm, the reverberation of the sun on the ruins is insupportable.

The donkeys stumble, the rubbish rolls away noisily beneath their tread, the bricks are chipped, the pottery is broken up smaller. Onésime has almost fallen off his steed into a hole, the edge of which gave way with a clatter on his imprudently approaching too close to it : he turns round and regains the road.

The Doctor and Jacques continue crossing these heaps of ruins, climbing the mounds, descending the slopes, and soon reach a hillock sufficiently lofty to command the entire plain.

To their right, on the other side of the palm trees, the Nile is resplendent in the sun, dotted with dahabichs with white sails ; to the left, beyond the cultivated fields, standing out against the palm trees in the foreground, expands the plateau of the Libyan desert, with naked, sterile flanks of a reddish yellow, a sort of calcareous wall running parallel with the river, forming a barrier, so to say, to the west, all bristling with pyramids : those of Ghizeh quite to the north on the horizon, and, more to the south, those of Abou Seir ; then, as they draw nearer, seated between his two mutilated sisters, the Step Pyramid of the " Black Bull," whose imposing silhouette dominates with sombre majesty over all this sadness scorched by the sun ; behind these the group of mutilated pyramids of Dashour forms, to the south, the limit of this immense city of the dead, slumbering in the silence of the desert. Between the Libyan chain and the Nile extends the abode of the living.

After a prolonged contemplation, Jacques and the Doctor regain the road as well as they are able. Onésime, who had gone off to quietly smoke a cigar and rest in the shade of the palm trees, remounts his ass, laughs a little at the two friends about their love for broken pots, and they continue trotting gaily along the road that takes them to Sakarah.

Near the walls, before a sort of low coffee-house, are some wooden posts supporting a roof made of a few planks, on which branches of sorghum, palm-fibre, old cages, broken jars have been thrown, and here a gathering has formed. Fellahcen sitting down are taking their coffee ; a young peasant woman, a Bedouin perched on his camel, two or three wretches drunk with raki or hashish, applaud with noisy laughter the foul contortions of a vile buffoon. The latter, a negro covered with tinsel, necklaces, bracelets, dances, imitating, in a way that leaves little room for doubt, the movements, attitudes, and smiles of an almeh. The sight is revolting.

At the gate of the village a pack of lean, hoarse dogs, with bristly yellow hair, receive them with deafening yelps. The blows that the donkey boys generously distribute to them increase the tumult. Onésime trembles for his calves.

Street at Sakarah.

Instead of entering the place they skirt the outer walls of its ramparts, which are very high and of a bright whiteness. Picturesque groups are camped along them.

Here is a blacksmith, shining with sweat, with his apron of buffalo hide, his head covered with a red skull-cap, black with filth and smoke ; he beats a bar of red iron on a very small anvil let in across the unbarked trunk of a tree, while a hectic urchin seems to be playing a toneless accordion, as he sets in motion the primitive bellows, which stimulates a meagre fire covered with cow-dung dried in the sun.

Here a family of unfortunates in rags has established its dwelling-place. Squatting on a heap of broken straw, which they share with three mangy dogs and a donkey covered with raw sores, they mutually free themselves of the vermin which devours them ; when the fingers are insufficient, they bite freely with their teeth, just like their four-footed guests.

The three friends pass at a respectful distance from the group. Farther on is a boat on the stocks : Arabs are calking it ; women beside them are mending the sails, torn in shreds.

Here is an old, grey-bearded weaver ; with a well-applied blow

from the back of his hand, he chastises the curiosity of a young fellah, his son or his assistant, who has so far forgotten himself as to look at the *roumis* instead of turning the wheel.

A knife-grinder with his great toe sets in motion his mill-stone, which is supported by two shafts inclined against a buttress; he is solidly built; his face is wan, and his look deceitful.

At each step are pictures full of originality and local colouring.

Near one of the entrances to the village, in a square shaded by a tamarisk, a score of natives are basking in the sun like lizards, seated or lying on a little low wall enclosing a meadow where a cow guarded

The tomb of the Sheikh.

by an old woman browses : at the appearance of the "Nazarenes" they rise, look at them maliciously, and exchange some words with the donkey boys. On the other side of the square, a great sycamore covers with its shade the cupola of an Arab chapel, the tomb of a revered Sheikh ; the cemetery is close by, and isolated tombs, built of clay mixed with straw, and whitewashed, rise around the tree and extend as far as the road.

Some of the Arabs have approached : from dirty check-patterned handkerchiefs hidden beneath their burnouses they draw out "antiques," the masks of mummies, beetles, divinities in bronze ; they do so with some hesitation at first, the sale of these antiquities being strictly prohibited ; then, becoming bolder little by little, casting aside

16

all reserve, they literally assail the travellers. Onésime, who remembers his mishap with the hand of Ouserkeres, dismisses them with voice and gesture; all his Arabic vocabulary is brought into play: "Emshi!" (be off); "Yallah!" (quickly); the gesture produces no effect, his Arabic makes them laugh, and "Antiquos!" "Baksheesh, ketir!" tickle his ears more than ever with lamentable recrudescence of tone.

A few surly curs show their teeth, and give a hoarse bark.

A saint in rags, bearing a standard in tatters, casts a terrible glance at them as he passes, which checks the smile that his peculiar appearance had brought to Onésime's countenance.

"The ugly brute," he murmurs, approaching

A saint.

Jacques. "There's a fellow that I would not care to meet at night at the corner of a wood. What a disgusting creature!"

"You speak of saints in a very disrespectful way."

"That a saint! That dirty beast?"

"Yes, a saint! See what respect they have for him! Our donkey boys kissed his hand as they passed; the other Arabs do the same; others devoutly put the hem of his filthy rags to their lips."

"Pouah! Are they not sick?"

"Bah! We also have our saints preserved in devotion and filth; Saint Benoit Labre, who lived on a dungheap, was not wanting in admirers. His exemplary dirtiness procured him canonisation; he picked his halo up out of dirt."

"After all, every one takes his comfort where he finds it; but, all the same, Mr. Saint has a bad eye. When he stared me out of countenance I felt cold all down the back."

Kéradec does not trouble about the saint; he is eagerly bargaining for a pretty bronze statuette of the goddess Sacht.

Reaching the border of the desert, the Arabs relieve them of their presence; only the owner of the goddess insists on selling it to the Doctor. He pesters him with his offers; his hand on the donkey's back, measuring his step with the pace of the animal, he pulls Kéradec at every instant by the sleeve, thrusting the statuette between his hands, taking it back, giving it him again. He perspires in great drops, displays a volubility that would be exasperating to any one but the Doctor, whom this tide of words leaves absolutely indifferent.

The heat has become suffocating. The reverberation of the sun on the ground, in the march through these waves of sand and multitude of pieces of rock, is quite distressing. Every now and then they perceive the summit of the Step Pyramid peep up. Onésime has not even the strength to complain; he does nothing but blow and mop himself. Jacques is in a hurry to arrive. Kéradec, as dry as a mummy, will not budge from the price of five francs that he offers for the bronze. When they reach the foot of the Step Pyramid the bargain is not yet concluded. Onésime is stewed in his own juice; Jacques is half roasted. They stop in the shadow thrown by the monument; men and beasts rest, and Kéradec ends by purchasing Dame Sacht.

After a collation that was too slight for their famished appetites, Ahmed serves coffee. Onésime, comforted and dried, finds his good humour again; and all three set out to make the tour of the pyramid.

" But, I say, how do you enter that box ? " inquires Onésime, who, returning to the point of departure, has not noticed the least trace of an opening.

" You don't enter it, Monsieur Onésime, or rather you enter no more, since a recent slip has blocked up the entrance."

The Step Pyramid.

" And you must be distressed, my dear Doctor, at this accident, which prevents you from investigating the inside of this good pyramid, from searching its entrails, and, like Cuvier, who reproduced from a collar-bone the figure of a race that had disappeared, from reconstructing from a calcinated thigh-bone or a bit of papyrus a theory demolishing that of a colleague.

" She was a clever person, this Ko-Kome, as you call her, who prudently avoided your indiscreet investigations. You are so enterprising, you men of learning, that she must have felt alarmed in her sense of modesty. You affirm with such charming looseness things that your condisciples contradict with such perfect ease, that to put an end to all reports, all interviews, the good dowager, jealous of her reputation, simply shut the door in your face."

"After having left it open sufficiently long to permit of its being inspected in the remotest corners."

" In those that she chose to let you see. Because you know some parts of her person, you must not conclude that you know the whole of it. I would wager that the sly dame has masked the entrances to one or two small trenches. This, they say, is the most aged of the pyramids; it must be the most cunning, and heaven knows what this contemporary of primitive times could relate to us if it would."

"Until it makes up its mind, and this Libyan Phryne casts away her last veils, this is what we know of it. It is, as you said, the oldest pyramid in Egypt, the most ancient monument on the earth. Its name is Ko-Kome, according to the hieroglyphic Ka-Kem, the ' black bull.' It dates from the first Thinite dynasty; it is thought that it was built by Ounephes; a passage of Manetho appears to confirm that idea. On the other hand, Mariette seems to be of the opinion that beneath this pyramid is the most ancient tomb of the Apis, bulls' bones having been found there in large quantities. Finally, the presence of several mummies that are not royal indicates that at one time it was used as a sepulchre for private people—for the high and mighty of the Court, no doubt."

" Fie! When one has had the honour of receiving the sacred remains of a Pharaoh or an Apis, to lower oneself to the point of protecting any kind of corpse, of no matter whom, is derogatory for a pyramid that respects itself!"

" Excuse it, Monsieur Onésime. It is the first time; it has not had the example of the others to guide it. And then it has so many peculiarities that distinguish it from them. First of all, it is not set according to the cardinal points. Then its base is rectangular, and not square; one of the entrances is on the south; it is built in five floors. All this gives it an appearance apart, well defined."

"And what is the arrangement inside?" asked Jacques.

"About the centre of the pyramid, on a level with its base, opens a large well descending to a great depth under ground, as far as the room of the sarcophagus, the residence of the Pharaoh or of the Apis. At this well terminate a number of corridors running in every direction. Four rooms and several niches exist besides that of the tomb. Sarcophagi, mummies, ox-bones, show what they were used for. Two of these rooms had the sides lined with a sort of mosaic of green-glazed tiles incrusted on a backing of stucco, and the ceilings ornamented with stars on a blue ground. On the floor lay vases of alabaster, marble, pieces of pottery, a skull, and gilded soles of feet. These objects, collected to be sent to a museum in Europe, met with the same fate as the sarcophagus of Mycerinus, which went to the bottom with the vessel that carried it.

"As to the sacred lake of which the Greek writers speak, the green fields that they place between the pyramid and the Libyan desert, where rose the temple of Hecate, where one saw the famous statue of Justice without a head, the gates of Cocytus and of Truth, and a number of other edifices, there is not the slightest vestige.

"Must we regret that there remains nothing of such a bewitching spot, or should we consider this luxuriant description a fresh proof of the exuberant imagination of the Hellenes ?   I leave to others the task of settling the question."

"They are to be heard with caution then, these Greeks whom you so greatly admire, Doctor ?" said Onésime ; "for you, in the face of such a precise affirmation of their manuscripts, you, the man of hypothesis, not to risk one on the existence of this Eden replaced by an ocean of sand. Decidedly the Greeks were nothing but frightful babblers."

"Yes, but they babbled so wittily that one almost pardons them their freedom in regard to truth. There are so many people who say true things so stupidly that they make themselves ridiculous."

"If our learned man in ' us ' of the German universities were here he could take that for himself. Wasn't the compilation that he made us swallow terribly indigestible ?"

"But what is that mass of ruins over there ? Is it a pyramid fallen in, Monsieur Kéradec ?"

"It is the mastaba of El-Pharaoun, the throne of Pharaoh, an unfinished pyramid. It is little better than a mound of ruins. It is necessary to guess that there has been a monument there. The rectangular base is correctly set towards the East. Mariette was the first to penetrate within it. It contained a royal sepulchre, that of King Ounas of the fifth dynasty."

They get on the donkeys again. Onésime grumbles, and with difficulty avoids falling off his ass, which stumbles and slips at each step. Hassan laughs on the sly at the sight of the despairing efforts of his master, and does not lose sight of him, in order, in case of need, to rectify too exaggerated a deviation from a vertical position.

Passing before the enormous mass, Jacques calls the Doctor's attention to the rubbish strewn on the ground.

The Mastaba of El-Pharaoun.

"The top is also covered; that, coupled with some blocks in position, might be considered sufficient to show that the pyramid had been completed, and that the upper part had fallen in."

In a quarter of an hour they reach the tomb of Ti. Leaving their asses, to the great relief of Onésime, delighted to stretch his legs a bit, they descend the path traced in the sand on a gentle slope, which takes them to the entrance of the mausoleum. On the pillars of the doorway stands out the figure, engraved in relief, of Ti, leaning on his stick of command; inscriptions give his name and titles.

"We shall find on these walls," said Kéradec, "all the details of his words and deeds."

"But these people, then, have always the stick in the hand?" asks Onésime.

" Yes," answers Jacques, " and, you see, nothing changes in the main

The dance of the stick.

in the valley of the Nile. The proceeding does not vary, if the people
are different. Pharaohs, Hyksos, Persians, Greeks, Romans, Arabs,

Mamelukes, French—all have flogged the fellah. He has always bent the spine ; you would say that his back was made for the stick, and *vice versâ* ; that there is an agreement between the two parties. Under the Pharaohs they even kept the feast of the scourge, and the stick dance of the present day is but a souvenir of that festival. The sons of Osiris have got accustomed to it, and are no sadder for that. Habit becomes a second nature, by atavism especially."

"Flogged and satisfied, and perhaps something else also, as in the story of La Fontaine. A strange people all the same ! "

" Bah ! The stick is somewhat the master in all countries," continued Jacques. " The policemen knock John Bull's head about.

Tomb of Ti.

in England, when he is refractory, and Bobby has neither a tender heart nor tender hands ; Brother Jonathan in America does likewise : the Prussian officers break their canes over the heads of their subordinates, they are so thick ! Austria copies Germany. In Russia they have the knout ; it is the courbash of the North."

" And in France ? "

" In France only marshals receive the stick or bâton, and if an entire lifetime, of which the years are marked by brilliant actions, can make them worthy of such an honour, faith ! they have not had it bestowed on them for nothing."

" Let us go now to the tomb of Ti, and see what is said of this original individual."

" He will himself give us all the information, Monsieur Onésime."

" Himself ? "

" At least, his scribes have taken the precaution of doing it for him. You see all this series of bas-reliefs ; it is a correct passport, a biography on stone, and with illustrations ! The entire life of the man is written there.

Statue of Ti.

" He commences by telling us that he has served under three Pharaohs, that he was their intimate, secret adviser, chief of the writings, and, moreover, invested with a high sacerdotal dignity, that of commander of the prophets."

" Is that all ? He was a little bit of an accumulator, this gentleman."

" He was married to a Princess of royal blood, Nefer-Hotep ; he terms her ' darling wife,' ' palm of love for her husband.' "

" How gallant they were, those Egyptian monsters ! Why not call her a sugar-plum, a lollipop ? But these commencements of centuries were very similar to our ends of centuries ; it's just like our ' souvenirs and regrets ' of Père Lachaise."

" Man is always man, my dear Onésime : a composition of some middling virtues, acquired with difficulty, and clumsily plastered on our individuality, and of a host of solid vices inherent in our nature.

" Virtue is an object of luxury, taxable like dogs ; it is a rare flower, delicate, fragile—a greenhouse plant that grows slowly, requires a great deal of care, and which the least draught may kill. They endeavour in vain to acclimatise it in man. It vegetates, languishes, and dies.

" Vice possesses a vitality that is hard ; it is a vivacious and resisting plant. Born with man, it grows vigorously and in all latitudes, like the Jew, and is so deeply rooted in us that it will never be torn out.

"Between the dweller in caves of pre-historic times, and him who lives on the Boulevards at the present day, the man of Cro-magnon and him of Montmartre, there is as much difference as between a bear's skin and an overcoat, a flint axe and a repeating rifle—that is all ! The same goods under another flag. Instincts and appetites have not varied. The law of the strongest is still the law of the human species, one half of which is always seeking to destroy the other. The only variation is that we do not devour our prisoners. It was the excuse of our cannibal ancestors that they fought to fill their larders, whereas we fight for the sake of fighting, stupidly ; and after the victory, we do not know what to do with our laurels ; we cannot even make a sauce of them, to serve up with the vanquished."

"That's true, and we return to our point of departure, in spite of our discoveries, our progress of all sorts, and what we term our civilisation, Monsieur Onésime."

"What ! to the age of stone implements, to the man of Solutré, the contemporary of the mammoth and the great bear ! "

"Perhaps ! Man's head becomes smaller every day, his muscles and chest enlarge ; animal strength develops at the expense of the brain, which diminishes in proportion. They wanted to load it too much ; it has acted like the camel, it refuses to advance."

" Then ? "

"Then we reverse the machine. Nature turns us out to grass again. She had bestowed on us a splendid gift, intelligence ; we have not known how to make use of it; we have done nothing but stupidity ; she withdraws it : she is right."

"But steam, electricity, are they nothing ?"

"No ! Not while one half of the world lives on the other half, while it is possible for a man to die of hunger with heaps of food before him."

"Monsieur Kéradec, you become lugubrious ; the air of this tomb is dangerous, let us hurry over it ; I would prefer you to talk to me of Ti."

"Willingly, it will be more interesting. Let us enter the apartments of Pharaoh's intimate. The pillars of this court must have formerly supported a peristyle, of which no trace remains. But observe these walls of beautiful calcareous stone of fine and compact grain ; how delicately they have been adorned ! The scenes depicted thereon, enriched by colour, are strikingly true. What delicacy in the lines of these bas-reliefs, yet so boldly scooped out ; how sure the hand ! What suppleness in the execution ! and what a sense of truth and observation, in spite of the intentional suppression of details !

"Built partly during the lifetime, and partly after the death of the person, this tomb gives us the best possible insight into the life of the Egyptians of that period."

Jacques is astonished. Onésime, even, is interested in all these naïve, gay scenes above all, scenes that have been lived.

"Here," explains the Doctor, "are statues of our dignitary ; they are placing them in boats, which carry them to the tomb he has chosen ; one of the bullocks destined to the sacrifice is seized, bound by the feet, and the servants are making ready to slaughter it. There, it is Ti himself, with his wife and children, overlooking the work of his people—some are loading sacks, others stuff poultry with paste balls ; farther on it is the farm and its dependencies—meadows where bullocks browse, pools where ducks dabble, flocks of geese, flights of pigeons, and a quantity of other birds of various kinds ; there are even gazelles and antelopes.

"We cannot pay a visit to the well, completely stopped up, leading to the sarcophagus, the entrance to which is here, in the centre of this court. This passage has the peculiarity, which must be noted, of being on a slope instead of vertical.

"Let us now take this corridor at the angle of the court. The different pictures that succeed each other on the sides represent the passage of the defunct into the other life. First of all it is the carrying of acacia and ebony-wood statues, the writing explains ; groups of musicians and dancers, bullocks that are to be slaughtered in sacrifice, servants bearing funeral gifts, baskets of flowers, dishes, salvers loaded with vases ; then it's the Nile with boats under sail, others containing the body of Ti and the funeral gifts, propelled by many oarsmen.

"Here we are at the end of the passage, at the door of the principal room. Let us enter. What a variety of subjects ! What life ! What movement in all these representations !

"Observe this vessel in dock, this action of ploughing, these oxen treading out the corn, others passing a ford conducted by a drover, these games on the water, these fish from which they are scraping the scales and are preparing. Here are acrobats, harpers, wild beasts being removed in cages. We find Ti hunting in his boat ; in the middle of the marsh he holds a bird-call, and throws at the aquatic birds a curved stick, a sort of boomerang, similar to what the natives of Australia use. Crocodiles and hippopotami are hiding in the reeds : an attendant harpoons one of the latter, and beside him a crocodile is struggling with another hippopotamus.

"There are troops of women with kouffas on their heads containing fruit, vegetables, wine, birds, animals. More sylvan scenes, and always Ti with his stick.

"There are painters—like you, Monsieur Jacques—sculptors ; then tanners, shoemakers, glass-blowers, and others. All Egypt passes here.

"On this western side, before these two false doors, were the statues of Ti and his wife : you will find them at the Boulak Museum.

"Now what do you think of your brother-artists of the time of Ti ? "

"I think them wonderful, and if they had not been condemned by an inflexible theocratical government to a defined, unalterable formula, compelling them to be ever recopying themselves, they would certainly have given us other masterpieces of exceptional originality.

"In their animal paintings there is a vast amount of observation and truth. The execution is at once summary and admirably executed.

"The suppression of details, the accentuation of special characteristics ; the firm, elegant delineation, where the line is irreproachably correct and elastic, give a particular cachet to their work, never to be forgotten.

"In representing human beings, their sculpture is less free; one feels that the priest has forced the hand of the artist, has traced him out a line, from which he must never deviate. The form displayed with exaggerated conciseness and absolute disdain of detail, the conventional stiffness of the lines, the similitude in the fixed, majestic attitudes, the identical expression of the physiognomies, their intended symmetry, envelop Egyptian art in a sort of mystic veil, which weighs upon the imagination and fatigues it.

"The imposing severity of the lines is hardly sufficient to excuse their stiffness; the serenity of the faces does not compensate for the vague fixedness of those uniform visages; finally, those sought-out attitudes of eternal repose, immobilising the gesture in these colossi, beset you like something contrary to nature. It would be quite a crushing monotony were it not so highly formulated."

"You are right; one feels that the artist has worked in prison, under the eye and at the instigation of a sacred scribe, of a therapenta, who imposed on him, along with a unique, hard, and stiff formula like his own monuments, the sacrifice of his individuality, stopping all initiative, all research, all progress, ignoring or casting from him all ideal, petrifying his genius in a definite, immutable, hieratic mould."

"Go on!" said Onésime; "your manufacturers of stone gods were not artists, at most they were stone-masons. Would not real artists have very soon sent these Mecænas of the vestry to Jericho? Do you think genius accepts masters or inquires its way? They have done *that* because they had only *that* in them, do you hear, my son! They were copyists, clever in caligraphy and nothing more; and yourself, refractory as you are to all discipline, abominable canvas-dauber, you would make a fine set-out if you were in the least degree obstructed in your ideas, if any one tried to put a break to the mad pranks of your brain.

"I prefer their minor painters of simple subjects, of still life. They are very monotonous, very lugubrious, with their everlasting mummies in boats, their gods with the heads of animals, and all the entanglement of their allegories and hieroglyphics; but still they are sometimes funny, one meets with some ludicrous scenes; it produces

the effect of a burst of laughter at a funeral, but it is amusing : this
scene of the payment of the impost, for example, representing mayors,
armed with the stick of course, bringing the ratepayers within their
jurisdiction before scribes, the tax-collectors of the period.

"One sees that Jacques Bonhomme, in all countries, has always
reluctantly paid his money and received blows, and that the poor man
must have his loins covered with callous skin.

Mariette's house

"They must also have been fond of good fare, judging by the way
in which they delighted in representing victuals.

"Just look at that goose: isn't it plump?　Doesn't it provoke
the appetite?　What round legs !　What a luxuriant stomach !　One
could almost eat it ! "　And Onésime softly felt the bas-relief of the
bird, and his pleasant face beamed all over.

" Were they truffled, or merely filled with chestnuts ? " he asked
apart.

" Only with little onions, my friend.　It was the vegetable the
Egyptians preferred."

" Their god ! " added Kéradec.

" It must have been divinely good."

As they chatted, they left the mausoleum.

" If you like," said the Doctor, " we will go and rest in Mariette's house, at two steps from here ; then we will visit the Serapeum."

After a short walk through some hillocks of sand, fallen-in tombs, from which a bleached bone, a mummy's bandage, the carcass of a jackal, occasionally juts out, they come in sight of the little house that serves Mariette as a shelter.

At their approach an old Arab with a white beard meets them, and conducts them under the large verandah preceding the house. Two other Arabs offer them rush-bottomed chairs, filtered water, and, shortly afterwards, some excellent coffee. The donkey boys stretch themselves out near their animals, Jacques produces his pipe, Onésime lights a cigar, the Doctor rolls a cigarette.

A Bedouin Camp.

CHAPTER XII.

Ghâwazi and Awâlin.—Their exile to Esneh.—Memphis.—Who Menes was.—
Whence came the Ancient Egyptians?—The god Phtah and his temple.—The
bull Apis and the honours rendered to him.—Onésime an augur.—He beats all
the prophets and disentangles the oracles.—His explanation of the signs of
the bull Apis.—A compromising moonbeam.—On sacrifices and the victims.—
Effect of the sun.—Greatness and decline of the city of Menes.—Mariette's
discovery.—Jacques and Kéradec explore the Serapeum.—Onésime reproaches
them with troubling by their noisy visits poor mummies who only want to
rest in peace.—A breakneck gallop to Bedrasheen station.

"IT is extremely nice here," said Onésime, who was sipping his
coffee astride on a chair.

"It only needs some Almehs and singers to pass a delicious afternoon beneath the shade of this verandah."

"Faith! they would be welcome; we have seen a great many
things, but no Almehs. It's a gap, a serious gap, in the course of our
studies of the crude."

"I thought you were disgusted with studies of life, after experience
of the fellaheen, male and female, during our journey from Alexandria
to Cairo."

"Ah! yes, I have had enough of those creatures, but the Almehs!
By Jove! that's another matter"; and Onésime stroked his beard
conceitedly and tried to look bewitching.

" You must wait until you are at Esneh, Monsieur Onésime, to find the dancers, in Arabic, *Ghâwazi*, and singers, *Awâlin*, which is the plural of Almeh ; and I am afraid that when you see them you will experience bitter deception."

Ghâwazi dancing the dance of the wasp.

" What ! Doctor ! the Almehs—excuse me, the Awâlin in the plural ; that's it, is it not ? "

" The Awâlin are the singers."

" I refer to the dancers, the—what do you call them ? "

" Ghâwazi."

" Yes, that's it, the Ghâwazi : are they falling into decay ? "

" Alas ! Yes. Like the Pharaonic monuments, the Arab mosques; like everything here but the Nile and the fellaheen."

" They are irremovable, like the Senators."

" Yes, and inalienable and unattachable, like the inheritance of a minor or sequestrated property. Abbas Pacha, under the pressure of the Mussulman clergy, drove them out of Cairo and relegated them to Esneh."

" Oh ! those priests ; they must always meddle with what does not concern them ! "

" It is true that the Princes, the high dignitaries, the rich, ruined themselves for them in a mad way."

" But don't they ruin themselves at home, in the same manner, for Ghâwazi of the Opera, who are much less interesting and quite as costly, if not more so ? "

" That may be. They are none the less fallen from their ancient splendour, and reduced to delight the people of Esneh and Cook and

Son's tourists. You will see them there dressed in long gowns, the
bosom covered with sequins, the hair plaited in a row of long thin
tresses, intoxicated with vermouth, in a filthy den, lit up by candles
fixed in the necks of empty bottles. On a mat spread out over the
beaten earth, to the accompaniment of rebecks and daraboukas, they
will perform before you, for a large baksheesh, three-quarters of which
will be taken by the dragoman, the dance of the wasp, or even of the
sword. There is a certain symmetry in their evolutions, consisting at
times in lascivious undulations, in voluptuous movements of the hips,
now abrupt and jerky, now very lithe, very soft, accentuated at
moments by a prolonged trepidation at the lower part of the
loins, and scanned by the sound of the crotali which they hold
above them in their hands, while the bust and legs are as motionless
as in a statue. It is quite the *vibrabunt sine fine, prurientes lascivos
docili tremore lumbos* of the daughters of Gades in the epigrams of
Martial."

"It's simply what we call in Paris the *danse du ventre?*"

"Nothing else ; and, besides, either of the three Consuls at Luxor
would take a pleasure in arranging for you to be present at one of
these little fêtes. For women of this sort are also to be found at
Luxor and in certain other towns of Upper Egypt."

"The Consuls ! "

"Yes, the English, French, German—Arabs, naturally. They will
have no scruple, either, in selling you false beetles, mummies, stelæ,
manufactured by themselves or under their direction ; and their brats,
who run about the room, will thankfully accept any baksheesh you like
to offer them."

"That's rather nice, that."

"Bah !" said Jacques, "at home baksheesh is called a tip, drink
money, or so ; the difference between them and us is that we have
several words to express the thing, and they have only one. A matter
of language."

"And your Serapeum, to return to your frightful Pharaohs," asked
Onésime, "is it very far ? "

"Two steps."

" Ah ! So much the better ! These marches and counter-marches through mummies' bones, broken jars, dirty linen, and a lot of old things that have fallen in, on a donkey that stumbles at every step, are fatiguing and not at all gay. Here, in the shade of this verandah, one at least breathes. And so those are the ruins of Memphis ?" he remarked, waving his hand towards the desert.

" Alas ! Yes, Monsieur Onésime, and yet God knows what an immense site Memphis occupied, the first, the most celebrated, the largest city of antiquity.

" It extended from east to west over the entire space comprised

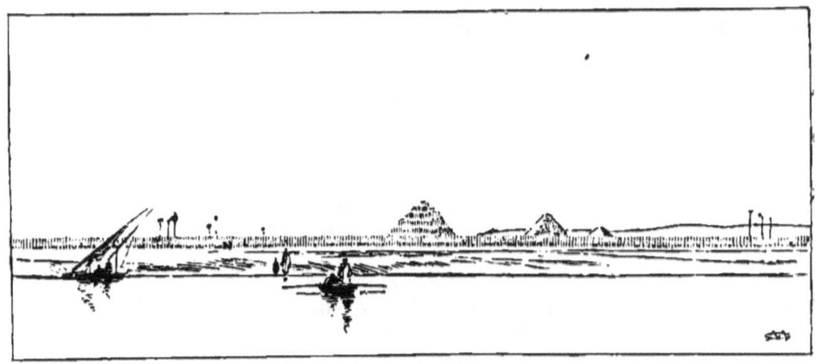

The Nile and the Pyramids.

between the Nile and the Libyan desert ; the pyramids of Ghizeh bounded it on the north, and those of Dashour on the south.

" Herodotus attributes the foundation of it to Menes, the first monarch after the age of fable. On the ruins of the theocratic system which he had just overthrown, he established military government and absolute and unique royalty. He diverted the course of the Nile to increase the area of the city, had a gigantic dyke built, the *White Wall*, the Dam of Kosheish of the present day, to secure it against inundation and attacks of the enemy, raised temples to the gods and regulated their worship, suppressing the privileges of the priests of Heliopolis, who were then all-powerful. The latter avenged themselves by having him devoured by a hippopotamus at the age of sixty."

"A priestly vengeance! But, Doctor, where on earth did this Menes come from, this happy soldier who, all at once, five thousand years before Jesus Christ, makes his appearance from no one knows where, raises by a wave of his wand an entire city with monuments, and after victory suddenly becomes architect and legislator for gods and men. A people at the commencement generally throw out feelers, and it is hard to believe that they accomplished such a prodigy, all at once, and at such a remote period."

"You forget that Menes did not find a nation in an embryo state, but a civilisation already old, a theocratic government firmly established, and merely substituted his authority for that of the priests, while continuing their work. That is the story related to Herodotus by the priests of Phtah."

"But you cannot believe what those hierophants, as clever as old monkeys, said!"

"One may suppose that, for several thousands of years before Menes, the Egyptians, isolated from the rest of mankind by the desert, which was difficult to cross, and by the sea, which was an impenetrable barrier, also having the advantages of an exceptional climate, of a valley of remarkable fertility, thanks to the regular inundations of a river unique on the face of the globe, sheltered from want, from intemperate weather, from warfare, must have developed more rapidly and under more advantageous circumstances than other nations less favoured by their geographical position."

"But of what race were these Egyptians?"

"Perhaps a branch detached from a red race of the plateau of the Himalayas, who, previous to their migration, had already mingled with a white race. This mixed people, at an unknown period, perhaps crossed the Isthmus of Suez and established themselves on the banks of the Nile, where they may have found negro tribes, whom they reduced to slavery, already installed here. The Copts are supposed to be the descendants of this first invasion.

"A third cross was produced by the conquered contributing a little negro blood to the red and white. This threefold mixture, increased by successive doses, in unequal proportions, of those three races, by infiltration as in the case of the Hebrews, by invasions as in that of the Hyksos, must, in a few years, have kneaded all these groups into one type, and have definitely constituted the Egyptian race."

" And Menes was ? "

" A white barbarian, a Scyth, a *Tamahou*, come from the North with a horde of warriors, who burst into the peaceful and religious valley of the Nile, and seized, as later on the Hyksos conquered by force, a country whose civilisation he adopted instead of destroying it.

" The syllable Ker, essentially Celtic, which you find stuck on to the names of several kings of different dynasties, is a certain indication of the Aryan origin of the conquerors Nekheropis, Nephekera, Kerpherès, Seberkherès."

" Ker-adee, then, Doctor! There are your ancestors become conquerors of Egypt. I can understand now your great love for the Pharaohs. You are their cousin."

" And you also, Monsieur Coquillard, for you are of the family, a Celt also."

" Crossed with a negro," said Jacques. " There must have been some *gri-gri* of the Congo among your ancestors."

" And you, you ill-licked cub," replied Onésime, " some Northern boar with red hair of the genus *homo rufus hyperborealis*, some laggard of the invasion forgotten in France."

" You both come from the same race," said the Doctor, laughing, amused at the frequent tussles between the two friends. " Monsieur Onésime is of the brown Celtic branch, the most ancient Aryan horde that emigrated to Europe. You, Monsieur Jacques, are of the second horde, the fair branch. You are a pure Gaul."

" Like Menes, who, no doubt, brought a god with him which he acclimatised in Egypt."

" He was satisfied with the one he found there, the god Phtah, to whom he raised a temple, which was enlarged and enriched successively under all the Pharaohs.

" This was the most ancient god of Egypt, ' Primitive fire.' the ' Father of the Sun.' He afterwards became the Hephæstus of the Greeks, the Vulcan of the Romans."

" Did Menes leave descendants ? "

" No, he lost his only son. In reference to this subject the people composed a song of mourning, the ' Maneros,' which was transmitted from century to century."

" In Egypt, as in France, all ends by song."

" When they sang it they placed a death's-head on the table."

" Those people always had an undertaker's gaiety."

" Phtah, the demiurgos, the *cabiric* artisan, passed as the creator of worlds, ' the Originator of all '; he was termed ' the Opener,' because he had broken the egg from which the sun and moon issued. Under the name of Phtah-Sokar-Osiris, he was the protector of the Necropolis of Memphis, and the word Sakarah is merely a corruption of his name Sokar-Osiris. It was he who gave the sun that had set the power to re-appear, the dead that of resurrection."

" A sort of precursor of Jove."

" The bull Apis, the animal that was consecrated to him,

The god Phtah.

was treated with particular care : he resided in the temple, reposed behind magnificently worked drapery, embroidered with gold and ornamented with precious stones, on a carefully selected litter. They gave him a mash of fine barley flour and peeled wheat, milk, pastry prepared with honey ! They spoilt him in every way.

" He had his harem of cows."

" The happy rascal ! "

" His mother, the cow that had dropped him, was no more taken to the bull, and shared, in a measure, the honours of which he was the object; she had her stall and her private attendants."

" And what, apart from the sweet occupation of allowing himself to be adored, were the duties of this worthy bull? For I suppose that

The bull Apis.

these honourable Egyptians did not entertain him so plentifully to do nothing."

" He delivered oracles, for he possessed the power of seeing into the future. Thus it was considered a favourable omen when he came and ate the food that was offered him in the hand. Those who consulted him previously burned incense before the window looking on to the yard where he was let loose at certain hours, placed on the altar a piece of money, and filled the lamps with oil; then, approaching their mouth to the bull's ear, they questioned him on the matters that interested them ; then, stopping up their ears immediately, and keeping them so until they were out of the temple, the first words that they heard when they were once in the street were considered to be the oracle's answer, and, as such, were received with respect."

" It was rather an original style of answer, but very elastic and passably intricate. Was not his worthy brother of Heliopolis, the bull Mnevis, less complicated in his manner of proceeding ? "

" He acted in the same way, as also did the bull Onuphis of Hermonthis."

" These fat prebendaries were everywhere then ? "

" There were only those three, but Apis, adored throughout Egypt, was more popular than his rivals. Onuphis, however, was not to be disdained. Macrobius relates marvels of him : his coat, it seems, grew the wrong way, and changed colour every hour."

" He must have astounded his parishioners, that chameleon ! "

" The inauguration of the kings took place in the temple of the bull Apis."

" This Memphis was the Rheims of the Nile, then ; the anointed of the Lord was consecrated there."

" With a little ceremony that was not without interest : they placed the yoke of Apis on the king's shoulders, and he had to pass down the street with this inconvenient apparatus."

" They cruelly avenged themselves for this affront, the scoundrels of kings, by making their subjects, those condemned to the pyramids for life, carry a heavier yoke."

" The office of Holy Bull was doubtless hereditary in the family of these lazy oracles. They must have formed a stock of Apis ? "

" Not at all. It was not every member of the bovine race that had the chance of becoming Apis : the aspirant to this title had to unite certain special and clearly defined characteristics. They numbered twenty-nine."

" And these signs were ? "

" He was first of all recognised by his coat."

" It was of your colour," remarked Jacques.

"His hair certainly," and the Doctor smiled as he looked at Onésime, "had to be black : on the forehead there must be a white spot of a triangular form, on the back the image of an eagle, on the right side a white crescent, under the tongue a wart or knot in the shape of a beetle, besides important secondary signs."

"But the coat of that animal predicted as clearly as daylight the destinies of Egypt."

"How is that ? "

"Oh ! it's very simple ! The triangular white spot indicates the triumph of Christianity and the overthrow of Osiris."

"And why so ? "

"I am ashamed to have to explain it to you. Is not the triangle a symbol for Christians, that of the Holy Trinity ? "

"Agreed ! But its white colour ? "

"Are not Christians Europeans, consequently white ? "

"Ah ! "

"The crescent signifies unquestionably the arrival of the conquering Arabs. Is it not so ? The eagle on the back, the victorious eagles of Bonaparte, the expedition to Egypt, the French who fell on the—backs of the Egyptians. One must be blind not to see it."

"And the knot ? "

"The knot in the form of a beetle, also ! That completes it. For persons who decipher hieroglyphics currently, your hesitation grieves me. The knot is an emblem of slavery—prisoners are tied; the beetle means that this slavery will last for ever—beetle, symbol of eternal duration."

"And the black coat of Apis ? "

"But you are more obstinate, more incredulous, now, than St. Thomas ! It was the mourning worn by Apis for their lost liberties. Do you understand now ? "

Jacques and Kéradec were annihilated. Onésime assumed in their eyes Olympian proportions.

"That is not all, gentlemen," continued the latter; "Onuphis also predicted their ruin ! A coat with hair growing the wrong way, a sign that events would occur which would make their hair stand on

Street in Cairo.

end ; change of colour every hour, a way of saying that they would see things of all colours. And I have not finished ! Mnevis accentuates the predictions of his two colleagues. His gilded horns are the Golden Horn, the Bosphorus, Constantinople—in a word, the Turks ! Bristling hair, confirmation of the oracle of Apis.

"And his comrade, moreover ! The lion with the luminous coat. the gilded claws ! Who does not recognise there the British Lion, and in the gilded claws the cavalry of St. George settling the fate of Egypt at Tel-el-Kebir ? Hey ! isn't that smart ? Is he sufficiently trampled on, your Commander of the Prophets, your old bouze of a Ti ! "

His two friends, recovered from their stupefaction, burst out into a mad laugh, in which Onésime heartily joined.

"I told you your great-great-grandfather was a *gri-gri*, a sorcerer."

"A sorcerer might pass, but not one in ebony wood."

"Ah ! Monsieur Onésime, if the last Apis had not been mummified long since, I should really think—— "

"That his double had entered your skin."

"Thanks for the compliment ; I look like a bull then ? "

"No ; but what a diviner ! "

"Ah ! that's in the family, my friend : it comes of itself, without an effort," said Onésime, in a modest tone. "It's by intuition. I divine, as you paint, without thinking of it ; it's a natural gift. But tell me, Doctor, our ceremony of the procession of the Fat Ox is, doubtless, a relic of the Feast of Apis ? "

"Yes, but we are much less exacting towards him than were the Memphites.

"Under a republican government, my friend, there are no privileges, even for animals; every ox can become Apis, as every soldier can become Marshal."

"Yes, but to play the part of Apis a decent abdomen is necessary."

"Like yours."

"And they eat the ox, anyhow, instead of giving him to eat."

"He must have been of illustrious birth, this creature favoured of the gods ? " inquired Jacques.

" He was born of a cow rendered fecund by a moonbeam."

" That moonbeam was very compromising for the virtue of Madam Apis, the mother.   It would be a nice question of divorce, at the present day, this indiscreet interference of the Divinity in private life resulting in a series of unwished-for and unexpected intruders in the family life of poor mortals."

" It's the privilege of the gods and kings.   The latter also had the right of taking certain liberties, as in the middle ages."

" He was the symbol of the constellation of the Bull," continued Kéradec.   " As soon as the ministers of the cult discovered a bull fulfilling the indispensable conditions, they built him a house on the spot, the doorway facing the east, and for four months they fed him on milk.   When the new moon appeared, the priests came to see him, and greeted him with a particular ceremonial ; a gilded vessel, provided with a sumptuous bed, was prepared to transport him to Memphis, and a procession of priests escorted him.

" On the way they stopped at Nicopolis, where he was fed on choice food, and during the forty days that he remained there, only women had the right to visit him, and behaved in a most indecent way."

" That was rather naughty on the part of a people who prided themselves on having invented wisdom."

" From there he was taken to Memphis, and placed in a delicious retreat, in the midst of a sacred wood close to the temple.

" Near at hand, in an elegant châlet, carefully selected heifers awaited the good pleasure of their lord and master.

" This was the Little Trianon, the Parc-aux-Cerfs, of the redoubted bull Apis ; it was quite Regency style.   In the evening the Sultan threw the handkerchief to her whom his caprice desired to make his temporary choice companion ; in the daytime, his bovine majesty had his great and small levees, gave his grand audiences to the public in the temple, listening to the complaints of his subjects and then delivering his oracles. This was a royal bull ! Louis XV. could not have done better."

" Certain authors, however, pretend that his habits were better looked after, and were less free, that he had a more respectable gynæcenm, that he was a monogamist and very reserved in his love affairs, only sacrificing once a year to them, and only bestowing his favours on a single heifer, who also possessed characteristic exterior spots which procured her that honour."

" Then he was less of a libertine than they made him out to be."

" When he went out, officers escorted him to keep back the crowd, and young children preceded him burning incense, throwing flowers and singing verses in his praise.

" They sacrificed bulls, bullocks, and calves to him, but never cows or heifers, which were sacred to Isis.

" These had to be pure, that is to say, red, without a black or white hair.

" To the sphragist was entrusted the care of examining the victim ; this done and found satisfactory, he sealed the animal by marking it with the imprint of a man on his knees, the hands fastened behind the back and a sword on his throat. It was then placed on a wood-pile on the altar ; the fire was lighted, and after having poured wine over the animal, they slaughtered it. Imprecations were cast upon its head, which was cut off, and Greeks were allowed to carry it away if they came for it. If not it was thrown into the Nile, the Egyptians under no circumstances eating the head of any animal."

" The bullock was then reduced to cinders ? "

" No, indeed ! Herodotus tells us that the manner of burning and cutting up the victims varied with the species of animal.

" In the case of the bullock they first of all removed the inside and threw it into the Nile. The feet, the neck, the shoulders were cut off, the inside stuffed with bread and honey ; raisins and figs were added; then myrrh, incense, and other aromatics, and the whole was sprinkled with oil. During the process of cooking, which was overlooked by the priests, the company mutually chastised each other until the sacrifice was completed and the victim cooked to a nicety."

" To give themselves an appetite."

" What then ? "

" The crowd treated themselves to a feed of beef-steak, roast beef, and rump-steak that would have put Gargantua to shame."

" Of course, not till after the priests had taken their share of the banquet."

" The best pieces ? "

" Naturally ! "

" Those good old hierophants ! "

" Father Apis must have lived to a ripe old age under such an administration."

" Alas ! Apis only lived for a certain time : that was the reverse of the medal. After twenty-five years he was slaughtered and cast into a holy well that was known only to the priests. If he died before the expiration of that period, he was buried with pomp ; his remains were placed in a chapel with brazen doors or in subterranean caves ; the ministers of religion shaved their heads, and the whole people went into mourning until a successor to the deceased Apis was found.

" The vulture was the symbol of Phtah, and the lion also represented him."

" But," inquired Onésime, " he must have had a wife of some kind somewhere, this Phtah, a companion, ' a palm tree of delight,' to speak as the gallant Ti, a little hen to incubate his celebrated egg and hatch those famous chicks the sun and moon ? One cannot make an egg all alone, after all ! "

" He had the third share of a wife——"

" A third share ? "

" That was unfortunately his lot. Kronos and Thoth divided the favours of the goddess Athor with him."

" The goddess with three husbands ? What a woman this goddess was, after all ! She also must have had a temple where she was adored."

" Yes, in the nome of Menilaïtes at Momemphis, as well as at Atarbechis, the city of Athor, which Strabo terms Aphroditopolis, the city of Venus."

" They must have been rather dissipated in those little nests ! "

" The Greeks knew of her in Egypt by the name of the ' Dark Venus.' "

" Because she sought out these little nooks ? "

" Rather, Monsieur Onésime, on account of the black veil that covered her."

" It served to hide her frolics."

" She was simply in mourning for her virginity, my friend. The hawk was her symbol, the cow her adored and venerated image ; the mouse and the dove were sacred to her."

" Now that you are edified in regard to these dear Apis we'll go and see their tombs, if you're agreeable ? " said Jacques, rising.

" Let's go," said Kéradec.

" Well, and you ? " Jacques inquired of Onésime, who did not show any sign of moving.

" Oh ! I remain ; I will wait for you here."

" You don't want to see the Serapeum ? "

" Faith ! no. Monsieur Kéradec relates all these stories of the past so nicely, your own sketches are so true to nature, that I prefer to listen to the Doctor's description of the Serapeum and to consult your album ; not to see it for myself. I get mixed up with my impressions, I cannot make them clear, whereas after listening to your explanation, Monsieur Kéradec, and looking at your sketches, my friend, the thing is engraved in my head and does not move. It's fixed.

" Proceed, gentlemen, do not let me detain you "; and Onésime, whose eyes commence blinking, indicates the Serapeum to them with a pretty wave of the hand.

Jacques and Kéradec set out laughing ; they understand that Onésime wants to have his little siesta, and they walk towards the tombs of the Apis.

From where they stand, Cairo and its Citadel with its two slender minarets can be seen in the background ; the city comes out very white, on the left against the deep blue sky, on the right against the tawny hills of Mokattam. The Nile sparkles at its feet, and is rendered still more luminous by the contrast of the burnt-ochre tones of the desert, which borders the Libyan bank. Here, at about two hundred paces from them, in the foreground, is an intensely blue lake, and on its banks a herd of buffaloes watched by two Arabs in the

shade, beneath a solitary tamarisk. The effect is striking in colour
and power.

"Memphis must have been a wonderful city," Jacques remarked to
the Doctor, as they approached the Serapeum.

"Unique! The city of Phtah, 'Akou Phtah,' which they
called the good port, 'Mannofri,' Memphis. That statue we saw
this morning, near Mitrahineh, half buried in the mud, was one of
the two colossi that Sesostris erected before the gate of the temple
of Phtah.

"Even after the invasion of the Hyksos, when Thebes had become

Cairo from the desert.

the capital of the Pharaohs, Memphis continued to prosper for a long
time.

"Its port on the Nile was the mart of Egypt, and of the East.
People assembled there by nationalities. In one part of the city the
Phœnicians had their houses of business, their temple erected to Venus
Aphrodite or Astarte; and the noise, the animation that reigned there,
formed a striking contrast to the calm and grave tranquillity of the
Egyptian city. Near the 'White Wall' was the military quarter, with
its numerous barracks.

"Its industry was renowned; its schools depending on the temple
of Phtah were much frequented and appreciated. From a strategic
point of view, it was one of the principal bulwarks of the empire, and

its famous fortress, the ' White Wall,' victoriously resisted long sieges and furious assaults at different periods.

"The founding of Alexandria dealt Memphis a blow; that of Fostat despatched it. Reduced to the state of a quarry, Memphis was abandoned for Amron's new city; the marble and alabaster of the Pharaonic or Greek monuments served to form the interior of the Arab mosques, the hewn stone was used for their walls, the gilded wooden beams ornamented the houses of the 'believers,' and its ruins soon disappeared beneath the desert sand, leaving nothing of Memphis but its half-buried Necropolis.

"Here we are at the Serapeum. At this same spot, forty years ago, Mariette, perceiving the head of a sphinx penetrating through the sand, had the surrounding ground cleared away, and recognised one of those statues that figure in the avenues approaching the great Egyptian temples. Hearing the Arabs say that similar statues had been discovered at the same spot, then remembering a passage in Strabo where a description of the Serapeum seemed to coincide with the aspect of the ground where he had commenced his excavations, he was convinced that he was on the traces of the celebrated temple, so famous in antiquity.

"He advanced the work with ceaseless activity. In two months the avenue was cleared; a number of other sphinxes, some intact, others mutilated, were brought to light, as well as the statues of great philosophers and literary men of Greece, arranged in a hemicycle terminating the avenue. The space between the latter and the hemicycle was crossed by a dromos, ending on the left at a temple of Apis flanked by two enormous sphinxes, on the right at the temple of the Serapeum, with its two crouching lions placed in front of its pylons. This dromos was bordered by a multitude of statues of animals, of groups of Greek statuary. Hundreds of small figures of divinities in bronze were found in the foundations of the temple.

"In spite of the falling in of the ground, which the great depth that they had reached rendered more frequent and dangerous; notwithstanding the obstacles of all sorts against which he had to struggle, Mariette, thanks to extraordinary perseverance, to invincible tenacity and energy, overcame all difficulties ; and, after eight months' constant struggle, attained the end of his labour. A final blow from the pickaxe of a fellah opened the entrance to the sacred hypogeum.

" Mariette relates his discovery in the following terms :—

" ' The tomb of Apis is a subterranean edifice, and when, on the 12th November, 1851, I penetrated within it for the first time, I confess that I was overcome with a feeling of astonishment, which after five years is not yet quite effaced from my mind.

" ' By an accident that I have difficulty in understanding, a chamber in the tomb of Apis, closed up in the year 30 of Rameses II., had escaped the spoliations of the monument, and I had the pleasure of finding it intact. Three thousand seven hundred years had not changed its primitive appearance. The finger-marks of the Egyptian who had closed the last stone of the wall built across the door were still on the cement. Naked feet had left their imprint on the layer of sand placed in a corner of the mortuary chamber. Nothing was wanting in this receptacle of the dead, where an embalmed bull had reposed for nearly forty centuries.' "

The doorway is already invaded by sand, and it is by slipping between the wall and an enormous granite sarcophagus blocking up the entry that they reach the principal corridor. The gigantic coffers, hewn in single blocks of basalt or porphyry, or simply calcareous stone, placed in these vaults roughly hollowed out of the virgin rock, look like the colossal coffins of a race of giants. They explore the vast subterranean galleries one after the other ; the magnesium light of the guide sheds bright rays around. These sepulchral chambers, these grand remains of a civilisation that has disappeared, deeply affect them ; they leave quite oppressed, and return in silence to Mariette's house.

Onésime, who had finished his siesta, was struck with the grave expression on their faces.

" Well ! my poor Jacquot, we look very sad, very dejected. What have the Apis done to you then, to give you both such a piteous appearance ? Did they receive you badly, the rascals ? "

"No, my dear Ouésime; but one cannot contemplate without emotion a place which for thousands of years was the object of the

Interior of the Serapeum.

veneration of the entire world. One feels somewhat giddy in the face of the abyss of centuries which separates us from those who built these sacred dwellings. We are a little upset, that is all."

" It's the past that rises in your throats and stifles you, gentlemen sepulchre-hunters !

" But why are you always thrusting yourselves among these beggars of Pharaohs, and endeavouring to make their acquaintance by force ? Why torment by your presence, why persecute, on every excuse, to the bottom of their funeral vaults, individuals who have taken a dislike to you ? It's senseless !

" Here are people who have made superhuman efforts to hide their burial-places and to prevent profane hands from pulling their bones about ; who have pushed precaution to the point of boring mountains and of raising factitious ones for the purpose of concealing their coffins there and sleeping their last sleep in peace. And your first care is to go and trouble their *tête-à-tête* with death, to turn their tumuli topsy-turvy, hunt them out in their dark holes, rummage in their affairs, despoil them of their bandages, prig their jewellery, collect their chaplets, thrust your noses into their prayer-books ; briefly, to pillage them. But it's burglary ! A matter for the Court of Assizes : violation of sepulchres, Article 360 of the Penal Code. Punishable with imprisonment and hard labour.

" And, to crown all, when you have once thoroughly dislocated the poor old bones of these good-natured, inoffensive mummies, who only ask for silence and oblivion, you write all sorts of unheard-of things about them, and indecently exhibit their shapeless remains under glass cases in your museums, where they are the object of the brutal curiosity and stupid comments of the crowd !

" You will own that there is here matter for vexation, and that one should not be angry with these unfortunate mummies for showing a little ill-humour ?

" I cannot be accused of excessive tenderness for the Pharaohs. Well, I feel overcome with pity when I see the ill-bred, off-hand way in which what remains of them is treated. I've no grudge beyond the tomb, I've not !

" Look here ! The wisest thing, now that you've put all the customers of this necropolis against you, is to be off at your quickest.

" Here, Hassan ! Ahmed ! Abdallah ! Hurry up ! Quick ! Put on the saddles ! " thunders Onésime in a stentorian voice, striking the palms of his hands together, after the Oriental fashion, to call the donkey boys.

In a twist of the wrist the animals are saddled, bridled, and brought to the foot of the steps of the verandah.

" And the pyramids of Dashour ? " exclaims Jacques.

" And the wells of the ibis mummies ? "

" It's a violent interference with us," says the first.

" A forcible abduction," chimes in the Doctor.

" It's anything you like," retorts Onésime, who is not of their mind.

He is hungry ; a good dinner awaits him ; they have just time to catch the train, and shall not miss it.

" There's enough for to-day of your pyramids, hypogei, mastabas, and the rest. I am dragging you out of your nightmare, tearing you from the pursuit of folly. You do not intend, I suppose, for the unhealthy pleasure of contemplating the layers of stones in a pyramid, or of counting the feathers of a stuffed ibis, to make us lose the train and swallow a warmed-up dinner ?

" By dint of roaming in those cemeteries, rubbing against those frightful tombs, you exhale a vague odour of corpse, you smell the sepulchre."

" And you the dinner."

" I have a delicate nasal organ, my friend, and not a depraved sense of smell."

" Come, let us be off. Don't let's quarrel with your stomach."

Urging forward their donkeys, who for their part smell the stable, they set out at full speed, raising a cloud of dust. " Gambetta " bolts, " Telegraph " is worthy of his name, " De Lesseps " flies. Onésime, borne along at a wild gallop, does not notice, in his hurry to get home, Hassan's diabolical " Ah ! " who has picked up a jackal's thigh-bone on the sly, and literally massacres " De Lesseps' " buttock with it. They pass like lightning before the mastaba of El-Pharaoun and the Step Pyramid, tear through Sakarah, laming fowls, dispersing flocks of turkeys, putting all the village in commotion and the dogs at their heels, to Mitrahineh ; the children fly, the women scream out crazily, everything gives way before them ; they dash in and out of Bedrasheen at breakneck speed, and tumble into the station in time to precipitate themselves into the train. At six o'clock they are at Cairo, in a café of the Esbekieh, drowning the disagreeable perfumes of the past in a social glass.

The port of Old Cairo.

CHAPTER XIII.

Kéradec leaves for Upper Egypt.—Jacques introduces him, on the steamer, to Sir Hugh and Miss Madge.—The Doctor is disagreeably surprised to meet Reptilius on board.—A trip to the Bazaars.—The Mouski. the Khan-el-Khalil, the Nahassin, the Serougieh, the Souk-es-Sullah, El-Ghourieh.—Along the Khalig.—What remains of El-Asker and of El-Kataï.—The legend of the Tent of Amrou.—Near the aqueduct.—Filthy feast.—Old Cairo.—Its port.— With the Howling Dervishes.—Their Mosque.—An ebony-coloured maniac, a fantastical Zikr.—In the Coptic town.—The Church of Sidi Miriam.—The Mosque of Amrou.—The legend of Omar.

THE Doctor, to the great grief of Abdallah, left for Thebes this morning. He had been kind enough to delay his journey for a few days in order to pilot his friends about a little and accustom them to the country; but, notwithstanding mutual regret, he could not postpone his departure any longer. So they are deprived of their delightful cicerone and good friend.

Notwithstanding his dives into antiquity, his excursions on the ocean of hypotheses, his habit of sinking the systems of his condisciples, he rapidly rose to the surface, and hastened to reinvest himself with the air of an agreeable person, to become once more an extremely witty talker, a charming companion, a man of many parts.

He did not exhale that smell of mustiness and old folio volumes

281

that the learned generally drag along with them. He chatted, he did not pontificate. People knew a great deal after each conversation with him without feeling that he was the professor giving the lesson. He possessed peculiar talent for bringing into prominence the slight baggage of which their knowledge was made up, and for allowing his own prodigious erudition to pass unperceived ; so much so that Onésime and Jacques were sometimes quite astonished that they knew so much.

On the steamer they meet some of their acquaintances of the *Saïd* —Sir Hugh, his daughter, and Miss Priscilla—who were to stay two months at Thebes. Jacques introduces the Doctor : as Sir Hugh is a bit of an Egyptologist, and both are perfect gentlemen, they will get on very well.

She is very pretty, Miss Madge, with her magnificent light hair, piled up at the back of the head in heavy coils displaying a brown-gold shade, and sheltering her temples and forehead, which are of exquisite purity, with a silken network of rebellious tresses quivering in the wind. You like her dark blue eyes under her beautiful nut-brown brows. Her small teeth, well-set, regular, sparkle with whiteness beneath her crimson and firmly outlined lips. Her nose is straight, delicately modelled, her chin shaped with rare correctness, her neck admirably proportioned. And over all what a splendid, warm, light carnation tint, with amber tones ! She is tall, slim, elegant ; the waist is supple ; the hand is beautiful ; the foot small, narrow, arched. She walks very erect, with infinite grace and perfect ease.

" When an English girl makes up her mind to be pretty she certainly does not stop half-way," says Jacques.

" And when she decides on being ugly," answers Onésime in a whisper, gazing at Miss Priscilla, " she goes to the extreme. It's all one or all the other in England."

Some of Cook and Son's packages are also there ; they are going to Thebes, probably to break off the tip of the ear of a colossus, and to make a paperweight out of it on their return home.

Just as the steamer was about to leave, Reptilius, in a great hurry, appeared on the quay, rushed on deck out of breath, and had some

cases of a strange form placed in his cabin. Dr. Kéradec turned pale at the sight of him, and up to the last moment appeared very pre-occupied.

There is something wrong between them; they reckon each other up with severity! What on earth can it be?

A last pressure of the hand; the steamer weighs anchor. Jacques and Onésime are alone; they feel they will miss Kéradec a great deal.

They return to the Esbekieh. Onésime goes to the hotel; and while he is writing a few letters, Jacques sets out for a stroll in the Bazaars.

He first of all follows the Mouski, that great artery which cuts the Bazaar quarter in two. The Mouski, the old Frank quarter, is the only street where the East mixes so much with the West without, however, being absorbed by it. They live side by side; they bow, speak in the morning on opening the shutters, in the evening on closing them. They offer each other tea, cigarettes, during the day, and there ends the connection.

The Mouski.

Here one sees establishments of all countries, samples of all people, who wrangle in all languages; it is a regular Babel Street. There is a dealer in French novelties, separated from an American dentist by the little shop of an Arab barber;

A domesticated negro.

an Italian retailing vermouth with a German druggist for neighbour, who chats with an Israelite money-changer to whom he has let a corner of his shop, and so on.

In the road, on the footpaths, a compact crowd, a rolling flood of folks always on the move, hailing from all latitudes: Fellaheen, Arabs, Nubians, Soudanese, Syrians, Turks, Greeks, Italians, Spaniards, Frenchmen, Englishmen, Germans, Americans ; all possible races defile there, all the colours of the rainbow are displayed there. And among this multitude are loaded camels, people on horses, donkeys, mules, victorias drawn by powerful steeds

at a trot, sayces driving the crowd aside by blows from their sticks, water-carriers, ambulant dealers, soldiers—something of everybody; with cries, hustling, and an infernal noise.

From the Mouski, or rather from the New Street, the continuation of the Mouski, one turns to the left down a small, narrow lane, and comes into the midst of the Bazaar of Khan Khalil, before a high gateway striped alternately white and red.

At the first glance one sees nothing inside the gate; the street is terminated by a great black chasm,

A soldier.

which seems a hole in the enormous white wall; it is made still
darker by the vigorous opposition of one
side of the gate, which is brightly lit up by
the sun. Little by little the eye recovers
from the shock produced by the sudden
transition from shade to light; the place
becomes illuminated gently, slowly, by insensible degrees, and one discovers in the
bluish penumbra of the immense arcade a
whole world of beings and things standing
out in a sort of light, filmy, transparent
vapour.

Beneath the arch, hooked on to the sides
of the walls, are diminutive shops. From
the edge of the raised pentices hang frightful
many-coloured rags; on the shelves are copper
utensils of all forms and sizes, coffee pots with
bewitching curves, little coffee pans with long
handles, perfume burners of rare elegance,
delicious ewers, and beside them two enormous chandeliers
for mosques.
All these things,
of red or yellow
copper, shine softly in the shade with
dying reflections of blue.

In the other shops more copper
utensils, but also other things: Persian
caskets, chiselled with an art and
patience that are astounding; sabres
with handles of rhinoceros horn, the
flexible and tapering blades of which
rest in red velvet sheaths, with copper
mounts and chains; lances; Circassian
or Saracen steel armour inlaid with gold;

Types in the Mouski.

tables fashioned in the form of ogees, all covered with incrustations of mother-of-pearl and ivory ; mosque lamps—in fact, something of everything.

Inside the shop, against this background of arms and knick-knacks,

shining in semi-obscurity, a handsome old man, his head wrapped in a turban as white as snow, in a silk gown striped yellow and white, showing a piece of waistcoat of apple-green colour, is squatted on a rich Smyrna carpet before a doll's table made of deal. With the aid of a punch and a small hammer he draws marvellous arabesques, with surprising dexterity, on a tray that has just left the hands of the beater.

Beside him a beautiful child in a blue gown polishes a pair of Mameluke pistols.

At the angle of the street facing this gateway, a dealer in old clothes is enjoying his narghileh and playing a game at "namr" with a neighbour.

A woman of Cairo.

At the opposite angle another display of copper ; verses from the Koran in green letters on a black ground hang in black frames against the walls. The devout owner, curled up in a corner of his den, has given way to the sweetness of the comforting "kief" in which he dreams of Mahomet's seven heavens.

This gate of the quarter gives access to one of the principal thoroughfares of the Bazaar ; a very compact crowd moves along there. It is tolerably broad, very high, protected by a roof made of planks, reed mats, trellis-work fashioned out of palm branches, thrown on beams reaching from wall to wall. The sun penetrates through a number of openings, spreading out in a thousand rays,

Manufacturers of pipe-stems.

presenting the effect of a forest of fiery spears thrust into the wall. In places only the bare beams remain, and rare planks falling into decay

Under a gate of the Khan-el-Khalil.

19

by age. The mats, made rotten by the temperature of the air, have disappeared, with the exception of a few shreds that dangle overhead. Then one perceives the deep blue sky ; in the sky black kites, vultures, hawks, describing circles, and, from time to time, a triangle of wild geese, coming from the north, pass by. The sun bursts in through these large openings, and on the whitewashed walls streams a sheet of dazzling light, rudely intersected by lines of shade from the beams.

The road is covered with a thick layer of sand and dust ; when it rains, it becomes a marsh.

On either side shops succeed shops in a double line, broken here and there by the great wall of a ruined mosque, the carved door of a shrine, or part of a brick wall, crumbling away at the base, which threatens to tumble down, gaping holes hidden by partitions of dis-jointed planks grey with dust, floors that have fallen in.

A merchant of pottery.

From time to time one passes beneath an arch with open double doors, the folds of which, a foot in thickness, are plastered over with a coating of filth, shining in the lower part where beggars have set their backs, dull above : they are sheathed in sheets of copper furnished with triple rows of nails. A coffee-seller is installed between them. A square niche hollowed out in the breadth of the masonry contains two or three cracked white cups and a saucer with lumps of sugar. On a stove, made on the spur of the moment with stones and a handful of plaster, sings a tin jug, and a tiny copper pan full of Mocha is being kept warm in the cinders.

Sometimes, at the bottom of a turn-again alley, one perceives a

An Arab beggarwoman.

lofty building of dressed stone, and a monumental door, the aperture of which is edged with interlaced ornamentation. A flap opens, and veiled women enter, accompanied by their slaves and bathing attendants. It is a public bath; it is a day reserved to women. They make appointments with each other there, burn perfumes, aloes, and benjamin, send for singers, and treat themselves to pastry and sorbets.

A number of narrow dark irregular streets bear on this principal thoroughfare. The buildings in blocks of dressed calcareous stone are very high; the corbels of the upper floors almost touch each other, hardly permitting one to catch sight of a gap of light or a square of blue sky.

The street is full of people; they come from all sides: it is a continual rolling wave, heaving, noisy, composed of most different elements. They hurry along, elbow each other, but not roughly, and show courtesy full of good humour.

This crowd is far less disagreeable than a European one; it is more civil, less morose, and, above all, does not exhale those strong and insufferable odours that are invariably emitted in gatherings of

Northern people. This peculiar immunity, enjoyed by Orientals, and in which the great eating and drinking Northern races, under their cloudy sky, in their damp atmosphere, do not participate, is the result, among the children of the Prophet, of frequent baths, constant ablutions, great sobriety, and of a splendid climate.

Bedouins, with hard physiognomies beneath their kouffiehs fastened tight round their heads, their ample garments in camel's hair striped white and yellow, walk slowly, erect, cold, impassive. Persians, with their delicate, effeminate features, in floating silk gowns, wearing high astrakan caps on their heads, with their painted faces, their dyed hair and beards, appear like dolls beside these rough children of the desert. Here it is an Arnaut, proud in bearing, the ends of his moustache twirled up in points, looking magnificent in his crimson jacket smothered with gold, with open floating sleeves, also sprinkled with gold and lined with pink silk, his skirt of well-ironed white muslin, embroidered gaiters, with an arsenal of arms in his belt. He makes the ugliness of a fat baboon-like Turkish functionary, in tarboush and stambouline, whose spare nether garment ill dissembles a pair of feet swollen with

An Arnaut.

fat, stand out very prominently. A sturdy Montenegrin, with arched nose, eagle eyes, accentuated features, bargains for an inlaid pistol. His eye sparkles strangely when he grasps the weapon in his dry, brawny hands. Farther on, seated at the edge of an Algerine jeweller's shop, a Maghrebin from Mequinez, white and pink, exquisitely clean, wrapped in the folds of his white silk haïk, handles with his slender fingers, with nails reddened by henna, massive bracelets manufactured in the Djurjura.

Then there are negroes from the Soudan, of a deep, dull black, sly

Abyssinians, Nubians with long wavy hair, with a simple piece of cloth round the loins, Arabs from Sinai in rags, their long guns on their shoulders, fellaheen men, women, children, old men, beggars, blind men, reciting a prayer through the nose, well-to-do townsfolk, followed by their slaves, and lost in the floating folds of their long pieces of black taffetas which they hold on their chests with both hands, loaded with rings and bracelets, displaying ostentatiously their heavy feet encased in European boots.

Amidst this clamorous multitude move sordid Jewish sarafs, water-sellers with goat skins on their shoulders, leathern aprons covering their knees, striking their copper goblets one against the other, venerable imams on richly caparisoned mules, whose gowns are kissed by the people as they go by. Sometimes a " saint," naked, filthy, appears gesticulating, vociferating the name of Allah, and the crowd opens before him out of respect, mingled, perhaps, with a little disgust.

At moments the traffic is suddenly blocked by a long string of camels, which advance loaded with thick pieces of timber, rugged stone, or enormous bales. They walk silently in the dust, which deadens the sound of their tread, with long strides and a horrible waving to and fro, exhaling an insupportable odour. Their heavy and incommodious cargoes, borne along in this oscillating movement, become regular rams, striking right and left, breaking in everything before them. Woe betide him who has not taken refuge in time in a shop, or some sort of recess beyond reach of these terrible catapults! The

A lady of Cairo.

furious pendulums manœuvre without a pause, upsetting horsemen, crushing them against the walls, jostling people on foot, overturning piles of material, pounding pentices, tearing away signboards. And the impassive beast continues its disastrous march to the end of the Bazaar, indifferent to the dismay that it produces, to the damage it causes, to the perturbation it brings always with it; insensible to the cries, to the maledictions, to the blows of its victims. When these frightful camels have passed the disorder is repaired, and the street resumes its usual appearance, until the arrival of another caravan, which will again put everything in confusion.

Just as Jacques was getting on his donkey, which Ahmed had been leading by the bridle behind him, he found himself face to face with his landlord and Onésime, who, as soon as he had got through his letters, had come under the guidance of the former, to find him.

Their host took advantage of the occasion to show them—a little too rapidly, unfortunately—some other quarters of the Bazaar. Crossing that of El-Ghourieh, swarming with shawls, cashmeres, cloths, muslins, from all countries, they next inspected the coppersmiths' gallery, the Na-

Types of the Bazaar.

hassin, a labyrinth of covered lanes, extremely dirty, horridly narrow, where you can with difficulty walk two abreast. In the Souk-es-Sacegh, goldsmiths, Copts for the most part, are squatting in their miniature shops, near enormous safes with drawers full of jewels. Some are fashioning gold and silver articles on very small anvils; others make necklaces and bracelets sparkle beneath the brilliant, covetous eyes of a customer seated at the edge of their store ; a third exhibits finger and earrings in gold.

Here they are at the Serongieh, among the saddlers, embroiderers, shoemakers.

Two steps from there they turn a street corner, and are in the famous court of the Carpet Bazaar. It is half covered with mats and shreds of cloth ; here, allowing a diffuse, soft, tranquil light to filter through ; there, giving passage to a powerful ray of the sun falling firmly on the scarlet ground of a prayer carpet, which glitters in the stream of brightness. There are piles of camel bags, some of brilliant colour, others of subdued tones ; small mountains of carpets come from all parts of the East. These velvety, silky ones, with shades blended together, come from Persia ; those coarser ones, with many

Babouche Bazaar.

stripes, from Rabat, Tunis, Kurdistan ; these long squares, with grounds of garance or soft blue, which serve the disciples of the Prophet in performing their devotions, have been woven at Smyrna or Bokhara.

They leave this corner, so marvellously lit up with colour, with regret, to go to Souk-es-Sullah, where all sorts of arms are glittering—

Court of the Carpet Bazaar.

long guns of the Berbers of Rif, with their stocks curled over, enveloped with leather, ornamented with ivory and copper nails, with barrels enriched with numerous silver rings; finely chiselled bronze powder flasks from Persia; pistols, blunderbusses, yataghans; quantities of arms, helmets, stirrups, spurs, incrusted with gold; something of everything up to the antique blades of the Knights of the Crusades, to which Arab handles have been adapted.

They return to the Mouski, then to the hotel. After lunch Jacques leaves Onésime at a café in the Esbekieh, where he has commenced a series of interminable games at dominoes. Ahmed assures him that to-day there is a *Zikr* of Howling Dervishes at Old Cairo. They go to Old Cairo.

Instead of taking the Boulak Avenue and that of Kasr-el-Nil, they follow the banks of the Khalig, which are much more picturesque than the broad straight streets of the Ismaïlieh European quarter.

Here is a graceful Mosque, half lost among the tamarisks and sycamores, there a pretty Arab fountain, farther on an enormous fig tree in the dilapidated court-yard of an old house, a group of

Fellah handling shadouf.

women filling *goulahs*, and another of men performing their ablutions. A fellah handles a *shadouf*, while a Berber consolidates with the hand the sides of the small trenches that convey water over a bit of a garden adjoining a hut of dried mud. A *sakieh*, manœuvred by two buffaloes, has been perched on the summit of a block of masonry which soaks in the water. There, you see a house on piles, of which the corbelled windows, furnished with *moucharabiehs*, bulge out over the canal ; through a trap door in the floor descends a pail to draw water from the Khalig.

Through narrow, barred openings in high grey walls one perceives the heads of women ; they smile, forgetting to hide their faces.

The bank is encumbered with bawling children, grovelling in the mud, rolling with the dogs.

Voracious, bearded vultures, on the wing, catch the refuse, flung out of the windows into the Canal, as it falls ; beneath them birds pursue dragon flies.

Lizards with golden backs, silvery bellies, sky-blue tails, run along bits of old wall, overgrown with the brambles of abandoned gardens, and great greyish rats, with long ringed tails, covered with strong, stiff, prickly hair, run across the path at every moment.

On the wheel of an old *sakieh* out of use, disappearing amidst a thick cluster of plants and shrubs, jerboas with hairy feet press against each other as if in search of warmth, and give utterance to little cries ; another, a solitary one, nibbles grain in the sun on a lump of stone.

On reaching the Square, and in front of the Mosque of Seïdeh Zeïneb, they quit the banks of the Khalig, and follow a road ending at a gate bearing the name of the Mosque. They are beyond the city.

They find the Canal again on their right, but what terrible desolation on the left ! As far as the eye can see there is nothing but a succession of mounds of ruins, the remains of the two towns which, with Fostat, were built before Cairo—El-Asker, in 750 ; El-Kataï, in 870. This last, the capital of the Toulonnides, spreads around the Mosque of Touloun. The destruction of these two places in the reign of Mostansir-Billah merely preceded that of Fostat, which, in 1168, was burned by the Saracens, in the fear that it might fall into the hands of the Crusaders. It never rose from its ashes, and from then Cairo, El-Kahirah, founded two hundred years previous by Gowher, a general of El Moez, Fatimite Sultan of Maghreb, became the capital of Egypt, and its houses grew up in proximity to the Mosque of El-Azhar.

Every one has heard of the legend connected with the building of Fostat. Amrou, with the assistance of the Copts, who at the instigation of the traitor Benjamin, Archbishop of Alexandria, had come to swell the ranks of his army, had just beaten the Byzantine troops, commanded by the Greek Makaukas ; had captured Fort Babylon, where the remains of the vanquished forces were shut up, by assault ; and, finally, had made terms with Makaukas, who had sought refuge in the island of Rhoda, after his last defeat.

He then decided on marching on Alexandria, and gave orders to strike his tent, erected near Fort Babylon ; but having learned that a couple of pigeons had built their nest at the top of it, he forbade its being touched, and set out to besiege Alexandria, which he captured after a gallant resistance on the part of the inhabitants.

When he returned to Fort Babylon the tent was still standing. It was then that he determined to erect round its site a new city, which he called Fostat—the tent.

The aqueduct which brings water to the citadel divides these barren mounds at a right angle with the road. The numerous birds of prey, attracted by the pestilential smell of the slaughterhouses placed in the midst of this arid steppe, render the aspect of the place still more ominous. Mangy, hairless dogs fight over heaps of offal, quarrelling with vultures, so gorged with food that they can hardly rise from the ground, for a few shreds of filth.

Buzzards, kites, whirl round with piercing screams, awaiting the moment to take part in the hideous feast. And such a horrible stench is thrown off by this unclean banquet, that men hasten to reach the head of the aqueduct, where the wind still brings them weak puffs of the nauseous miasma.

Donkey boys and camel drivers, lying down amidst their animals in the shade of an old sycamore, do not seem in the least affected by this sickening breeze. They possess such an eclectic sense of smell !

They reach the first houses of Old Cairo, Masr-el-Atikah, by an avenue of tamarisks. They pass beneath low arches, alleys of trellis-work overrun by vines ; here and there a block of stone, an overthrown column, encumber the roadside. A thoroughfare on the right leads here to the bank of the narrow arm of the Nile, which separates the island of Rhoda from the mainland.

A little farther beyond the view is admirable. From the bank, where a number of small boats, *canges*, dahabiehs, barges, craft of various sorts are fastened, the Nile extends in all its majesty for a considerable distance towards the south. On the opposite bank one perceives, behind a long curtain of dark palm trees, the pink pyramids, standing out against the grey-blue sky, and, in the near foreground, thousands of yawls with white sails ploughing the river under the influence of a strong north wind.

It is the port of Old Cairo, very picturesque, very active. Along the quays are hewn stone, sacks of corn, bundles of sugar-cane and *dourah*; the ground is sprinkled with broken straw; everywhere are planks, sleepers, staved-in cases; fastened to stakes stuck in the mud are vessels unloading. Here, there are two craft joined together by ropes and a flooring of beams, heaped up to the height of a first floor with pottery. This cumbersome cargo is maintained by a strong net with large meshes, which entirely covers it. There is

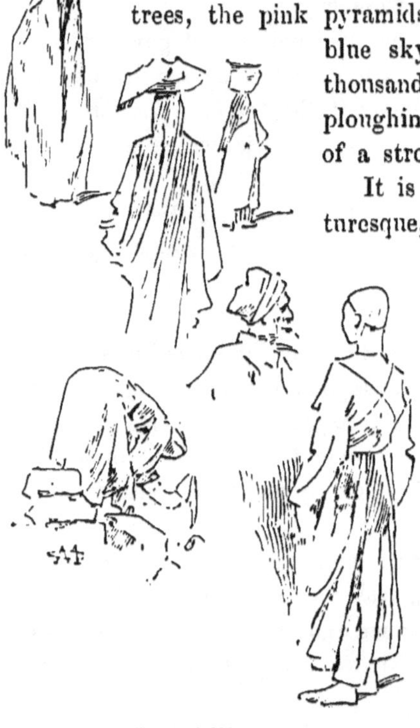

Types of Old Cairo.

another double vessel containing a mountain of straw, a freight of barley. Then there are dahabiehs from Assouan, with goods and passengers from Nubia and the Soudan, a ferry passing between Bedrasheen and Old Cairo, loaded enough to make the boat sink. There is everything in this Noah's Ark—fellaheen men and women, Bedouins, negroes, asses, camels, overwhelmed by the weight of their bales, cases, cages of fowls, *kouffas* of fruit. The people all grumble, and gesticulate in an inconceivable way. A *reïs* squabbles with his sailors, a fellaheen woman quarrels with the ferryman, a camel that has got its bales off its back and is dragging them behind by a cord, causes dismay on all sides, bellows frightfully, donkeys roll with their saddles in the mud, and amidst this topsy-turvydom swarms of children as naked as worms increase the clamour by their deafening yells.

They regain the principal thoroughfare, and finally, quite at the end of the town, come to the *Tekké* of the *dervishes* at the Mosque.

A small low door gives access to a spare garden. Rose trees in full bloom entwine their branches over the bowers made of reeds ; black currant bushes, with yellow flowers, pomegranates, rose-laurels, grow everywhere. One or two tamarisk trees shade the courtyard, at the bottom of which opens the very simple, very dilapidated door of the Mosque.

In this courtyard a strange creature gives himself up to contortions while pronouncing the name of Allah. He is a negro. His head almost disappears beneath an immense white turban surmounted by a yellowish rag. He is as black as night, his skin is shiny, his eyes sparkle

A saint.

strangely, his large half-opened mouth permits of one seeing his small teeth, which are remarkably white ; the expression of ferocity and exaltation on his countenance is frightful to behold. On his scarlet gown, embroidered with gold, hangs a scimitar enveloped in linen ; a Morocco *djellabah*, with a large hood, all patched with odd pieces, covers his shoulders. He clasps in his hand a long flute, from which he from time to time draws a sharp note.

At our approach his haggard eyes sparkle ; he repeats with

ferocious and painful volubility, that almost resembles a sigh, a phrase in which the name of Allah occurs constantly ; Ahmed kisses the hem of his garment. He is mad, but quite inoffensive. Two *dervishes* quietly say a few words to him, which have the effect of calming him,

Panoply of arms in the *Tekké* of the dervishes.

and Jacques enters the Mosque, where he joins some other Europeans who are penned up in an angle of the building. A very polite Arab offers him a straw-seated chair.

There are a dozen ladies and gentlemen. Some English ladies pull out their notebooks, their diaries, and watch for their impressions as they come, to carefully inscribe them there, rigorously, with the date, the exact hour, according to a well-regulated chronometer, when this important event took place. Some elderly parties are accompanied by their dragomans, tall, strapping Syrians. They are full of attention for their mistresses, who thank them with little movements of the eyes that are indiscreetly significative.

The room is large, square, bare. At the angles plaster alveoli, fashioned circularly in sloping gradations, con-nect the plain parts with the curved; a broad frieze of a geometrical design serves as plinth to the dome; light comes from rectangular barred windows placed above the frieze.

A dervish.

Before us, in a Gothic arch some feet deep, arranged in the thickness of the wall, are hanging pikes, axes, halberds, reaping-hooks, iron maces, chains, pincers, spits, cutlasses—all the imple-ments of a prison of the Inquisition. In the wall on our left is sunk a semi-circular arched niche, the *mirhab*, with interlaced work, ornamented at the angles by two Doric columns. It may measure four feet in breadth by eight feet in height. Near the left column is a flowing green flag, a corner of the material being secured by a nail fixed in the wall; on the other side are displayed a series of squares of cardboard, on which are written quotations from the Koran.

A dervish with fine, regular features stands erect before the *mirhab*. He wears a tall, round black sugar-loaf hat on his head, surrounded at the base by a turban wound very tight, and is clothed in a long dark floating gown, very full, open down the front. A second gown, underneath, of mauve silk, shows, at the top, the points of his jacket of a tender blue; below it, the ends of his orange-coloured trousers. He grasps a small flute in his elegant, well-taken-care-of hand; from time to time he carries it to his lips, produces from it a soft, ethereal note, and indicates on the spot a giddy turn of waltz, in a space no larger than a crown piece.

Beside him the musicians try their instruments. One is squatting down, a *darabouka* between his legs; another, standing, strikes with his fingers on a sort of large flat drum; a third is on his knees before a tambourine, which he beats with a pair of small sticks rounded at the ends; the fourth, seated on a small form, blows in a clarionet or hautbois. Behind these are three or four other musicians with cymbals, viols, rebecks.

Around them, in a semi-circle, the arms falling at the sides, stand

Howling dervish.

some thirty howling dervishes in long gowns of different colours, fastened tight round the waist with a red silk sash; for head-gear green, white, bright crimson turbans, fezzes, tarboushes, woollen or linen caps. Their babouches are behind them on the mats; they have naked feet, and one sees the bottoms of their trousers, that descend to the ankle. Most of them have hair of extraordinary length, dyed with henna and falling to their knees. They are of all ages.

At a signal from the chief, who turns slowly round with his arms crossed on his breast, the musicians play a dull, strange, plaintively modulated melody. The dervishes all uncover at the same moment, and, bending the loins, balance themselves slowly at first, from front to back, in one general movement, pronouncing in time at each jerk the name of " Allah ! " Little by little the swinging motion is accelerated, the voices are raised, the see-saw motion is accentuated still more, the voices burst out. At intervals the shrill, sharp, piercing note of the little flute is heard above the sound of this rumbling wave, starts like an arrow, and seems to penetrate the flesh; the cymbals ring amidst the hollow roll of the daraboukas. The oscillations become precipitate, the voices hoarse; then, finally, in the paroxysm of intense excitement produced by this music, the broken, wild rhythm of which acts powerfully on their nerves, a prey to savage, delirious exaltation, furious, white with foam, out of their wits, almost rattling,

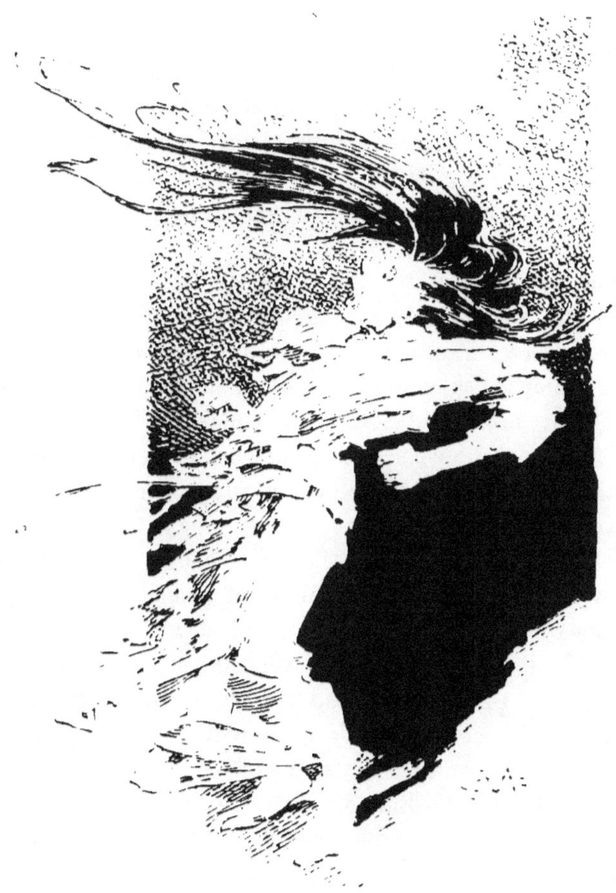

Howling dervish.

they twist themselves in frightful contortions, and always with that regulated, terrible, bewildering, all-together swing. Their bodies bend fearfully; their hair whips the air, sweeps the ground; the voices yell the name of Allah in a scanned measure, a threatening roar, going always crescendo.

The ladies with the pocket-books have found the performance shocking and the howling dervishes disgusting, which does not prevent one of them, on leaving, from dexterously taking a pair of scissors from her pocket and cutting a lock from the mane of one of the dervishes on the sly—a souvenir, to corroborate the impressions. The ladies with the dragomans have almost fainted in the arms of their Mamelukes. They depart, very much affected, very red, supported by these handsome men, striped from head to foot with gold lace.

The company walk in the little garden. Dervishes are seated beneath the trellis-work smoking cigarettes, drinking tea; they offer some to the visitors. Those of the *zikr* are not long in making their appearance. They are calm, smiling; not a single drop of perspiration falls from their bronzed faces; their hands do not tremble; the breathing is regular, the voice clear; they are in perfect possession of their faculties. One can hardly realise it after their violent gymnastic exercise of a little while ago.

At the moment of leaving, Jacques thanks the chief of the dervishes, who, with the grand manners of people of his race, offers him a delicious cup of Persian tea, perfumed with peppermint, in a crystal cup. He is exquisitely polite, even refined. He escorts Jacques to his donkey, gives him a final and very courteous greeting, crossing his two hands on his chest; and Jacques, with his donkey and donkey boy, makes his way towards the Mosque of Amrou.

Ahmed points out to him, on their left, a block of houses, surrounded by high walls pierced by gates. It is the old Coptic town, and the fortifications enclosing it are those of ancient Babylon, the fortress where Rameses II. detained his Assyrian captives, where the Roman legion entrusted with the duty of holding Egypt under the domination of the Cæsars was garrisoned.

They advance towards one of the entrances of this refuge of Egyptians who have remained Christians. The gate is more than a foot thick. It is a rampart rolling on hinges. The streets are singularly narrow, damp, dark, and repulsively dirty. The light hardly passes through these lofty walls, which almost touch each other. They are bored with barred openings in the form of loopholes. Disjointed moucharabiehs hang threatening above your head; you dabble in nauseous pools, slip over putrefying offal; you burst the expanded bellies of dead cats with a tread, and horrible stenches exhale from this uncleanness.

It is with difficulty that one is able to make a way among the ragged children eaten up with vermin, with bad eyes, and a complexion the colour of lead. They follow you, rub against you, slip between your legs, touch your clothes with an over-hasty movement, eagerly feeling your pockets.

Tall, thin, veiled women, with hard features, foreheads tattooed with a blue cross, eyebrows blackened with *koheul*, lean against the wall with the stiffness of statues to allow you to pass, the eyes fixed, the hands extended. Old, sordid men, with black or blue turbans, exhibit repulsive ulcers to excite compassion. From all these rises a vile, stuffy smell that makes you feel sick. One hastens to escape from such ambient corruption.

After ten minutes' walk in a labyrinth of streets, an inextricable entanglement of courts, crossways, blind alleys, they pass under some arches, and halt before a barrier of disjointed planks—the entrance to the Coptic church of the Virgin Mary, Sidi Miriam, and the guardian shows them in.

It is lugubrious, black, dirty. Partitions in tolerably well-worked wooden mosaic separate the three naves, formed by a double row of columns, from the edifice, built in a basilic form. Niches in the walls, incrustations of mother-of-pearl and ivory on the woodwork, polished by time and the backs of the faithful, heads of apostles painted on a gold ground, in the Byzantine style, Greek crosses, and that is all, with a close, sharp, dry, penetrating smell and the vile uncleanliness that is general.

Jacques gives the *boab* a few piastres, and they get out of this *mellah* quickly, followed by the clamour of the inhabitants demanding bakshcesh.

At last they are in the open air; they breathe, and soon come before the Mosque of Amrou, the Gâm-'a-Amr, the first mosque built by the Arabs in Egypt in the year 21 of the Hegira. It is the most complete type of Arab art at its origin, the most faithful representation of the primitive mosque.

From the outside, this square, grey, powdery mass, flanked by its two minarets ending in points, having only one gallery, is imposing in its simplicity.

A door in the form of a trefoil leaf, surmounted by an ogival window, opens under one of the minarets into a first court. When you enter the second immense court, surrounded by its galleries, its forests of columns, you feel penetrated by the magnitude of the conception which presided at the erection of this monument of the piety of the first believers, and very much struck by the great silence, the absolute solitude, that reigns here.

The colonnades, with three rows of pillars on the north and south sides, are half in ruin, and on the west there remains only one arcade. The sanctuary is against the façade, turned towards the east, facing Mecca. These interminable straight lines, through which an attenuated light sports with effects of shade and brightness of an harmonious soft grey, produce within you a singular sensation of calm, repose, reflection.

All these columns of a single piece of granite, of marble or porphyry, of different sizes and forms, were torn from the Greek and Roman temples of Heliopolis and Memphis, and set up indifferently as to style. A Corinthian capital faces an Ionic volute, a composite one adjoins a Doric; some of the columns have even been placed head downwards, the capital serving as a base; others, too short, have been raised by a stone socle. An entire scaffolding of beams, fixed in between the stones of the arches, serves to maintain this multitude of pillars.

Ahmed conducts Jacques to the middle of the sanctuary, near the *mirhab* and *mimbar*, in carved wood, where stands the famous column bearing a white vein, which passes for being the mark of the courbash of the Khalif Omar.

Mosque of Amru.

This, according to tradition, is how the thing happened. The Khalif Omar was reciting his evening prayer at Mecca. When he had ended, his thoughts went to Amrou, who was building the Mosque by his orders. He gazed in the direction of Cairo, and perceived that one of the pillars just set up in the edifice was wanting in stability and badly dressed. The Commander of the Faithful immediately ordered a column lying at his feet to go to Fostat. It trembled, but did not quit the ground; at the second injunction it slightly oscillated, without, however, making up its mind to leave. The Khalif, irritated, struck it with his courbash, exclaiming: "In the name of the all-powerful and merciful God, go!" This time the obedient column moved, and, launching into space, came and stood in the place of the defective pillar.

In the sanctuary Ahmed also shows the columns of the ordeal— a magnificent pair standing pretty close together. He passes between the two shafts with tolerable ease, and urges Jacques to follow his example. The latter hesitates to make the trial, for while he does not possess the circular amplitude of Onésime, he has not the thin spine of a house-top cat like Ahmed. It appears that it is only true Believers who can undergo the ordeal victoriously. If such be the case, there must be a multitude of lean people in Mahomet's Paradise.

In the south-east angle of the Mosque rests the body of Amrou in a rectangular stone tomb, beneath a pointed top, supported by small slender columns.

In the centre of the immense bare court one perceives, like an oasis in the desert, the fountain for ablutions, quite diminutive, with its palm tree and cluster of acacias.

Ahmed endeavours to make Jacques understand, with a great many gestures and a few French words, that this fountain communicates with the Zem-Zem well at Mecca. As a proof in support of it, he assures him, by the beard of the Prophet, that pilgrims from Cairo having, one day, while on a pilgrimage to the Holy City, let fall a chaplet in the said well, found it on their return in the fountain for ablutions of the Mosque of Amrou.

Jacques gives Ahmed to understand that he is quite of his opinion, that it is beginning to get late, and that if they wish to get back before night they have no time to lose. Then, digging with his heels on both sides, he returns to Cairo by the Gate of El Karafeh, the Mahomet Ali Square and Boulevard, and reaches the Esbekieh just as the cafés are being lit up for the evening.

Tombs of the Mamelukes.

CHAPTER XIV.

The Bazaars again.—The way Onésime operates.—The *môristan* of Kalaoun and his Mosque.—That of Nas'r-Mohammed.—Round about the Mosques.—The perfumery bazaar.—An old quarter.—The tombs of the Mamelukes.—El-Achraf-Ynal. — El-Ghouri. — El-Barkouk. — El-Achraf-Barsebaï. — Kaït-Bey. — The Mosque of El-Azhar.—The Boulak Avenue.—The snake charmer.—The animal showman.—The Boulak Museum.—The rooms in the Museum.—The mummies of Deïr-el-Behari.—Fabulous antiquity of the Egyptians.—The Boulak Port. —The island of Ghezireh.—The Ghezireh drive.—They leave for Upper Egypt.

DURING the two weeks that have passed since the Doctor left, Jacques and Onésime have done nothing but trot from one to the other of the four cardinal corners of Cairo. They think each time that they have seen everything, and every day discover something new that requires their attention.

Their favourite promenade is the Bazaar. Every one knows them there ; they are welcomed with affable politeness and many bows; are offered innumerable cups of tea, and shown wonderful things. First of all, they are asked exaggerated sums ; it is the custom, and they are caught like every one else. It is a sort of tax levied on ingenuousness, the first surprise of the newly disembarked. But, little by little, they discuss, bargain, the pretensions are lowered, and now they pay reasonable prices, about the same as those of the country.

Onésime has a wonderfully smart way of doing business to the seller's advantage. On the other hand, Jacques, ever since he was so outrageously robbed in a transaction at the commencement, will not hear of any more bargaining. This is very humiliating for his companion, but so it is. He gossips for hours with the dealers, who all understand a few words of French, offers them cigarettes, inquires after their family, gives them some advice on matters of hygiene, instils his good humour into them, and dazzles them with his superb verbosity. Finally, he proves to them, what they know already very well, that their goods are frightfully overpriced, places in their hands the third of the sum asked for, gravely takes possession of the purchased article, hands it to Hassan, who promptly slips it into his leather bag, and continues the conversation unmoved, deaf to the protests of the vendor. The dealers are naturally a little surprised at this off-hand way of ending the difference ; but the purchaser, as a matter of fact, has at least given the value of the article, and as they are good customers, there is laughter on both sides, and the matter is settled pleasantly.

Door of the Mosque of Kalaoun.

This morning they are taking their usual turn in the Bazaar, and are going to pay a visit to the mosque and *môristan* of Kalaoun and Nas'r Mohammed.

This group of monuments in the midst of Khan-el-Khalil is most picturesque. From the exterior the mosque looks very pretty, with its lofty walls striped red and white, surmounted by its imposing minaret,

A street of the Bazaar.

rather bulky, with superposed terraces, square at the base with an octagonal terrace, and ending by a cylindric drum with a circular gallery. The bewitching arabesques of the drum, the delicacy of the elegant open sculpture of the balconies, atone for the rather heavy aspect of the building as a whole. A display of charming ideas, arranged with undoubted taste, affords ample compensation for the irregularity in the plan of the edifice.

You enter by a high door giving access to both the mosque and the hospital.

The mosque is decorated with more extravagance than art. An octagonal canopy, supported by slender marble columns, covers the old Sultan's body. Finely carved wooden railings surround the tomb. Visits are paid to the relics of Kalaoun: his turban which heals headaches, his silk kaftan which drives away fevers, his leathern belt which brings back luck to the penniless. Women come to ask him for male children ; mothers bring their babes in order that they may speak early.

A public writer.

On leaving, under the arcades, groups of fellaheen men and women and Arabs argue in a lively way with lawyers ; a public writer, installed on the shaft of an overturned column, seems very busy with the clients surrounding him.

The hospital, the *móristan*, situated behind the mosque and tomb, is connected with these buildings. They do not enter it : the place is very well conducted, they are told, and has accommodation for about a hundred patients. Lunatics were also shut up there at one time in rooms set apart : they have now a special house at Boulak.

The streets bordering on the mosque are very much frequented and encumbered by ambulant dealers. Here a country woman is squatting down between a cage of fowls and a basket of eggs ; there is an old Jew, who is seated on a boundary stone, a bundle of sticks on his knees ; farther on a Syrian, his head wrapped up in a coloured handkerchief, is selling a *moja* ; there is a cake-seller in a blue gown, or a confectioner with his urchin customers weighing out a few ounces of nougat. An auctioneer, bowed down beneath the weight of garments and things of all sorts, moves about with his eyes and ears on the alert : he almost disappears under his goods.

With three or four rugs on his head ; a piece of clothing rolled round his neck ; carpets, jackets, embroidered stuffs, on his arms ; chains, bracelets, pistols, in his hands, he accosts you, follows you

The perfumery bazaar.

for whole hours, leaves you for another customer, rejoins you, begs, insists, asks exorbitant prices, reduces them a little, more still, and ends, while laughing, gesticulating, bawling as loud as he possibly can, by selling you something, and often at a moderate price. Groups of Bedouins walk along indifferently, carrying antelopes' and rams' horns on their shoulders, which hook you as they pass.

At the perfumery bazaar, near here, women, seated on a form before a shop, talk a great deal, purchase little, and gaze eagerly when

Tombs of the Mamelukes.

a European of the fair sex happens to come along. The shopkeepers, almost all Persians, the eyes enlarged by antimony, the beard soft and carefully combed and trimmed, attired in silk gowns, with pointed hats on their heads, perfumed, obsequious, are smoking cigarettes, extended on soft carpets.

Beside the *môristan* rises the mosque containing the tomb of Nas'r Mohammed, son of Kalaoun. Its elegant gateway, of a Gothic aspect, is remarkable ; the harmonious lines of its minaret, covered with arabesques, surrounded by well-sculptured galleries, stand out in bold profile of a fine mould.

The two friends leave the Bazaar to visit the Necropolis of Kaït-Bey, commonly, but improperly, termed the tombs of the Khalifs.

The real site of the sepulchre of the Eyoubite Khalifs, independent sovereigns of Egypt from the ninth to the twelfth century, was rather where the Khan Khalil now stands. When the Bazaar was built under the Baharite Mamelukes, the tombs and the remains they covered were carried outside the city, and thrown pell-mell amongst the ruins. An exception was made for that of Es-Salah-Eyoub, the last sovereign but one of the Eyoubite dynasty. His son was assassinated by the chief of his guard, El-Moëz, the founder of the family of the Baharite Mamelukes.

To get to the Necropolis, Jacques and Onésime follow the zigzag of very narrow streets, excessively peopled, of a quarter that has preserved all its physiognomy of other times almost intact. There are delicately sculptured gateways, very well preserved moncharabiehs displaying charming fancy, corbels supported by beams worked with perfect art, the edges of which are as sharp and neat as if they had just left the hands of the sculptor, and a large stirring, active, gay population.

One never tires of admiring the expressive features of these bronzed, energetic, meek, dreamy, and never vulgar heads—or contemplating the light gait, the easy movements, the assured step, of these figures full of irresistible charm.

The desert commences at the Gate of El-Nas'r. After a short laborious walk in the sand, where the asses sink in noiselessly to the middle of the legs, they are in the Necropolis of Kaït-Bey.

The impression felt at the grandiose spectacle of these rows of mosques, these tombs full of harmonious lines, with ornaments of exquisite delicacy, elegant minarets, cupolas of so pure a curve, is indelible; and when the setting sun illuminates these marvels of architecture by a final beam, the lofty walls glitter with tones of purple and gold, the slender minarets are lit up, the angles of their balconies catch the light that glides along the sculpture, accentuating the reliefs, deepening the shades, and the cupolas, beneath the network of their lace arabesques, sparkle with a myriad of flashes.

In face of the splendour of these ruins, crumbling slowly beneath the action of centuries and the carelessness of man, amidst the incomprehensible indifference of the descendants of those who built them, one feels an unutterable melancholy.

Onésime himself, who is not very easily moved, is slightly touched, no doubt out of sympathy for his friends the Sultans.

The Gate of El-Nas'r.

"I do not know," he remarks to Jacques, "but in contemplating these masterpieces which are hopelessly lost, I feel something undefinable like sadness."

"We are in mourning for these monuments, the ruin of which is near at hand."

"As one weeps beforehand for a friend whom the doctors have given over—isn't it so?"

"Something like that."

" Bah ! After all, the responsibility rests with the Arabs."

" With the Arabs ! " says Jacques, shrugging his shoulders ; " why, they are children, the Arabs, and consequently irresponsible, and it is to us that belongs the duty of elevating this race."

" Its monuments first of all ; for if we do not very soon give these poor old things crutches, they will not last very long," answers Onésime, "and that is the effect of the stick on the backbone of a nation—it softens it. Ah ! those beggarly Pharaohs, those inventors of the stick and the way to use it, as our dear Doctor pretends that they invented everything, if I had hold of them—— "

Pending the moment when Onésime would get hold of the Pharaohs, the friends continue across the Necropolis. On the way Onésime stops before the Mosque of El-Achraf-Ynal, attached to that of El-Ghouri by a long wall broken up by openings ; its pretty minaret in floors and graceful cupola have bewitched him.

Here they are facing the vast and splendid Mosque of El-Barkouk, the glorious Sultan who, on two occasions, stopped the Mogul Timour-Leng in his victorious march. The opposition between the severe lines of its lofty walls, with layers of red and white stone, crowned by loopholes in the form of the trefoil leaf, and the elegant silhouettes of its two minarets of different form built up in floors, joined one to the other by intelligently combined corbels, has a most happy effect.

The court, full of rubbish, plants, brambles, with its fountain for ablutions in ruins in the centre, presents a grand aspect with its surrounding of porticoes. Those on the west form two rows of galleries, those on the north and south only one, and those of the sanctuary on the east three, with six pillars each. The *mimbar*, in deliciously-cut stone, is a marvel.

The room where the tomb is has the lower part of its walls covered with marble ; it contains the stone mausoleum, very simple, surrounded by a delicately worked balustrade of wood. The angles are connected with the curved parts by pendentives, which slope up in stages to join the base of the roof. The dome has a charming effect, with its windows flanked by ornaments, its interlaced work, its bands of Cufic letters.

They pass by the half-ruined Mosque of El-Achraf-Barsebaï without entering ; its minaret, devoid of any ornament, has little interest, but its cupola is very pretty, and sculptured with great refinement.

A moment afterwards they find themselves in a poor dilapidated village with low mud houses. Along the street are a few shops with rags hanging from their pentices, and orange-sellers ; in the square camels lying down, asses, tattered children, old men seated on a form of dried earth, the frontage of a low coffee-house, and facing them the Mosque of Kaït-Bey commanding all the village. It is with difficulty that from the narrow square one tries to get a general view of the monument, which is surrounded by hideous buildings, and so to form an idea of the beauty of its proportions.

Its graceful cupola is charming, with the relief of its network of arabesques; and its minaret, shooting up with its projections, its offsets, its endless embroidery on stone, its balconies, has a boldness, a purity of line, that are surprising.

A staircase with disjointed steps leads to a high door, which recalls, on a small scale, that of the Mosque of Sultan Hassan. The interior court, open to the elements, is all paved with marble mosaics, and communicates with the sanctuary, a step higher, by a beautiful horse-shoe arch. The ceiling of the sanctuary is carved, painted, and gilded wood, in exquisite taste ; the rose-windows are cut in the massive stone in rare perfection. But all this is falling in ruins, is crumbling away bit by bit, like everything in the East.

On their return to the square, Onésime sends Ahmed and Hassan to fetch coffee, which is drunk without quitting the stirrups, and they re-enter Cairo at the fall of night by the Gate of El-Ghoraïb.

The next morning they are strolling again in the Bazaar. They go there quite naturally, by instinct, as a clerk goes to his office. They exchange politenesses with their acquaintances, majestic old men, very cunning, in pink, lemon-coloured, or pistachio-green silk gowns ; or filthy, shrewd, wily Jews : they absorb a number of cups of tea and coffee. Onésime does business.

They are now going to visit the Mosque of El-Azhar, " the splendid " ; one of their friends in the cloth bazaar has offered to take them there.

Tomb of Kait-Bey.

Originally founded by Gowher-el-Kaïd, the general of the Fatimite Sultan of Maghreb, El-Moëz, in the year 970, it was later on rebuilt and successively increased in size at different periods by the Sultans Bibars, Kaït-Bey, and El-Ghouri. It has always preserved the double character of a mosque and university, which it possessed from its foundation, when the Khalif Aziz - Billah endowed a college there. The reputation of its schools, directed by the most celebrated doctors in theology and Mussulman law, was universal, and even now students flock to it from all parts of the world.

It is here that they still warm up the fanaticism of the neophytes to white heat : here that the password is received by the chiefs of certain sects, who then disperse among all the convents, the *zaouïas* of the Mussulman world, the affiliated of which— the *merbouts*—by their inflamed preaching excite the populations, and pro-

The Mosque of El-Azhar.

voke those constant religious risings, so terribly repressed by the ruling Powers.

They soon perceive the minarets of the mosque, and a narrow street brings them to the principal door, recently restored. Their guide enters first of all, and returns a few moments afterwards with a sheïkh, whose presence will spare them a host of difficulties: after an exchange of greetings, they follow him.

Two sanctuaries open on either side of the entrance passage, which leads to a first and very small court, where the students, squatting down on mats, are being shaved. From there they pass into the grand court, surrounded by colonnades, supporting lofty brick walls covered with a coating of stucco. The sanctuary is imposing, with its thousands of columns of granite, marble, porphyry, of Greek or Roman origin, and its innumerable lamps.

An Ulema of El-Azhar.

The porticoes on the north and south serve as schoolrooms for the pupils; partitions of wooden bars separate the groups of different nationalities in quarters, *rouags*, having each their superintendent, the *nagher*, and their professors under the high direction of a head-master.

All the nations, all the races of Islam, are represented here: Turks, Persians, Kurds, Hindoos, Syrians, Arabs from Hedjaz, Maghrebins, Algerines, Tripolitans, Nubians, negroes from the Soudan and Kordofan.

They are all here: those of the north and those of the extreme south, those of the west and those of the east; the Ottomans of Stamboul, the blacks of the Sahara, the inhabitants of Maghreb-el-Aksa, and Hindoos from the banks of the Ganges. Turks, Mongols, negroes, Hindoos, white, yellow, black, red, they have all forgotten their country, their difference of origin, their special character, their peculiar affinities.

Maintained by the Koran in a formidable cohesion, trained by stern discipline, subjected to inflaming practices, they form but one nation—a threatening fanaticised army, always ready to rush upon Europe at the voice of a Mahdi, or a Moslem impostor of any sort.

Grouped by quarters, they come to follow the classes, listen to the lessons of the learned Ulemas, commenting on the Koran, teaching it according to the four rites—malekite, chafeite, hanafite, and hanhibite—practised in Egypt, explaining the laws of the Prophet. Boarded at the mosques, they also receive a slight monthly allowance and oil for the lamps. Gathered together in circles, holding their tablets in their hands, lying or sitting on the mats that cover the ground, they learn aloud by heart verses of the Koran, which they recite in a drawling and monotonous tone, with that strange swinging of the body that is peculiar to Orientals. Others listen attentively to the explanations of a doctor in theology or a professor of law who has his back to a column. This one, on his knees, turns over the pages of a huge book placed on a stand. Others, rolled up in blankets, are extended on the ground half asleep. One is deafened by the immense hum of all these voices dissolving into one unique, dull, intense, incessant clamour—made giddy by the perpetual oscillations of these thousands of turbans.

They look at the new-comers, murmur a few words that the latter do not understand—no doubt a malediction upon these dogs of Christians, which their guides repeat *in petto*; but the party move about without difficulty.

The sheïkh then conducts them to Zawyet-el-Oumidn, the Chapel of the Blind. A special fund, taken from pious legacies, is set apart to keep these unfortunates, who also follow the classes of the school, and are not the least fanatical among the pupils.

Between the lessons the students unite in groups, converse with visitors, receive their relatives, nibble a cake of doura or a tart. One purchases an orange, another a lot of figs, a handful of dates, of a strolling dealer, who will retire when the classes recommence. Water-sellers make their copper goblets ring.

The Mosque of El-Azhar was the last refuge of those in revolt on the occasion of the insurrection in Cairo against Bonaparte, two months after the city was captured. Having barricaded all the issues, they obstinately continued the struggle. Batteries placed on Mokattam swept them down; they refused to surrender. At length the grenadiers, having surrounded the mosque and opened fire against it, the rebels, taken between two attacks, fearing to be buried beneath the ruins of the building, already shaken by the cannon-balls, surrendered at discretion to the "Sultan of the cannonade."

The sheïkh reconducts them to the door with a number of salaamliks. Onésime bows to him in Oriental fashion, like a real son of Islam; Jacques thanks him as well as he is able; and they leave him to his studies and his pupils. At the Bazaar their cicerone offers them a cup of tea in his shop. They purchase some knick-knacks of him, and return to the Esbekieh.

After a rapid snack, Jacques leaves Onésime, who has a revenge to take at billiards, and sets out for Boulak with Ahmed.

The avenue which leads there is very much frequented. There is a great traffic of carriages, horsemen, persons on foot, porters, asses, camels. The thoroughfare is broad, has plenty of air; but one is blinded by the dust. They soon reach the Khedive's stables, turn to the left to go to the Museum, and are at Boulak. Crossing the streets of this suburb, they think of the terrible resistance that its inhabitants in revolt maintained there against Kleber, a struggle in which his soldiers had to take each house by assault, to engage in a combat in every street.

Farther on they pass rapidly by an animal showman and his unfortunate victims—an equilibrist goat, monkey gymnasts, a learned dog, and donkeys—poor beasts that he atrociously torments.

Here they are at last at the Museum, that incomparable collection got together by Mariette by dint of energy and perseverance, and so zealously continued by Maspéro.

In the courtyard are sphinxes engraved with the name of Thotmes III., sarcophagi, a colossus of Rameses II. in pink marble, other colossi of kings in grey granite, the statue of a woman covered with the peplum in white marble, a pedestal of Arsinoe, a somewhat defaced cippus.

In the absence of the Doctor to initiate Jacques into the hidden mysteries of all these monuments, Mariette's clear and learned notice serves to guide him through the venerable remains of old Egyptian civilisation.

In the small hall are a fragment of a stela, a Greek head in white marble, a bust of a Roman emperor in red porphyry.

Sphinx of the time of the Hyksos.

In the large hall you notice, among other objects, a head of Pharaoh covered with a *pschent* in black granite, bas-reliefs, stelæ, inscriptions, mummies' coffins, tables for offerings, a *naos*.

The room of the Ancient Empire! Here one finds the most ancient monuments of Egypt: a sarcophagus in pink granite; the sepulchre of a certain Konfou-Ankh, a functionary who lived six thousand years ago; panels of wood carved by a masterly hand; upright stones of the doorways from the tomb of Hoti; a wooden stela from that of Scheri;

another monolith stela of the tomb of Sabou. They are articles of remarkable execution and precision of touch ; it is the work of a people in full civilisation, and not the rude attempts of a nation in its infancy.

The Hyksos Room contains the only monuments known of this period that can give us some information about the invasion of those Asiatics, who, after having put Egypt to the brand and sword, held it for more than five centuries under their domination.

In the Centre Room are objects of all sorts — religious, funeral, civil, historical : bronzes of Osiris, Isis, Horus, Anubis, Ammon ; a porcelain of Typhon ; a faïence of Thoth ; a statuette of Neïth in lapis-lazuli. And here are funeral rituals, beetles, bolsters, sandals, mummies of ibis, and the famous wooden statue of the Sheïkh El-Beled with his stick in his hand. Finally, the beetles with royal cartouches, pails, vases, a vessel in massive silver, an axe, a statue of Chephren in diorite, supremely majestic, Cheops' stone, a full-length statue of Osiris.

Statue of Sheïkh El-Beled.

The Eastern Room possesses beetles, cases of mummies, Canopus vases, pectorals, amulets, statues of the Ancient Empire, arms of all periods, furniture, utensils, clothes, bronze tools, axes, knives, and scissors.

In the Jewel Room one remains a long time before the glass case enclosing those of Queen Aah-hotep : bracelets of gold and pearls, earrings, a splendid gold necklace in repoussé of marvellous workman-ship, and rings ; a fly-flipper, and an axe in cedar-wood, of which the handles are completely covered with leaves of gold ; a boat and its crew in massive gold ; a superb alabaster statue of Queen Ameniritis : and the two statues in calcareous stone of Ra-hotep and Nefert, contemporaneous with King Snefru of the third dynasty—the two most ancient statues known of the Ancient Empire, and consequently of the world.

Then, finally, here are the famous royal mummy boxes which Maspéro has just discovered at Deïr-el-Bahari in the plain of Thebes. They are here in the Eastern Room, hardly unpacked. Most of these mummies are so well preserved, that after more than three thousand years one can still clearly catch the expression of their features. Maspéro, who is present, gives Jacques some information concerning the mummies, after having related the details of the discovery.

They are the Theban Sekenen-Ra-Taaken and Queen Ansera of the seventeenth dynasty. Sekenen is the Conqueror of the Hyksos, the hero of the War of Independence against those Asiatics. He must have died on the field of battle, struck down by two terrible blows : one, probably a cut from an axe, which split his jaw ; the other a thrust from a lance, which must have penetrated above the arch of the right eyebrow. He bears an expression of intense suffering on his face, and has bitten his tongue in his agony.

Tall, slim, muscular, he has a long head rounded by black hair, deeply set eyes, a straight nose, large at the base, cheeks bulging out, the maxillary glands being very pronounced.

Beside him is Ahmes, his descendant, then his son Amenhotep, Queens Ahmes-Nofretari, Aak-hotep, Houtimos, Prince Se-Amen, Princess Set-Amen, Kings Thotmes I., Thotmes II., Thotmes III., all of the eighteenth dynasty.

Of the nineteenth dynasty we have Rameses I. and his son, the old Seti I., builder of Karnac. The head of this last is stamped with great intelligence, his white teeth are remarkably preserved, and the ends of his fingers indicate that he suffered from gout. His son Rameses II.. the great Sesostris of tradition, bears a striking resemblance to his father, and possesses his robust vigour. The head is elongated and small ; a few locks of hair cover the skull ; the forehead is low and narrow, the eyes are close together, the brows short and thick ; the

nose is long, thin, very much curved; the cheeks stand out prominently; the chin, which comes very forward, is furnished with a few
rare hairs; the mouth is small with thick lips; the teeth are worn;
the ears stand out, and are pierced. The expression is not very
intelligent—it is even brutal—but it has an air of command, resolution,
and pride that are astounding. Rameses III. is the attenuated likeness of his father, with a little more intelligence, and less coarseness.

The twenty-first dynasty gives us Queen Notem-Maut, King
Pinotem II., the grand priest Masaturti, the Queen Athor-Hount-
Tani, the Queens Makara and Isi-Em-Kheb, the Princess Nasi-
Khonsu, the Prince and priest Tatf-Ankh-Nebseni, the priest Noi-
Shounau.

Besides the coffins and the mummies, more than five or six
thousand other smaller relics are here: royal papyrus; cupboards in
papyrus, containing, one, princesses' wigs; embalmed sheeps' legs and
calves' heads, vases that served for libations, a cupboard belonging
to Queen Makara and her daughters, and a swarm of other small
objects.

And now, before these mummies dating from three thousand years,
in face of these sculptures of the ancient empire of Ra-hotep and
Nefert, six thousand years old, in presence of the Sphinx of an
unbelievable age, so far is it lost in the night of time, to how many
thousands of years must we go back for the commencement of the
history of Egypt?

The Sphinx is its oldest known monument, as it is the most perfect
in point of proportions, lines, and audacity of execution. It is the
result of an art arrived, if not at its climax, at least at a high degree
of perfection. Other masterpieces of its period must exist, buried
beneath the sand, perhaps lost for ever; for it cannot be the sole
monument of its period. Is it the last word, the summit of art
in those distant times? Does it mark a commencement of decline
which continued with the first empire and went on always increasing
until more recent periods? Chance alone, by uncovering some day
another monument contemporaneous with this colossus of calcareous
rock, might give the solution to the problem, and perhaps the priests

The shores of the isle of Gheateh.

of Egypt were right when they made the origin of Egyptian history ascend more than thirty thousand years.

From the terrace of the Museum, the supporting wall of which bathes in the Nile, the view is splendid : opposite is the island of Ghezireh, with the long line of palm trees that covers its shores, with its boats at anchor or drawn up on the banks ; to the left, the river speckled with craft, the Kasr-el-Nil Bridge in the background ; to the right, the Nile extending northward, broad and imposing.

Leaving the garden, Jacques and Ahmed proceed to the port and walk along the quays. Impossible for anything to be more lively, more animated, than this emporium of all the commerce of the north and south of Egypt.

Multitudes of vessels lie side by side along the shore : canges, dahabiehs, steamers, yachts, transports, and rafts.

From the south come the vessels from Assouan loaded with senna, gathered in the desert by the warlike Ababdiehs ; elephants' tusks, rhinoceros' and antelopes' horns from Darfour ; courbashes of hippopotamus hide from Sennaar ; skins of jaguars, zebras, and giraffes, arms and necklaces from Khartoum.

Dahabiehs with elevated poops advance ; they hail from Esneh with ivory, ostrich feathers, acacia gum, nitre, transported across the desert by caravans from Abyssinia ; coffee and incense from Arabia ; spices, pearls, precious stones, cashmeres, silk, from India, arriving by the desert of Kosheir.

Transports from Kenneh, composed of two boats lashed one to the other by cords with a common flooring, discharge their lofty and fragile cargoes of pottery ; *bardaks* of porous earth to keep water of the Nile in, pitchers, amphoræ of all sizes and all forms.

Edfou sends its pipes, its charming vases in red and black clay, elegant in form, with gracefully modelled ornaments.

And there are heavy barges from Fayoum, the land of roses, filled to the top with rye, barley, cotton, indigo ; dahabiehs full of carpets, woollen stuffs, flagons of rose-water, mats made with the reeds of Birket-el-Keroun.

From the north come rice from Damietta, doura and maize from the province of Charkieh.   Alexandria forwards its goods from Europe and Asia : Syrian tobaccos, Persian carpets, draperies from Aleppo, Smyrna, Damascus, heavy freights of wood cut on the mountains of Karamania, millions of bushels of dried grapes which will be converted into brandy, provisions of dried fruit, Turkish tobacco, soap from the islands of the Archipelago.

Sailors of all countries, all colours, all races, naked or dressed, in a bustle without a pause, run like cats through these piles of things, climbing to the yards, hoisting the sails, raising enormous cases, moving heavy bales of cotton, rolling great tuns of oil, filling vats with pitch, vociferating with horrible imprecations, quarrelling, exchanging blows ; while others, lazily extended in the bit of shade of a yawl heaved high and dry, lunch on some figs, or smoke their narghilehs.

And in the midst of this din, there are donkeys bending beneath their burdens, on whom blows are being showered; camels abominably loaded, moaning frightfully and refusing to rise ; donkey boys who storm, camel drivers who yell, carters who slash the bellies of their cattle with blows of the whip.

Fellaheen naked to the waist discharge a corn-boat ; others empty rough stone from a barge.   Here it is a dahabieh that they are repainting ; its reïs overlooks the work and discusses with an American the price of a voyage to the second cataract.   There is a yacht at anchor carrying the British flag, admirably kept in order.   Its exquisite cleanliness ill accords with the filth of the native craft.   The crew, in dark blue jerseys and little black caps with streaming ribbons, calm and cold, smoking short white Irish clay pipes, contemplate with disdain the clamorous mob of Arabs.   Or a steamer of Cook's Agency leaving for Thebes, a yacht of the Khedive, a boat crossing over among the flotilla of small craft and vessels, passes under way at full sail on the immense river.

They escape from this tumult, and with difficulty regain the street which runs parallel to the Nile ; they follow it to the bridge of Kasr-el-Nil, which they cross, and, turning sharply to the right, find themselves at Ghezireh, opposite Boulak.

A high dyke planted with palm trees borders the bank ; groups of decayed mud houses, hung all over with old clothes ; broken cages, branches of sorghum, broken pottery, rubbish of all sorts, scattered over the ground, are seen through the trees—in those hovels live fishermen, bargemen, poverty-stricken folk. Here and there is a sort of shop of clay and planks, where they sell raki, coffee, oranges, maize cakes, and things without a name. To the right, on the slope which descends to the river, small vessels are drawn up ; sailors mend sails, repair damaged old sloops, calk a craft, or re-tar it ; others seated or lying down, at the bottom of a boat at anchor, smoke cigarettes and drink coffee.

On the other side of the road, to the left, are sheets of water formed on the low land by the inundation ; farther on is the avenue of Ghezireh bordered by sycamores. They follow it on their way back. This is the promenade of the Champs Elysées of Cairo. There is hardly any one out to-day, but on Fridays and Sundays all the world of fashion drives here : victorias, horsemen, hired carriages, asses, mules, pedestrians, Europeans, Arabs, passing to and fro in picturesque variety.

At the hotel Jacques finds Onésime, who is awaiting him with impatience ; he has received a telegram from the Doctor, who urges them to join him at Thebes. To-morrow a vessel of Cook's Company is leaving. They hasten to engage a cabin. Ahmed and Hassan are disconsolate at losing their customers. A good baksheesh somewhat calms their regret, and a serious letter of recommendation, which the two friends hand them at their request, almost completely consoles them. Abdallah has already an excellent master, whom the Doctor procured for him before his departure.

To-night, Jacques and Onésime have taken their farewell dinner with their landlord. His servants have conveyed their trunks to the boat ; to-morrow they will be on their way to Upper Egypt.